Magic Lessons

Center Point
Large Print

Also by Alice Hoffman and available from
Center Point Large Print:

Faithful
The Rules of Magic
The World That We Knew

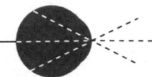

**This Large Print Book carries the
Seal of Approval of N.A.V.H.**

Magic Lessons

ALICE HOFFMAN

CENTER POINT LARGE PRINT
THORNDIKE, MAINE

Love all, trust a few, do wrong to none.

—WILLIAM SHAKESPEARE

PART ONE

Transformations

I.

She was found on a January day in a field where the junipers grew, wound in a blue blanket with her name carefully stitched along the border with silk thread. There was a foot of snow on the ground, but the sun was strong and whoever had named the child Maria had most assuredly loved her, for the wool of the blanket was of a very fine grade, certain to keep her warm, and she'd been well cared for, not lacking for comfort or food. She was a quiet baby, but as the day passed she began to fuss and then to cry, doing so unfailingly and with great effort, until at last a crow came to perch on her basket, peering at her with its quick black eyes.

That was how the old woman discovered the abandoned child, staring at a bird nearly as large as herself, fearless and wide-eyed from the start. Maria was a beautiful baby, with pitch-black hair and pale gray eyes, a silvery shade so unusual the old woman wondered if she wasn't a changeling, for this was a place where strange things happened and fate could be a friend or a foe. Changeling or not, Hannah Owens carried the baby back into the woods, singing as they went, the first human words the baby would remember.

The water is wide, I cannot get oe'r it
And neither have I wings to fly
Give me a boat that will carry two
And I shall row, my Love and I.

O down in the meadows the other day
Agathering flowers, both fine and gay
Agathering flowers, both red and blue
I little thought of what love could do.

In the child's first days at Hannah's cottage, the insistent bird beat his wings against the cloudy, pitted glass window, doing his best to be let in. He could not be chased off with pails of vinegar and water nor with shouts and threats. One could hardly toss stones at such a loyal creature. The crow had been allowed to stay and was called Cadin, a name derived from Maria's baby talk name of *Cawcaw*. Whenever the weather turned foul, he settled onto the wooden perch kept beside the sooty fire. There he cleaned his gleaming feathers and kept a sharp eye on Maria.

"I suppose he's yours," Hannah had said to the baby in her basket when seven days had passed and the crow had not left his post on the fence surrounding the garden, not even to eat or drink. "Or perhaps you're his."

10

Hannah knew full well that you do not choose a familiar, it chooses you, bonding with you in a way no other creature can. Hannah, herself, had long ago made a pet of a she-cat that had followed her everywhere, a pretty marmalade-colored tabby with lovely markings, a beloved familiar that was in tune with her thoughts and desires. On the day Hannah was let out of prison, she found the cat nailed to the door of her house in the village. That's what her neighbors had done while she'd been imprisoned, as well as robbing her of the few belongings she'd had, a feather mattress, some pots and pans, a quill pen. Hannah carried the cat with her into the woods, and buried it in the green hollow where she had camped before her cottage was built, a glade she called Devotion Field where bluebells grew in the spring and celandine shone through the last of the winter frost in a carpet of white and yellow stars. The beauty of that meadow reminded Hannah of the reasons to live in the world, and the reasons to mistrust those who saw wickedness in others, but never in themselves. The natural world was at the heart of her craft; what grew in the woods could harm or heal, and it was her obligation to know the difference. It was part of old Norse tradition, *Seidhr*, that had been brought to England in the ancient times. This was green magic, visionary in nature, blending the soul of the individual with the soul of the earth.

Holly should be burned to announce the end of winter.

Rowan, sacred to witches for protection for making spindles and spinning wheels.

Hazel will lead to water.

Willow is sacred magic, transporting the soul.

Yew signifies life, death, and rebirth, used for bows. Beware: the seeds are poisonous.

Ash is sacred and healing, the leaves make a tonic for horses.

Apple is the key to magic and is used for medicine, love spells.

Birch, write spells on strips of bark and they will reach their intended.

Pine tree sap is a salve for pox and spotted fever.

The leaves of the larch tree boiled as an ointment for wounds and cuts.

Hemlock will cure swellings and sores.

It was indeed good fortune that the child had been found by Hannah and not by another, for there were many in Essex County who would have disposed of an unwanted baby as easily as they'd have drowned a cat. Hannah was a kind and generous soul, and she didn't think twice before giving the baby a home and, as it turned out, a great deal more. She stitched a blue dress for the child, for good fortune and protection, and tied a strand of blue wool around her ankle.

Residents of nearby villages and towns believed that among the good and decent folk there were hidden servants of evil who caused children to die of pox and fevers and could curse the land so that it lay fallow. What people believed often came to be, and blame was placed where it was imagined. This was the year when two comets streaked across the sky for mysterious causes and a volcano that had begun to erupt at Mount Etna in Italy would soon spread ash as far as their own village, so that it seemed to snow in March. Within a year, two poor souls in London were infected with the plague, with more and more falling ill each day. People wore masks and locked themselves in their houses, yet the illness still found them, sliding under doors, it was believed, or flowing through windows, but in truth the disease had been brought from house to house by doctors who didn't know well enough to wash their hands. By 1665 the city would lose sixty-eight thousand inhabitants.

When Maria turned two, the Great Fire of London destroyed seventy thousand homes in a city of eighty thousand, and smoke filled the air for the entire month of September. Birds fell from the sky and children coughed up black phlegm, a sign they would not see their next birthday. The world was a dangerous place where people were punished for their sins and most believed that good fortune depended upon a measure of faith and superstition. These were years when cruel and unexplained things happened, and kindness was a rare and valued gift, one that Hannah Owens happened to possess.

There were those in the county known to practice the Nameless Art, spells and rituals handed down through the generations by cunning folk who knew more than most. These women understood the mysterious nature of medicine and love and did their best to pierce the veil that separated men and women from knowledge that might save them from ill fortune and disaster. They could mend a broken heart as easily as they could cure a fever, but they did so discreetly, for women were blamed for much of the world's troubles, and there were known to be witches in this county.

More than twenty years earlier, Matthew Hopkins, a young man from the village of Manningtree on the banks of the River Stour in Essex County, had begun his wicked hunt for witches. Aided by the Earls of Warwick and Manchester, he became the witch-finder general, and was paid a lordly amount for sending women to their deaths. What made for a witch was in his hands, as if he alone could see through the spectral curtain and pluck out the evidence of evil. A mark on a woman's hand or cheek, a bird at her window, a dog or cat or some other creature that would not leave her side, a book of magic found in a cupboard or discovered beneath a straw mattress, an embittered neighbor with a grudge and a story to tell. Such was the manner of proof, especially when it came to poor women without a family or a champion.

In the time of the witch-finder, it was believed a witch could be ensnared by nailing her steps to the ground so that she could not flee, and iron traps made to catch fox were set out, for it was well known that a witch's powers decreased when she was near metal. Some witch-hunters actually nailed women's feet to the ground and left them to try to escape. If they were able to evade their captors, they then needed to dab rosemary oil on the spot where the nail had entered them while invoking a spell of protection and vengeance: *This cannot harm you on this day. When you walk, you walk away. When you return, all your enemies will burn.*

Still, protection was hard to find. Three hundred suspects were charged; one hundred of these poor souls went to the gallows, having been tested by being tied to a chair and tossed into a river or pond to see if they would drown or if they would float like a witch. It was a test that was impossible to win. Hannah Owens had been fortunate to have escaped a hanging, for the trials were stopped and the madness was broken, much like a fever, suddenly and for no apparent reason, other than the fact that logic finally prevailed. The accused were let out of prison, grateful even though there were no apologies or explanations, and certainly no reparations. Hopkins died in his twenties of the coughing disease, said to have been contracted after he had been swimming. There were many who were overjoyed to hear that he'd been damned with his own version of drowning, his lungs filling with water that had sunk him as surely as if he'd been tied to a stool and forcibly immersed in a pond. On the day he was buried, scores of women in Essex County celebrated with bonfires burning and mugs of ale poured and enjoyed. As for Hannah, she'd had a cup of tea on that day, made of a mixture she had blended to give herself courage during these dreadful times when a woman couldn't walk down the street without fear of being accused of misdoings, especially if a book was found in her belongings, or if she could read and write her own name.

Although the mania had died down, mothers continued to tie their babies to their cradles to make certain they wouldn't be stolen in the night, setting bowls of precious salt on their windowsills to protect those inside. Men nailed

16

upside-down horseshoes above barn doors to ensure that their luck wouldn't run out, for they privately feared that a witch could ruin any strong man's health by placing a strand of his hair or his fingernail clippings under the eaves of a house. Children were taught never to speak to strangers; should they stray and be bewitched, they must shout out numbers backwards as a way to break the enchantment. Those unfortunate children who did go missing were searched for with pitchers of goat's milk, said to be a witch's favorite drink, and many times children who had been spirited away appeared at the door late at night, with burrs in their hair and no practical excuse to give their mothers, other than a thin apology and a claim they'd become lost in the woods and could not for the life of them find their way home.

Hannah Owens lived apart from the delusions and bad intentions of men, as deep in the forest as possible, in a small cottage hidden by vines. She'd had it built by a local carpenter, a fellow no one would hire due to a deformity at birth, a simple, honest man who later claimed the old woman had blessed him and given him a salve she had concocted from her apothecary garden that had made his withered arm bloom and become whole again. The roof of Hannah's house was thatched and the chimney was platted with reeds and clay, with a pot of water kept near the hearth in case a spark should catch the reeds on fire. The path to her door was made of uneven blue stones, hidden by shrubs. So much the better, for the difficult going provided protection from prying eyes. And still, women from town and from the neighboring farms managed to find their way when the need arose, setting the brass bell to ringing when they knocked on the door.

Hannah knew the woods as well as anyone. She knew that counting the knots on a lilac bush could predict the number of cold spells and that if you lit a bit of snow with some tinder and it melted quickly the snow on the ground would soon disappear. Nutmeg opened the heart, lily was useful for rashes, and arnica could make a man burn with desire. When a baby refused to be born or would not nurse, when a child was ailing and feverish, when a husband strayed, when a candle burst into flame of its own accord, marking a spirit lurking nearby, women came to Hannah Owens' door, and for the price of some eggs, or a pitcher of goat's milk, or, in the most difficult cases, a broach or a ring, a remedy could be found.

Maria grew up watching such transactions, always after night fell, for no one wished to be seen at the witch's door. Hanging on the wall was the Lucky Hand, an amulet shaped into five fingers, made from moss, preserved on Midsummer's Eve with the smoke of a bonfire, which would protect the house from bad luck and ill fortune. The women who came calling sat at the kitchen table where bread was kneaded and hens were butchered and babies were born, often after a difficult labor. By the age of five, Maria had been taught how to turn a baby in its mother's womb, how to grind a bird's bones into a powder to combat sleeplessness, how to identify the symptoms of a fever or a pox. She had been given close instructions on which herbs were best to gather, carrying them home in a basket or in the skirt of her long apron. Wood avens to cure toothache, black horehound for nausea and monthly cramps, salted leaves that could be used to dress and heal the bite of a dog, elderberry and cherry bark for coughs, dill seeds to be rid of hiccoughs, hawthorn to disperse bad dreams and calm a frantic heart, and nettle, which made a fine soup, to treat burns, infections, and inflammations. Maria only had to touch a clump of nettle once without gloves to learn her lesson. Even after Hannah had rubbed the crumpled leaves of the jewelweed plant to calm the afflicted skin, Maria avoided those stinging plants forever after. From the start, the girl was a quick learner. She didn't have to be hurt twice to be wary, and she knew early on that love could be either a blessing or a curse.

• • •

The women who made their way through the woods most often came for one thing. Time and time again, it was love. Love everlasting, young love, love defiled, love that caused aches and pains, love that left bruises and red welts, love wished for desperately, or love to be rid of as quickly as possible. Often Hannah wrote down the desired result and placed the bit of parchment in her spell box. She cast her spells while lighting a candle. White for health, black for expunging sorrow, red for love. Prick the third finger of the left hand with a silver needle to bring back a lover. The power of a spell increased with the waxing moon, and decreased with the waning moon. Time mattered, devotion mattered, belief mattered most of all. Maria sat by the hearth, which was hers to tend, for she had her own tinderbox and could start a fire in a flash. From that warm and cozy spot she watched Hannah scan the pages of her book filled with remedies and spells, careful to take note of the potions and powders that were prescribed: amulets of apple seeds and menstrual blood, doses of henbane that could bind a couple together, or, if used to excess, could cause delirium or death, the heart of a deer or a dove that brought about devotion even in the most feckless and untrustworthy of men, and fragrant verbena, which, depending on its use and what the user desired, could bring a man to you or cause him to be impotent.

"Remember one thing," Hannah told Maria. "Always love someone who will love you back."

PRACTICAL MATERIALS

Candles.

Essential oil. Lavender for calming. Sage to purify. Rosemary for remembrance. Rose for love.

Salt, garlic, stones, thread, talismans for fortune, love, luck, and good health.

Always meet and depart from inside a circle.

Honor the twelve full moons in a year from December until November: Oak, Wolf, Storm, Hare, Seed, Dryad, Mead, Herb, Barley, Harvest, Hunter's, Snow, and the thirteenth moon, always most special, the Blue Moon.

Silver coins, pure water, willow, birch, rowan, oak, string, knots, mirrors, black glass, brass bowls, pure water, blood, ink, pens, paper.

Nettle will give protection and return evil to sender. Apple for rebirth and immortality. Holly leads to dream magic but can be poisonous, Black-thorn can return evil to the sender. Ferns call rain, but fend off lightning. Feverfew to ward off illness. Worm-wood is poisonous, but can be used for divination. Belladonna, though poisonous, can cause visions and give the power of the sight. Mint on your windowsill will keep away flies and bad fortune. Lavender for luck.

Hannah Owens was unusual not only for her kindness and herbal knowledge, but for the stunning fact that she could both write and read, a rare skill, for a working woman in the country was expected to have no more formal learning than a plow horse and ninety percent were illiterate. Hannah had been an orphan herself, but she had been raised in the scullery of a royal house to do kitchen work, and there the tutor for the family's sons had taken it upon himself to allow her into the library and teach her to read. As soon as Maria was old enough, Hannah taught her precious talents to the child on stormy nights when the weather was too awful for even the most lovesick women to come to the door. They sat in the light of a lantern and drank cups of Courage Tea, a blend of currants, spices, and thyme, made for protection and healing, a mixture that needed to steep for a long time. It was an elixir that made it clear one should never hide who one was. That was the first step toward courage. In this way, magic began. The crooked black letters looked like nothing more than circles and sticks, and then all at once, after weeks of attention, they became words that took on the shape of cows and clouds and rivers and seas, a miracle on the page, drawn with ink made of oak seeds, or plant sap, or animal blood, or the damp ash of charred bones. There were sympathetic inks that few knew of; a scribe could write with one and it would not be seen until a second ink was used, or when lime juice, milk, or vinegar were brushed onto the paper, and then, after heat was applied, the message would suddenly be visible.

This was true magic, the making and unmaking of the world with paper and ink.

It was said that if any of God's creatures could think like a man, it would be a crow, for they have minds that never rest. Cadin was a great collector and brought back all manner of treasures discovered in the surrounding villages and towns, found at the great estates as well as the laborers' hovels, spied from above by his bright vision of the world below. What belonged to others was fair game for him to steal, and rich or poor made no difference; they all had some-thing worthwhile. He could flick in through a window and flit out again, or dive into a trash bin, or pick through a garden. Buttons, spools of thread, coins, children's poppets, horse hairs, and once, on a bright blue day when he could see farther than any other beast or man, he brought back a hairpin, clearly stolen from a lady in a castle, a lovely, intricate object that had tiny rubies set into the silver. Maria, now nearly eight, was in the meadow when Cadin swooped down to drop this miraculous find at her feet. He had been somewhat wounded in his attempts at stealing the treasure he now offered, and there was a small scar on his head.

Maria wore a blue skirt and a woolen bodice with narrow sleeves, along with stockings Hannah knitted and a linen smock. The child was still as fearless as ever. What fell from the sky, she was happy to collect and examine.

"Oh, look, Hannah," she cried. "My Cadin's a robber."

Hannah came around from the apothecary garden as Maria was studying the pin that had been cast into the tall grass. In the girl's hands the silver turned black in an instant, as if brushed with dark paint, though the rubies shone more brightly because of her touch. Hannah clutched the leeks she had gathered to her chest, and felt an ache inside her bones. The wide-brimmed straw hat she wore to protect her from the sun fell from her head, and she didn't bother to go after it. What she had long suspected had now been shown to be true. She'd felt it from the start, that first day under the junipers when she spied the baby in her basket, a rare sight that had spread cold pinpricks along her spine. As she'd unwrapped Maria from her blanket, she'd spied an unusual birthmark in the shape of a star, hidden in the crease of the girl's inner elbow. Right away she wondered if this was the cause of the child's abandonment, for bloodline witches were said to be marked in such sly, concealed places, on the scalp, upon the small of the back, at the breastbone, along the inner arm. It was one thing to learn magic, but quite another to be born with it.

Ever since, Hannah had kept watch for telltale signs. Over the years omens had appeared, one after the other, clear evidence of the child's unusual nature. As soon as she could speak, Maria could predict the weather, just as a crow can tell when a windstorm will come, often beginning to fly erratically hours before the first gusts. Maria could taste snow in the air and know the skies would open before rain fell. She had the ability to speak backwards, an unsettling trait, and it sometimes seemed she could converse in the language of birds, calling the crow to her with a sharp clacking sound, and chattering with magpies and doves. Even the cheeky sparrows came to her when called, and sat in the palm of her hand, calmed by her presence and comforted by her touch. When only a babe, she cut her finger on a thorn bush, and the blood that spilled onto the ground had burned through the grass, turning it black. That was when Hannah first felt her suspicions to be correct, but if she wanted undisputable proof it was now right in front of her, for silver turns black when held in a witch's hand.

"I ruined it," Maria said, frowning as she showed off the blackened hairpin.

"Nonsense. You've made it far prettier. See how the red stones glow?" Hannah had the girl turn around so that her long hair could be gathered and tacked up with the crow's pin to keep the tangled mass atop her head. "Now you look like a queen."

Later Hannah caught the girl staring in a hand-held mirror. It was black painted glass in which a person could see her future if she knew what to look for. Some called it scrying or prophesizing, but it could only be properly handled by a true witch. Hannah chuckled when she saw how entranced Maria was by her own countenance, for clearly the girl had the gift of sight. Still Hannah feared for her fate, for this was the day when Maria realized she would be beautiful, for all the good it would do her in this cruel, heartless world.

Whatever her heritage might be, there was magic in Maria. At eight, her letters were more shapely than Hannah's. At nine, she could read as well as any educated man. Had she been allowed access to books in Latin and Hebrew and Greek, surely she would have learned those ancient languages as well. Hopefully, her canny intelligence would benefit her when she was on her own, a future Hannah fretted over, and the cause of many sleepless nights. A child unprotected was at the mercy of those who wished to ill-use her. As the ultimate protection against the merciless ways of fate, Hannah began work on the only legacy she could give the child, a personal journal called a *Grimoire*, meant for the eyes of the user alone, a book of illumination in which cures and remedies and enchantments were documented. Some called such a text a Book of Shadows, for it was meant solely for the use of the writer and the formulas within often disappeared when looked at by a stranger. The first *Grimoire* was said to be *The Key of Solomon*, perhaps written by King Solomon, or, far less impressive, by a magician in Italy or Greece in the fifteenth century. The book contained instructions for the making of amulets, as well as invocations and curses, listing the rules for summoning love and revenge. Solomon was believed to have been given a ring engraved with a pentagram that had the power to bind demons, and there were those who said that the angel Raziel gave Noah a secret book about the art of astrology, written on a single sapphire and brought with him on the Ark. *The Sworn Book of Honorius*, an ancient magical treatise Hannah had found in the royal family's library when she was a girl, advised no woman should be allowed to read its incantations and invocations. Those women who could read were revered and feared, for they were the most skilled in love magic.

Magical practitioners were everywhere in England, in the court and in castles, but magic books were forbidden for the poor and for women. There were searches for magical manuscripts belonging to women, which were often found hidden under beds, or, to avoid discovery once doubt had been cast upon the writer, floating in rivers or thrown onto burning pyres so that their magic would not fall into the wrong hands. Spells and magical symbols were written upon parchment, then tucked into the folds of clothing or into the food of the intended objects of desire. But it was a woman's personal book that was most important; here she would record the correct recipes for all manner of enchantments. How to conjure, how to heal, including those illnesses that had no name, how to use natural magic to bind another to you or send him away, and how to use literary magic, the writing of charms and amulets and incantations, for there was no magic as coveted or as effective as that which used words.

Whereas Hannah's *Grimoire* had vellum pages and a wooden cover, the book she fashioned for Maria was a true prize, a magical object in and of itself. It was made of real paper, dearly bought from a printer in the village. The cover was black and bumpy and cool to the touch, unmistakably supernatural in nature, made of a most unusual material. Cadin had led her to the shallows of a nearby pond where she found a large toad floating on the calm surface, already cold and lifeless when Hannah knelt to hold it in her hands. For those who were uneducated, toads were full of evil magic, and witches were said to transform themselves into toads if need be. This toad's fate would be to guard a treasure trove of cures and remedies.

As Hannah walked home in the fading dark, the toad's skin sparked with light. This made it clear that a *Grimoire* formed from this creature would have its own power, and would give strength to the written enchantments it bore. Any spell would be twice as potent. Hannah prepared the leather that very night, secretly, and with great skill, salting the skin before stretching it on a wooden rack. Overnight the toad-leather grew twice as large as it had been, taking on the form of a square, which signified the mystical shape of the heart, combining the human and the divine, and representing the four elemcnts: fire, earth, air, and water. It was an omen of power and heart-break and love.

When presented with the book, on Midsummer Night in the year she turned ten, Maria cried hot tears, the first time she could recall doing so, for although witches are said to be unable to cry, rare occasions cause them to do so. Maria was swept up by raw emotion and gratitude, and from that day forward she cried when she was flooded by her responses, burning her own skin with her dark, salty tears. Never in her life had anything truly belonged to her and her alone. She marked this day forever after as the day of her birth, for it was, indeed, the formation of the woman she would become. Her fate was tied to this book as if her future had been written with indelible ink. On the first page were the rules of magic, ones Hannah declared they were obliged to follow.

Do as you will, but harm no one.
What you give will be returned to you threefold.

From then on, each day was a lesson, with more and more to study, for it seemed there might not be time for all that Maria must learn. Hannah had begun to hear the clatter of the deathwatch beetle inside the house, the dreaded creature whose sound echoed in times of plague and famine and illness, predicting the end of a life. One could never be sure whose life was in peril, but on this occasion Hannah knew. After finding a small neat hole in the wall beside her bed, set there from the creature's burrowing, Hannah held up a burning twig to smoke out the beetle with yellow sulfurous fumes, but it did no good. If anything, the clicking grew louder, deafening at times, for there was no way to prevent a death that has already been cast, as every man and woman who walks the earth is bound to know when their own time comes.

Perhaps the girl had foreseen Hannah's death before Hannah herself had, for Maria worked harder than ever, studying by lamplight, doing her best to ascertain if a curse could be reversed and a death unmade. At ten she was old enough to be aware of the unkind ways of the world. She'd heard the stories Hannah's clients told, and had seen those who were too ill to be saved by any means. She knew that life and death walked hand in hand and understood when Hannah confided that a *Grimoire* must be handed down to a blood relative or destroyed upon the owner's death. Magic was dangerous if set in the wrong hands. At the hour of her adoptive mother's death, Maria must burn her book even before she accom-

31

panied Hannah's body to the burying ground.

She had begun her own book, with Hannah's lessons taking up the early pages, and these would always remain a treasure. Maria wrote carefully, with curving, near-perfect script, using ink made of the bark of hawthorn and oak trees and the ashy bones of doves she had found strewn in the grass. Maria made a bond with doves, as she had all birds, and much later in her life, she would be grateful she had done so.

FOR LOVE

Boil yarrow into a tea, prick the third finger of your hand, add three drops of blood, and give to your beloved.

Never cut parsley with a knife if you are in love or bad luck will come your way.

Salt tossed on the fire for seven days will bring an errant lover home.

Charms for wandering husbands: feather, hair, blood, bone.

Prick a candle with a pin. When the flame burns down to the pin, your true love will arrive.

To win the favor of Venus in all matters of love gather a white garment, a dove, a circle, a star, the seventh day, the seventh month, the seven stars.

To study love with an expert is a great gift, and yet Maria wondered why, with access to so much power and magic, Hannah had spent her own life alone, without love.

"What makes you think I have?" Hannah didn't look the girl in the eye when she spoke, perhaps for fear of what the sight would allow Maria to intuit, things that were best kept private. There are secrets that must be held close, and most of these have to do with the wounding of the human heart, for sorrow spoken aloud is sorrow lived through twice.

All the same, Maria didn't let her questions go unanswered, and now she was even more curious. "Haven't you? I've seen no man come near."

"Did you think I had no life before you came along?"

This notion only caused Maria's interest to pique. She pondered that statement, her mouth pursed, deep in thought. Contemplating her own personal history, she had begun to wonder who she'd been before she was left in Devotion Field on a snowy day. Who had given her life and loved her, only to have left her in the care of a crow? Did she resemble her mother or her father, for surely every individual who was born must have parents. She noticed then that Hannah's eyes were damp, and not because of the sun's glare. That was when she knew the truth about Hannah.

"You did know love," Maria declared, quite convinced. She didn't just presume such a thing, as much as she read it in the air, as if Hannah's past was made up of letters set into a book and that book was the world they walked through.

They were deep in the forest where Hannah was schooling Maria on how to hide should the need arise. Ever since the days of the witch-finders, it had been necessary to plan an escape at all times. Birds lived in such a manner, settling into the thickets so deeply and with such complete silence not even a fox could spy them.

Hannah gave the girl a sharp look. "You're not invisible if you talk."

Maria crouched beneath the junipers, barely breathing, not far from the place where she'd first been found. She knew the value of silence. Cadin was perched in the branch above her, equally quiet. Perhaps he had the sight as well, as familiars are said to do. He had not spent a single night away from Maria from the time he'd found her in the field, and Maria always wore the blackened silver hairpin the crow had brought her as a special gift. Sometimes she imagined the pin in a woman's long red hair; perhaps it was a vision of the original owner. Whatever its history, the hairpin was her most valued possession, and would be all her life, even when she was half a world away from these woods.

"Bring me something wonderful," she always whispered to Cadin when he set off on a flight, and she patted the feathers of her beloved thief. "Just don't be caught."

On the day of invisibility, he went off when they were finished hiding, winging across the field. It was very warm and the leaves on the willows were unfolding in a haze of soft yellow-green color. The ground was marshy all around them and ferns covered the heathland. On the way back to the cottage Hannah said, "You're right." She looked straight ahead as she spoke, but she had an open expression on her face, as if she were young again. She was remembering something she had done her best to forget.

Maria hurried to keep up with her. "Am I?"

Being told she was right was a rare treat, for Hannah believed that character was built when it was assumed that a child was most often wrong and still had much to learn.

"He was a man like any other, an earl's servant who had seven years to work off his debt. That is what poor men must do, and I didn't fault him for it. I was willing to wait, for a year is only as long as you let it be, but then I was arrested. They said I used my skill at writing to send letters to the devil and that I had a tail and that all men were in danger when I walked by, not because I was beautiful, I wasn't, even I knew that, but because

35

I could cause their blood to boil or go ice cold. I suppose they made it worth his while to turn against me, for after my trial was over, he was a free man with coins in his purse. He was the one who said I had a tail, and that he'd chopped it off himself so that I might appear to be a woman rather than a witch. He gave them the tail of a shrew and vowed it was mine, and if a fool is believed then those who believe him are even bigger fools."

Maria thought over this new information. "So that is love?"

Hannah glanced away, as she did when she didn't wish to reveal her emotions. But she needn't have bothered attempting to hide her sorrow, for Maria could sense what a person was feeling so strongly she might as well have been able to hear someone's deepest fears and wishes spoken aloud.

"It can't be," Maria decided.

"It was for me," Hannah told her.

"And for me?"

"You looked in the black mirror. What did you see?"

It was a private matter, but this was a time for truth rather than privacy. "I saw a daughter."

"Did you now? Then you'll be a fortunate woman."

"And a man who brought me diamonds."

Hannah laughed out loud. There they were in

36

their ragged clothes, half a day's walk from the nearest village, with nothing precious between them, save for their wits and Maria's stolen hairpin, as far away from a man with diamonds as they could be.

"I wouldn't be surprised by anything that happened to you, my girl," Hannah told Maria. "But I believe you will be amazed at the turns of fate, as we all are when it comes to our own lives, even when we have the sight."

A church bell rang miles away. Maria had never been to the closest village; she had never seen the blacksmith's shop where irons were cast, and knew nothing of constables, or churchwardens, or toll-takers, or surgeons who believed in using leeches and live worms and foxes' lungs as cures, and medical men who disdained folk remedies. Hannah placed her faith in washing her hands with clean water and her strong black soap before any examination, and because of this she lost far fewer patients. None, as a matter of fact, except those who were too far gone for any remedy, for things without remedy must be without regard. She made her own black soap every March, enough to last the year long, burning wood from rowans and hazelwoods for the ashes that would form her lye, using licorice-infused oil, honey, and clove, adding dried lavender for luck and rosemary for remembrance. Ladles of liquid soap were poured into wooden molds, where they hardened into bars. Maria had written down the recipe in her *Grimoire*, for this soap was most often asked for by the women from town. They said a woman grew younger each time she used it; if she had sorrows the soap washed them away, and if there was an illness in the house it would not spread, for the herbs in the soap defeated fevers and chills. It was the sort of recipe one could add to however one saw fit. Mistletoe for those who wished for children. Vervain to escape one's enemies. Black mustard seed to repel nightmares. Lilac for love.

This year, there was a coughing illness in the village, and people still feared the wave of fatalities that had passed among them only a few years earlier when the Black Death was everywhere. Small towns had disappeared entirely, with none left behind to bury the dead, and cattle soon enough had made their homes in abandoned houses where there were no roofs or windows or doors. In their village, women turned away from the doctor, for he had never been to school and believed in bloodletting and using stones and petrified wood to discern both the illness and the cure. Instead, they came to Hannah, in the night, along the path where the ferns were green and sweet, so that the world seemed brand-new, and anything seemed possible, even salvation.

Wash your hands with lye soap before
treating the ill person.
Horehound, boiled into a syrup, for
coughs.
Tea of wild onions and lobelia to soothe.
Beebalm for a restful sleep.
Vinegar elixirs stop nosebleeds.
Eat raw garlic every day and a cup of hot
water with lemon and honey.
For asthma, drink chamomile tea.
For chills, gingerroot tea.
Licorice root gathered from the riverside
for chest pain.
Dragon's blood from tree bark and berries
of the Dracaena draco, the red resin
tree from Morocco and the Canary
Islands that can only be found in one
market in London and can cure nearly
any wound.
A live snail rubbed on burns will help
heal the blisters.
Feed a cold, starve a fever.

In the summer of 1674, a time of unusual heat, a woman with red hair arrived at the cottage. As fate would have it, she brought the future with her. She knocked at the door, and Hannah said, "Come in," even though she seemed to hesitate.

Bad news often came this way, without warning, on what appeared to be nothing more than an ordinary day. The visitor had on beautiful, muddy clothes. Her shoes were made of kid leather, dyed red, decorated with buckles, and she carried a cloak made of fine blue wool, fringed with the fur of a fox. She wore a linen gown dyed scarlet with madder root and a silk, corded petticoat. Yet beneath her lovely, ruined clothes, purple bruises bloomed upon her skin, and there were marks left from a rope that had been tied around her wrists. From her place by the fire Maria stared at the red-haired lady. The stranger was so elegant, with a pretty, calm voice. She said her name was Rebecca and that she needed to spend the night. Hannah allowed her to sleep on a pallet of straw, knowing that though good deeds should bring good luck, such results aren't always the case.

The red-haired lady announced she was in search of a remedy to quench her husband's fire for her. Hannah explained to Maria that the lady was running away from her husband, which was a perilous proposition, especially when there was another man in the picture, the one she truly loved. She needed a cure to protect her and allow her to leave her wedded life.

"Is this what love does?" Maria wished to know.

"That's not the name I'd give it," Hannah responded.

"Is it so different than your man, who claimed you had a tail?"

"Perhaps not, but at least he was a coward and never set his hands on me."

In the morning, after a quiet night of sleep, their visitor was in better spirits. Hannah crafted an amulet of apple seeds. She then added mandrake, the heart of all love potions, first mentioned as such in Genesis, referred to as Circe's plant by the Greeks. The roots of this plant grow in the shape of human limbs, combining the aspect of a dragon and a man. It was so powerful that some refused to pick it themselves, and instead attached the plant to a rope wound around a dog's neck, so that the dog would be party to the mandrake's wrath when it was pulled from the earth, for the plant screamed when it was taken, its roots torn from the comfort of the soil in which it grew. Rebecca admitted she had cast a spell on her husband years earlier. She had bound him to her, bewitching him with the Tenth Love Potion, a spell far too dangerous for common use.

> Wrap a red candle on which his name and yours is written on red paper, soak in dove's blood and burn through the night. Saying the words:

> Love conquers all, so it must be. Let him burn with love for me.

41

My lover's heart will feel this pin, and his
    devotion I will win.
There'll be no way for him to rest or
    sleep, until he comes to me to speak.
Only when he loves me best, will he find
    peace and with peace rest.

The incantation must be recited while stabbing a dove's heart with seven pins on the seventh day of the week. For the use of the Tenth, an enchantment too strong for the usual manner of dissolving spells, Rebecca had paid a steep price. She could not undo the magic she had called onto herself, though she had tried for more than ten years. To change what she had wrought, Rebecca needed help from another woman, one who was adept at magic and could reverse the spell entirely. Hannah was that person, a master at the Nameless Art. After she made the charm, she wrote Rebecca's name and her bewitched husband's name on a white candle coated with myrrh oil. She then had Rebecca say: "I burn this candle as a token of the spell that binds our love. Let this magic now be broken by the gods above."

Hannah wrapped the candle in white cloth, for pure intentions must be cloaked in pure fabric, then she brought her visitor to the nearby pond, where she flung the candle as far as it could go. Maria stood behind Hannah and Rebecca as they watched it sink. They could all feel the spell breaking apart, as if dust were sifting down from the sky. For one wild moment, all three danced in a ring, forgetting the many trials of this world. Rebecca then insisted she must wash the mud and bloodstains from her clothes. She did so, and then set them to dry on the twiggy branches of the low-growing shrubbery. Rebecca wore several amulets and charms, acorns and agate strung on red thread and a brass circle onto which a pentacle had been etched. On both her wrists she wore spells that had been knotted and woven into bracelets for protection. It was summer and so hot the birds remained in the shadows.

Careful, the sparrows told Maria, warning her not to go near. Cadin took one look at Rebecca and flew away, making certain to keep his distance, but Maria was entranced by the stranger who was so alluring. Hannah gave their visitor a bar of black soap, and Rebecca walked to the shore, past the reeds, into the cool green water. She was still wearing her undergarments embroidered with blue thread, but they could see enough of her to spy that behind one knee there was a red mark in the shape of a crescent. Maria stepped closer. She, herself, had the mark of a star on her arm.

Hannah always had Maria wash with water from a bucket, never from the pond, but now Maria longed to take off her clothes and bathe.

43

Hannah grabbed her by the arm and said, "No, you mustn't. Water reveals who you are."

Maria had never been allowed to go near the pond, but now she felt the call of the cool water. She noticed that every time Rebecca attempted to dive under the surface it was no use. Again and again she sprung back up and clearly was too buoyant to dive or swim beneath the currents. She gave up, washed with the black soap, then floated back to the shore. She drifted like a lily pad, with no effort, a spoiled, beautiful flower.

"What's wrong with her?" Maria asked.

"Her kind can't be drowned. She's a bloodline witch. Whether it's wrong or right is not for us to say. She has magic in her."

Maria thought this over as she watched the woman dress, for her clothes had already dried in the sunlight. The black soap had caused her to appear even younger and more beautiful. But witch or not, she was still covered in bruises. She should have come earlier if she'd wanted a cure for her husband's love, as so many women before her had done, but perhaps she'd been prevented from running away. Runaways were dangerous. They brought trouble on their heels. Maria could smell it brewing. It smelled like blood and fire.

"I'll be gone soon enough," the lady Rebecca assured them as they walked back to the cottage. Her silk petticoat rustled, and she was lovely to look at. She'd brought death with her, as the enchanted often do, yet she was so captivating that Maria found herself charmed by her all over again. When Rebecca rested her hand on the girl's head, she noticed the hairpin. "Look!" She bent down so that Maria could see the back of her head. "I have one like it. I used to have another, but I was a fool and lost it to a black bird that was upon me before I could be rid of him."

Maria bit her lip. Surely this was the work of Cadin's thievery. "You can have this one," she was quick to say. "Then you'll have two again."

"I'm grateful, but it gives me pleasure to see you wear it. Let us vow to wear them every day."

Later, as Hannah was fixing supper, Maria came to help her. They had eggs from their hen, and mushrooms from the woods. Hannah did not eat beef or lamb, and they would have a vegetable soup for their dinner served directly from the cast iron pot. Maria was too curious to stop herself from asking, "Why did she come here? If she has her own magic, why doesn't she use it?"

"Working magic for yourself is tricky. It should be something you use to help others. If you use it for yourself, it can backfire and bring you untold troubles. As you may be able to tell, our visitor is not exactly selfless. She set an unbreakable spell and now regrets what she did. Let that be a lesson to you." Hannah knew exactly who this woman was. She had seen a spool of blue thread in the satchel the lady carried, and a pile of tarnished silver coins. "It's likely she's come for more than a spell."

Maria furrowed her brow, confused.

"Just because you lose something doesn't mean you don't want to see how it's turned out," Hannah told the girl.

"And has she?" Maria asked.

"She's seen how right you turned out, hasn't she?"

That was when Maria knew. The stranger was her mother.

Hannah glanced at the girl's shining face. It was never a good idea to place one's faith in someone who was by her very nature undependable. Rebecca's presence meant there was trouble ahead. There was a reason she hadn't come to see her child before now. She'd had other things on her mind. Love for some people was like that, easy to slip on and off.

"I don't think she'll be here much longer," Hannah assured Maria. "Now that she's seen what she's come to see she'll be gone by morning. And don't expect her to say good-bye."

When Maria returned to the pond to wash the supper dishes, she crouched down and dipped her fingers in the silky water. She was usually a well-behaved girl, but now she hastily stripped off her clothes, leaving her shift, her skirt, and

46

her smock on the ground. She felt the prick of a strange sort of freedom as she stood there in the damp evening air, doing as she pleased. Maria had never before questioned her situation. She was Hannah Owens' girl. But perhaps she was something more. She stalked through the reeds, quickly, before she had time to lose her nerve. Frogs splashed away from her and small fish darted into the depths. When she was knee-deep, she threw herself in. She floated perfectly without effort or skill, exactly as Rebecca had. Curious, she climbed onto a rock. She closed her eyes and leapt, her heart pounding, wondering if she would sink to the mucky depths. Instead, Maria landed so hard on the surface of the water that it took her breath away. Try as she might, she couldn't sink. When she staggered onto the shore, Maria shivered as she pulled on her clothing, not because of the night air, but because her situation had become quite clear to her. She could not be drowned.

Rebecca left while they were sleeping, just as Hannah had predicted she would. Twice she had managed to come to this place. Once when her daughter was born, when she ran off through the snow, and now again when she wanted to see how the girl had grown. She was not the sort of woman to say farewell.

Hannah and Maria awoke when they heard the

door close behind her, and as it did, the future became the present and the present became the past. The witch had only stayed a night, but one night was all it took for her husband to find her. This wasn't love. Maria knew that without anyone telling her. It was ownership and revenge. They could hear horses in Devotion Field, and the barking of hounds, all of which gave Hannah time enough to pack what mattered most in a leather satchel. Cheese and bread, a change of clothes, Maria's *Grimoire*, a sprig of juniper for protection, a spool of blue thread, packets of herbs, the makings for Courage Tea, the painted black hand mirror, along with the fine wool baby blanket that had been in Maria's basket when loving hands abandoned her.

Hannah took Maria as far as the pond. They had hustled so quickly that they were soon out of breath. The sky was clear; a perfect day. Hannah had vowed never to leave her home, but the girl had her future ahead of her. She was told to run until the forest ended, then to keep on through the fens until she reached the sea. This wasn't a country for someone with her bloodline. She'd do better in a new world, one where a woman wasn't considered worthless.

"But where will you be?" Maria begged to know.

"I'll be here where I belong. They couldn't drag me back to the world I used to know." Hannah shoved her own *Grimoire* into the girl's hands. No one gave up such a treasure unless her own end was near. "Burn this as soon as you can. And whatever you do, don't come back here."

FOR REVENGE

A wax figure cast into fire can cause damage or death.

A curse thrown to bind a man to the place where he stood.

Nightshade, wolfsbane, foxglove, yew, fire.

The bones of a bird baked into a pie of thorns.

When Rebecca's husband arrived, the death-watch beetle came out of the wall and sat on the threshold of the cottage. Its appearance came as no surprise to Hannah, who had known all along that her time was near. There were ten men in all, half of them his brothers, worked up into a fury of rage. They immediately took Hannah for a witch and tied her to her front door. They nailed her shadow to the ground so she couldn't escape. These men knew a cunning woman when they saw one. Give her a chance and she'd poison you or seek to do you harm. She might look old, she might walk with difficulty, but even more than most women she was not to be trusted.

49

When questioned about the red-haired lady, Hannah simply said, "She's gone home. If you think you want her, you'll regret it."

Rebecca's husband told his brothers to leave Hannah where she was as they burned down her house. What was the life of one old woman worth? Nothing to these men. They thought she couldn't fight back, but she could. Sparks flew everywhere, and in no time the apothecary garden beside the house caught fire, including the plants in the poison garden that Maria had learned not to pluck from the earth. Yarrow and black nightshade, wolfsbane with its purple hooded flowers, foxglove that could slow a heart, yew, lords and ladies laden with poisonous berries, all went up aflame, their dark fumes breathed in by the very men cheering on the blaze. The husband of the red-haired lady, a man named Thomas Lockland, had come closest, so he might shoot an arrow through the witch's heart, and because of this the poison affected him more than the others, leaving him unable to speak or move or see. Smoke soon caught in his men's chests; they began to cough and retch, then were beset by dizzy spells. They did their best to run for their lives, but in the end they all lay sick in Devotion Field. Though none ever truly recovered, not a single one died on that day, for what you gave to the world would come back to you threefold, and what Hannah was most proud to give to the world was a ten-year-old girl who had more knowledge than most grown men, and more courage, as well.

Maria had not done as she was told. It was a lesson she'd learned from Hannah. Do what you know is right. She watched from a hillside and wept as the house burned. When it was over, and the men had gone, she went back to add Hannah's *Grimoire* to the fire. The smoke was green as it arose in spirals into the canopy of trees. It was a lifetime of knowledge given back to the world from which it had come. Maria saw a glimmer in the grass, the brass bell that had been attached to Hannah's door. She took it with her so that she would always remember to keep her door open to those in need.

By evening, Maria had reached the fens, where the land was so marshy and wet the hem of her skirt was sodden and her leather shoes were soaked through, for she was ankle-deep in mud. She carried the satchel Hannah had packed held high over her head to keep it dry as she followed the path of the crow, westward. She wept to think of Hannah and her tears turned hot and burned her cheeks when she thought of Rebecca, who had caused the end of one fate and the start of another.

She was so close to the sea that when Maria licked her lips she tasted salt. There were different kinds of birds here, gulls and terns that wheeled through the pink-tinged sky. Soon the water she walked through was brackish, and all along the shore small crabs burrowed in the mud. Maria climbed a tree in which to safely rest for the evening, and from that high vantage point she could see blue in the distance, the miraculous sea. There was her future before her.

She already knew that the past was over and done.

She would never again watch another woman burn.

II.

A crow can recall every route it has ever taken, and Cadin had been this way before. Crows are messengers, spies, guides, companions, harbingers of luck, deliverers of trinkets and treasures, tireless in all ways, more loyal than any other man or beast. This one had been connected to his mistress from the time she was a baby in her basket of reeds, which was why he knew her thoughts and wishes and was aware of the destination she wanted most. A familiar is such a creature, an animal or bird that sees inside to the very soul of its human companion, and knows what others might not. What fears there might be, and what joys, for it shares the emotions of its human partner. They were on their way west, to the house where Cadin had found the silver hairpin, which he'd daringly plucked from its owner's long red hair, though she'd cursed him and thrown stones into the air aimed at him, managing only to graze him. He'd avoided her when she'd come to Devotion Field, bringing her troubles with her, but now he was headed directly toward her. He knew she was a complicated woman, and crows do not judge harshly, unless they have good reason to do so.

They had come to the Thames estuary, where the footing was as much water as it was land, a river of grass. Once or twice Maria felt herself pulled down into the rich mud that had claimed so many souls who had dared, and failed, to cross here, but she could not sink. It was not in her nature to do so, and for that she was grateful. Her dress was soon enough soaked, but no earthly difficulties troubled her. She had seen something no girl her age should see, the murder of someone she loved. The violence she'd viewed had changed and embittered her. If she had been a child before, she was no longer. Her eyes were darker, an ocean gray; her mouth was set in a fierce, unyielding line. She was bitter, and in some ways stronger than before. A stormy cloud-clotted sky didn't cause her to take shelter or find rest. Rain didn't stop her. She was on a path she had decided upon as she watched Hannah tied to her door. With each step, Maria was more resolved. She raged at a world that would allow such injustice to occur. How could the rural, verdant beauty all around her be the domain of such cruelty, a place in which the larks chattered despite the dangers they faced, unable to keep silent as they sang the praises of the sky. Maria knew now that she was not like those around her. Why that should be, she now wished to understand. All she knew was what Hannah had taught her. Life was worth living, no matter what fate might bring. That was why Maria went forward. She had decided to find her mother.

Rebecca had returned to the manor house at the edge of a vast parkland that had once belonged to a king, unaware of her husband's attack on Hannah. She assumed she would find him at home. She intended to act as if nothing was wrong, hopeful that Hannah's spell had done the trick, making him fall out of love with her, so he was willing to let her go. But her husband wasn't at home, and frankly she was grateful not to have to face him. A king's fortunes could fail, and so had her husband's. Thomas Lockland had royal blood, diluted by hatred and drink. Theirs was a case of love gone wrong. Such things happened even to the wisest of women. Rebecca had been young when she met her husband-to-be, at an age when she saw only what the outside of a man revealed. She was inexperienced enough to assume what they had was love because she wanted him, and want can be a hundred times stronger than need, and a thousand times stronger than common sense. She used the Tenth Love Potion, an enchantment only fit for those so desperate they did not fear the consequences, and there were always consequences. The payment for this potion was dear, and had, in the past, cost the user her well-being; it was the one that could turn a person inside out and destroy one or both parties. Desire, if handled incorrectly, could become a curse.

It had been easy enough for her to bewitch him, but what was sent into the world came back threefold, so strong it was tainted. She had wanted him to burn with love for her, and burn he did, three times as much as anyone should, with a vicious passion that did more damage than Rebecca would have imagined possible. In time she had turned to another man, her one true love, and she'd kept that love a secret. This was the reason she had hid her pregnancy, concealed beneath shifts and cloaks, and why she had gone into the woods by herself to give birth, already having decided she must give the child away before Thomas took the baby from her. Perhaps Rebecca was too selfish to be a good mother; all the same, she wanted to ensure that Maria would never have a taste of the brand of love she herself had known, in which a woman was all but owned and had no choice as to her own fate, with or without the use of magic. She used blue silk thread to bring good luck when she initialed her own garments, and she did the same on the woolen blanket for her baby girl. Each day she had wondered what had become of the child, and if she had inherited the skills women in the family were known for. She had traveled to see who Maria had become, even though it meant risking the wrath of a man she feared.

On the evening when Cadin brought Maria to the manor house, Rebecca was celebrating being alone. She had loosened her hair and had begun to drink the rum imported from the West Indies that her husband kept under lock and key, for she could open the catch with a flick of her wrist and a hairpin. Thomas Lockland's brothers were currently ailing after breathing in the fumes of the poison garden, and Thomas, himself, was unable to move or speak, in such a state his family worried that he might lose his life. He had been brought to his family's home, north and farther from the sea, so that his sisters could care for him. The Locklands had no cause to trust Rebecca, who had already planted the apple seeds from the amulet Hannah had crafted, so that in time there would be an orchard where the variety of apple called Everlasting brought true love to anyone who ate the fruit grown in this valley. Rebecca was grateful to be alone in the huge, drafty house, and even more grateful to be rid of her oppressor, for magic can only do so much when an initial spell has already been set.

As the night fell, however, she felt a nest of nerves coiling around her heart. That evening at dinner, a spoon had fallen, a sign that meant company was coming, something Rebecca most assuredly didn't want. She had been a selfish girl, but she was a cunning woman and she knew that everything came in threes, including death. She took a bowl and filled it with water and ink, and there she saw Hannah, nailed to her door, and Thomas in his bed, suffering from poison. Rebecca feared that she, herself, might be the third one to be afflicted. She was waiting for death to come through the door, perhaps her husband's sisters would send their own husbands and sons to come here and fill Rebecca's boots with stones before wrapping her in chains and throwing her into the river where the weeds grew tall as a man and the rushing current led to the sea.

The knock on the door was light, however, not death's hand, but the tapping of a bird's beak. It was the crow, the robber who had been here many times before. Women who are unlucky in love must throw their silver out the front door if they want to improve their fortunes, and Rebecca had often done so. There was a field of silver, tarnished from the witch's touch, and the meadow appeared glazed with light when the moon rose. It was a perfect treasure trove for a curious crow.

"Leave here!" Rebecca demanded, for she recognized the creature that had been cheeky enough to take the comb from her hair. If she wasn't mistaken, he still had a scar on his head from one of the rocks she'd thrown to chase him off.

Cadin knew what this woman was capable of, and he flew away, his wings obscuring the rising moon. Rebecca stepped over the threshold, one hand over her eye so that she could see him well enough to spell him and be rid of him once and for all. But then she spied Maria and all else fell away. There was the baby she'd left in Devotion Field, now a dark fury of a girl in sopping clothes, her black hair in knots.

Rebecca went to meet her daughter halfway. The grass was damp and she left footprints behind, each one turning as dark as some of the choices she had made. In truth she was anxious, for the girl was an unusual creature; even Rebecca, who usually cared only about her own affairs, could see that. Talent is something you're born with. It's a gift and a curse, and it's often cause for jealousy from those who are without it, although in this case, Maria's talents brought Rebecca a good deal of pride. She was a mother, after all. She might not look like one or act like one, yet she had a mother's heart. Great power was something to be celebrated.

"Why did you give me away?" Maria called out with more emotion than she wished to reveal, for this was the question she'd been carrying inside her ever since she'd come to learn that Hannah was not her mother.

"For your own safety." An excuse was an excuse, but this one was true.

"To protect me from my father?"

Maria was too clever to accept an easy answer. There was no reason for Rebecca to lie anymore, and even if she had, Maria would have known. It was clear the girl had the sight. What was to come was in the corner of Maria's eye, so that she spied both the present and the future. A death, a blessing, a love affair. She could see it all, and the world knew it and responded to her. White moths were collecting in the grass all around her. Doves gathered in the branches of one of the oldest elm trees in the county. Robbers had been hanged from its branches; the tree had turned blood red wherever a rope had been tied, and the ground beneath it was red as well. No grass grew here. The Lockland family had a legacy of greed and cruelty, and even the trees knew their history.

"My husband was not your father," Rebecca admitted in a soft voice.

"But surely I had one." Maria's face was pinched. She felt twisted inside. Hannah Owens had been her family, and now she felt alone in the world. "Or perhaps you no longer remember who he was, as you failed to remember that your husband would punish whoever might help you. Your men came to kill the woman who raised me." Maria met her mother's gaze, unafraid. She blamed Rebecca for Hannah's death, and it was in her nature to speak her mind. She could already tell, her mother might be more learned when it came to magic, but of the two, Maria was stronger.

"I did not mean for that to happen," Rebecca vowed. "She was a good woman. That was why I left you with her. I never thought my husband would be able to follow my trail." Rebecca's red hair nearly reached to her waist. She was vain and she always had been, but her expression showed heartfelt remorse. "I laid out cayenne, pepper, and lavender to confuse his dogs. I thought he'd prefer his drink to me and that he'd be too filled with rum to find where I'd been. That was my mistake. I underestimated the power of the Tenth. I know I can't undo what has been done, but even if I am at fault, I wish you would stay with me. If you ever have a child and lose her, a tragedy I wouldn't wish on any living soul, then perhaps you will forgive me."

Maria scrutinized the house, three stories of pale stone with a cobbled courtyard, the home of the Locklands for over two hundred years. She looked at her mother, who had given birth by herself in a snowy field despite her fine manor house, and who had initialed Maria's blanket with blue silk thread spun halfway across the world by glowing worms that turned into moths with bright wings.

Perhaps it was meant to be. Maria would take a chamber on the second floor. The largest one, with a lock on the door so she could have her privacy, for magic was a private affair, even between mother and daughter, and magic was all she cared about now.

Although Rebecca could neither read nor write, when it came to matters of love, she was an expert. Her *Grimoire* was filled with runic marks, the ancient alphabet of alchemy. She used these symbols to denote which herbs to use and which to avoid, which spells were best to recite in the waning or waxing of the moon, to bring forth the power of the earth and sky, incantations which were dangerous in a novice's hands. She taught Maria the eight lesser love charms, and the Ninth Potion, which was so potent one must wear gloves during its preparation. The Tenth Potion was the one she herself had used, and she did not recommend the use of that enchantment. If she knew Maria had copied it into her own *Grimoire*, at the very back of her book, she did not say; she only told her daughter to be vigilant. There were sinister aspects of magic, and what you brought into this world was your responsibility, to deal with forevermore.

Rebecca herself was drawn toward the dark, what some people called left-handed magic, and she certainly didn't care about any man's wrath, even after her years with her husband, who had known enough about her skills to set out a circle of salt around her and tie her to an iron chair before he beat her, for salt and iron deplete a witch's talents. Of course he would want to change her once he knew what she was; that was the way their love first unraveled. Rebecca knew how to blind a man and how to make him see again, what herbs would help to bring on a pregnancy, as well as those that would end that condition. Rebecca was as acquainted with the many forms of magic as she was with the corners and walls of her own bedchamber. She was a seeker of revenge, fearless since her first day on earth. She, too, had grown up as a motherless child, and because of this Rebecca had learned to survive by her wits early on. Her own mother was a witch who had disappeared after her daughter's birth. Rebecca was an outcast from the start, for her father did not wish to have her in his house-hold. It was no mistake that Rebecca had left her daughter in Devotion Field rather than with a nurse, as she had experienced the terrors of such a childhood. For what was perceived as a bit of magic—a white deer that came to her, unafraid; the sight of the red crescent mark on her leg— she'd been slapped and beaten by her nurse, then locked in a dark room until she learned to keep her talents to herself. The nurse had granted Rebecca one meal a day, unless she stole from the pantry, which she always did. She thanked that horrible woman now. The nurse had taught her how to survive, and Rebecca made her way on her beauty and her talents to the home of the Locklands, but she had wanted a real home for her daughter. She'd heard of Hannah Owens and her remedies and had chosen Hannah to raise her child with kindness and a gift for the Nameless Art. Now, after all these years, she had the chance to mentor the girl herself. Rebecca felt that she was Maria's proper teacher, with access to private knowledge known only to the women in their family. They'd come from a long line of women whose blood burned black in the snow, who could cure or wound with words and herbs, who spoke to birds and bees, who changed the weather and were either feared or respected by their neighbors.

Studying under her mother's tutelage, Maria wrote down lists of herbs and useful plants in her *Grimoire*, along with remedies for sorrow, illness, childbirth ailments, jealousy, headache, rashes, desire. There were other spells, not medicinal treatments, but spiritual, ancient enchantments that began with the Hebrew word *Abracadabra*, I create as I speak, taken from the even earlier Aramaic chant, *Avra kadavra*, It will be created in my words. Some spells were too dangerous to use, unless there was no choice, for they could wound the practitioner as well as the object of their conjuring. Spells for revenge or survival, in which the spell maker's own blood was used as ink to ensure that only she could read the words.

Sympathetic magic, using poppets and lifelike figures, and, when revenge was involved, pins and hooks. Poisons that were tasteless and odorless, but stung like a wasp before they could be noticed. Black magic, red magic, blood magic, love magic. Rebecca divided both the world that she walked through and the world that was unseen into these categories. Maria kept her book under the floorboards beside her bed. No women came here asking for Rebecca's help even if they might have wished for it. They were all too frightened of her. She did not mind if a subject had to take ill, or die, in order for her to get her way. A pin in a poppet, a vial of blood, a bird bled to death on the hearth—all of it was in her book, brought to bear when deemed useful.

There was a distance between Maria and her mother, for they were still strangers to each other, and they saw their place in the world quite differently. Maria had grown up learning to help those in need, while Rebecca thought only to help herself. Still Maria was interested in all Rebecca had to teach her. They were blood relations, after all, and one often knew what the other was thinking before the words were spoken aloud. Each also had the ability to keep secrets by throwing up a screen that blocked her most private thoughts. Shared blood didn't account for everything. They were different as night from day. Maria knew in her heart that if she'd been the one in that snowy field, she would have never left her child on her own.

FOR LOVE GONE WRONG

Vervain eases the pain of unrequited love.
A cobweb on a door means your beloved
    has been untrue.
To bring about passion: anise seed,
    burdock root, myrtle leaves.
Amulets for luck are made of blue beads,
    dove feathers, mistletoe, wishbones.
All spells increase with the waxing moon,
    decrease with the waning moon.
Place two eggs under the bed to cleanse
    the atmosphere—destroy afterward.
    Do not eat or you will swallow bad
    fortune.
A mirror beside you reflects back the evil
    eye.
For protection against love: black cloth,
    red thread, clove, blackthorn.

In the year 1675, when Maria turned eleven, there was another epidemic, of smallpox. Some towns and villages were emptied of all of their inhabitants, and the doors to houses swung open and robbers ruled the roads. It was a sorrowful and ruthless time. All the same, Rebecca often disappeared at night. It seemed she had a destination she would not or could not refuse when it called to her. She tossed a cape over her shining hair, gazed at herself in the painted black mirror that revealed the future, then ignored her fate and did as she pleased. She was headstrong and had always been so, especially in matters of love, as had been true for her own mother. The women in their family had the talent of the Nameless Art, but Rebecca admitted, they all had difficulties with love. They were prone to ignore the rules and the warnings inside their own hearts and heads. Love could ruin your life or set you free; it could happen by chance or be a well-planned decision.

When Rebecca returned in the mornings after her nights out, there were brambles in her clothes and her hair was unbraided. She had marks on her throat and shoulders, as if she'd been bitten by some animal, and she was so overheated she had no need of a cloak. Even at Maria's young age she knew there was only one reason for her mother to vanish and to spend all of the next day asleep, with the door to her room bolted shut. Night after night she disappeared, wearing her finest clothes, black crinolines, red dresses, and red boots. One dew-drenched morning when the sun had not yet risen, Rebecca returned to find Maria waiting for her in the Silver Pasture, which was littered with spoons and candlesticks and platters, all tossed out the door to bring her luck.

Cadin had presented Maria with three strands of black hair, and when she held them in her hand she knew her mother's secret.

Rebecca stopped where she stood when she realized Maria was there to greet her in the foggy morning. She had been caught red-handed, as if she were the wayward girl and Maria the strict caretaker. Her boots were slick with mud and she had a fresh bite mark on her throat, as if someone had mistaken her delicate flesh for an apple. She raised her chin, defiant. She had been a willful girl, and that trait didn't often disappear.

"Do you want to ask me a question?" she asked her daughter.

The girl was growing up, and quickly. It was already possible to see the woman she would soon be. Dark and far too curious for her own good. She came to judgments easily, and held a grudge, and was fiercely loyal. She'd had her first blood, therefore some might call her a woman already. Certainly, she had more skill than Rebecca would have imagined possible. Maria was a weather witch and could stop rain by standing in a downpour with her arms uplifted. She could melt the drifts of snow that she walked upon. Cures for fevers, love madness, insomnia, bad luck, all were within her reach. Neighbors from the nearby farms came to see her, out of her mother's line of sight, waiting anxiously beside the empty barn where Maria dried herbs. Rebecca believed magic should never be shared or bought; for her it was a bloodline talent, meant for family members alone. But Maria had learned otherwise from Hannah. What gifts you had, you were meant to share. What you set out into the world came back to you threefold. If a child was ill, if an old woman was losing her sight, if a family knew suffering, she was willing to do what she could on their behalf. She charged nothing, but accepted whatever they gave. A silver spoon, a currant cake, a copper coin.

Now as her mother approached after being gone all night, Maria held up the strands of hair the crow had brought her earlier that morning. They were the exact same color as her own hair, black as midnight, but coarser. She knew exactly who they belonged to. The man who'd been responsible for her life. She could sense who he was. A man who lived in shadow, who did as he pleased, who could convince people he was one thing, when he was someone else entirely.

"I thought I had no father," Maria said.

"No official father."

"But a father all the same. One you have come from right now." When she gave Rebecca the dark strands of hair, her mother held them with a rare tenderness and stored them in a locket she wore around her throat.

A farm boy came riding by, tentative and

nervous as he neared the house where people in the village said there lived not one witch, but two. One might curse you, one might cure you, but two had the power to do as they pleased, and there'd be no defense against them. In this world, witches were best to be avoided at all costs. Still, the boy did as his master had instructed. His horse was old and nearly lame, but the boy rode him as quickly as he could. No messenger wanted to be caught and questioned by Rebecca Lockland.

"That boy's horse has a tail as black as your hair," Rebecca said as she watched the worried rider. "Perhaps the old stallion is your father and you're only half-human."

Maria had her hands on her hips. She did not like to be taken for a fool, even by her own mother. "If there's one thing I know for certain, it's that the non-human half was inherited from you."

Mother and daughter were more than ready to quarrel as they faced each other in the field. But they had begun to pay closer attention to the boy, who leapt from the horse to nail a piece of parchment to the door, then jumped back onto his old steed to race out of sight before Maria and Rebecca reached the house. Out of breath, Rebecca tore the paper from the door and handed it to Maria to read.

"Your husband's family claims this house and will come for it and all of your belongings tomorrow," Maria told her mother. "They are legally entitled to everything, as your husband is ailing and in their care."

A single woman might own property, but a wife was entitled to nothing, and the proclamation came as no surprise. The Lockland house had been a prison, and Rebecca was glad to have good reason to leave it. She had another life to live elsewhere. They went to pack up all that mattered to them, which as it turned out, wasn't much. Maria took a change of clothes and her *Grimoire*, along with pen and ink, the black mirror of divination, and the bell from Hannah's door. Rebecca gathered some jewelry, along with a pistol that had been a favorite of her husband's and the rest of the blackened silverware. If they stayed here, they would likely be sent to Bridewell Prison, where as paupers and women alone they would be set to work and kept confined, perhaps for the rest of their lives. The wisest move was to flee as far from Essex County as possible. It was always best to step into the future while it was still waiting for you. In fact, there was a man who was Rebecca's past, present, and future. For him, Rebecca had planted a night garden that bloomed after dark. Angel's trumpet, moonflower, night jasmine, evening primrose, all waited for the moon to rise.

Both Maria and Rebecca wore skirts that were ankle-length, best to wear when riding, and neither bothered with petticoats that would only be dragged in the mud. Before they walked outside, Rebecca placed the second hairpin in Maria's hair.

"You might as well let him see you at your best."

"How do you know he's coming here?"

"We have made a decision to leave here. The Locklands will come for this place, and we can't be here when they do. As for your father, he's always been waiting for me."

Maria took him to be her father the instant she saw him approach. His horse was black, as was his hair, and he wore a long overcoat and black velvet breeches that had once been elegant, but now were threadbare. It was clear that witches didn't frighten him. He shouted out for Rebecca, a grin on his face, and in return she called him Robbie, such a sweet name in her mouth she sounded like a girl again, the one she'd been on the day she'd first met him, when he'd been a member in a company of players, often taking the part of the hero, and she had been rapt all the while she watched him, certain that he was the one for her.

He'd turned to crime during the plague years, when theaters were shut down due to illness and Puritan beliefs. Many of Shakespeare's plays hadn't been revived until recently, and then, in altered form; still there were rogue companies of

72

players, and some would still hire Robbie despite his history and his bad reputation in the theaters of London, where he had stolen from some of his contemporaries, charming them as he did so. As time went on, he became more of a thief than a player, and he couldn't return to his true calling. All the same, he thought of himself not as a robber, really, but rather as a man portraying a robber, and in this role he had excelled. Horses were his specialty, and the hearts of women, and other men's savings.

When he noticed Maria, he gazed at her, curious, but asked no questions, merely nodded a greeting. She was such a solemn creature, with her black hair parted down the middle and her pretty, somber mouth in the shape of a black rose. He would not know how to describe her, so he merely shook his head. He was quite marvelous at speaking other people's words, but otherwise could not express himself. Some men are tongue-tied in that way; they need a prompt that allows them to release their emotions, unless they are in bed with a woman they love, and then they reveal themselves in a thousand ways. Maria gazed at her parents as they embraced. She herself would want more. A man who talked, who could speak for hours and still be worth listening to, as he told stories of his own making. A man who listened to what you had to say.

Most times this particular man, called Robbie

73

for as long as he could remember, tried not to think about all that he'd done in order to survive in the world. Robbie had brought with him a horse for Maria to ride, recently appropriated from a local farmer, and he took Rebecca onto his own. At last he had the love of his life beside him, and for him this was enough. Thieves have hearts and souls, and his heart was pounding. Before they left, he took a flint, and with a spark he lit some hay wrapped around an arrow. He shot the lit arrow into the door of the house, then shot six others similarly made through the windows. He'd done this very same thing in a play once, one about the son of a king who yearned for vengeance, but then the flaming arrows had been aimed into a bucket of sand offstage. Now he clearly took pleasure in what was a very real act. When he smiled, his face changed; he was as handsome as a boy again, and Maria could see why her mother loved him so.

"There's my gift to you," he told Rebecca as the flames went up.

Even though the grand stone house would be standing when the lord's family came to make their claim, everything inside would be burned to ash. That was vengeance, pure and simple, for all the years her husband had stolen from them.

They went through the estuary, riding south. At times the horses were chest-deep in water.

It was a glorious golden day. Riding behind her parents, Maria could hear a spray of her mother's laughter, a beautiful, musical sound. There seemed a sea change in Rebecca now that Robbie had come for her; she was not a witch, merely a woman in love. Clearly she allowed her raw emotions to lead her astray. Maria thought of all the things she should have asked during the time she'd spent with her mother. She'd gathered knowledge about enchantments and remedies, but no knowledge about their own history. How they had come to be the way they were. What trick of nature were they? Why did their blood burn black? Why should they avoid water at all costs if they could not sink? For some, witchery was a choice, but not for them. It was in their very nature, and they must do their best with it, but how did a woman survive when she would surely be judged again and again? Now it was too late to ask. The future was upon them, and Maria could see it would split in two, their fates diverging as they went their separate ways.

Every once in a while the man who was Maria's father would turn to gaze over his shoulder at her as if he continued to be surprised that she existed. There was clearly no room for her; the love between her mother and father was exclusive and couldn't contain anyone else. Some love is like that; it only has room enough to fit two people, who can only see one another and include no one else. The love between them was the reason her mother could leave her in the snowy field, to hide Maria's cap of black hair so that no one would suspect who the baby's father might be. He'd never been apprehended as a robber, but he wouldn't have escaped Thomas Lockland's murderous rage had Lockland ever found out the truth and discovered his wife had a lover. As good an actor as he might be, Maria's father would never have been mistaken for an innocent man.

They rode for a very long time, and when at last they came to the sea, Maria was both terrified and thrilled. The water stretched out before them, a wild blue field of waves. The sound was deafening, the possibilities enormous. There was another unknown world beyond their own, and frankly Maria was done with England, and had been since the fire in Devotion Field. She was glad that Cadin was on her shoulder, her one true friend, for the world seemed very big and she felt young and small. They stopped at an inn to take some food. Robbie went inside while Rebecca waited hidden in a yew hedge, so she would not be recognized should her husband's family come searching after they found the manor house burned from the inside out. Robbie brought out some meat and bread and cheese. Maria fed the crow, but took nothing for herself.

"Do you wish to starve?" the man who was her father asked.

He said it more out of interest than concern. His eyes were pitch-black, and he had a wide mouth and high cheekbones, as she did. He was so handsome that women in London often followed him down the street; some fainted at the sight of him, as if he were the hero in the theatricals they'd seen come to life. A smile played at his lips as he spoke to Maria, for her presence continued to puzzle and amuse him. She was a great beauty, and in his experience that would bring her both good fortune and grief. In many ways Robbie was a simple man, and he stood in judgment of no one. He knew what Rebecca was and did not fault her for it. A witch was a funny thing, particularly when you loved her. If not for Rebecca, he would not be in the strange circumstance of trying to rescue a black-haired girl who stared at him with cold eyes, when they should have already left the county. He wished he could write a drama that would tell the story of the night when he first saw Rebecca and came under her spell. She was already married, not that it mattered to either one of them, for their love for each other consumed everything in their way, that much was clear to Maria.

"Tell me, girl," he said to this strange daughter of his. "What is it you want in this world?"

"I wish to have a life that I can claim for my

own, without paying for the crimes of my mother and father," Maria told him. "Where do I go to do that?" When she squinted, the present was transparent, and she could view a future where Cadin flew above her in a different world, a place where every plant was one she had never seen before, a land in which there were trees with thorns and trees bent over in the wind, trees with blood-red leaves and those with branches as white as snow.

They were not far from a harbor, and gulls wheeled across the sky. The city of London was nearby, and smoke rose from the city's chimneys in great black clouds. A city such as this was a wondrous and terrible thing where anything could happen. It was the place where one could find the end of her days or the beginning of her life. And yet Maria knew that this city was not the place where she would find her future.

Rebecca had come to stand beside her man. "That's why we're here," Rebecca told their daughter. "So that you will have a life of your own. It's your future we're thinking of. We're sending you away."

"I can't say I'm surprised," Maria said with dark bitterness. What would they want with her when they were so involved with one another?

Her parents exchanged a look. She was difficult indeed. Still, she was theirs, and they meant to see she was safely away from Thomas Lockland's family, who might wish her ill. There was a far-off place called Curaçao, a Dutch Island where she might have a future that was very different from the solitary life in the fens that Hannah Owens had known. She could remain in a place where a woman alone had no rights to her own life or she could agree to her parents' plan and travel half a world away where anything might be possible.

"Fine," Maria said, grabbing for a crust of bread. The truth was, she was starving. She'd met her father, and known her mother, and had been lucky enough to have been found by Hannah Owens. Now she was ready for a life of her own. "I'll go where you send me, but the crow comes along."

They went on to Southampton, and in a shop near the docks, Rebecca bought her daughter parting gifts: a heavy woolen cape and a pair of boots for her journey. Maria slipped off her ragged shoes made of worn leather lined with wool. She was delighted with her gifts. The cloak was soft and lovely, and the boots were a pure wonder, red leather, made in Spain. Every witch should own a pair, whether she worked in a field or walked through the halls of a manor house.

Rebecca was happy that she had pleased her daughter with her purchases. "I know you better than you thought I might," she said cheerfully. "We're of the same blood and we favor the same things."

In her way, Rebecca loved her child dearly, but what you give up you can learn to live without, even if it causes you heartbreak at the start. Whether you are mortal or not, you go on, even if sorrow nags at you. Rebecca did not bequeath her *Grimoire* to her daughter, but then Maria had not expected her to do so, for it was still in use, and Maria had written down all of her mother's knowledge in her own book. Instead, Rebecca gave her a leather bag which included several packets of useful herbs, beeswax candles, and a spool of blue silk thread, all for the creation of amulets and potions.

"Never be without thread," she told the girl. "What is broken can also be mended. Remember that in your dark days, as I have." There was also a bag of oranges from Spain bought at a market and worth their high price. "This will keep you well and healthy on board a ship. Take my advice and stay away from men for as long as you can. Love is trouble, and trouble is love."

A fine bit of guidance from a woman who'd so thoughtlessly loved the wrong man not once but twice. Even here, along the docks, where life swirled all around them, she couldn't take her gaze away from Robbie. Likely it was true that the flaws you saw in other women you didn't notice in yourself. Love everlasting, love wished for desperately, love that walks in through the door, love that is a mistake, love that is yours alone.

Robbie had fashioned a bargain with the captain of a ship from Amsterdam that, in his opinion, would favor everyone, including himself. Now that the deal had been struck, he was waiting with the horses, more than ready to go. He let out a low whistle and bowed, the most handsome man in three counties. Rebecca grinned and waved, as if her heart were in her hand. Anyone with even a bit of the sight could tell there would surely be trouble ahead.

"Is this what love is?" Maria asked her mother, who was gazing at Robbie on the pier.

"Oh, yes," Rebecca said. "I'd die for it."

In fact, she would. When Robbie was caught by the sheriff for crimes he had committed, she would be hanged alongside him, not for witchery, of which she would have likely been found guilty, but as an accomplice to horse theft, a crime with which her man was well acquainted. When there was gossip about Rebecca—she had herbs with her, and wore talismans on her wrists and at her throat—the jailers clasped iron shoes on her feet, and as witches are helpless in the grip of that metal, she could not work her magic, she could only weep tears that scalded the ground beneath them. Robbie would give a speech that many in the crowd, especially the women, would remember for years to come. He'd speak of a love that would never end, about the world they shared and the heaven they would share as well.

He would quote from *The Tempest*, a revival of which he'd had the honor to be a part of, though his words to Rebecca were so heartfelt, everyone thought they were his own.

> *Hear my soul speak:*
> *The very instant that I saw you, did*
> *My heart fly to your service.*

The crowd would listen appreciatively, for they were fine words, indeed, and many of the women would applaud, but they would hang him all the same. Rebecca could see bits and pieces of the event to come when she looked into a pool of water in the gutter. Still, that awful occurrence would not be for months, and the time they had together was precious, and part of a bargain Rebecca was willing to make. "Love is not always under our control," she told her daughter.

"It will never be that for me." Maria was already wearing the red boots, and although she adored the gift, she would avoid her mother's path at all costs. She vowed she would never let love rule her life.

Mother and daughter said their good-byes on the dock, embracing one another, their true feelings surfacing. Despite all the time they had been apart, they had similar hearts, surprisingly easy to break, but they were strong when it mattered and it mattered now, for they both understood that they would not meet again.

The world was so much larger than Maria would have ever imagined, and all that lived in the sea seemed enormous as well: the creatures that swam alongside the ship spouting foul-smelling water, and slithering dark things that clung to the hull, fish whose mouths were filled with teeth, scaly sea snakes and blue crabs pulled up in nets overflowing with dark purple seaweed. At night the stars tore through the black sky, and when it rained the world itself seemed upside down, with water above and below. Strong men cried and called for their mothers during the worst of these storms, and fish leapt onto the deck to escape the roiling waves, but Cadin clattered into Maria's ear that they merely needed to stay alive, nothing more. Take a breath, hold tight, and soon enough the sky would reappear, blue as glass, and the men would return to work, not remembering how they wept for their mothers' arms. These same sailors did not soon forget that Maria could announce a storm before it appeared on the horizon, any more than they would forgo her remedies, for she was soon enough known to be a healer, and many of the men had learned to come to her when they were ill. She might have been in danger from their rough ways, for even at her young age she was a woman in most of their eyes, but no one dared to harm her or search her out in a dark corner. She knew more than most women twice her age; they could see it in her eyes, their own fates reflecting back to them.

Maria knew to use spirits of turpentine to prevent lockjaw, salt and molasses for a salve used on deep cuts that might otherwise poison a man's blood, black or green tea steeped with boiling milk and nutmeg for dysentery. If a man among them had hurt Maria, he would only be damaging his own chances at completing the long journey whole and well. She was valued, and although none would admit it aloud, all the crew felt fortunate to have her aboard.

FOR SEA TRAVEL

Hyssop tea will rid a man of worms.
Basil will preserve fish.
Borage can heal abscesses.
Ginger and vinegar for sores.
Mint for toothache.
If the cat on board sleeps in a coil, the weather will be bad.
If the sun rises red, there will be rain.
Do not take salt from another person's hand at the table, or you will both have bad luck. If salt spills, throw a pinch over your left shoulder.

Blue thread sewn onto every piece of clothing, for protection.

Hannah had taught Maria how to keep weevils out of the biscuits, and for this the cook and all the passengers were extremely thankful. Rats could be done away with by the use of monkshood, caraway was good for spider bites, peony root guarded against storms, nightmares, and lunacy, for there were those who were made mad by the endless rush of the sea. Because of those she had cured, Maria was thought to be a saint by some, although there were others who were certain she was a witch, for sailors were a superstitious lot, and their traditions included attempts at seafaring magic. A silver coin was always placed beneath the mast, a page of paper was never to be torn in two on board, a brand was used to mark wooden masts to drive out evil spirits and keep the vessel safe in storms. Cadin, who might have been deemed unlucky, or perhaps seen as a harbinger of death and destruction, was welcomed when Maria insisted he was a black albatross. Although none of the sailors had ever heard of such a creature before, they all knew there were marvelous, new things to be found in the world every day, and since an albatross brings luck to sailors, no one dared to challenge Maria.

The captain, a Dutchman named Dries Hessel, who always wore a knee-length coat treated with tar and animal grease for waterproofing, did little that did not bring a profit. That was why he'd allowed the girl on board. He'd arranged to sell her for sixty shillings once they reached Curaçao, a good bargain, considering he'd paid Maria's father only forty for her. A player in the theater survived as he must, and the captain of a ship assumed it was also his right to do the same, even when the object he sold was a person. Maria would be an indentured servant for a period of five years, and whoever bought her would own her outright during this time, then be legally responsible for freeing her on the appointed date that ended her servitude. That the girl had used her blue thread to sew up a wound Hessel suffered when a windstorm drove a splinter of the mast through his flesh had done nothing to change his mind regarding her fate. Nothing was free in this world, not a breath, not a life, not a journey.

Many on board were Portuguese refugees who had paid whatever price necessary for their passage, as they pursued an escape from persecution for their faith. Jews were not allowed in Spain or Portugal, or in England or France, and so they had set off for the New World, practicing their religion in secret until the time came when they at last found a place that offered a safe haven. Those who crossed the ocean wished to have the freedom to be true to themselves. For now, they were simply called the Portugals. They had brought dried codfish with them, and cheese made with thistle powder to set it rather than jelly from the hooves of animals, the rind covered by paprika to prevent rot. Maria learned their language, for she had an ear for such things, and made certain to help those women brought low by seasickness, with a spoonful of ginger paste and a slice of orange, carefully doled out to the ailing women and their children, for even the smallest taste of fresh fruit was a tonic. She listened to their stories, and observed them when they lit a candle on Friday at sunset, for candles were dangerous at sea, just as religion was dangerous on land.

At night Maria wrapped herself in her cloak and watched the stars appear in the sky, one by one at first, then whirls of constellations pricking through the darkness in a brilliant ceiling of light. How immense and beautiful the world was, especially to a girl who had never even been to town while growing up, never seen a shop or a market or a church filled with people as the bells rang on Sundays. She wished that Hannah could stand beside her on the deck of the ship and feel the future as she did, as a place where a woman might command her own fate. She was grateful that she had been found in that field of snow, and raised by a woman who was truly kind, just as she was grateful that her mother had given her the gift of sight. What was before her was still a mystery, even when she looked into the black mirror, for she had changed her fate when she came to cross the sea, although some aspects of the future remained the same: the daughter she would have, the man who brought her diamonds, the snow in the branches of the trees. When she saw bits and pieces of the time to come, she knew she would find the sort of freedom her mother and Hannah hadn't known. There had always been women who commanded the same talents as Maria, and most had taken refuge from the world so they would not be tested by drowning. If a witch floated she was proclaiming her pact with Satan. If she drowned she was innocent, for all the good it would do her to be dragged, lifeless and bound, from the depths of a river or pond, often wearing iron shoes nailed to the soles of her feet. Maria's predecessors would have thought her mad to be so far out at sea, with nothing but the waves around her, but she was convinced she had nothing to fear from water, only from men who saw evil where there was none.

On windy days, when it seemed the ship might take to the sky and the sailors tied themselves to the deck with ropes so they wouldn't rise up into the whirling air, Maria kept Cadin safe inside her cloak and fed him bits of cracker. A ship was a terrible place to be as the weeks went by, with less food and water and all manner of pestilence, lice and rats, lightning and storms. There were times when those on board thought the end was near. Men who had never prayed before did so, many in a language none of the sailors could decipher. Women blessed their children and held them tightly so they might walk into the nets of death side by side. But Maria could see enough of the future to know they would reach their destination. She looked in her black mirror and saw that the sun would be stronger than any of the passengers would have thought possible and the streets would be made of red dirt and the trees would flower in every season.

"Hush," she told the Portugals' children when they cried. "We've almost reached the other side of the world."

When they arrived, it was exactly as she had seen it would be, a land of oddities and miracles. The passengers looked out and blinked in wonder at where their journey had taken them. The cactus towered thirty feet tall, thorny acacia bushes bloomed with vivid lemon-colored flowers, and the divi-divi trees were bent over in the wind so they might look up to heaven. The children said these trees were little men wearing over-coats. There were yellow and orange birds in the sky, troupials and bananaquits, along with kingbirds and flamingos and hummingbirds no larger than bees that passed by a person's ear and left that individual's head ringing with a soft buzzing sound. There were birds that only flew at night, nighthawks and nightjars, black shadows in the dark and the dusk that drank dew from leaves as big as saucers. People of all sorts could be found here due to the Spanish slave trade and the settlement of Sephardic Jews. Many had on modest traditional clothing, long skirts called sayas worn over pants and shirts with combinations of two or three patterns.

A young woman named Juni, only a year or so older than Maria herself, was waiting on the dock, sent to hurry her along. Juni clapped her hands and called out a welcome in Dutch, in disbelief when she realized that Maria knew little of that language. "You had better learn to speak as we do," Juni advised, in English now. "Or maybe you have the right idea; this way you don't have to listen to what Mr. Jansen says."

The captain handed Maria her papers, which stated that she belonged to the Jansen family of Willemstad. She was to work for them until the age of sixteen, at which time Maria would be a free woman. She now understood that her father had sold her into servitude; he would likely say it had been for her own protection, and perhaps he meant no harm. She was a girl on her own after all, with nothing to her name.

"Are you free?" Maria asked Juni as they

walked side by side on the dock crowded with fish vendors and sailors, some of whom had no allegiance to any country and sailed only for themselves, pirates and traders of the roughest sort.

"I'm the same as you. Not a slave and not free. That's another way of saying we're nothing."

Juni's skin was a warm brown and her black hair was as long as Maria's. Her African mother had been bound to the Jansens' household as a slave, and her great-aunt had been granted her freedom only after working for the family for thirty years. Juni herself was a servant, and had been so all her life, since the time she was born, with no papers that affixed a time to her servitude. To Maria, that sounded like slavery.

"You have no papers?" Maria asked. "No date for your freedom?"

Juni was extremely beautiful, and men of all sorts stared at her as they walked along. "Mr. Jansen holds on to them for me. I'll be free when I marry."

But in fact, each time a suitor came around, Mr. Jansen found fault with him and sent him on his way. It didn't matter if a man was African or Jewish or Dutch. None would do.

"*Niet goed genoeg,*" he would say every time. *Not good enough.*

"I plan to never marry," Maria announced. She had seen a daughter in her future, but no husband.

91

Only the man with the diamonds, who, as they walked along the wooden dock, under clouds of parrots, seemed an impossible fate.

"That's what you say now," Juni responded. "Just you wait. If you're married you won't be a servant."

"I'm not certain I can be that now," Maria said, a scowl on her face.

"We do as they tell us until they go to bed, then we do as we please."

Maria had never had a friend and had never seen a need for one, but now in this faraway place she was grateful that Juni had a kind heart and had taken her under her wing.

"Do what I do, say what I say, and you will be fine," Juni assured her.

It was easy to see how enchantments might be brought about here. The sky wasn't blue in the early evenings, but instead there was a palette of color that ran from rose to deep violet to cobalt to ink. There were sixty-eight varieties of butterflies on the island, including large orange-and-black monarchs and tigerwings that only flew in the shade. The air was moving and alive, and when the wind came up suddenly it was a soft, dark breeze filled with salt and the tang of seaweed. Trapped in his carrying case, Cadin called to be set free. "Not right now," Maria told him. "You'll be out soon enough."

"Mrs. Jansen wouldn't like a bird here. She'll

say it's filthy and will ruin her house," Juni warned, not that Maria cared.

"Mrs. Jansen doesn't need to know."

Juni smiled at her then. The new girl seemed more interesting than most, and she thought she would be pleased to see how the household was provoked by someone who didn't seem concerned with their rules.

As soon as Maria was rid of her grimy clothes that she had worn day in and day out, and had washed with strong soap and water so hot it stung, she began her new life. She was only a girl and exhausted from her journey, but she would do as she must in order to survive. There were two other servants sharing their chamber, sisters from Manchester, England, who had only another year to work off their debt.

"We'll be gone in the blink of an eye," the sisters boasted simultaneously, for they had the habit of saying the same thing at the same time. They thought they were better than Juni because her mother had been a slave, and better than Maria, who was so young and inexperienced.

Maria waited for the other girls to go to supper, then she hid her *Grimoire* beneath the floorboards before going off to explore. She knew well enough to keep her bloodline a secret, for her talents could bring her luck or misery. It was a curious place she found herself in, the opposite of all she had known. Where there had been darkness, there was now light. Where there had been a solitary life, there was now a bustling household. Much of the living space was outside, and as she crossed the courtyard she marveled at how in this arid, subtropical land there could be a garden that was so lush. She walked along a path that was bordered by mangoes and Jamaican apple trees and brilliant flowering aloe vera speckled with yellow blooms. It was here she set Cadin free. She had crafted an amulet to wear around her throat with a single black feather, so she knew he would always be called back to her, no matter how far he might go. The bird studied her from the branch of a guava tree, then rose into the dusky air of this new world of theirs. By now it was evening. The moon itself seemed different here, glowing with pale silver light. In the salt flats there were miraculous birds, flamingoes, white and scarlet ibis, green herons, great blue herons, and the black-crowned night heron that cried in the dark as if it were a woman pleading for her life. But of all of these, it was the robber crow that was most beautiful to Maria, for he had more compassion than any man she had ever met, and far more loyalty.

At supper, Maria was served *funchi*, a soft corn-meal dish, along with a small bowl of *stoba*, a spicy stew flavored with papaya, leftover from the Jansen family's dinner. It was a large household, the Jansens and their three daughters, all nearly grown and looking for husbands. Juni and the sisters explained there was more than enough work for them all; they were pleased that Maria had come to stay. As for Maria, she was polite and cheerful, for Hannah had always said there was no need to ever let anyone know what you were thinking. Why be punished for your thoughts or beliefs? Maria believed no one should have her life signed over to another, but she kept quiet, knowing that, in the end, she would do as she pleased. To amuse the other girls she told fortunes by examining the lines on their hands. She had informed them that for women the right hand was the fate they were born with, but the marks on the left hand told the story of what they had experienced, the choices that had changed their original fates. The heart line was always most interesting; it was the mark that showed who was selfish, who would be content, and whose heart would be easily broken. She told them all they would fall in love and marry, which was true enough, leaving out the details they wouldn't wish to hear: who would fall in love too easily and who would find sorrow and who would make a choice she would later regret. The Manchester girls were pleased with Maria's special talent and called her their little sister. Little sisters would do well to be cunning, and it was wise for Maria to get along with everyone, at least for as long as it suited her, and it would have to suit her until she was free. She had one last precious orange left from those her mother had given her, and this she shared with the other housemaids before they fell into their white metal beds, the girls so happy to have her among them that no one complained when she left the window open on warm evenings to make certain that Cadin could always come home.

III.

No one knows where time goes, all the same it disappears. Maria had turned fifteen in this strange land that still seemed like a dream. Every color was vivid, and when she stood in the brilliant light she sometimes found herself yearning for the dark green of the forest where ferns turned black in the frost. She didn't wish to be a servant, she wouldn't wish it on anyone, still she continued to do the work expected of her, seeing to the list Mrs. Jansen gave her each morning. She had become an excellent cook, and had learned to leave and enter a room without making a sound, walking barefoot on the tiles so as not to disturb the members of the Jansen family. Maria combed the Jansen daughters' hair, washed in rum to keep it strong, and stitched their wedding dresses. She learned that eggs would keep well in limewater, that quicksilver beaten into egg whites could poison bedbugs, that lamp wicks would not smell bad if the cotton wick yarn was rinsed with vinegar, then dried in the fresh air. She was taught to shake carpets rather than sweep them and to wash silk dresses in green tea to restore their shine. During the day, she kept her eyes lowered and kept her mind on the tasks at hand. At night, however, she did as she pleased after Mr. and Mrs. Jansen went to sleep on the sheets she and Juni had washed with a harsh soap composed of lye and ashes, before they were hung out to dry in the garden, to ensure that the fabric would smell sweet, scented by fresh air and the clouds of fragrance rising from flowerbeds.

Who she truly was, she kept secret, a stone she had swallowed, those talents and traits she had inherited from the nameless women who had come before her. Maria never revealed how she knew to take in the laundry just before rain began to fall, or how she managed to chase the rats from the garden with a bit of white powder, or why she left garlic, salt, and rosemary outside their chamber door, to protect those inside from ill will. Certainly, she never explained why she refused to venture into the ocean when on their free Sunday afternoons she and Juni went to the shore. The day might be glorious, the sea might beckon, but she knew what would happen to someone such as herself in the water. She would float no matter what, and in doing so, she would reveal her true nature. This was why Hannah had kept herself hidden in the woods, and why Rebecca showed her talents to no one. It was a dangerous world for women, and more dangerous for a woman whose very bloodline would have her do not as she was ordered, but as she pleased.

On hot nights Maria and Juni escaped through the window so they might prowl the island. They were young and the heat made for restless sleepers. They were alive and wanted more than the room they lived in and the interests of people other than themselves. They'd grown close, for now it was only the two of them. The Manchester sisters, Katy and Susannah, had worked off their debt, and had then been free to marry the first men who came along, wretched suitors Maria warned them to deny. She looked into the sisters' tea leaves and into their palms and told them to wait, there would be other men to choose from, or perhaps it might be better to set off on their own lives. The sisters hadn't listened, and they'd married two silent, gloomy brothers. Their lives had changed very little since they had worked for the Jansens, only now it wasn't a grand house they cared for, but wooden shacks near the harbor, one wedged next to the other on stilts above the blue sea that rotted the floorboards and left a silver sheen of salt over every dish and chair. When the trade winds came up, the sisters had to nail their furniture to the floor and tie themselves to the decks of their houses with jute rope. Their husbands were off fishing most of the time, and for that they were grateful, for they treated the sisters badly; sex was for the husband's pleasure and women were not to speak back to men. Maria visited the sisters and brought them crisp red apples, an unusual fruit in this climate, for which she'd paid dearly. She told the sisters to prick the fruit with a needle as they said their husbands' names, then bake the apples into pies which, once devoured by the men, would bring about kindness and a bit of consideration from the sour, ill-tempered sailors they'd wed. After that the sisters embroidered a blue shawl for Maria, and every bird on the island was sewn into the fabric, for both sisters owed her a huge debt of gratitude, and later both would name their first daughters Maria so that they said that name a hundred times a day with love and devotion.

On nights when Maria and Juni climbed out the window to poke around and look down lanes and sandy paths, they felt more fortunate than the Jansens' daughters, who wore heavy silk dresses and undergarments constructed with bones, and tight shoes that left blisters on their feet, and were rarely allowed to go out on their own, even now that they were married and living in their husbands' homes. Juni was called upon by young men and boys who were dazzled by her beauty, but no one noticed Maria. She'd learned a lesson from Hannah and Rebecca, and to protect herself from love she wore a black petticoat under her dress, the hem stitched with blue thread, the fabric washed with cloves and blackthorn. She knew how to walk in the shadows so she wouldn't shine in the darkness. No one looked at her twice.

Often Maria and Juni borrowed the donkey kept in the stable with the family's horses. They called the sulky creature *Slechte Jongen*, "Bad Boy," for he would balk and refuse to carry them home, forcing them to pull him along with a rope to ensure they'd be back in time to start the family's breakfast. They were almost children again when they urged the donkey to keep moving, holding their stomachs, keeping their hands over their mouths so their laughter wouldn't rise into the air. But their world was not one meant for children, only for obedience and work. It was an island where some people had everything and others had nothing, and you could judge who was who from the shoes that they wore, the color of their skin, and whether or not their eyes were kept downcast while walking on the winding streets.

On some nights the girls visited the caves north of the city where escaped slaves had hidden, often until they were nothing but bones. Between 1662 and 1669, twenty-four thousand slaves had been shipped through Curaçao by the Dutch West India Company and the Royal African Company in Jamaica. These caves had been sacred places for the original people of the island, the Arawaks, all gone now, murdered or killed off by disease or shipped to work on plantations on other islands. The original people had left behind drawings that were more than a thousand years old. It was here, where marvelous renderings of the life they had known or imagined had been etched into the rock, that Maria often lit a white candle in memory of Hannah Owens. She was grateful for the years when she had been hidden away from the rest of the world in Devotion Field, and for the gift Hannah had given her when she taught her to read and write.

The plantations on the island were worked by slaves who would not be granted their freedom for another hundred years. For them, reading was considered a criminal offense. Reading was power, just as Hannah had said, and those who gave books to slaves were arrested. It was a time of evil, when people were owned and women were treated no better than they had been across the sea. Still, there was magic here. *Brua*, a name derived from *bruja*, Spanish for witch, had been brought from the shores of Africa, used for healing by practitioners who were said to help those possessed by spirits with the use of amulets and spells, and were called upon by those who searched for revenge or begged for mercy or needed to find what was lost. Maria had stumbled upon the remains of such a meeting.

A circle drawn in the sand, amulets of beads and shells and feathers set out within the sacred space. When she mentioned her find to Juni, she was told that Juni's great-aunt, Adrie, practiced *brua*.

"Take me to a meeting," Maria said.

"Never," Juni told her.

Juni's great-aunt had warned her to mind her business when it came to magic, advising that a woman always paid dearly for her interest in such matters. Still, Maria was persistent. When she'd stood inside the circle she'd felt a surge of power.

"I won't ask for anything else," she promised Juni. "We can just watch. I'll do all the house-work for a week. I will never divulge your secrets."

Juni's secrets consisted only of kissing a few young men and occasionally avoiding their mistress by hiding in a tall bureau; still a friend was a friend. Eventually Juni gave in and brought Maria to the meeting. On the night of the ritual, they held hands and watched from behind the tallest mango trees. The singing was beautiful, as if the angels had gathered in the clearing, with high, clear voices that echoed through the gleaming blue evening. The clients came one by one, many distraught and in tears—grieving parents, women in love, men who needed to escape from a bad situation. When the hour grew late, the group dispersed. Maria and Juni were bleary-eyed, yet they had made a pact, and they now crept into the circle of sand that had been cast, so that they might examine the amulets that had been left behind, for both the living and the dead. Seashells, stones, packets of seeds, small white bones. They were so intent on the discovery of these magical objects they didn't notice they weren't alone. Juni's great-aunt, Adrie, came from beyond the hedges. Adrie had the sight, and one of these two young ladies was about to find herself in trouble. Juni's great-aunt signaled for them to come forward. She was very old, known to be a *curioso*, a healer, famous for her teas. She was well aware that in this world it was best not to trust anyone who wasn't a blood relation. It was one thing for her great-niece to be here, quite another for a stranger to spy on them.

"Why did you bring her here?" she asked Juni, her eyes on Maria. She saw a young indentured girl who owned nothing of her own. But there was something more to her. Adrie saw the mark inside the girl's elbow.

"She's my friend, Auntie," Juni explained. "We were only watching."

The old woman shook her head and clucked her tongue, sure of herself. "She's a witch. Stay away from her."

Juni laughed, equally sure of herself. "Would she clean the Jansens' house if she were a witch?

Would she see to their laundry and draw their baths? No witch would do that."

"Of course she would. Didn't I do the same?" Adrie turned to Maria and looked directly into the girl's silver eyes. "Don't come back here."

"I honor what you do," Maria said.

"Do you?"

"Yes, I admire your skills, and I'm good at keeping secrets."

"I'd better not see you here again," Adrie said, which held a very different meaning than her first response. It wasn't an outright no, merely a warning not to be caught. "And don't let me hear you talking about this to anyone."

They had gotten their permission. The girls watched the meetings from a distance after that, just close enough to hear the incantations. Adrie ignored them, until one night, after the gathering had ended, she signaled in their direction. The girls came forward, nervous. "Just the other one," she told Juni. When Maria approached, Adrie patted the ground. "Why do you come here?"

"Because you know so much," Maria said.

If Adrie was flattered, her stern expression didn't change. "You're not a blood relation. Why should I give my knowledge to you?"

"I'll use it," Maria told her. "I'm not afraid of it. The woman who raised me was like you. I learned from her, and I wish nothing more than to learn from you."

After that Juni went out with her suitors at night, and Maria spent her time with Adrie. She added her lessons to the *Grimoire*. There were lists of plants, those that could break a fever, those that could set a man's imagination on fire, or could ease a woman's childbirth. There were recipes for revenge and for love, for health and well-being and to fend off curses.

CURAÇAO CURES

Soursop tea made from a glossy green tree with yellow-green flowers, cures insomnia, infections, and keeps away lice.

Mampuritu, a slender weed for tea to cure for nausea and cramps.

Kleistubom, a creeping weed with an extract helpful to ease prickly heat.

Lamoengras for fever.

Caraway cures the bites of poisonous scorpions and centipedes.

Wandu helps with an easy delivery of a baby, also good for the blood and improves memory and strength.

Tawa-tawa, a tea made from the hairy plant found in the grassland, a cure for Dengue, called Breakbone Fever, that stops bleeding inside the body.

"You may be a witch, but remember you're a woman as well," Adrie told her. By gazing into a pan of still water, she'd already seen several mistakes Maria was destined to make. The wrong man, the wrong trust, the wrong vow, the wrong curse. It was so much easier to see another person's future than it was to understand your own. Even when you kept your eyes wide open, the world would surprise you.

Maria tucked a packet of lavender inside her dress to protect herself from evil, but in all this time she had not once thought to protect herself from love. Maria knew it happened to other women, but she never expected it to happen to her. She had renounced it and had made a vow to always do so. She recalled how many lives her mother had ruined because of love; she remembered that Hannah's beloved had turned her over to the authorities. But fate could be beyond a woman's control, even a woman who had the sight. She paid no attention to the dark bits of the future flickering in every mirror she passed, pulsing like fireflies in reverse, black sparks of regret. Her dream had always been the same since she had come to Curaçao: to be a free woman, one who could do as she pleased, bowing to no master. In only a few months that time would come to pass. She would no longer sweep another woman's floor or brush her hair, or bring beer and warm milk to a man who called her *meisje*, Dutch for girl, because her name didn't matter to him so he never bothered to remember what it was.

When the first of January finally arrived, she would start a bonfire on the shore to mark the end of her contract. She would let it burn all night long.

Everything might have been different if she hadn't walked into the dining room at nine in the morning, a room she entered every day to polish the silver, which she did wearing heavy cotton gloves, and sweep away the red dust that filtered inside even when the wooden shutters were closed. Had she come an hour later, had she chosen to first set to work on preparations for dinner, had she done the washing and not waited for the afternoon sun, fate would have shifted. As it turned out, she was prompt. The day was blistering, and she had on her blue skirt and blue bodice, for blue was the color servants wore, since the dye was so cheap. Still the dress showed off her lovely shape and was short enough to show her long legs. She threw a passing glance at herself in the mirror above the sideboard. Oddly, she saw a glimpse of her mother's reflection instead of her own. It was a startling sight that stopped her cold. True, she resembled Rebecca, with the same cool gray eyes and delicate features, though she was already taller and far more skilled at enchantments. But even a witch can possess a woman's flaws, and a woman's desires. Maria thought she knew what was to come, but she was wrong. Anyone can fall in love, despite vows to the contrary. Any woman can make a mistake, especially when she is young, and sees the wrong man through a haze so that he appears to be something he's not.

Maria wore her long hair piled atop her head, held with the hairpins no one would suspect to be silver, for they appeared to be black, and were thought to be worthless. In her position it was best to have nothing, and all that she had she made certain to keep concealed, including the fact that she was now fluent in Dutch and Spanish and Portuguese. She was barefoot; her red boots were made for snow and foul weather, not heat and fair skies, and called attention to her differences. All of the housemaids went barefoot, priding themselves on how tough the soles of their feet were. It was an island of people who could survive an arid land, like the iguanas in the desert that could go weeks without water. This was not a place for the faint-hearted, and the beauty of the island belied its trials. The winds could raise a man into the air and toss him back down half a mile from where he'd originally stood. Rain rarely fell, and when it did it was collected in barrels, and even then it carried the taste and sheen of salt.

On the day she met the man who changed her fate, Maria had come from the sun-drenched courtyard, her skin still warm from the glints of sunlight sifting through the leaves. She always hated to leave that lovely spot, with its painted tiles and a fountain that was the home of three golden fish that hid beneath a lily pad whenever Cadin was near. She was dizzy, her head filled with sun, when she came inside to find a man gazing out the window at the sea, as if it were the enemy that divided him from everything he was accustomed to, pine and birch trees, fields of sheep, a house with black shutters closed against winter storms, a red fire that burned all night long. Even before she saw his face, Maria sensed he was the man she had seen in the black mirror. In the mirror he had been walking away, and so she had never spied his face, but he was tall and he wore a black coat, and he had been at sea, staring out at the waves, much as this man now did.

Caught off guard, she stopped where she was and began to recite an incantation that would prevent her from suffering the fate of her mother and so many of the women who came to her at night, when the Jansens were asleep. Women searched her out when they saw that a candle was burning in her room, when the nightjars flew from tree to tree, when the thorns on the hedge were said to be so sharp they would reach out to you as you walked along the path and wound you in places so deep you would never recover, piercing your throat, your sex, your heart. Most women in Willemstad knew that Maria Owens attended to love that had been lost, love that was broken, love that was meant to begin but hadn't, love that had become a fever despite every remedy.

They came to her and she was bound to help them, as Hannah had, but who was she to go to?

Cadin was outside tapping at the window. He was relentless and frantic. All the same, Maria didn't let him in. She knew what he would tell her. *Burn mandrake in a brass bowl. Write his name on a candle and throw it far into the sea. Repeat three times: Fly away as fast as you can.*

She thought of the way her mother had looked at her father, as if nothing else mattered. It was dangerous for a woman to give up her power. Under her breath, Maria uttered the first verse of an invocation she had learned from Hannah as she sat by the fire in a place she might have felt she had only dreamed, had she not had Cadin to remind her of who she was and who she would always be. She was the woman who couldn't be drowned, who had fled from fires and the country where a woman couldn't be free. It was an ancient conjure Hannah had found in a book of Agrippa's *Occult Philosophy*, perhaps part of a powerful manuscript called *The Fourth*

Book. It was among the most potent charms and incantations Maria had copied into her *Grimoire*.

You are not mine, I am not yours, you have no power, I walk where I wish, my heart is protected.

"You are not mine," Maria said under her breath. But she had no pins, no red thread dyed with madder root, no rosemary, no St. John's wort, no mandrake torn from the ground, no myrrh oil, no will of her own, and she stopped the chant before it was complete, in mid-sentence, leaving herself defenseless. That was when he turned to her.

I will never love you, she should have said—it was the last line of the invocation—but instead she stood there like a fool, not unlike the women who came to her at night, their faces damp with tears, their minds made up, convinced they would walk through a door they knew full well should be kept bolted shut.

Maria told Mrs. Jansen she grew rue in the garden to keep away flies, without mentioning that it also checked lust, something her clients often wanted to feed to their men, along with a tincture of wild lettuce to reduce longings. Perhaps Maria should drink such a mixture herself, perhaps she should bathe in lettuce water, as she had suggested to others in dire situations, for the pale green water was helpful in extinguishing desire. Instead she stood where she was, and that was how she came to tie her life to John Hathorne's, despite the fact that she had sworn she would never belong to any man. Love begins in curious ways, in daylight or in darkness, when you are in search of it or when you least expect to find it. You may think it is one thing, when in fact it is something else entirely: infatuation, loneliness, seduction.

John Hathorne had been so deep in thought he hadn't noticed her presence until he turned to see her. At first he believed he might have conjured her, for there were people who said a dream could be brought to life in the waking world. He had faith in the goodness of God, but he was also certain that life was a mystery and that one must fight against the forces that opposed mankind. All the same he was a man of thirty-seven, with a man's flaws and weaknesses. He had never seen a young woman who was as captivating as Maria, and what was even more charming, it was clear she didn't even know she possessed the power to enchant.

"I've acted in error," Hathorne murmured. It was something he would say forever after; he would say it in his sleep, in his own bed at home, and on his last day on earth.

He was more than twenty years older than Maria, but that made no difference. He was tall, quite handsome, with distinctive features and an intense gaze. She saw the person he was at that very moment, the one he'd become ever since he stepped onto the dock here in Curaçao. He'd let go of the darkness that was always pooled inside him in his Massachusetts life, and along with it the burden of being his father's son, for William Hathorne had come to the new world in 1630 and was one of the first men to establish the Massachusetts Bay Colony. The elder Hathorne was a well-known, respected magistrate and trader, an assistant to the governor and a deputy representing the town of Salem for many years, a fierce persecutor of the more freethinking Quakers, a man who owned most of Salem Village. Everything John had done was to please William Hathorne, but the upright man John had forced himself to become had flown away like a night bird upon his arrival on the island and left him to return to the person he'd been as a boy, before he, too, had become a magistrate trained to judge others, before he'd taken over the family shipping business in which every cent must be accounted for, and every bargain must be in his favor.

He'd come to the house to take coffee with Mr. Jansen before they continued on to the Jansens' warehouse, where they were to discuss their trade, but the courtyard had confused him, and he'd found his way to the dining room rather than the study and had entirely missed Jansen, who by now, annoyed to have been kept waiting, had already left for the docks. Jansen wasn't the only one who was frustrated. Hathorne himself felt the trip would likely be a waste, and it had been, until he saw Maria Owens, who was wearing a blue ribbon in her hair for protection and luck.

Hathorne was a man from a county north of Boston, who often traveled into the White Mountains, so called because they were said to have snow all year round. He had a house in Newburyport and another in Salem. His ships brought iron ore and lumber from Massachusetts to trade for tobacco and sugar and coffee in Curaçao and Jamaica. He had undertaken this trip to better know his business and understand how it might further prosper. He thought of the Antilles as places to be tolerated, full of uneducated, superstitious people, but as soon as he stepped off the ship he felt a sort of enchantment. The blistering heat had overwhelmed him, and the palette of endless blues was blinding in the stark light. The charm and heat of the island brought up a welter of emotions that Hathorne was unused to experiencing. New England was a place of darkness and, in the evenings, of fear. Wild beasts roamed the mossy woods, and the native people were angry at how much land had been stolen and settled. Where he came from, every moment must be accounted for, in the meetinghouse and at home, and punishments were fierce. There were the stocks for those who were known to commit crimes concerning both legal matters and matters of faith. There were rules that were never to be broken. But here on Curaçao, he felt himself to be a different man, and that was the man Maria stumbled upon in the dining room.

She saw him not as he had been, or would be, but as he was at that very minute. He had been listening to the birds outside the window, and he stood in a block of yellow sunlight when she first spied him. Now that they were face-to-face, he ran a hand through his dark hair, confused by his own strange emotions. Hathorne looked younger than his age and he felt as if he was no more than twenty. He was not a man who easily let his appetites arise, and now he supposed it was joy he was experiencing; perhaps it was a gift to feel this way. Certainly, it was a feeling that was most uncommon. He came from Essex County in Massachusetts, named after the very place from which Maria fled in England, an omen she would not fully understand until much later, when she stood in a green field outside his house, a cold ocean away, a place where the ferns turned black in the winter, and evil was seen by those who lived their lives with fear and intolerance.

"I've somehow made a mistake. I've missed your father and I should be at the warehouse. If you could direct me, miss, I'll be on my way."

Clearly, he had made yet another mistake, taking her for a member of the family.

"I'm happy to guide you there," Maria offered. She had laundry to see to in the huge pots in the courtyard, and Juni would be waiting in the kitchen so they might set preparations under way for that evening's dinner, but instead she went back out through the garden, the man from Massachusetts following closely, drawn by what he would later swear was pure enchantment. He'd been warned that black magic was invoked in the caves by the sea on this island and that pirates were welcome in the city of Willemstad, especially if they spent gold stolen from Spanish ships. Yet as they walked under the inkberry trees, on their way to the harbor, he forgot the life he'd led. He forgot his house with its fine pottery brought from England, and the people who lived in that house in rooms that were continually gloomy throughout the year. In summer, the air was filled with flies and gnats. In winter, darkness fell at four in the afternoon. But that was there, a world away. He squinted in the sunlight and stayed close to the girl. She smelled of lavender and salt. Once or twice she gestured to chase away a black crow that seemed to follow her, wheeling through a slice of the sky, then careening down toward Hathorne, so that he might have believed it was his enemy, if birds could think and feel and plan such things. He

117

didn't yet know the girl's name, but he couldn't take his eyes off her. This is how it felt to be free of everything you had been trained to do. *Be cautious, be sure of yourself, be careful of outsiders, beware of women who have the nerve to meet your eyes, who think they're your equals, who do as they please, who please you as well, who will never do as they're told.*

Maria glanced behind her when they reached the sea. The water was blue-green and clear enough to see the shadows of large, lumbering shapes cast onto the white sand by the creatures that swam beneath the waves. John stopped to kneel so he might better see them. He was wearing leather boots made in London that cost more than what most people on the island earned in a year.

"A monster," he said of the huge sea animal that came nearer the shore.

Maria crouched beside him. He saw that she was barefoot, and that the skirt of the dress she wore was hemmed with blue thread.

"Sir, I'm afraid you're mistaken," she told him. "That is no monster. It's a turtle."

Hathorne grinned at her, then pulled off his boots. "We'll see about that."

He must have been enchanted, for he leapt into the sea fully clothed, wearing his loose linen shirt and his trousers and even his coat. Only a man possessed would do such a thing. He was so

118

far from the darkness of Massachusetts anything seemed possible. The water was warm and the current helped him along. He remembered feeling this way when he was a boy, at the sea in August. He approached the turtle, for that was what it was, and ran his hands over its bumpy shell, then swam beside it, gliding through the flat water, then floating on his back, his eyes half-closed, a smile on his lips. Hathorne had large, handsome features and a smile that changed his expression so thoroughly he might have been another man entirely. He was inside of a dream, not thinking how he would explain his drenched appearance to Mr. Jansen, not thinking of anything at all other than this island, this woman, this moment he was in.

"Now I see what it is," he called, joyous. "It is a miracle."

Maria knew what was happening. She tried to recite a spell backwards, but the words dissolved in her mouth. She remembered that Hannah had said it was difficult to set a spell upon oneself. And now, if she wasn't mistaken, it was already too late.

After his swim, Hathorne climbed up a ladder to the dock, soaking wet, but laughing. "I think I look to be the monster now."

Perhaps he was, for a man tells you who he is the instant you meet him, all you have to do is listen, but when he leaned in close to kiss her, she stopped thinking altogether. When a man kisses a witch, all the coins in his pockets turn black, but Hathorne didn't notice until later, and he thought the salt air had been the thing to turn the coins, and he frankly didn't care after that kiss. As for Maria, she was surprised that his kiss had burned her mouth. Hannah would have warned her to be careful, had she been there.

What burns is best left to turn to cinders. Be wise and stay away.

There were eight guests at the dinner party that evening, too big an undertaking for Maria and Juni to handle. Two cooks had been brought in; one of them was Sybil, a servant who lived down the lane, and the other was Adrie, for the family had always said she was the best cook on the island. Indeed, she was lauded for her *arepa*, a dough made of ground maize, and for her red snapper, as well as her delicious *keshi yena*, a slave dish now favored on the tables of the wealthiest merchants, though it had been originated by the poorest residents of the island, using rinds of cheese and table scraps, and was now made of fine cheese and spiced meat.

"This is the perfect time for us to poison them." Adrie laughed as she kneaded the dough in which she would wrap the fish. She worked so quickly her fingers seemed to fly.

"Not tonight," Maria said, knowing that what-

120

ever you put into the world came back to you threefold. "There's a man at the table who doesn't deserve poison."

"And there's one who does." Much to Maria's surprise Adrie added, "You know why Mr. Jansen never lets Juni go? Look at her face and you'll see." It was true that Juni resembled their master more than any of his three daughters. "Open your eyes, girl. Look at the guests you serve tonight and you'll know that man who owns this house isn't the only bad man at the table." Adrie didn't look up, but merely salted the fish. "I knew it the minute he walked by. You've got the sight, you should use it."

Maria served dinner, carrying a blue-and-white tureen from Amsterdam, wearing her best silk dress, one that had belonged to the Jansens' youngest daughter. It was a pale sky-blue, the same shade as the walls, so that she appeared to be more shadow than woman. A maid should not be seen. Indeed, none of the guests paid the slightest attention to her, and when the visiting daughters and their husbands wanted a drink or a plate of food they gestured to her as they would to a dog. She was embarrassed that Mr. Hathorne would now know she wasn't a member of the household and would see her true circumstances. Tonight she had refused to go barefoot, but instead wore her red boots. Let him see who she truly was. Let him back away from her if that's what he wished to do.

Cadin was tapping at the window, but Maria was forced to ignore him. She was in service, and if the family knew she kept a black bird under their roof they would be furious. There were no crows on the island and black animals of all sorts were considered unlucky. Besides, Cadin had taken an instant dislike to John. Perhaps he was jealous, as familiars often were, for they wished to be closer to their human companion than any-one else. Maria wagged her finger at the window. *Go away,* she thought, although the farthest the bird went was to the branch of a nearby tree.

When Maria brought the platter of fish to present to John, he most certainly knew she was there. Clearly, she was not a daughter, but a housemaid, not that this seemed to bother him. He quietly said, "Is this turtle?"—a sly reference meant for her alone. He glanced at her and there it was, the connection between them, a thread that pulled them close.

"No, sir, but if you'd prefer turtle, I'll see what I can do."

Hathorne laughed and shook his head. "This is fine. But I forgot to thank you for showing me to the docks."

"When I was 'miss.'"

"You're still 'miss.'" No one was listening to them. "You will always be that to me." He spoke softly and in earnest when he asked her to meet him in the courtyard. He pleaded, saying *"You must, you must,"* which was not at all like him. He himself seemed surprised by his ardor. But on this night he was so outspoken, he quickly turned to observe the others around the table, and was relieved when he saw they hadn't noticed his behavior. "Please, miss, meet me there."

When Maria could get away, she did so. She blushed to think of what she had conjured up, the first man to be in love with her. She was fifteen, the same age Rebecca had been when she first spied Thomas Lockland. Maria left her apron on the counter next to the pile of dishes in the kitchen, and she didn't respond to Adrie's disapproving expression. Men went to war and women fell in love, heedless and for reasons they might never understand. She could stop this and put it to rest right now. She could make an amulet for protection and speak the words that would keep him away; she could fashion an image of him and bury it in the earth outside her window where the centipedes nested, and he would never return. Instead, she ran a comb through her hair, and found her way to the courtyard. *Turn back,* something inside her said, but there was an element of defiance in her soul ever since the fire. Rebecca had told her that life was short and she should do as she pleased.

They met beneath the Jamaican apple trees,

which bore pear-shaped fruit with red skin and white flesh. Cadin was perched in one of the boughs, and he created such a racket that Maria waved him away. But before he obeyed her, he dove at the stranger in a flutter of feathers, knocking the hat from Hathorne's head.

"That's a foul creature," John declared.

"No more than I am," Maria said, hurt by his estimation.

"If you believe so, then I'm mistaken." By then the bird had flown from the garden and was no threat to him. "He must be another miracle."

"He is, as a matter of fact."

"If this is your opinion, I will agree."

"Will you?" Maria was pleased.

He might have agreed to anything at that moment, for he received a kiss for agreeing with her, and then many more. Juni was asleep, her face to the wall, when Maria finally came to bed. The Jansens were in their chambers, sprawled out on newly pressed sheets woven in Amsterdam. Maria sat at the window when she returned to her room, her hair undone, her mind racing. She knew nothing about this man and yet she had given herself to him. This was what had befallen her, a madness of sorts, powerful and potent, brought on without a potion, without a spell. She did not wish to understand her mother's actions, which had always seemed foolhardy and irresponsible, and yet she did.

This is the way it happens. You walk into a room with blue walls. You kiss a man in the garden. You feel your heart and bones and blood. You wait for him like a bird in a cage.

On the second night they were together John vowed that he loved her, on the third night she was his, on the fourth night he gave her a sapphire on a silver chain that she said she would never take off, on the fifth night he brought her a small packet of diamonds to do with as she pleased. This was what she had seen in the black mirror, her future and her fate. He had presented her with what seemed an impossible gift for a girl such as herself, and yet here were seven small diamonds, shimmering in the palm of her hand. This was her future, a man who promised to cherish her. And so she let him slip his hands beneath her dress in a dark corner of the courtyard, she let him do whatever he pleased, for he said she was his heart's desire, that he would always adore her. She told him that when they lived together she would plant lilacs outside the door; she would make a special entrance so that Cadin could come and go as he pleased; she would always wear blue, because Hathorne favored it so. Five days of dreams can seem like years, that was how well she thought she knew him. She did not need the sight, and instead let her heart lead her. But on the sixth night he didn't appear. Maria sat in the courtyard until the sunrise of the seventh day, a number that represents all that is good and all that is evil. There were seven heavens and seven deadly sins, for seven was the most magical number of all, the one that led to wisdom, even for those who would rather remain blind to the truth.

On all other nights Cadin had been locked away, at John's behest, for they had become enemies. The crow had done his best to chase Hathorne away, dropping stones from the sky and diving to pull his hair. *Beware,* Cadin had cried, but crows are proprietary creatures and Maria had paid him no mind. Now she went to her room and got down on her hands and knees beside her bed to reach for the black mirror. She had a sinking feeling even before she took the cloth from the mirror and peered into the glass. There was a ship in a cold gray sea. There was a black heart in a garden, among a tangle of weeds. With a single glance she knew the truth. He was gone.

She made her way to the inn where John had been staying, but it was too late, and now that she was clearheaded, with the sight returned to her, she knew it before she found his room was empty. She went to Jansen's warehouse, and up to his office. No one working there tried to stop her. Not when they saw the dark expression on her face.

"*Wat is er mis?*" Jansen asked when she appeared at his door. *What is wrong?*

Maria looked in a panic. Her hair was uncombed, her feet bare. This is what it did to you. This illogical, wildly impractical emotion.

"*Waar is je gast naar toe?*" she demanded to know. *Where has your guest gone?* She didn't sound like a housemaid, rather like a woman betrayed, and such women do not care if their voices rise or if they stare straight into a man's eyes. Jansen closed the door and stood to face her. He was a big man and he shouldn't have been anxious.

"*Wat is jour zaak daar?*" When Maria left, he would acquire another girl to replace her, and hopefully the next one would be more restrained. *What is it your business where Mr. Hathorne has gone?*

Although she legally belonged to Jansen until January, Maria didn't care what he might think of her, and she certainly didn't fear him. She knew more about him than he would have liked, and perhaps this was why he always grew uncomfortable under her heated gaze. Jansen was well aware she didn't admire him, and that irritated him. He had never especially liked her, for in his opinion, she should have kept her eyes lowered and done as she was told. People said she talked to a black bird that followed her to the market, sometimes in her language, sometimes

127

in his. Now here she was in Jansen's office when she was meant to be at work in his kitchen.

It had begun to rain, a hard, green rain that would cause mudslides in the northern hills. Maria shivered in the sudden cold wind that burst through the window. She herself had caused the rain, and all over the island small sorrows would grow and children would fuss for no reason so that not even their mothers' voices could comfort them. They had never seen rain this color before, and some young women collected it in pots so they might wash with it, for green is love and luck, just as it is jealousy and envy.

"*Hij is teruggegaan waar his thuishoort*," Mr. Jansen told her with equal amounts of meanness and pleasure. *He's gone back to where he belongs.*

Massachusetts. The cold, gray sea. The house with black shutters.

Maria left the office without another word; she ran along the pier and didn't stop until she reached the spare chamber that she shared with Juni. She did not know how to reach Hathorne. All she knew was that he lived in a county called Essex, named for the place she had left far behind. To stop wanting him she wrote his name on a white candle and threw it far out to sea, but it was not enough. A witch's love is not so easily erased. She drank lettuce water, poured whiskey in an iron pot, bathed in salt and vinegar and then with anise seed and bay leaves, and still she could not rid herself of her emotions. Hannah had warned that it was difficult, perhaps even impossible, to work magic upon yourself. The enchantment to forget him would not take.

She worried that he had been lost at sea, as so many were. Or perhaps he had been taken prisoner, or had contracted a disease and could not leave his bed in Massachusetts, not even to write her a letter. Soon enough she herself fell ill, sick to her stomach, vomiting and unable to keep any food down. When she realized her condition, she went to the beach and, in a fury, threw herself into the waves, but she merely floated back to shore, her hair a mass of tendrils trailing out behind her. In that soft sea she realized there was a reason she had known to trek through the Thames estuary, a reason why she had crossed the wide, cold sea. She was destined to save herself, with or without magic. She was destined to face her own future. She had already seen this daughter she would have in the black mirror.

January came to mark her five years of servitude. She went to Mr. Jansen's office to collect the official papers that declared she was a free woman. Jansen scanned her face with cold eyes, glad to be rid of her. Juni had been influenced by Maria and was now a dreamy girl who often didn't come when she was called. The neighbor's servants vowed that Maria worked spells, and could speak backwards, and wandered late at night in the caves where there were spirits. They could believe whatever they wished; Jansen knew exactly who Maria was and he didn't care for it one bit. She was sixteen and pregnant. There was no need to know more. The baby had quickened and Maria could already feel it moving inside of her.

"I want the same for Juni," Maria announced when she was set free from the family. If not, she explained, she would go to Jansen's wife and tell her the truth she had learned from Adrie. A man should take care of his daughter, and Juni should be given a small house outside Willemstad, one of the many he had acquired. "Hire a housemaid and pay her," she suggested. "It's time for Juni to have her own life."

Jansen cursed Maria Owens, not that it did him the least bit of good, for he feared the knowledge she had. Anyway, she kept lavender in her dress and blue thread stitched through the hem of her petticoat and was protected from his wrath. When she walked away, she owed him nothing. She was happy to move in with Juni and Adrie, who agreed that the three would share a roof. Though the house Mr. Jansen had allotted Juni was tiny, they would make do.

Maria made Hannah's black soap when the moon was waning, adding local ingredients, aloe vera and hibiscus. It was a hot night and Maria was burning up, using the largest iron pots in the house. The soap was so fragrant bees awoke, birds sang at an hour when they should have been silent, and fussy babies suddenly slept through the night. When she was done making the soap, she fell into her bed and didn't wake for eighteen hours. It took a huge amount of energy and focus to make this soap, and because of this who-ever used it would benefit and appear younger, perhaps by as much as ten years. In the morning, women from Willemstad and from all over the countryside came to buy the bars wrapped in brown paper, tied with string. Even Adrie was impressed by the profits Maria brought in. She tried the soap herself, and when she looked in a mirror she was surprised to find she was as pretty as she'd been as a girl.

For three months they lived together, happier than they'd been for a long time. When there was a chore to do, they decided when it would be seen to. They awoke when they wished to, and washed sheets and clothes for themselves, not for the Jansens. Time was slow, with each day a pleasure, but time speeded up and took over eventually. The baby arrived on a night when the moon was hidden behind clouds. It was the windy season, unpredictable spring, but soon the wind died down, which signified good fortune to come. What is a daughter but good fortune, as complicated as she might be. Maria dragged her straw pallet outside, then drew a circle in the dust around her chosen birthing place as protection from evil. Cadin settled onto a low branch, watching every move she made with his sharp eyes. It seemed a long time since he'd found a baby in the snow, wrapped in a blue blanket, her hair as black as feathers. Now the night was hot, and the earth was sand, but the blanket set out for this baby was the same one Rebecca had stitched late at night in the Lockland house. Hannah had folded the blanket into the bottom of Maria's satchel, dusted with lavender to keep away the moths. As the labor began, Maria took up a pair of scissors. She held up her long black hair that reached to her waist in a single braid and cut it short enough to graze her shoulders, unusual for a woman in this time and place. To have a child she knew she must make sacrifices and this would be the first of many.

On this night she forgave her own mother who had labored alone in the snow and had left her child behind for her own good. In doing so, Rebecca's heart had hardened. Still, she was the one Maria called for when the worst of the pains came. Adrie told her to breathe and she did so. The old woman had brought a hundred children into the world during her long lifetime, and Maria herself had seen dozens of babes born on Hannah's wooden table and had often helped with the birthing. Hannah had tied knots in a rope, then cut the rope between those knots into pieces, a spell for an easy birth. Here there was no such tradition, and the labor was hard. Maria asked Juni for a bowl of water, and when she gazed into the bowl it was black and deep. This was the moment when the worlds opened between life and death, the future and the past. She saw a man in the snow who longed for her, and a house ringed by a garden where nightshade and mandrake grew, where the lilacs were so sweet bees came from all over the county to drink from them. She threw the plait of her sheared hair into the fire to mark the death of her old life and the start of the new life to come. The smoke was red, a bloodline passed down from mother to daughter for as long as time existed.

It was March 20, and she wanted her baby to be born before midnight. March 21 was known to be the unluckiest day of the year. Juni and Adrie spread salt on the earth to banish spirits who might wish the baby ill. By then Maria was cursing the world that had made her a woman. But when the child at last arrived, at eight minutes before twelve, everything changed. She had seen her daughter's face in the black mirror when she herself had been a child, but she hadn't expected to feel as she did now. Nothing else mattered.

"Beautiful," Adrie said with approval. All of Adrie's friends came to view the baby, old women who, too, had once been beautiful. But this baby was something more. They could all tell that was the case, even the ones who were nonbelievers; the most practical, logical, down-to-earth women praised this new life. There was no mistaking that this child had the sight. Her eyes were silver, her hair as red as Rebecca's. On the back of her left hand was a black mark in the shape of a half moon, the sure sign of a witch.

The baby was soon enough safe in her mother's arms, wrapped in the blanket stitched with blue thread. Because the future seemed to have opened on this night, and because Maria's heart had opened as well, she called her daughter Faith. If Hannah had been with them, she would have spoken the truth for Maria to hear on this day that was like no other.

This is your heart that you hold in your hands, be careful with it, don't lose it, and don't forget that I loved you the same way even though you weren't born to me.

When Faith was five months old, Maria kissed Juni and Adrie good-bye. She wept to leave them, for they had offered her only kindness; all the same her fate awaited her, and she packed her satchel, sewed the diamonds into the hem of her dress where they would be safe from thievery, then went to the docks to search for a ship that would take her to Massachusetts. Before she left, she'd made a pot of Courage Tea, for she would require courage to find her way across the sea. Adrie had fashioned a small traveling basket made from reeds for Cadin, which he hopped into when Maria whistled.

None of the American ships would take her on, for a baby was not welcome on board, and its cries and ailments were said to bring nothing but bad luck. Fortunately there was another possibility. The Jews here had founded the first synagogue in this part of the world, and the first cemetery was founded in 1659, called *Beth Haim*, "House of Life," where the tombs were made of coral. Their settlement, the Plantation of Hope, had flourished; still many of their people had taken to the sea, carrying Torah scrolls from synagogues that had been burned to the ground in Spain and Portugal.

Many were merchants and translators and traders, but some of those who were sailors were actually pirates whose targets were Spanish ships; they felt it was their duty to take revenge on the country that had tortured and murdered their people. The Portugals were after gold and goods, but they also were known for transporting books, including outlawed literature that was said to incite slaves. There had been those who boarded their ships to steal their bounty, only to find wooden crates of books, worthless to some, a treasure to others.

There had been Jewish pirates reported by Josephus in the first century, and Jews had often lived at sea, especially when there was no country that would allow them entrance. Sinan, who sailed with the famous Barbarossa, had done his best to smash the Spanish fleet. Yaacov Kuriel had led the fleet, until he was imprisoned during the Inquisition. Many of these men had gold studs in their ears, often to mark a life that had been lost. They often hid their true identities, though there were some who recognized the gold chains they wore with charms imprinted with the Hebrew letter *Hey*. They made sausage from chicken, so if they were challenged and asked to eat pork to prove they were not of the tribe of Israel, they had their own false meat. These men journeyed to the ends of the earth, with many going as far as the Barbary Coast, where they often threw in with Moorish pirates in North Africa, who lived on a diet of blood rice, made with the blood of the lamprey eel, a creature older than the shark, a living fossil.

The sailors were a rough lot who felt they had little to lose, other than their own lives. Adrie had told Maria to stay away from them, but when Maria was turned down by the other ships, she searched out the captain of a schooner called the *Queen Esther*, bound for New England. The ship was set to trade in Newport, Rhode Island, where there had been a Jewish community since 1658, but the first port would be Boston, for there was a great market in that city for the rum they carried in the hull, huge barrels that gave off such a fragrant aroma sailors on board were said to grow drunk even when they hadn't touched a drop.

The captain, Abraham Dias, was about to suggest that Maria go home, keep her daughter safe, and leave the sea to men, when his son Samuel collapsed on the dock. Samuel wore a heavy black coat decorated with buttons made from the backbone of a shark, and beneath that a waistcoat, a heavy linen shirt, and leather breeches. Even though the day was fine, he was so ill that he shivered in the bright sunlight, his olive skin turning ashy, dark hollows beneath his eyes. Still, he was a handsome man, with a tough, lanky body and a sailor's strong arms and back. His long, densely black hair was slicked back and tied with a leather string. He wore three pieces of gold in the inner flap of his ear, marking the lives of three people he'd loved and lost to the cruelty of the world. He was young, having recently turned twenty-three, a number he'd always considered to be lucky, although he'd begun to wonder about his luck. He'd recently been stricken by dengue, a disease many called breakbone fever, for it caused the afflicted person's bones to ache as if they were indeed breaking with pain that was unbearable. Frequently, those who had been stricken hemorrhaged and spat blood. In the end many went blind and lost all ability to move. There were those who took their own lives rather than endure the agonies the fever caused. Some who survived vowed that the illness made them feel that they'd been made of glass and a hammer wielded by a thoughtless enemy had been used to shatter them, body and soul. The disease was contracted in swampy mosquito-ridden areas, and the islands nearby were rife with such places, marshy landscapes where clouds of insects rose into the dull illumination of the dusk, turning the sky into a fluttering dark that was more dangerous than most battlegrounds, with casualties initiated by an enemy the combatants had never spied.

Samuel Dias was leaning against the railing of the dock, his eyes glazed with pain. He could be charming or brash, depending on what the occasion called for, and was such an excellent navigator there were those who vowed he used black magic to guide him, when in fact he had a deep knowledge of mathematics and of the constellations that he used to map both the sky and the sea. Abraham Zacuto, a Jewish professor of astronomy and navigation, had created a table of celestial positions that allowed sailors to find their way even when they could not chart by the position of the sun, and most explorers had a tradition of sailing with Jewish navigators and mathematicians on board. Samuel Dias had been born in Spain, escaped to Portugal, then had been raised at sea. He had dark, gold-flecked eyes, and could speak six languages; he would have been more than happy to talk to a beautiful woman such as Maria if he hadn't been struggling for breath. Samuel could taste blood in his mouth, and when he looked into the sea he spied a black eel turning in its death throes and thought perhaps it was a sign and that he was foreseeing his own demise. He'd vowed right then that if God granted him life he would change his ways. He was wild and young, but that didn't matter anymore. He was in the hands of the Almighty, and, if he should survive, he would start life anew as a more serious, less arrogant man.

Maria studied him, observing his pallor and the blood he spit upon the dock, then turned to his father. "Take him on that ship and he'll be dead before you reach Boston." She sounded utterly sure of herself, so much so that Samuel Dias had begun to listen to her despite the attack of pain that left him straining for the next mouthful of air. "Unless you take me with you," she added. "I won't let him die."

She had the ingredients for a breakbone fever cure that Adrie had taught her. It had been added

139

to her *Grimoire* with ink drawn from the stalks of vibrant coral-colored hibiscus so that the written remedy was nearly as red as blood.

Abraham Dias didn't trust Maria. He was a practical man who'd never meant to go to sea, and had now been to all corners of the world. He knew a witch when he saw one. Maria carried a black bird in a cage and she spoke her mind, as if she were a man. If the truth be told, he didn't trust anyone who wasn't a blood relation, but his son begged him to allow Maria to travel with them. For once in his life, Samuel was truly afraid, though he tried his best not to show his raw emotion. "How can it hurt us to take her with us?" he asked his father. He had seen this disease affect other men. They often bled to death and became empty shells, with white eyes and white skin, like the walking dead local people spoke of. When he died, as all men must, this was not the way he wished to leave this world.

"She has a child," his father said. "A ship is no place for a babe. Most likely this woman only wants passage to Boston and will say anything to get what she wants."

Samuel gazed at Maria and she looked right back. He took her in for the first time, really seeing her. She did indeed look like trouble, but he kept this to himself.

"Let us take that chance," he told his father, and Abraham had little choice but to agree. This

140

was his beloved son, his only living child, and he would agree to anything that might save his life.

Samuel had Maria and the baby stay in his cabin rather than on deck, where straw-filled mattresses were strewn about for the crew and their safety might be in question.

Maria took the baby directly to the small, airless cabin, before either man could change his mind. There was a bunk for the ill man, which he could barely climb into, and a hammock where Maria and the baby could sleep. Right away Maria boiled water over a flame and made Tawatawa tea, using the powerful herb that looked like nothing more than grass.

"Isn't that what you feed to goats?" Samuel asked in a thick voice. He was sweating out his disease and had drenched his linen shirt. Samuel hadn't valued his life enough, and now he was filled with regret. He'd seen other men die— frankly, he'd been party to some of their deaths when it came to fighting the Spanish at sea—but he'd never actually considered that the moment of his own death might come while he was still a young man.

"Then you'll be my goat," Maria told him, as she touched her hand to his forehead. "And you'll eat the grass I give you."

She'd known that his fever would be high, for it always presented to her as a red aura circling the afflicted individual, though she never would have known from his behavior. Samuel Dias refused to show his suffering, although when she went for more water, and he thought she couldn't hear, he moaned and cursed his state of being and her heart went out to him. A ship was a dreadful place to be ill, suffocating in the cabin, freezing and damp on deck. Maria fed Dias a spoonful of tea every hour. She demanded she be given all the papaya on board, then ground the leaves into a tincture for him to drink. When her patient had regained some of his strength, she fed him slices of the fruit, which he ate from her fingers. Maria often kept Faith in her lap when she treated Dias, and the baby mimicked her mother's motions, patting Dias on the head.

"You're not afraid she'll catch my disease?" he asked.

"You can't become ill with breakbone from another person, Goat," Maria informed Dias, using her pet name for him. "Only from the insects in the swampland."

"How are you so sure?"

"It's easy to be sure about the truth. Even a goat should know that," she teased.

She continued to feed him the tea made from weeds that he had complained about at first, but now he drank the brew willingly, no matter how bitter. He was feeling stronger in a matter of days. He had faith in Maria, a mad, joyous rush of feeling which often made him laugh out loud, for at last the fever was breaking. And then one day, the pain eased, the hammer stopped, and he was no longer glass. Without either of them noticing, he grasped her hand. That was when it happened, the heat between them. There she was wearing little more than her shift and her apron, her legs bare, as if the two had taken up living together. Maria drew away and saw to feeding Cadin some fruit for his supper. She wondered what he thought about this man. "Do you mind if I let my crow out of his cage?" she asked. Poor Cadin had been trapped in his basket watching their every move with his quick eye. "He'll eat any mosquitoes that come near."

When Dias agreed, she opened Cadin's door. He quickly flew up to perch on a beam, clacking happily, gazing at Dias with a bright, friendly glance.

"You travel with a crow rather than a husband," Samuel said thoughtfully. "The crow I understand. He seems a clever fellow. But where is your man?"

Maria made a face. "Is it your business?"

Samuel gestured to the sapphire she wore. He felt a stab of jealousy. "Was it Faith's father who gave you the gem?"

"You seem like a clever fellow as well if you've figured that out," she teased. "Almost as smart as Cadin."

"Is that a compliment? If it is, I'm grateful."

A broad grin broke across Dias's face, the first Maria had seen during his illness. She blinked and took a step away. Why did his expression affect her so?

"You're going to him in Boston," Samuel guessed. "And he knows you're arriving?"

"Not yet." She was not the sort to tell a lie, even when it might have ended the conversation.

"And do you even know where he is?"

"Essex County," she said primly, as if it were a proper address.

"Essex County and Boston are not one and the same. This is a vast land, Maria. It's not the island of Curaçao."

She threw him a dark look. "You ask too many questions."

"So I've heard," Dias said.

He sensed that something wasn't right. He certainly had known men who led a woman on with false information, those who had two wives who never knew of each other, those who left in the middle of the night, disappearing with all the household valuables. Dias squinted at the stone this man of Maria's had given her. He knew the worth of gems, and this one had no spark. The blue was an empty color, dead inside. "I'm not sure this is genuine."

Maria laughed out loud. "I see what you're doing. You just want to make trouble. He's a Puritan of high moral quality."

"I know men, and I'm sorry to say a Puritan is a man like any other. A man who disappears is either dead or wishes you to think him so. Perhaps it's best if you do."

Maria gave Dias a sidelong glance. "You talk too much," she told him.

"I thought women liked men who talked," he said, knowing he would annoy her and wanting to do so for reasons he was only beginning to understand. "That's what I've been told."

"Really? How many women have told you that? A hundred?" she teased. He had such dark eyes it was best for her not to stare into them for too long.

"I haven't counted," he admitted. "But I will now if you're so interested."

"I'm not," she was quick to say.

"Good. I would hate for you to be jealous."

"You don't have to worry about that, Goat. Just worry about living long enough so there will be a hundred and one women who have told you lies."

He laughed, enjoying sparring with her. She was not like any of the women he'd known, for she was unafraid to argue, and she often bested him, making him feel a fool, the color rising in his face, until all other women were forgotten.

At night Maria curled with her baby and sang her to sleep, the same tune Hannah once sang to her.

The water is wide, I cannot get o'er it
And neither have I wings to fly
Give me a boat that will carry two
And both shall row, my Love and I.
I leaned my back against some oak
Thinking he was a trusty Tree:
But first he bended, and then he broke;
and so did my false love to me.

Maria studied the child's face in the pale light that filtered through the small, shuttered window. She had the red hair of her grandmother and Maria's own wide, generous mouth and gray eyes. Her features were narrow, as her father's were, with high cheekbones and a straight nose. Despite these resemblances, she was unique, a rose of a girl Maria could study for hours on end.

"All sleepers should dream as she does," Samuel Dias said one night, for he was often awake till all hours, thinking about the life he'd lived, knowing how closely he had walked beside death. The child reminded him of what was good in the world, and he often told her stories his own mother had told him. There was one about a cat that was far more clever than its master, and another about a wolf who had been a man until he'd been placed under a spell, and still another about a child lost in the woods.

"Hush," Maria told him. "Try sleep for yourself. That's what you need."

146

Maria closed her eyes and imagined Faith in a large garden, the one she had seen in the black mirror, where trees bloomed with white flowers and lilacs grew beside the door. She was in that vivid garden, in the midst of her dream, when Cadin woke her before the first light of morning. He tapped at her and made a harsh clacking noise. There was the wretched sound of struggling, as if someone had been caught in a net. In an instant, Maria was wide-awake, her heart pounding. Samuel was having convulsions. She left the baby in the hammock and went to throw her arms around Samuel to ensure he wouldn't harm himself as he thrashed around. The fever was still in his body, it always would be, and there would be times when it would return unexpectedly. Illness had robbed him of some of his strength; he was gaunt, in a weakened state, otherwise Maria would have never been able to hold him down. He shouted for her to let him go, as if in her arms he was in chains and not merely in her embrace, but she held on until he quieted, finally exhausted by the fit brought on by his disease.

"You'll be fine," Maria told him, as she stroked his head. "You're here with me."

She filled a pan with water from the rain barrel outside their door, then slipped off his shirt and washed him with cool water and black soap, her hands stroking his chest and arms. His body ached so badly he thought this must be what it

147

was like when a prisoner was placed on a rack, then stretched beyond all reason. Dias turned his head so that she would not see that he wept. He had done things in his life that were cruel and terrible, actions he didn't wish to share with anyone and might be paying for now if God's judgment was upon him. He'd been a robber and a thief. He'd been with women he remembered only too well and those whom he'd completely forgotten. All the same, he wanted Maria. She looked at him and knew. After that, she kept her hands to herself. She had promised herself to another, and she wasn't one to break her word.

"Maybe you should give up on me," Samuel said. She was still beside him and he could feel her heart beat. His own heart was jumpy and uncontrolled, ruled by fever. "Don't worry, my father won't throw you overboard. He's a better man than he appears to be. He's likely due a better son."

By now Samuel was exhausted. Maria knew that an illness became worse before it was better. To help with his cure, she made him talk, for that encouraged him. That was who he was inside, a man who loved stories.

"Do you want the one about the wolf or the cat?" he asked.

"The one about the goat," Maria said. "Tell me about you."

And so he did, although he rarely spoke of

the past, and for good reason. Once, when he was a boy, he'd had a family, a mother and two sisters, but that was long ago. He and his father had left Portugal and traveled to Brazil, but the Inquisition had followed, and soon the sea was the only place left for them. For more than ten years, they'd commandeered Spanish ships and fought the people who had so cruelly murdered and expelled their people. Because of this, Samuel hadn't counted the dead for whom he'd been responsible. This very ship had been taken from the Spanish navy. Though father and son had begun as thieves, they now were respectable traders. All the same, they continued to consider anything belonging to the Spanish to be fair game. When the winds were bad, or when trade was difficult, they wouldn't think twice about returning to their original line of business.

"Do you judge me for this?" he asked Maria.

"My own father was a robber," Maria admitted. "So I can hardly judge." It was less offensive to say Robbie was a thief rather than to admit he'd been a player in a theater troupe.

When Maria asked what had happened to Samuel's mother and sisters, he shook his head.

"My sisters were converted and married to men they didn't know. My mother was burned."

First they burned the books, then the people who wrote them, then those who read them. They burned books about medicine and magic, books in Hebrew and in Spanish and Portuguese. Samuel's mother could read and write; she was a healer and a midwife, and had written a book of cures, but there had only been one copy and it had been destroyed. That was why Samuel and his father always transported books, even those that had been outlawed by slave owners in the West Indies.

"I'm glad I memorized my mother's stories," Samuel said. "That way they can never be forgotten."

Maria felt a tightness in her chest when she learned the fate of the women in his family. She only hoped he hadn't seen what she had seen in England, the last moments of a life engulfed in flames. She'd decided she would hem all of his clothing with blue stitches, to protect him from ill intentions.

"A woman like my mother is frightening to those in power," Samuel said.

Maria understood that a woman with her own beliefs who refuses to bow to those she believes to be wrong can be considered dangerous. In the county where she'd grown up in England they would call her a witch, they would say she had a tail and spoke to Satan, but in Spain and Portugal they would say that the Jews had dark powers, that they could control the seas and stars, they could work magic to curse people or keep them alive.

• • •

The voyage passed as though it were a dream. Once Samuel Dias began talking, he didn't stop. He spoke about Brazil and Morocco, and of the great flocks of birds in Africa and the beaches in Portugal so hidden a man would never be found, and of islands in the middle of the sea where the only residents were the turtles. He told her of places where men wore scarlet scarves and painted their eyes with kohl and women dressed in silk and calico, their heads covered. In time, Maria talked as well, admitting that her robber father could recite entire plays without taking a breath.

"But why would a man in his right mind memorize another man's words instead of speaking his own?"

"That's what a player does." Maria shrugged. "He pretends to be someone he's not."

But wasn't that what they were doing? He pretended to be a man who hadn't spent his life running away, and she pretended to be a woman who could reveal her true self. And yet they talked, so much, they didn't notice when the seas changed from blue to gray. Whenever Samuel's pain was at its worst, Maria went to his bed, her body folding next to his. She wrapped her arms around him so he wouldn't thrash in his fits of anguish. He was ablaze with fever, although his other symptoms—the headaches and rashes and bleeding—were gone. Night after night, she went to him unbidden, despite her vow to do otherwise. It was a dream, she told herself. Only in the fleeting hours of dimming light, the hours when it is said the soul can travel freely, did she come to his bed without shame, wishing to be nowhere but where she was, in the wide and glittering sea.

As they neared Boston, and his health improved, Maria came to know Samuel's stories, as she knew him. She hadn't understood how her mother could love a man who could only speak words written by others, and was pleased that Samuel was nothing like her father. Here was a man who was filled with words, and Maria found she was intrigued. It occurred to her that Hannah had raised her to value words above all else. Samuel could not stop talking, and she could not stop listening. One night as they drifted off to sleep, she thought she heard him say *Don't leave me,* but by daybreak she'd convinced herself she'd only imagined his plea. Men like Samuel Dias didn't say such things, and neither did she; they had both been hardened by burnings, and had good reason not to trust the world.

Cadin often settled down beside the ailing man, making a nest in his quilt, allowing his feathers to be stroked when he usually only let Maria near. The bird was at least sixteen, and likely

152

had aches and pains himself. Whenever Samuel turned his head, Cadin tried to steal one of the gold earrings he wore.

"One thief knows another," Samuel warmly said to the bird. He had a deep affection for the creature by now. "What happens when you let him free?" he asked Maria.

"He comes back to me." She felt choked up for some reason, which was not at all like her. She told herself it was the closeness of the room, the flame on which she cooked a broth of fish bones to strengthen Samuel's constitution.

"Of course," Samuel said. "Why wouldn't he?"

Samuel would have come back to her as well and he knew it, without a chain, without a cage, but he said nothing. There was no point in doing so, even though he had found the blue thread marking all of his clothing, stitches he examined with confusion and tenderness. There was another man, one who Samuel suspected was a liar at best, for he was convinced the sapphire was false, and only a false man gives a gift that is a lie. All the same, whoever he was, he was Faith's father and most likely a man who didn't spend his life at sea, and therefore a better man than himself.

Most were grateful for the sight of gulls wheeling across the sky, the sign that land was near, but Samuel refused to look outside. He let his assis-

153

tant use the charts he himself had plotted. They followed the coast northward, for they would unload their cargo of rum in Boston and Newport, then replace it with goods in New York, all manner of cloth and tea and spices, along with English pottery and French wine. By now, Faith was speaking a few words. *Momma, Caw Caw*—for Cadin—and *Gogo* for Samuel Dias, her baby talk word for Goat.

"Is that my name?" He'd laugh when the baby nodded, a serious expression on her face. He turned to Maria. "I think you've been talking about me."

"I have not," Maria insisted, although, in fact, she often did and had a song that made Faith clap her hands with joy.

What should we do with the Goat?
Shall we feed him supper, shall we give
*   him tea, shall we wake him up or let*
*   him sleep?*

As it turned out, Dias had overheard. He didn't know whether to be pleased that Maria sang about him, or hurt that she thought of him as little more than a pet.

"What should we do with the Goat?" he sang, with more darkness than Maria would have expected. "Shall we let him live or watch him die?"

"I want you to live or you wouldn't be here. That was the bargain in exchange for my travel."

"Is that so? If you hadn't felt forced to help me you wouldn't be here?"

Maria was confused. "You knew the terms. You were there on the dock."

He turned his back on her then, clearly wounded. That night she could tell he was only pretending to sleep. When he truly slept, he talked in his dreams, recalling everyone he had known and every country he had been to, all he had lost and all that he'd found. Lately, when he did sleep, he had begun to say her name. A single word and nothing more. Maria only.

"You're insulted," Maria said to him. She had tried to slip into bed beside him, but he made no room for her.

"If I hadn't been ill, you would have had nothing to do with me?"

"But you were ill, and I was with you."

"So it was." It seemed he was nothing more to her then a bargain to fulfill. He kept his back to her, and when she climbed in beside him, he moved away when she tried to slip her hands under his shirt. He was burning still, but now he was hot with anger.

The rain fell and turned into mist. The sky was gray and the sea grew rough as they traveled north. When a disk of sun broke through, it was possible to spy cliffs, and seals sprawled upon the ledges of the rocks. In the very far distance there was a haze of green. Massachusetts was indeed huge and wild.

"You've done as you promised," Abraham Dias told Maria as they neared the coast, pleased by the outcome of their agreement. He had his son, alive and well, and he thought more highly of Maria than he would have imagined. He almost seemed jaunty, wearing a leather cap that had been treated with animal blood and grease so that it would be waterproof, a grin on his sunburned face.

"So have you," Maria responded. She carried the baby. As always Faith's bright hair was a beacon on this dark ship. "Thank you for bringing us to Boston. I know it was against your better judgment."

"I judged wrongly," he admitted. "Will he now be well?" Dias asked of his son. Though the old man was tough, his deep love for his son was evident.

"As well as ever," Maria assured him.

They both laughed. Samuel had been a difficult, argumentative boy with a mind of his own, and he'd grown to be a difficult man who never shied away from a fight.

"So he is himself again," Abraham Dias said, relieved. His son was his heart, and Maria understood, for she held her heart in her hands, a red-haired little girl.

Samuel was strong enough to be back on deck, and back at his maps as well. Navigators were prized on ships, for without them all was guesswork, and the northern coasts were littered with wrecks that had not avoided the reefs and rocks. He still tired easily, and was often chilled, wearing his black coat even on fine days, but he appeared healthy, as he must have been before breakbone fever seized him. He made certain to avoid Maria, sleeping on deck with the rest of the men covered with tarred sheets of linen to protect them from rain and seawater. Now that he had his health and freedom returned to him, it turned out he didn't want either one; he would rather be ill if that meant Maria would still take care of him. He was no longer angry, he was hurt, and that was worse.

As they approached the Massachusetts harbor, Maria could see a city of docks and streets that followed the old paths where cows still wandered freely, where markets sold cod and oysters and clams. So many houses were being built that the clatter of hammers echoed constantly. Huge white clouds were strung as if on a clothesline and the harbor was thick with ships. Maria was on the deck with Cadin, at last freed from his cage in the open air, when Samuel approached. He had a slight limp due to the pain in his legs, but it was only noticeable to those who knew him. It had been days since they'd spoken.

"You're setting him free?" They usually spoke in English, but now Dias spoke Portuguese. His voice was more musical and more urgent, and his questions and intent were harder to ignore. He almost seemed like a serious man. After his illness he had come to understand time in a different way. It was not endless, as most young men believed it to be. There was so little of it he could hold it in his hands, and still it slipped away, even as he stood in the pale sunlight approaching Boston Harbor, beside a woman he didn't wish to lose.

"He was always free," Maria said. "I told you that."

When Cadin lifted into the sky, they watched him wing toward the shore. Boston Harbor was cold and gray even on a summer day. Dias had been stitching as sailors often did, and he'd made Faith a little poppet doll that she was delighted to be given.

"Keep it safe," he told her, and the little girl nodded solemnly and clung to the doll. When Samuel went to the quarterdeck to help guide the ship to shore, the baby called out to him, but he didn't answer. Samuel Benjamin Dias, navigator and robber, the man who liked to talk so much he continued to do so in his sleep, had become quiet on this day, as if afraid of what he might say. He'd been too many places and lost too many people to think there was a point in a drawn-out parting. He was gone before Maria knew it, leaving her there to consider what her new life might be once she found John Hathorne, for in truth, she could no longer picture his face. When she closed her eyes, all she saw was Samuel Dias, which clearly was a mistake.

He did not leave the ship after it docked. He told his father they should turn toward Newport as soon as their trading in Boston was done. There was no reason to stay. Maria looked back and saw him at his maps. Perhaps he was too busy to say his good-byes; he was meant to study the seas and stars and there was nothing for him here on land. A man who talked as much as he did knew when he'd reached the end of a story, even though there are those who insist that once you save a life, that person is tied to you eternally. Maria might have gone to him and asked for him to explain himself and tell her what he wanted of her, but it was too late. There was the city of Boston and beyond were the green hills of the second Essex County.

This was where fate had led her.

PART TWO

Talisman

I.

Summertime in Massachusetts was sticky with heat and plagued by thunderstorms, and August was the worst of it. Even a weather witch could do little here when faced with the oddities of nature. Occasionally, hailstones as big as a man's hand would fall with a noisy splatter, pelting against roofs and cobbled walkways. The streets ran with waste, and temperatures rose until people were unable to sleep at night. Overheated men roamed the city, courting trouble; proper women slept without a stitch of clothing and dreamed of lakes and streams, often waking with their hair wringing wet and pools of water mysteriously appearing on the wooden floor beneath their beds.

Yet, despite the troubles the season brought, every soul in the colony agreed that summer was far too short. No one wished for a New England winter. Winter was severe in every acre of this region, bleak and much more fierce than winters in England, so cold that harbors froze solid. There were those who believed this new country was too frigid for Englishmen, many of whom perished in blizzards, freezing in their own beds. The native people vowed that every ten years there was no winter, but that the years in between made up for that blessed time. It was a land of extremes and there seemed to be more of everything here, both disaster and promise, and mothers whispered that was the cause that there were so many twins in the Massachusetts Bay Colony, for all here was doubled, even human life.

The land itself was huge, endless, some people vowed, with uncharted territories of wilderness said to be overrun by beasts and natives that the settlers had betrayed and now feared. Essex County itself was large, with many towns and villages. Until Maria could discover where John Hathorne was, she would remain in Boston, boarding near School Street, where the first public school, Boston Latin, had opened in 1635. As always, she kept the window open for Cadin, so that he might come and go as he pleased. He continued to bring gifts for Maria, from every neighborhood in Boston. Bullets, fishhooks, a blue pearl, scallop shells, colored glass, a key that seemed to fit any door. The crow perched in the rafters of her room, but at night he seemed to know that she was lonely, for he slept beside her, making a nest in the blanket, lulling her to sleep with a clacking sound. Several of Cadin's feathers had turned white by this time, and Maria worried over him, although crows could easily live to be twenty, and in rare cases, such creatures had been known to survive for thirty or more years. *Do not leave me,* she whispered to the crow, the same words Samuel Dias had so often said in his sleep, not that she would think of that, or of him, or consider what he had meant to her.

There was a teahouse in her lodgings, and in exchange for room and board, Maria was employed as a cook. She knew the basics of Hannah's simple cookery, and she quickly learned the American specialties favored by their customers. Odd as these dishes were to her palate, she soon grew accustomed to the strange food she ladled out each evening. Cod and mashed potatoes, baked beans that had been soaked in cold water overnight and were then cooked for hours with salt pork, stewed pumpkins, yellow and green native squashes, pot pies of every sort, boiled clams, cherry and plum puddings, as well as a dish known as Indian pudding, a great favorite of Faith's, for it was a heavenly mixture of scalded milk, Indian meal, molasses, cinnamon, and ginger. Maria had learned to tell the difference in the fish she used; cod was good for boiling and had white stripes, and haddock was best for frying and had black stripes. On Tuesdays she baked Shrewsbury cakes, buttery and flavored with rosewater. On Saturdays there was bird's nest pudding, made of cored apples and egg custard. Best of all were Sundays, when she fixed apple fritters, battered apples fried and coated with sugar and cider, or on special occasions, an apple pie, Faith's favorite. For those who had a taste for tart desserts there were slices of cranberry spice pie flavored with nutmeg and cinnamon, or hard gingerbread, which kept well for weeks. Courage Tea was always called for, especially when a woman had a difficult decision before her or when the right words could not be found although they needed to be said.

Every morning Maria made her daughter a breakfast of gruel, oats settled in cold water, boiled with raisins, sugar, and a pinch of salt and nutmeg. Faith was an early walker, and by the summer's end she often toddled about from table to table, with her favorite poppet in hand. Maria laughed to think that her doll had been sewn by a sailor who had fought battles at sea and thought nothing of engaging in bloodshed. She was reminded of Samuel's charm and his open smile, and his reckless brand of self-confidence that had made her laugh out loud, for in his opinion, there was nothing he could not do. She looked at the poppet and thought perhaps this was true. Sailors had endless time at sea, hours in which they took up what were ordinarily considered the female arts. They fashioned extraordinary boxes

166

decorated with shells, knit scarves, learned to sew.

Maria recalled the times she had slept beside Samuel when he was burning with fever, and closer to death than she'd let on. She still missed their intimacy. All that talk, all those stories, were like a river she had dived into. She told herself it was only natural to think of him, for they had held each other, and had once or twice done more. But perhaps her thoughts were drawn to him because she had saved him and her connection to him was not unlike someone who had rescued a dog from an icy pond or a bird from a tangle of thickets, nothing more.

Faith often called out for the sailor, puzzled by the fact that he was no longer in their lives. Maria would then shake her head. "He's out at sea," she'd tell the baby. When the child would not stop calling *Gogo,* Maria brought her to the wharf. She gestured to the harbor and the waves beyond. "That's where he is," she told her daughter. "He's gone."

Secrets were hard to keep, even in Boston, and word of Maria's talents soon spread through the city, with each client telling the next her address. These referrals were knots in a rope, buds on a tree, birds that sang to summon others who might need a tonic or a cure. Soon a line of women waited at the back door after dark, their shawls drawn over their heads, for no one wished to be recognized if a neighbor happened to pass by. Some called Maria Owens a healer, others said she was a witch. Those who feared magic came for her help anyway, regardless of what their fathers or husbands might say had they known their daughters and wives had come to a woman who was an expert in the Nameless Art. The ill, the old, the lovesick, the brokenhearted, the abandoned, the hopeful, the cursed, the fevered, the fallen, all arrived after dark, when the streets were empty, and the harbor quiet, and rats ruled the city. As always, most came for love. Maria wasn't surprised, for this had been true in Devotion Field, and Hannah had always said lovesickness afflicted most of those who came to her door. In many cases a simple cure would do. The most reliable love potions were the ones Maria had learned watching from a corner as Hannah worked her magic. A woman could plant an onion and keep it on her windowsill; she could write her own name and her intended's on a white candle and burn it without ever extinguishing the flame; she could braid a strand of her own hair with her beloved's and keep it under her pillow. When the eight lesser charms had been tried and had met with failure, Maria turned to the Ninth, which did no harm and could not force love, but instead gently invited it to walk through the door.

9 oz. red wine
9 basil leaves
9 rose petals
9 cloves
9 apple seeds
9 anise seeds
9 drops of vinegar
Combine all ingredients on the 9th hour
    of the 9th day of the month. The effect
    is strongest when performed on the
    9th month of the year.
Stir nine times.
Let the one who drinks this wine grant me
    true love divine.

The Tenth Love Potion, the one Rebecca had cast upon Lockland, was written down in Maria's *Grimoire*, but she had made an oath never to use it, not for any woman who came calling, no matter how desperate, and certainly never for herself. It was a spell written in blood, able to turn a person inside out with raw emotion, and it could not be reversed without grave consequences. The Tenth was a dangerous spell, as much of ancient magic was; it called on elemental powers that could turn one's beloved's heart to stone if the slightest error was made in its creation, and the ingredients could cause complete havoc if not used correctly.

Hannah had done her best to correct these effects for Maria's mother, but in the end she had merely reversed it. The opposite of love was hate, and Thomas Lockland had that emotion in his heart when he burned down the cottage. The Tenth was said to be unbreakable, and nothing in this world should be so, for all that is and ever will be must change.

The winter of 1680 in Boston was one that consisted of hard work and days that grew dark at four in the afternoon. The temperatures were so cold that bread rattled on the plate and people wore every item of clothing they owned at the same time, one layer over the other. It was a bad time to search Essex County for John, and Maria decided to stay at the boardinghouse until the weather turned. During her time of employment she and the proprietor, Mrs. Henry, had grown quite close. Both were women on their own in the world, after all, and both were willing to open the door to anyone in need. Maria's talents were evident, and the line outside their door grew to be surprisingly long. There were those who must set two eggs, never to be eaten, beneath their beds to clean a tainted atmosphere, and those who were to use black mustard seed to repel nightmares, those who were told to use vinegar for husbands who could not perform in bed and were told to feed their men chestnuts and oysters to inflame desire, those who asked for Be True to Me Tea, for straying husbands. Still others came for a remedy of garlic, salt, and rosemary, the most ancient spell to cast away evil. Many wanted Maria's teas, concocted late at night by lantern light. Fever Tea was composed of bayberry, ginger, cinnamon, thyme, and marjoram. Frustration Tea was made of chamomile, hyssop, raspberry leaf, and rosemary. Courage Tea was the great favorite, Hannah's old recipe, and pots of it were served day after day.

When Mrs. Henry looked at Maria, she saw a healer, not a witch, and she would always be grateful for the lily-of-the-valley tea Maria had used to stop the older woman's heart from fluttering one night when she fell faint. Mrs. Henry swore she would surely be in her grave if not for that curative; she opened her heart to Maria and her charming little girl, and was happy to share her own cures.

BOSTON REMEDIES

Honey and milk for worms.
Salt and molasses for cuts.
Huckleberries boiled for stomachaches.
Balm of Gilead buds boiled into a paste
    for wounds.
Dark blue violets as a tincture for mouth
    sores.

Chickweed prevents toothaches.

Table salt and vinegar, fermented, for colic.

Castor oil, milk, and sugar for a children's tonic.

Maria had confided that she was in search of a man, like so many women who had been forsaken by husbands and fathers who had come to the New World promising to send for them, then disappearing into cities or the wilderness. This came as no surprise to Mrs. Henry. Women in search of men were nothing new in Boston. There were signs tacked to lampposts and on market stalls with descriptions of lost husbands, which sometimes included the image of a face, drawn to the best of the bereaved's abilities. Maria could often see where the missing were when she set out a pan of water for scrying, and she gave out the addresses of lost men, many of whom didn't wish to be found; she warned her clients that sometimes it was best to let the lost remain so, for they might not be pleased once their loved ones were located.

Try as she might, Maria could not see John, not in the water and not in the black mirror, which she kept carefully stored in a piece of blue flannel so that it would not break. Hannah had told her that when a person looked in the mirror she would see what she must, not what she wished to see.

John was never there. She could only see him in her daughter's features—the high cheekbones, the lanky arms and legs, the particular way she laughed with her head thrown back, exactly as her father had when he stepped into the turquoise water and found the world to be a miracle.

It was Mrs. Henry who directed Maria to Salem. By then it was early spring and Faith had passed her first birthday. The ice was melting in the streets, and as always at this time of year the harbor was filled with ships. A customer returning from London mentioned he was on his way home to Essex County.

"How many people can there be in one county?" Mrs. Henry said to Maria. "Perhaps he'll know your man."

Maria brought the gentleman a bowl of her apple pandowdy, apples baked in a crust, a delicious end to his dinner, and when he thanked her, she asked if perhaps he might have heard of a man named John Hathorne. Indeed, there was a well-known magistrate in Salem by that name, a man of wealth. "It's a strict village with Puritans setting down their rules not just for themselves, but for everyone."

Maria had no fear of rules, and she thanked the customer for his help.

"Now I'll lose my cook," Mrs. Henry said sorrowfully when she saw the expression on

Maria's face, for one didn't need the ability to see into the future to comprehend what would happen next.

That night, Maria had difficulty sleeping. When at last she fell asleep, she dreamed of a ship at sea. In her dream she held her *Grimoire* in her hands, open to a page on which a map had been spun out of stars. It was a map she couldn't read, and she was as lost and alone as she had been in the field of snow when Cadin found her and sat on the rim of her basket, refusing to leave her. And then she was no longer alone. Hannah sat across from her in her dream, as real as she'd been on the last day they had spent together. Their boat drifted in a vast and endless sea, but there was great comfort in being in Hannah's presence, even in a dream.

Fate is what you make of it. You can make the best of it, or you can let it make the best of you.

The fish swimming beneath their boat were huge, dark shadows, but Maria paid them no mind. Stars fell from the sky. Clouds appeared, gray and swollen, promising storms. The world was cold, but there was a flame burning inside her. Hannah leaned forward to whisper.

Life is not what you think it is. Remember that. Remember me.

When Maria woke, she had already decided she must leave for Essex County without delay.

174

Her future was waiting for her and it would be best for her to discover what was in store. She had most likely stayed too long in Boston. She wondered why she had been unable to find John Hathorne on her own, for she had sighted countless lost men for so many women. There was a problem that thwarted her, that much was evident. She set to work baking a love cake, using the recipe Hannah had taught her. It was a skillet cake, made over the fire, and as it baked, it turned from white to red. She set it out to cool, but an hour later returned to find that the cake had been devoured by ants. It was a dark sign, but one she ignored as she threw away what was left of the cake.

Believe what the world shows you, and make no excuses. See what is right before you. Instead, Maria told herself that it was impossible to control all living things and all occurrences. Not even magic could do that.

There was farmland ringing Salem, with fields of grass and black-eyed Susans, and farther in the distance, a deep forest of ancient woodland. Spring was madness in New England, all the world come to life at once. Pine, oak, chestnut, plum tree, elm, walnut, ash, witch hazel, and wild cherry all grew here. There were mallows and white hellebore in great profusion in the marshes, used as a curative for wounds and aches, and clusters of loosestrife with vivid purple flowers. In the shadows, there was nightshade, black henbane, wormwood, and bloodwort.

The North River flowed inland and there were marshes and tide pools dotting the land. Salem itself was bustling, and was always so, no matter the hour. This seafaring community had been settled in 1626 at the site of a native village, and was the second oldest settlement in Massachusetts, named after the Hebrew word for peace, *shalom*. It was here the first Puritan church had been built by those who'd fled England in search of freedom, but once the refugees arrived in a land they claimed as their own, they became as intolerant as their persecutors had been. They insisted upon purity that did not deviate from their beliefs, ensuring that all would live within the Scriptures as they saw them, rejecting the ways of sin practiced in England. The soul was said to be divided into two halves, the immortal half, which was male, and the mortal half, which was female, set in place by Eve's original sin. It was women who were more likely to carry sin, to keep it in their hearts, to veer from the path of the righteous. The settlers believed with utter certainty that the world to come was predestined; some were condemned to hell in an unbroken fate that could not be altered, while others would receive God's grace no matter what their earthly deeds might be. The only mercy that could be shown was divine. It was not for men to forgive; they were merely to enforce the rules of God, and make certain they were obeyed. Deviation from the rules meant severe punishment—lashings, whippings, the stocks, prison, being sent into the wilderness.

Women in Essex County were not allowed to wear fine clothes, for such attire might awaken the evil impulses of both demons and men. Female members of the community were expected to dress plainly in austere gray dresses of a color known as liver. Brown and indigo were sometimes used, for the dye was cheap, but only the wealthy wore black, for it was an expensive color to produce. Vanity was not allowed, and silk and lace were considered sinful; there were to be no scarves and no embroidered needlework. There had recently been cases in the nearby town of Newbury of women who had been arrested for wearing silk hoods. Long hair was outlawed, for it called up unwanted desire; there were to be no kid gloves or silk-laced shoes, no gold or silver jewelry. Puritans placed meaning in the color of clothes. Black symbolized humility; russet and brown, made from madder root dye, was the color of poverty; gray meant repentance; and white, the color of caps and cuffs and collars, was purity and virtue.

Wickedness could easily be found in this part of the world; hands must be kept busy to prevent evil deeds and to keep God's favor, which many thought had been lost when there were several years of failed crops and famine. It was in God's name that the Puritans made their attack against the native people and the French, a vicious endeavor called King Philip's War, named after the Wampanoag chief who had taken the name Philip and led a bloody uprising that had lasted fourteen months. The English took what they wanted and felt was divinely given to them, land they claimed for God, but kept for their own use. One must be careful to keep oneself in God's light and not in the devil's darkness. Women must keep their eyes lowered, their voices soft. They must not ask for what they did not deserve, or think themselves above others, or pursue any vile needs or desires.

Mrs. Henry had told Maria to keep her head covered so that her glossy black hair wouldn't be seen. Puritans rejected beauty in a woman, Mrs. Henry warned, just as they feared independence in the sex they deemed responsible for Adam's downfall and the trials of all men who had followed. Maria carried the baby on her hip and Cadin in his case made of reeds. From the start, the crow made it clear that he was unhappy with their destination, clattering nasty clicks, as if scolding his mistress. Cadin put up such a racket that at last Maria paused on the street to open his cage. He peered at her with his glittering eye, sulking as he had on the day when Rebecca Lockland had knocked at the door, as annoyed as he'd always been when John Hathorne had come to call in Curaçao.

"Go on," she urged when he glared at her with fierce disapproval. Cadin would always be her dearest friend, but perhaps he was jealous of John; certainly he had never taken to him. "You asked to be free. Go have a look at this town."

The crow disappeared above the rooftops, a black streak in the sky. If he didn't wish to help her find John, so be it. They'd make amends; they always did, for they had similar temperaments, cool and mistrustful, but ultimately, forgiving. She had decided she would no longer have doubts. A black heart could belong to anyone, and she would ignore the image she had seen. This was the day when she was to step into the future. She wore a serge dress, hand-stitched by Mrs. Henry for the occasion, dyed with blue composition, an inexpensive dye made of indigo and sold as a liquid in small glass bottles, a common enough color in Boston, but one which stood out here in Salem, where the women most often wore gray. She had on her red boots, still as good as new, and in her hair were the blackened silver hair clips that she considered to be good luck, even though a witch makes her own luck, and silver meant less to her than remembrance. Her lovely face shone in the sunlight, perhaps

179

even more than it might have elsewhere, for sunlight was a rare occurrence in this city.

Maria had brought along some johnnycakes for Faith to eat on the journey, and some salt cod for herself, and as they went along the road she'd picked handfuls of ripe blackberries. Although the baby was hungry, Maria's stomach was a nest of nerves and she couldn't bring herself to eat. Whenever she closed her eyes, she saw herself holding a black heart in her hands.

Turn it over once for love, twice for betrayal, three times for heartbreak.

Maria was young, her looks striking with her black hair, silver-gray eyes, and slim, reedy body. *Puritans are men,* Samuel Dias had warned her. *No matter how many prayers they say.* Instinctively, she searched for a woman's help, which she found when she approached an inn on the wharf. When she mentioned Hathorne to a barmaid there, she was directed to Washington and Court Streets. If Maria was in search of the magistrate, that was where he would be found, at the court or city hall. His house was on Washington Street as well.

"But if I were you I'd avoid that place," the barmaid confided. She was a Dutch protestant, and did her best to live in the Puritans' world. "They've got their rules and we'd do best to stay far away from them."

Maria followed the directions she'd been given. She stood on a corner of the cobbled street and observed a row of elegant houses. Better to find him at home, she decided, as they'd found one another in the blue dining room in Curaçao. She would know which house was his when she came upon it. As she closed her eyes, she saw it in her mind's eye, a large house with black shutters that were thrown open on summer mornings before the heat turned brutal, the cloudy windows where he stood to watch snow fall on dark winter days. She felt the tug inside her and there she was standing in front of John Hathorne's house, a world away from the country of heat and light where they'd met, where women went barefoot, and men were willing to jump into the sea-green water, and no one who saw such behavior would give it a thought.

The bricks in front of the house were patterned in diamond shapes, a formation that is said to bring bad luck, but Maria would not think of luck. Still, the mark on her inner arm had begun to burn, as though it were a star that had fallen from heaven to earth. When a witch's mark burns, she had best be aware of the dangers that surround her, for it is a warning that should never be overlooked. Hannah had taught her not to ignore her intuition, telling her not to look away or think all will be well if she wished it to be. *Pay attention, pay heed, listen to the voice inside.*

The two large elm trees in his yard displayed a peculiar black leaf. When the leaves fell in autumn, a black carpet led to the gabled entrance-way, but in summer they provided a welcome bower of shade. When Maria approached, the leaves that had only recently unfurled began to fall as if autumn had come early. She could see nothing through the small casement windows with leaded diamond-shaped panes. To summon John to her she rubbed her wrists with lavender oil. She had a pocket full of bird bones, gathered from the grass of grazing land in Boston, then strung on a bit of rope that she wore around her wrists. They were spells for love and for remembrance. She wore Cadin's black feather in a charm at her throat.

They waited for nearly two hours, until Faith grew cranky and hungry. Little Faith was not as patient as Maria had been as a baby; she had a bit of a temper, as red-haired children often do. Maria hushed her, but some things have only a single remedy. Because the baby needed to be fed and because there was nowhere else to go, Maria made her way up the path to the garden, where she sat in the sunlight, the baby at her breast. Someone had carefully tended the kitchen garden here, planting seedlings of parsley and chervil, summer savory, thyme, sage, and spearmint. The black leaves continued to fall, their shapes forming black hearts in the grass.

• • •

As he approached the house, John Hathorne spied a crow in the tree. A chill went through him even though the day was fine, or at least it had been until this very moment. He had a true distaste for such creatures, and had ever since Curaçao when that horrible pet of the Jansens' housemaid spat stones at him. Hathorne was accompanied now by the captain of one of his fleets of ships, scheduled to leave soon for the West Indies. A stone hit him as they spoke of sugar and slaves, grazing his cheek and drawing blood. He gazed upward and there was the vicious feathered beast. Although few men could tell one crow from another, he swore it was the same foul bird he'd known in the West Indies who had taken pleasure in tormenting him. It was the glint in the creature's eye that gave him away, the way he held his head, proudly, as if he were as good as any man. If it was the bird he knew, it occurred to him that he was being threatened. He quickly made his excuses to the captain; he was so sorry to change their plans, but they would have to speak in the morning. He professed to be ill, and perhaps he was. Certainly, he couldn't think straight and his gut was lurching. Like many in this world, he had two souls residing inside him: the man he wished to be and the man he actually was. Here, in Essex County, he was the man he'd been trained to be, his father's son, a magistrate who did not stray, whose judgments were cast upon others, never upon himself.

He saw a woman's figure in his own garden and was completely baffled. It was as if a wolf had come to lie beside the hollyhocks, or a lynx had climbed upon the roof, or worse, a witch had followed him across the seas. It was she; he knew her as he'd known the crow. His deeds had come back to haunt him. He rubbed his eyes hoping the vision would disappear, but the scene remained the same: a woman wearing red boots, which were outlawed in this town, intent on the child in her arms. He had never imagined her here in this landscape where the clouds billowed and the sky turned gray late in the day and black leaves fell. They fell now, as if the trees had been shaken and the world had fallen apart and not even seasons knew their time and place.

She was still a beauty, but he was now the other man, the one he'd been born to be, his father's son, and Curaçao was only a dream to him. He considered his own behavior on that island to be a mystery. Men were undone in mysterious ways; they stopped thinking and only felt when they wanted what didn't belong to them, and they often did as they pleased in a strange country where rose-colored birds stood on one long leg in a blue-green sea and the women could bewitch you if you weren't careful, if you didn't keep your head and remember exactly who you

184

were—a man who owned ships and wharfs and warehouses and a house with black shutters, whose father and grandfather had been men of honor, all magistrates, all respected citizens who kept their word and made certain others kept theirs. These were men who would never have leapt into the sea fully clothed, shouting with joy, grinning like a fool, as if a demon had entered to use the darkness inside of them for ungodly purposes.

Maria sat beside a bank of tall, snow-white phlox. Nearby, in the kitchen garden, fennel and purple cabbage and radishes would soon be grown. There were no lilacs, as there had been in the vision in the black mirror, but surely she could plant them when she was John's wife and this was her house. She would have Persian lilacs in shades of purple and violet and blue, with blooms so sweet women passing by would stop, unable to go any farther, called to the spot as if their names had been spoken aloud.

A bee came to examine Faith's hair, red as a flower in the bright sunlight. Maria sent it off with a polite nod. "Be elsewhere," she whispered, and it happily complied. In the tree with black leaves, Cadin was clacking and tossing down pebbles. Maria gave him a dark look, but otherwise paid him no mind. She could not let a crow make her decisions. Her fate was her own, and she would most certainly make the best of it before it made the best of her.

She set her sleeping baby in the grass. To call John to her, she took a laurel leaf from her satchel and held it in the palm of her hand, then set it on fire with a single breath, not minding that she scorched her own skin. The smoke was thin and green, so fragrant it was impossible to ignore. She said his name backwards, chanting beneath her breath. From behind the gate he felt the thrill of seeing her again. She was like no other woman he had ever seen or known, and when she called to him he felt his desire in the pit of his stomach. Sins were committed every hour of every day, and it was clear that this woman was unnatural in some way. But who among them had not committed a sin? The eternal torments of original sin had waited for mankind from the moment Adam ate the apple, which was handed to him by Eve, an act that proved to him and his brethren that women were spiritually inferior to men, weak with human frailty, sinful at their core.

John entered the garden and closed the open gate behind him, always bad luck. He was wearing the same black coat he hadn't bothered to take off when he swam alongside the turtle, when he didn't know the difference between a miracle and a monster. It had been laundered with hot water and lye soap and yet there was still sand in the seams. He looked at Faith, dozing in the afternoon light. She might be anything at all, an angel beside the snowy phlox, a wicked changeling sent in the guise of a red-haired girl, but her features were not unlike his, the same narrow nose and high cheekbones. She was merely his child. He softened then, and perhaps he smiled, for as Maria gazed up to see him she believed she saw his heart beating beneath his black coat.

Maria turned her attention to the bee that now came to sting Faith. The child let out a cry so filled with shock and pain that the sparrows in the garden took flight all at once. For a moment the sky was dark as the leaves from the black elm fell to litter the path as if they were bats falling from the branches. Maria quickly removed the stinger from her baby's arm, then rubbed some lavender oil on the rising welt. "Hush," she told the child. "All better." She picked up the dying bee and cast it into the bed of phlox. Some creatures do not care how polite a person might be, they will hurt you for no reason, and then all you can do is heal yourself with whatever ingredients are necessary.

John's heart was twisted in two between what he wanted and what he must do. He took her hands in his and drew her to her feet. He embraced her then, and so it came as a surprise when he said, "We must leave this place."

"What do you mean? I've brought you your daughter."

Hathorne gazed at the child's hair. It was a time when many people believed red-haired women to be witches and imagined those with freckles had been marked by the devil, especially if they were left-handed, another evil trait. Redheads were said to be violent in temperament, false in nature, evil in intent. But this darling baby smiled up at Hathorne. "Gogo," she said in her sweet voice.

Maria laughed. The babe thought Samuel Dias had returned. "No, no. This isn't Goat. He's another man."

At the mention of a man, and one with a name that called Satan to mind, Hathorne flared with jealousy. What was his was his alone, even when he wasn't certain he wanted the prize. "Am I not her father?"

"Yes, yes," Maria assured him. Dias was her patient, nothing more. A friend, perhaps, a confidant, the man of a thousand stories, far away and out of mind. The one she embraced in bed, the one she allowed to kiss her until she was burning, but she always stopped him before she was completely his. There was John to think of, and loyalty, and their daughter. "Of course she's yours."

"Then we must go now. For safety's sake."

He led her from the yard, the baby still whimpering. When at last they reached the far end of the street, Hathorne drew Maria into a doorway so he might kiss her. Once begun, he could not get enough of her, though she held the baby in her arms. He knew that his desire could be his undoing. He was not young, though he was handsome enough so that women in town failed to lower their eyes when they passed him by, daring to smile and perhaps take his arm so they might make their interest clear. But those were inappropriate flirtations, nothing more. This was an enchantment, and he, who judged others harshly when they came before him in his chambers, did not judge himself for his wrongdoings. A spell was at work, and as he had leapt into the water in Curaçao, he embraced her now, but only for a moment, for this was not the time or the place.

They went to the edge of town, past the fields and woods so dense it was difficult to navigate through the branches. Though many trees had been cut down as more and more land was cleared for Indian corn and other crops, the forests were still deep. Salem seemed destined to grow until it met up with the forest and claimed all the land, but for now, it was still a mysterious and dangerous place. There were great gray owls in the trees here. Gnats filled the air and poisonous plants grew nearby—stalks of horse nettle and chokeberries and toxic wild cherries that contained cyanide. It was dark and damp and so green the world seemed black. Black hearts grew in the lacey leaves of ferns, and there were mushrooms in the shadows, and black forget-menots that were already wilting in the sunlight. As they walked, John explained that his father was a stern, overbearing man and that here in Salem the court and the magistrates would consider a child born outside of marriage a crime. He could find himself in jail, for this world was different than Curaçao, with rules that couldn't be broken. Without marriage, a child would always be an outcast. Here, he explained to Maria, people looked for monsters, not for miracles.

"What is there to do?" Maria said, her mood darkening. Perhaps it was the unfamiliar landscape that made it seem as though the man was unfamiliar as well. And yet, Maria believed that now that she and Faith had arrived, Hathorne would change back into the man she had known. The man who had fallen in love with her was inside of him. "Our child exists," she said. "Who could fault us when there wasn't time to marry?"

Faith's encounter with the bee had exhausted her, and she had fallen asleep on her mother's shoulder, her face hot and streaked with tears. Every now and then Maria patted the baby's back.

"They might fault us," Hathorne said. "But we do not need to fault ourselves."

He looked at her the way he had on the island, and Maria was relieved to see the man she had known. She followed John, who was so tall he cast a shadow before him. He had taken her hand and she could feel his heat. They went on through, past the elms and the wild cherry trees already laden with fruit, with its poison seeds. He knew of an abandoned cabin often occupied by hunters in autumn, but deserted in all other seasons. Maria and the baby would be safe there until he could sort out what to do about his family. They were far enough from town, Hathorne said. *Hidden,* Maria thought. *Not fit for the company of others.*

When they arrived, Maria peered inside the cabin. Leaves covered the floor, ashes filled the fireplace, and pottery was broken and scattered about. Cutlery, left unwashed, had been strewn upon a small wooden table. In a corner were straw pallets and several threadbare woolen blankets. Once inside, Maria found a spoon to cast out the door, as her mother had done time and time again, to be rid of bad luck. But the spoon was tin, not silver. It didn't turn black in her touch, and rather than being flung into the distance, it landed at her feet, clattering upon her red boots. A dozen crows were in the trees, but Cadin was not among them. He was making himself scarce, and in doing so he made his annoyance evident, as it was whenever she was with John.

The baby was bundled in her blanket with Maria's name stitched at one corner and Faith's name stitched below her mother's with the blue thread Rebecca had given her. Blue for protection and remembrance. Hathorne embraced Maria fiercely; he would have had her right there if she hadn't stopped him. His hands were all over her, so hot they burned her skin. She thought of the laurel leaf aflame in her hand; she'd called him to her, but now she backed away. *Do good among them,* Hannah always said, *but do not expect the same in return.*

"If they have set out rules in this town, let us act by them," Maria said.

If marriage was what this world insisted upon, then marriage it would be. Here, in these woods, in the second Essex County she had known, Maria thought of Hannah's burning house. Most witches feared water, but Maria feared fire. She thought of the day when Lockland and his brothers arrived, when the air had filled with the stems and petals from the poison garden. Her eyes had burned for days afterward, perhaps from the billows of smoke, perhaps from the tears she couldn't shed. It was so easy to make a mistake in matters of love. So many women had made their way across Devotion Field, convinced they must make the wrong man their own. Maria had done her best to help those who came to her in Boston, even the ones who knew they should let go of love. Now she asked for marriage, even though she thought of another man. There was a cure for this, she knew, but to set a spell upon herself was dangerous, and she could stop such thoughts by sheer willpower if she tried. *O Amor* meant sweetheart, darling, flame, love. That is what Samuel Dias had called out in his sleep, and it was only now that Maria realized he might have been speaking to her.

"My pledge remains the same," Hathorne told her. For now he would bring all she might need to stay in the cabin: bedding and pots and pans, baskets of apples and onions, ginger and butter and eggs, odd vegetables Maria had never seen before. He returned the next night and the night after that. They took a late supper together cooked over a fire. Before she'd left Boston, Mrs. Henry had taught her how to fix Salem Pudding, a favored dish made of flour, milk, molasses, and raisins, all boiled for hours, and how to make a quick meal of johnnycakes with Indian meal and flour, one egg, a little sugar, and salt and soda. John praised the tea she made and said it gave him the strength and courage to try to set things right.

In time, Maria relented, and while Faith slept, she took him to her bed, the straw pallet where hunters camped after the leaves turned, when they came to shoot deer and wild fowl. Spring passed into summer, and some evenings John could not get away. On these nights there was nothing but darkness and the flicker of the fireflies, creatures unknown in England. They rose amid the trees in globes of pale yellow light, signaling to one another. *Is this what love is?* Maria might have asked Hannah Owens, who'd been betrayed by a man who claimed she spoke with Satan and had sworn to the judges that beneath her skirts she possessed a tail. *Is love not more than this?* she might have asked her mother, who pledged her life to a man who'd charmed her with words that weren't his own. She knew something was wrong, even within her own heart, but then John would return, as though he'd never been gone, full of apologies and promises. It was his family, he explained, and their austere view of the world that was at issue, and the differences between them. Maria had not been raised in any church, she did not live by the tenets of Puritan beliefs, she had a child without the benefit of marriage. She would not be accepted, and yet he returned. He could not stay away, he told her. *Was this love?* she might have asked herself, if she hadn't feared the answer.

On nights that she spent alone in the second Essex County, she couldn't help but wonder if she had been the one who had mistaken a monster for a miracle. She was a world away from Devotion Field, far from everything she had known. She could hear owls and the sound of deer mice in the pine needles. At night, when she was alone in her bed and John had left her, she could hear her own heart beat. She had seen this before, a woman

194

arriving at Hannah's door, love gone sour, love gone wrong, love that wasn't love at all.

October came quickly, a glorious month when the fields turned yellow. The leaves might appear green in shadow, but when sunlight pierced through there were threads of scarlet and orange. So many pigeons crossed the sky they blocked the sun from sight, and the day seemed as if it were night. Maria felt there was a power in this place as she knelt by the lake that was said to have no bottom. The twiggy shore was home to birds she had never seen before—scarlet cardinals, red and black woodpeckers, flickers, white owls sleeping in the hollow trees. She imagined she felt as Hannah had when she left the world of men and crossed through Devotion Field to enter into a world of magic and silence. The only sound she heard was the song of the earth when she lay in the yellow grass. Perhaps this was a blessing, for during this time the lines on her left hand began to change and she saw for herself that if you had the strength, you could change your fate.

The crows stayed on past autumn, as they always did. They would remain all through the coming snows, fearless creatures that they were, eating winterberries and snatching eggs from henhouses, managing to survive. Through the autumn, rumors spread about a young woman living in the woods. People said she was fearless, for it was a wild, thorny woodland, with creatures that had never been seen in England. Spikey porcupines, deer that were twelve feet high and thought to be so strong that the teeth of their fawns were strung into necklaces by the native people for babies to wear when teething. There were beaver that were said to contain both sexes, whose powdered tails were mixed into wine by those who claimed to be physicians and swore the false remedy would cure stomach ailments, and fox with pelts that were silver or red or black, and bats of all sorts flickering through the night. Raccoons that lived in hollow trees could open the doors and windows of houses in town, as if they had human hands, then slip inside to steal flour and day-old bread. Ground squirrels were so ravenous they would devour entire fields of corn, inspiring farmers to pay two pence apiece for each one killed and brought to town hall. What woman would live in such a place with a young child other than a sorceress, or a wild woman, or a witch?

One blue evening when the flocks of sparrows and warblers were beginning to migrate south, Maria saw a huge dark creature of more than three hundred pounds standing in the lake in solemn silence, sniffing at the chill in the air. Perhaps there were monsters in Essex County.

Surely people here believed in such things. Wolves that would track a man for weeks and devour him whole, poisonous snakes that favored young women and were said to hide beneath their beds, birds that drilled holes in the wooden planks of a house as if they had knives on their beaks, rabbits that turned from brown to white when the snow fell, magicked in front of your eyes. People in town vowed that a sea serpent resided in the leech-filled lake where Maria and her child bathed. The native people had always believed there was a mysterious creature in the depths, one that had dragged itself inland from the harbor when the countryside flooded in a storm surge and tides engulfed the forest. Perhaps this was nothing more than a story told to chase the English interlopers away; all the same, even after the original people had been dispatched from this area, not a single child from town would dive into that lake, not even on the most stifling days when a swim was the only tonic that might cool heat-struck boys. Instead, they would stand at the edge of the water, throwing rocks, not a one venturing any deeper than his toes. Local men had searched for the serpent with no success, and some of these individuals had disappeared; because the lake was bottomless, they were never seen again, leaving their wives and children to mourn their losses.

Cadin had made himself at home in these

woods. He often disappeared to scour the town for treasures to bring home— a shoe buckle, a carved wooden top, a silver thimble that immediately turned black in Faith's hands, for magic ran through her. She could call the birds to her with a single reedy cry, and at the lake the leeches never dared to come near when she waded into the cattails, clasping her mother's hand, for Maria warned her not to go too deeply into the water. Once Faith found a toad, withered and close to death, but when she gently picked it up and held it in her palm, the creature revived. Panicked, the toad leapt from her hand and disappeared into the bramble bushes. Maria happened to see this event and she was filled with a deep pride. Her daughter was a natural healer.

Had he been there, Samuel Dias would have applauded all of Faith's endeavors, for she always shone in his eyes. Faith still sang the Portuguese lullabies Samuel had sung to her. "Gogo," Faith said in a serious tone as they picked blackberries that grew near the shore, for the berries had reminded her of the man who had always shared the fruit Maria had insisted he eat to help him recover, including papaya and mangoes and berries, holding them out to Faith and applauding when she ate the berries.

"He's far off at sea," Maria told the baby, though it was really herself she was reminding that Samuel Dias was not part of their lives.

· · ·

Winter came early, with huge flakes falling nearly every day, and nothing had changed.

Three times a month Maria tramped through the dark, past the pear orchards, carrying her sleeping child so they could meet at Hathorne's warehouse on the dock. She wore black so that no one would take note of her. She took narrow paths at a late hour, though they were icy, and she shrunk into the shadows. Still she was not invisible, and as she made her way one cloudy night, the moon slipped out suddenly, and thinking she was a crow swooping through his fields, a farmer shot at her, peppering her coat with buckshot. Fortunately Maria was only grazed on her arm, and Faith went unscathed, though she startled in her mother's arms. Before she could stop herself, Maria uttered a curse. "Let he who tried to wound me be wounded in turn."

The next morning, the farmer vowed witchery was at work. Moles had burrowed up through the hard, frosty ground and a gang of crows descended upon his house. One of the crows had made its way down the chimney and had caused a ruckus in his parlor while his wife screamed and covered her head with a quilt. "There was a witch," he told anyone who would listen. "You wait and see," he said. "She'll come for you as she came for me, a woman who can turn herself into a black bird."

Every time Maria was with Hathorne there was a flicker in her heart, an ache beneath her ribs, as if a spike of metal had lodged inside her. He was more distant each time; he turned his back to her as he dressed. The black mirror had shown her fate, a man who brought her diamonds, as Hathorne had. All the same, she recalled Hannah's words, that she must always be careful to love someone who could love her back.

You make love what you want it to be, Hannah had told her. *You decide. You walk toward it, or you walk away.*

Maria recalled the women who had crossed Devotion Field driven by love they couldn't renounce, even when it had ruined them. And then one night she knew the answer to her own question. This wasn't love.

Maria Owens turned eighteen during her first winter in the second Essex County, the coldest winter in more than forty years. Harbors froze solid and the snow was so deep that horses in the pastures drowned in drifts that were eight feet tall. People who lived on farms far from town would not be seen until the following spring. Time was passing more quickly all the time. Faith was growing up here, just as Maria had grown up in the woods of the first Essex County, in England. This was where they lived, with or without John Hathorne, and Maria hung Hannah's brass bell just outside the door; when the wind came up the sound of the bell comforted her. She made the best of what she had. She chopped wood every day, and was lucky to have potatoes and onions and winter apples stored. When she ran out, she began to frequent Hatch's General Store, where she traded dried herbs for provisions. Anne Hatch, the grocer's wife, often added something special for Faith, a bit of molasses candy or a packet of sugar to help teething. As always Cadin followed along, but he waited for Maria in the tallest trees, for unlike his mistress he had never made this place his home.

The sky was black and pricked with stars when Maria went to the lake to chop ice for their drinking water. As she knelt, she spied the future written in the black ice. She saw herself tied to a chair, and John walking away in his black coat, and diamonds falling from her hands. She saw a tree with huge white flowers, each one the size of the moon.

Try as she might she could not tie these images together. Hannah would have said that women often didn't understand what they didn't truly wish to know, and perhaps Maria knew the truth already, for she wasn't surprised when one night she trekked to the harbor only to find the door to John's warehouse locked. She waited, but he never appeared. Each night she listened for his steps, but when the brass bell outside her door rang, it was only sounding for the wind.

When March came around, Maria celebrated Faith's second birthday alone with the baby, fixing a pie from apples she had stored in a barrel, adding the last of the cinnamon she'd brought along in her herb box from Curaçao. Faith was a wonder. She could hold full conversations, and was well behaved, a true helper in gathering herbs, a darling who listened to Maria's retelling of Samuel Dias's stories about a cat and a wolf and a child who had been lost in the woods.

Know who you are, Hannah had told her. *Know what you are,* Rebecca had said.

By now she knew exactly who she was. She was the woman who decided to walk to town on the day the snow melted, even though Hathorne had warned her not to come.

"People will not understand you," he'd told her. "The way you look, the clothes you wear, what we are to each other."

"What are we?" she had said, her face hot.

"We are what God will allow us to be," he'd said, which was not the answer she'd wanted.

It was spring, with the world suddenly alive and green, magicked back to life. Maria walked quickly, for it was mud season as well, and she didn't wish the muck to stain her red boots. On Washington Street, Cadin dove down from the sky, pulling out strands of her hair until she waved him away. Clearly he disapproved of the path she took. But a crow was a crow, and a woman a woman, and there were some things she believed he couldn't understand. She had written a letter with ink made from her own blood. It was a last attempt to see if John would do the right thing.

The house with the black shutters was only steps away. The black elms were festooned with a thousand dark buds that would soon unfurl into heart-shaped leaves. Maria was standing beneath the tree when she spied a woman and a young boy on the other side of the fence, there in the warm spring sun. Ruth Gardner Hathorne and her boy, three-year-old John, were seeing to the garden. Ruth wore a white cap, her blond hair hidden, her fair skin blotchy from hours of gardening. It was then that the new black leaves began to fall. The elms could not abide Maria, nor she them. A wet gust of wind came up and blew the fallen leaves away. She had seen Hathorne walk away from her in a vision where there was black water and a black heart lying broken in the grass. She'd discovered the reason he could never stay with her, why he kept her on the outskirts of the city, why he had begun to avoid her. All along he'd had a wife. Even a woman with the sight can be taken for a fool in matters of love.

Maria could not take her eyes off Ruth Gardner Hathorne, whose parents had been Quakers, persecuted for their religious beliefs by the Puritan magistrates of Salem. They had been forced to leave Massachusetts and had followed Ann Hutchinson to Rhode Island, leaving behind their fourteen-year-old daughter, Ruth. Thirty-three-year-old Hathorne had taken the girl in, then had married her. Ruth was now nineteen and her son meant all the world to her. Hathorne had betrayed them both, on Curaçao and now again, and there was reason to burn with anger. The leaves around Maria's boots caught fire and turned to cinders, and the sparks flew down chimneys all over town, so that women had to drench their fireplaces with pitchers of water.

Ruth had a basket on her arm as she cut the first of the season's parsley and sage. She'd urged her son to keep out of the billowing phlox, the first buds to bloom in this season, but he only grinned and let out a joyous whoop before disappearing into the tall white flowers, trampling a few on his way. He was a naughty, delightful boy of three, whose father would soon take a cane to him for his own good, for headstrong behavior was not tolerated. The little boy came up to the fence, and when he realized he was not alone, he wrapped his hands around the posts and stared at Maria, for she appeared to be an angel hiding behind the phlox. There were petals in her hair, so that the black strands were woven through with white, as if winter had already returned after only a few days of joyous, muddy spring. The boy had John's dark eyes. Faith's, on the other hand, were silvery gray, her mother's eyes, but paler still. Faith waved at the boy and he stared at her, considering. Their features echoed each other's. Straight nose and small ears, their father's high cheekbones, his pale coloring, marked by ruddy cheeks. Maria crouched down and slipped the letter between the railings of the fence. If this was her enemy, there had never been a sweeter one. She flung the child a smile, which he was quick to return.

"Be a good boy," she said in a soft voice. "Give this to your father."

John's son nodded with a serious expression, a child who knew nothing of the cruelty of the world. But he saw the black leaves falling and the crow that came to perch on the woman's shoulder, and in this town even someone at such a tender age looked for evil everywhere, not trusting a stranger's smile. Perhaps she was not an angel after all.

Maria put a finger to her lips. "Don't forget the letter."

When his mother called to the boy, Maria learned he had been named for his father, lawfully his only child. Maria turned and ran, Faith riding on her hip.

Love was the thing that tore you apart; it made you believe the lies you were told, obvious as they might be. It was nearly impossible to see your own fate while it was happening to you. It was only after, when what's done had been done, that one's vision cleared. She thought of the man who had turned against Hannah, and of her mother's husband, trekking across Devotion Field with his brothers and revenge in mind, and of her father, so handsome and vain he hadn't thought twice about selling her into servitude.

Love is what you make of it, and she had made it into her undoing. As she walked through the farmland ringing Salem, the rows of wheat she passed withered in the fields. Her hair was in knots, her complexion pale. She thoughtlessly tore her flesh on thorn bushes, and the blood that fell scorched the grass she walked upon. In her arms, Faith patted at the tears streaming down her mother's face, but a witch's tears were as dangerous as they were rare, and they burned the child's fingers. Even Faith, whose touch could heal a bird with a broken wing, couldn't heal her mother's despair. Nothing could give her back the time she had wasted on a worthless man.

They went to the lake, where Maria knelt to dash water on her face. Surely John would answer her, for a letter written in blood has consequences for both the writer and the reader. You could not forget what you had read. He would have to answer. Faith was his child, after all, and deserved his name and attentions. What his response would be, no one could foretell, for a man's fate changed every day, depending upon his actions. When Maria gazed into the still, black water, she could see pieces of what was to come. The tree with white flowers, the woman in the lake. Summer would come, and the world would grow greener, and, she could already see, John would disappoint her. She realized it had never been love between them, for you cannot love someone you can never know.

Perhaps his neighbors had told him that a woman with black hair had been seen peering into his garden, speaking with his son, with some insisting that she seemed to rise above the bricks. They said that a black bird had followed her, often a sign of bad luck and a harbinger of death and disaster. Everyone noticed she was not like any other woman in town; she wore blue rather than gray, with no bonnet covering her hair, and her leather boots were red. It was clear she did as she pleased, despite the magistrates' rules. If indeed she was a witch with bad intentions, she could have easily had her revenge; she might have stolen the Hathorne boy and left a changeling in his place, a faceless poppet made of straw. Even an ordinary woman who had been betrayed might have started a fire in the garden, a flame that would have quickly spread to the roof and the gables. But Maria did no such damage.

Revenge was not in her nature. She knew full well that whatever she sent into the world would come back to her threefold, be it vengeance or kindness.

Cadin, however, wasn't as generous. When Hathorne came home at the end of the day, he was puzzled by the small gray rocks on his roof, tossed down as if some imp had marked his house for doom. This past winter he had done his best to leave behind his other life, the one in which he'd been enchanted. Whenever he yearned for Maria, he went out to a shed behind the house, removed his coat, then his loose linen shirt, and he beat himself with a rope, leaving marks on his back to remind him of the failures of the flesh. He had considered speaking with his father, that stern and illustrious man who had led troops to victory in King Philip's War against the native people, and was said to be the most upstanding man in Massachusetts. But he knew what his father would have told him: even a fool must pay for his wrongdoings. John was not ready to pay, and yet what was done could not easily be undone. There was proof of his sin after all. There was the child.

When John stepped inside his house, he spied a letter on the table in the parlor, folded and sealed with melted candle wax.

"What's this?" he asked his wife.

"The boy says a witch gave it to him." Ruth

208

had been worrying all day, ever since little John had deposited the letter into the basket of herbs. The woman who'd given it to him had had a black bird with her, their son had said, and she wore red boots. Weren't these the signs of a witch? Ruth had kept the shutters closed and the door locked. She made certain their son remained in a small chamber that had no windows, where he would be safe. There was evil in this world, just as there was good, and it didn't hurt to be careful. Ruth had never spoken back to John, or discussed what had happened to her parents, but she wasn't a fool. Something was wrong. She'd washed her hands three times after touching the letter. She had a sinking feeling inside of her, as if she'd swallowed rocks. She'd heard stones pelting against the roof all afternoon, and she shuddered with each one that was thrown. Now that her husband had at last come home, she kept her eyes downcast, as she always did when speaking to him. He had rescued her from the fate of many Quakers, and she felt she owed him everything. Why was it then that her heart hurt as it beat against her ribs?

"Our boy is telling you a story." Hathorne addressed his wife as he might a child, doing his best to convince her as he spoke, and convincing himself as well. "Don't be silly." He opened the letter, unfolded the message within, then quickly refolded the parchment and slipped it into his coat. "This is pure nonsense," he told his wife. "Nothing more."

He went to his study and latched the door, letting his wife know he was not to be disturbed. Ruth was accustomed to doing as she was told and asked no questions even though she had taken note of his dark expression. She thought that he might be writing a sermon, for he often spoke in church, or perhaps he was drafting contracts for his shipping business, when in fact, he had locked himself away so that he might burn Maria's letter in a brass bowl. The smoke was foul and red, and yet it made him feel something, a rush of desire, what he'd experienced in the tiled courtyard in Curaçao, the raw emotions of a reckless fool. He sat there with a throbbing headache, sprawled in a leather chair that had once belonged to his father. He knew that men must pay for their mistakes, for even men who tried to do good in the world were touched by original sin. Wicked actions sprang from a few moments of weakness in the face of the sinful ways of the world and all its indecent enchantments. Women could destroy men, he was sure of it, as Eve had tempted Adam. This was the reason women were not allowed to speak in church. To merely look upon them could cause vile thoughts, and soon enough such thoughts could become deeds. Hathorne believed that God and his angels moved through the mortal world, but the devil walked among them as well.

That night he fully admitted to himself that he had erred and veered onto a dark and unexpected path. Hathorne made no more excuses. He had sinned. He fell into a sort of madness as the two sides of him warred, the one who was the man who swam with a turtle, the other his father's son. He stood at the window, looking into the dark. Halfway through the night, when the stars had filled the sky, Hathorne considered breaking faith with everything and everyone he had ever known and imagined taking Maria and their child back to Curaçao. But those treacherous thoughts lasted for only an hour or two, a heedless period of sin and lust, during which time he forgot he was a man with a family and a duty to the world in which he lived. Hathorne went to the shed and beat himself until his back was bloody and he gasped with the pain he'd inflicted upon his flesh. He could not do as he pleased. This wasn't the land of the turtles and rose-colored birds, but a world whose only palette was black and white, where it was hard to think or move or breathe, and sleep was often impossible, for with sleep came dreams, and that was something he must avoid.

People said that a black bird was circling the magistrate's house each and every day. It dropped stones, one after the other, and there was a pelting sound that echoed down the street.

By summer, crowds came to Washington Street so that they might stand on the corner and gawk. Most people believed such an event portended a curse, and neighbors began to close their shutters, as Ruth Hathorne had done on the day the witch first appeared, even though the heat had become oppressive. Bad fortune could move from house to house, it was contagious, and if there was magic it was best to lock oneself away.

The crow stole flowers from gardens, and when he spied children's shoes left on porches so that the mud on their soles could dry, he took them, too. He pulled open shutters and flew through windows to steal silver wedding thimbles, given here in lieu of rings, for a ring was nothing more than vanity and a thimble could be put to good use. Women's fingers bled as they did their sewing, and they found themselves weeping and wishing they'd had another life, for the crow reminded them of who they might be if they'd been allowed to make their own choices. The crow was so brazen he pulled the white caps off their heads as they walked to church on Sundays. He woke newborn babies from sleep with his clattering, and set people's nerves on edge. John Hathorne watched the crow from his garden and decided that something must be done. Time and time again, the crow perched in the tree with the black leaves, as if announcing John's guilt. He could not have this creature denounce him in the face of others.

Hathorne gathered the men in town to say the crow was more than a pest. He was a creature sent by evil powers, an evil they must resist. They went out with their rifles, stalking through the fields that separated Salem Town from the forests where not long ago these same men had pursued the Wampanoags, murdering and beheading as many as they could find. The settlers felt this land was theirs now. They'd taken it in battle, and a crow was not about to spook their families and get away with what was not merely mischief, but clearly something darker, something that boiled the blood. Large numbers of crows had been roosting in trees at the edge of town, and to men intent on murder, one dead crow was as good as another. It would do them well, they soon decided, to kill one and all. They walked past rye and corn, and alongside wild blackberries and saplings that would become pear trees, if they weren't broken by these men's boots. They walked past the wild red lilies that grew nowhere else. Across the sky there were banks of clouds. A hunt made men feel they could protect what was theirs; spirits were high, and for miles it was possible to hear the hollering and shouts that rose up.

They waited through the heat of noon and the dullness of a stifling afternoon into the falling dusk, when the air was thick with black gnats. By then an odd silence had settled, something uncomfortable. Still no crows flew overhead. A band of men was sent ahead to flush out the birds, Hathorne in the forefront, for his neighbors were fighting evil on his behalf. Privately, he wished Maria's crow would simply disappear, and take her along, like a fever dream that vanished in a blink. But just as darkness was about to fall, a huge number of crows came flocking from the north, a thousand or more. At once, the men began to fire their rifles. They shot wildly and blindly, and several grazed their fellow bird-hunters by accident. One fellow was shot through the throat, and he lay in a pool of his own blood, and not even a kerchief tied around his neck could stop the gushing. The men went wild when they could not rouse their fellow hunter, and they set to firing off rounds as if in war. John sank back from them, for he stood out in the crowd; he was the tallest among them, and the wealthiest, and the reason why there had been a death on this day. He knew how easily people could turn on each other, how a man could be a hero one moment, and the cause of resentment the next. How he wished he had never been to that cursed island, or gone to sea, or told Maria about Essex County. And yet he imagined leaping into the blue-green water, thousands of miles from here, in a land where no one followed the rules set forth, where a sin might float like a flower in a fountain and a man was free to do as he pleased.

Maria heard the mayhem. The guns, the echoes of death, the calling of men and of birds. She had no choice but to leave Faith asleep on her pallet, so she might run through the dark, barefoot, in her blue dress. The first of the season's fireflies drifted by, globes of light flickering among the blades of grass, then rising and falling between the trees. Maria felt danger all around her, burning like salt in a wound. It was then she realized she had not seen Cadin all day. She felt her heart beat as fast as his.

As she came upon the pasture, birds were plunging from the sky, a black rain of feathers. When a crow dies, the others band together and search for the killer, mobbing those responsible. Scores of birds attacked the men from town, diving beak and claw into the fray, their hoarse calls striking fear into the hearts of many of those who had believed themselves brave for the cowardly act of shooting at unsuspecting birds. Maria felt her arm burning, and it was only then that she realized her blood was spilling onto the ground, black and burning. In the mad volley of bullets and buckshot, she had been shot. She backed into the trees, breathing hard, feeling much as she had on the day she hid in the forest and watched Hannah's house burn. She murmured a spell of protection, in Latin and backwards, quoting from Solomon's book of magic, and as she did the men's guns began to misfire. She called to the sky, and banks of roiling clouds appeared in the west, moving in like a wave at sea.

The crows realized they could not win the fight against the barrage of gunfire, and in response they split apart into two groups, half flying east, the others west. Crows could not be eaten or baked into pies, for their meat was dark and gamey and foul, and their harsh feathers weren't used in pillows or quilts. They were worth nothing to these men and had only been killed because they were considered pests and scavengers, because it was decided they were evil beings. The men collected hundreds of bodies, whooping with joy, when all that they'd done could have been accomplished by a gang of ten-year-old boys armed with their fathers' rifles and slingshots. There had been no reason for this to come to pass, but what was done was done and couldn't be undone. Even a witch knows this. There are not spells for many of the sorrows in this world, and death is one of them. You cannot bring back those who have stepped into the next world, and should you try, they would not be the same beings that had once been, but rather they would become unnatural creatures, created by dark magic and desire.

Maria found Cadin in the tall weeds, a black heart lying still in the grass. The men in the field couldn't tell one crow from another, but she knew her dearest friend immediately. She tore the skirt of her dress and wrapped him in the fabric and wept as she did so. Her cries could be heard as far as the wharf, as far as sound could carry, even at sea, and the men collecting crows stopped what they were doing, feeling haunted. Many believed that a female crow was mourning the loss of her mate. A hush fell over them, even though they were soaked with sweat. They had been elated by their hunting madness, but even the most thoughtless among them now felt pricked by fear, embarrassed by their foolish acts of cruelty.

Beneath a pear tree, where he stood in the dark, John Hathorne knew exactly what he'd heard. A woman's anguish that was louder than the gun-fire, louder than the last calls of the crows in the sky. He knew her voice, and why shouldn't he? He was the cause of her grief.

She couldn't bring herself to bury Cadin and leave him forever earthbound. Instead, she set a fire on a flat ledge not far from the lake and burned his body. The smoke was as white as the snow had been in Devotion Field on the day he found her. Her dear black heart, her companion, her familiar, her friend. She sank down and sobbed and didn't leave his ashes until first light. By then the wind had carried him into the sky where he belonged.

Maria had been weakened from the metal bullet lodged in her arm, for iron is a bane to witches. In the countryside of England, iron chains were kept in every prison, with cuffs small enough to fit a woman. Maria went to the cabin, and while Faith was still sleeping, she took up a knife to dig out the bullet, though her hand was bruised as well. As she did so, she spoke backwards, asking for justice for Cadin. She made a poultice of balm of Gilead and boiled sage to dress her wound, then fixed a sling for her arm, using the shawl embroidered with birds from Curaçao, the country where it had been so easy to dream of miracles. She wound a white bandage over her hand, but it didn't hide the bruise in the shape of a crow that had risen on her skin.

When she went to Hathorne's house, the two silver hairpins were in her hair, one from Cadin and one from her mother, the sort of adornment Puritan women were forbidden to wear, not that such rules mattered to Maria. She wore a black dress, for she was in mourning as surely as any widow. As she walked down Washington Street, her daughter in her arms, the neighbors peered out and began to whisper. People were drawn into their yards, waiting behind the hedges to see what would happen next. Over two hundred crows had been shot, and there were those who vowed that Maria had been among them, and that she wore the sling to disguise what was not an arm, but a wing. "Shapeshifter," the neighbors whispered. "Look at the hem of her skirt," they said. She had walked through the fields and there was no mud clinging to her. Surely this had been done by magic, they insisted, and there were those who vowed that every night Maria flew above the treetops, flinging stones upon roofs. Some people said that the red-haired daughter of hers was a demon, not a girl.

Maria knew what they thought, and as she walked by their houses, she ran a stick along their fences, the sound clattering. It sounded as if crows were calling, and the noise sent chills down people's spines. Doors slammed shut. Windows rattled. Soon the street was empty.

She stood in front of the house with black shutters and knocked on the door, calling out for John Hathorne. No one answered, so she pounded harder, breaking a tiny bone in her hand that would always cause her pain on damp days. With Cadin's death, something inside her had changed. Now she knew she had read the black mirror incorrectly. Perhaps she'd been won over because although she'd been a servant, John seemed to have seen her as something more. Or so she'd wished. She had fallen under water, under a spell, in love with love. She had seen it happen a hundred times before, as she sat in the dark listening to Hannah's advice to the women who came to her door. *Is it the man you want, or the feeling inside you when someone cares?*

In the parlor, Hathorne heard his name called. It sounded like a curse, for it was said forward and then it was reversed. When he didn't appear, Maria looked in the window and saw a figure peering out. Ruth Hathorne, soon to have her second child, which she prayed would be another boy. Ruth's heart was racing. She knew a witch when she saw one. Even Ruth's little son had known her for what she was. Now the woman had taken a strange black book from her satchel and was reading from it, her lips moving quickly. Ruth knew that books had power; that was why she secretly studied letters so that she might read the Scriptures. But this woman at their door was clearly expert at reading, and therefore even more dangerous than Ruth had first imagined. She hid her son in a wardrobe and told him to be quiet. "If a woman in a black dress comes for you, do not go with her," she said.

Ruth had never demanded anything for herself and had never before raised her voice, but now she called for her husband in a frantic tone. "Come here now. She's looking for you!"

Maria could hear Ruth Hathorne cry out behind the locked door. *Good,* she thought. *He'll have to face me. He'll have to accept Faith as his own.*

By now, Ruth was too frightened to go look out the window; instead, she held a looking glass up to the street, to reverse any spells this witch might set upon her. Her mother had come from the west of England and had taught her folk medicine that she kept to herself, cures her husband would never have approved. Tonight she would bathe with salt and vinegar to cleanse herself and insure that evil thoughts could not cling to her. But Maria held no ill will toward her, only pity. They were sisters, really. Had they held up their palms, one beside the other, the same love line would have run through each of their hands until the middle of their palms, when the lines were diverted. *This is how he'll hurt you, this is the way you will blame yourself, this is your salvation, this is what you can see if you open your eyes.*

Hathorne came into the room in a fury when he heard Ruth demanding that he deal with Maria Owens. Was it his fault he'd been enchanted? He was a victim as much as Adam had been, tempted into sin. "Why have you not sent her away?" he asked his wife.

Ruth threw him a desperate look, but he insisted.

"It's woman's work," he said. "Just as you send away a peddler."

Ruth whispered a prayer to protect herself as she opened the door. She wore a gray dress, with her cap covering her hair. She was pretty and pale and confused, but most of all she was frightened.

"He said you must go away," she told Maria. Her voice sounded small and weak, even to her own ear.

"I'm not here to hurt you." Maria felt a tightening in her throat. She was the woman she had never expected to be, someone who had broken another woman's heart. "Please understand. I didn't know about you."

"I beg of you." Ruth closed her eyes, as if by doing so she could make this dark-haired beauty vanish. She did not wish to see Maria's eyes; people said they were silver, like a cat's. "Don't harm us."

Maria took Ruth's hand and Ruth's eyes flashed open. Her eyes were so pale, so blue. They could feel the heat of one another's blood. Maria let go. All she wanted was for this woman to hear her.

"Let him tell me himself," Maria said, "and no harm will come to you."

Ruth went inside and closed the door, her heart hitting against her rib cage. She was little more than nineteen years old, a motherless child, and now the mother of John Hathorne's only son. Her own beloved mother had whispered in her ear before she and Ruth's father were exiled to the wilderness of Rhode Island: *Trust no one but yourself.*

John was waiting for her, his expression wary. Tonight he looked older than his years; she could see the man he would be as he aged, his looks gone, his humor turned dark, a man who sat in judgment of all others. When you make certain choices, you change your fate. Look at your left hand and you will see the lines shifting into what you have made of yourself.

"Well?" he said.

At fourteen Ruth had been grateful that he'd married her, for she'd had no one, and knew nothing of the world. All she knew was this town. The elm trees with their black leaves, the bricked streets, the houses with their wooden shutters, the fields where the crows came to eat corn, the harbor with its boats straining to be free of their moorings, the endless winters with blizzards of snow. He'd told her to close her eyes and pray the first night they were together. He'd said not to cry, for it would displease God. She had done as she was told on that night and ever since, but now she lifted her chin when she spoke to him.

"She will speak only to you."

"For that I blame you," Hathorne muttered.

"And I you," Ruth said in a soft voice.

At last he went outside wearing his coat, his face set in a dark expression. He had not seen Maria for who she was in the bright light of Curaçao, but he most certainly saw her now. He'd heard of such creatures, women who were beyond God's watch and were said to devour a man's soul and make a mockery out of decency.

His wife's erratic behavior was one more mark of her power.

"You're not to come here," he scolded Maria. He knew the neighbors were watching. They were always watching in this town. He stood on the other side of the fence.

"What coward asks his wife to do what he fears to do?"

"We cannot quarrel. No good will come of it."

"And yet you came to me often enough." Maria's words caused the color to flare in his face. "Would you have ever told me you had a wife?"

There were features Maria possessed that he'd never noticed before, suspicious qualities. A black mark in the inner crook of her elbow. Silver-gray eyes that glinted in the dark. Hair that was black as a crow's feathers. Her arm in a sling. Black leaves falling out of season, gathering at her feet.

"And now you've killed him," Maria said.

"It," he said. "It was a crow."

"If only you had shared his qualities, you, sir, would have been a better man."

Rather than respond, Hathorne reached into his coat and took out a purse. Would he dare to pay her for her heartbreak with a bag of silver? *Every woman is a fool at least once in her life,* Hannah had told her.

"For my services?" she said in a tone he had not

heard before. She was not a weak girl he could command, though he had done his best to control the situation. She was something more than that.

"I have a ship leaving tomorrow," he told her. "This will pay your way. I gave you the sapphire and the diamonds, and now this silver. Surely that's enough." He lowered his voice. "I suggest you do as I say. We are not in Curaçao now, miss."

Maria nodded to Faith, carried in her arms. "And yet here is the evidence of that time."

Ruth was at the window, behind the cloudy glass. She forced herself to watch, not through a mirror but with her own eyes. She would not dare to step out of her house without her husband's permission, having never gone beyond the confines of her own property unless she was on her way to the market or to church. Later, Ruth would not ask John anything about Maria when he at last came to bed. She would say nothing and bite her tongue, but now she gazed out and imagined she was free, a bird, a ship, a woman on the street with her hair uncovered.

"Don't think I don't know what you are," Maria said.

"And what is that?"

"A liar, sir."

You can always tell a liar, for he will not look at you when he speaks, and often he has white spots on his fingernails, one to mark every lie he's told.

225

But no man enjoys being called by that title, even if it's the truth. Hathorne took Maria's arm, but she pulled away. She was not about to do as she was told, as if she were the one who wore a white cap and stood behind the window, too fearful to leave her own yard.

She spilled out the purse he'd given her. Ten silver pieces. A year's payment for a washer-woman or a servant. The moment she touched the coins, the silver turned black. She could see his panic as he observed this witchery.

"You had best never return," he said.

"You have it wrong," Maria told him. "*You* had best stay away from *me.*"

That same night, Maria unwrapped the black mirror and looked into the glass, for at last she could see clearly. She spied herself without the sapphire necklace. She recalled what Samuel Dias had told her, that to his eyes the stone did not appear real. She removed it and went out to the lake, where she set it on a ledge of rock. Then she took her *Grimoire* in hand, the spine of the book in her grasp as she brought it down, smashing the jewel. The stone shattered into a thousand pieces, as glass does when struck, for the gift had been paste and nothing more, as false as the man who had given it to her. Where there was one lie there would always be another. She slit the hem of her skirt, scattering the diamonds on the rock. She stood to stomp on them with the weight of her boot. They shattered also, worthless paste, trinkets meant to buy her love and nothing more, breaking into bright bits of dust.

When you look into your own future, you may see only what you want to see, and even the wisest woman can make a mistake, especially in matters of love.

She'd had the wrong man all along.

Tell a witch to go, and she'll plant her feet on the ground and stay exactly where she is. Instead of doing as she's told, she'll take a knife to her arm and let her blood drip onto the ground, and in that way she will claim the earth for herself and for her daughters and for all the daughters who follow her. It is the future she's claiming, the right to be a woman who can do as she pleases.

When Maria returned to the cabin, she took out the book, for what is written will open the world itself. As she paged through the *Grimoire*, she thought of the woman who took her in on a snowy day and gave her the Owens name, who had shared all she knew about the Nameless Art. *Own your own life,* Hannah had told her. *Never depend on others. Protect those closest to you.*

When she went to the courthouse, Maria was mindful that a woman in her situation must not call attention to herself. Not yet. Not now. She wore a white cap she had sewn, using the white cotton lining of the bodice of her blue dress. She had affixed white cuffs to a gray shift so that she would appear more presentable. Her hair was pinned up so that no one could spy that it was not long enough to knot into a braid but sheared at chin length, as if she were a boy. A legal document was worth little, for laws are made to serve the men who create them, and are rarely meant to honor women, but land is difficult to take away from the rightful owner. She kept her eyes lowered when she went before the magistrate, and she spoke softly. Be careful what you say when you come before such men, for they will find guilt in innocence, and evil in what is most natural. The magistrate approved of her manner of speech, and he allowed her to buy the acreage she camped on, for it was considered worthless. She used Hathorne's silver, for unlike the gems, these coins were real enough, and it gave her pleasure to know the man who wished her to vanish had made it possible for her to own land. That same day her ownership was recorded in the book of deeds and stamped with the clerk's initials. Married women could not own property, but a woman without a husband was free to do as she pleased.

Maria Owens did exactly that.

II.

By the age of five, Faith was a charming, well-behaved girl with talents all her own. She had already learned that judgment was everywhere in their world, and one should keep one's private thoughts and deeds and attributes to oneself. Her mother warned that being different could cause grief, for men often destroyed what they didn't understand. When the child asked who her father was, for surely she must have one, Maria simply said that some things were best not to know, and that, whoever he was, he had a darling child.

Faith understood that theirs was a world of secrets. She told no one that she could start a fire simply by imagining a red flame or that she could leap from the roof and land softly on the balls of her feet. She could call birds and fish to her, and because of this she soon discovered that certain rumors in town were, indeed, correct; there was a serpent in Leech Lake, a large gray-scaled eel-like creature she soon trained to eat crusts of bread from her hand. She told no one about his existence, for already she had witnessed how men handled any creatures they deemed to be monsters. This winter, she had spied two hunters dragging a she-wolf from her den; they murdered her in the snow, along with her pup. Wolves were outlawed in the colony, and men went about killing them one by one, as they did with the native people. One of the first laws the Puritans had passed in 1630 was to place a bounty on wolves, and that included Indian dogs, which looked to be a mixture of a wolf and a fox. A black wolf's fur was worth the most, and the poor mother wolf had a coat of that color. Faith had been hidden behind the bramble bushes, her hand over her mouth so they wouldn't hear her sobs. It was a terrible thing to have witnessed, and it changed who she was. She felt her difference tenfold, and the part of her that was human was ashamed of humankind.

Another pup, overlooked by the hunters because he was so small and weak, soon emerged from the den. His half-opened eyes were silver-gray, the same shade as Faith's own, and his coat was pure black, all the better to slip through the night unnoticed. He went to Faith as if he'd known she was waiting for him, and that she could be trusted, and that they belonged to one another. Faith raced home carrying the tiny surviving pup. Maria gave Faith a leather glove filled with goat's milk for the wolf pup to drink, sucking on a hole cut in the fingertip. Faith kept the wolf in her bed that night, to make sure he stayed warm. She named him Keeper, for she didn't intend to let him go. Sometime after midnight the pup ceased whimpering, and soon they were dreaming the same dream, girl and wolf alike, a dream of blood in the snow, and of warm milk, and of a bed in which to sleep without worry or fear.

In the early morning, Faith carried Keeper through the dark to the little shed where they kept two goats, and filled the glove with milk. Maria found her there once the sun had risen, asleep in the straw with the wolf by her side. She recognized a familiar when she saw one. Such a creature must always come to you on its own. You cannot choose it, it must choose you. Once it does, it will be loyal for the rest of its life, as Cadin had been.

"Wolves are killed here," Maria told her daughter that day. "But if you call the creature a dog, then a dog is what it will be."

Faith nodded solemnly. She knew that people in town stared at her red hair, thought by some to be a mark of the devil's own, and gawked at her mother's red boots. Everything they were must be a secret, and the same was true for the wolf. From the very first day, when Keeper was a tiny half-blind pup, he did his best to follow Faith wherever she went, refusing to be parted from her, fiercely loyal. She laughed and called him her little goat, for he soon enough ran to the goats in the barn, wishing to be fed, and he played with the tolerant creatures, biting at their hooves and running beneath them, until, having had enough, they butted him and chased him from the barn. Maria wondered if her daughter remembered the man they'd called Goat, for she still slept with the poppet doll he'd made for her. Maria had never told anyone how close Samuel Dias had come to death, a mere breath away. Even then he had continued to talk, as if there would never be enough time to say all that was inside of him. His stories had often seemed like imaginary tales of sea monsters and storms, but his advice to Maria had been true. He'd warned her to be careful in Massachusetts, for men would be men, especially in such a self-righteous place as Salem, and judges would continue to judge those who came before them.

Once Faith had learned to read and write, Maria brought out the *Grimoire*, their greatest secret, kept in the kitchen under lock and key, in a bureau drawer with a false bottom, so that even if someone jimmied open the drawer, they'd come upon nothing more than two large wooden spoons.

"This will belong to you someday," Maria told Faith.

Faith was delighted with this news. "Which day is that?"

"A day when you're very grown-up and I'm a very old woman."

Maria had hired a carpenter who went from town to town. He chinked the holes in the walls of the cabin, then rebuilt the shed for the goats so that it would no longer shake in the wind and he helped Maria to lay down a path of blue stones that reminded her of Hannah's cottage. When Maria claimed there was an underground stream nearby, the carpenter had grudgingly dug their well, surprised when he hit a pool of fresh, clear water.

"It's a talent to be able to find water," he told her. It was said only witches could do so, for they could not drown and had an affinity with water that people used against them. There were those who said they could smell water, and that water had the scent of sweet iris to such women. Maria planned to pay the carpenter with the last silver coin, but instead he asked for her help in exchange for the work he'd done on the house. He had unending headaches and his hands had begun to shake. In time he would not be able to earn his living. He had figured out that Maria Owens practiced the Nameless Art, and if she could help him, there would be no debt to pay. Maria gathered barley and vervain from her garden to boil, then wrapped the mixture in white cloth to place on the man's forehead. She said words in a language he didn't recognize, both forward and backwards it seemed. He could not keep his eyes open, and he slept all night in the barn with the goats, without nightmare or dreams. In the morning, his head was clear. He came back to thank Maria. "You have a rare talent," he said solemnly.

That was when she knew what her future would be. Maria would forsake love entirely, and turn her talents to the healing arts. She lit a lantern on the porch that the carpenter had built, and then she waited. She was far from town, but the lantern could be seen by anyone wishing to venture this far. They would spy the yellow light, and then the fence, and then the garden that was carefully tended, and they would know they were welcome.

A SIMPLE WITCH'S GARDEN

Sage, for headache.
Summer savory, for colic.
Green wormwood for wounds, mix with vinegar or rum, then apply.
Hyssop, for the lungs.
Colt's foot and flaxseed, for coughing.
Motherwort, to quiet the nerves.
Sweet balm tea, for fever.
Horseradish, mixed with warm vinegar for aches in the feet.
Mallows, steeped in milk for dysentery.

Savory, to give good fortune.

Parsley, to see the future and make wise
    choices.

The shopkeeper's wife, Anne Hatch, who had always been so kind to Maria, was the first to arrive. Anne was not more than twenty and her husband, Nathaniel, was near fifty. It was not an unusual match in the colony; men often had three, perhaps even four wives, for so many were lost in childbirth. But it was not a good marriage. Anne feared her husband, for he treated her badly; all the same she left her bed to walk alone through the fields, turning into the dark wood to reach the cabin that many said was enchanted. People in town hadn't forgotten Maria Owens. They saw her when she came in once a month to do her shopping, the little girl tagging along with her black dog at her side. Maria always wore a blue dress and those red boots, which some people said were the color of blood and others insisted were the color of roses. "Hold your breath when she passes by," mothers told their children.

On Maria's market days, Ruth Gardner Hathorne always went to her gate to watch her, as did most of the women on Washington Street. They never spoke a word or greeted Maria; all the same, they felt drawn to this stranger. What might she do for them if they asked? What was there to be found outside their own garden gates? The magistrates had allowed Maria to own land in Essex County; still, it was strongly recommended that no one speak to her, and if anyone should befriend her that person would also be suspect and run the risk of an inquiry. People swore that one day there would be proof enough for her to be brought to trial for witchery. "What makes her think she can defy laws and protocol?" the women whispered among themselves.

Anne Hatch went up the porch steps, even though her frantic heart was hitting against her ribs. She had been orphaned; first her mother was taken by a fever, then her father was lost in King Philip's War. She should have been grateful to have a man pick her out of the workhouse where she'd been sent by the Overseers of the Poor, but after the first night with her new husband there was nothing to be grateful for.

"Bless me," Anne Hatch whispered to He who watched over her. Her hands were shaking. "Do not judge me for what I must do," she asked of the Lord.

Maria had made soap earlier that night and the kettle was in the yard, the embers beneath burning a pale red. The brass bell sounded in the wind and she knew someone had arrived. When she answered the door, her hair was wringing wet, for she'd just washed away the cinders with a pitcher of lake water. She wound her wet hair into a twist, which was kept in place with her silver combs. The hour was late and her girl was in bed, but the leggy black dog growled at the visitor, who shrank back.

"He's only a pup," Maria assured Anne. When she told the dog to hush, he did as he was told, curling up beside the little girl's bed. Maria had been expecting a visitor, for the broom had fallen only an hour earlier, which always meant company was coming. She had already brewed a pot of Courage Tea.

They know what they want, Hannah had told her. *Ask the right questions and you'll get the right answers. Even those who have been afraid to speak aloud will tell the truth when they must.*

"I shouldn't be here," Anne said apologetically. She looked back at the door, and for a moment it seemed she might flee. "It's late."

"Perhaps it's not too late, but of course you're welcome to come or go as you like."

Anne steadied herself. Once he knew she'd gone, there would be hell to pay. This was likely her only chance to escape. "I'll stay."

Maria gestured to the table so they might sit together. She was not yet twenty-two, but that was two years older than the unhappy young woman before her, and by now Maria knew a thing or two about love. She understood the situation as soon as Anne removed her jacket and unclasped the hooks on the front of her dress.

237

Anne raised her chin defiantly as she showed herself, but even before she did, Maria knew what would be revealed: bruises in the shape of blooming flowers, the same color as the ones marking Rebecca on the day she came to see Hannah Owens. In Boston Maria had been called upon for cures and love magic. This was something entirely different.

"He does it to punish me when I'm slow or stupid," Anne said. "If I charge the wrong price or burn supper or when I speak too loudly." She had thought of murdering him in his sleep, but she hadn't the heart for such things, only the imagination.

Maria gave the shopkeeper's wife a salve of calamine and balm of Gilead for her bruises, and an amulet made of blue glass beads and blue thread for protection.

Anne Hatch shook her head, displeased. "This isn't a strong enough cure for my problem."

The women stared at each other. To come this far alone, a woman must be willing to take a risk. What she wants she must want desperately. Maria wished to have nothing to do with the pains of love; still her heart went out to Anne. In point of fact, this wasn't love, but love gone wrong, a different story entirely.

"What did you have in mind?" Maria asked.

"I need poison," Anne said softly, her chin up, her eyes meeting Maria's.

There were many toxic potions that could be made from the local plants: hogweed, lily of the valley, castor bean, tansy, bittersweet nightshade, mountain laurel, yew leaf, white baneberry, henberry, horse nettle, pokeberry, pure cyanide in the pits of wild cherries. But what was done could not be undone, and vengeance always returned to its maker.

"Neither one of us wants death on our hands," Maria told her. "It would come back to us and extract a price we wouldn't want to pay."

Anne's eyes were swollen from crying. "How then am I to be rid of him?"

"You have to be certain this is what you want." Maria looked over her shoulder. Faith was still sleeping peacefully. "Once he's gone, he won't return."

Anne Hatch smiled then, the first smile in a very long time. She was ready to begin.

Maria had Anne cut a lock of her hair to burn in a brass dish. This was the end of an old life and the beginning of a new one, and the transition must be marked. From black cloth and red thread a small poppet was fashioned, stuffed with blackthorn and cherry bark, and then Anne's husband's name, *Nathaniel*, was stitched upon the cloth. Anne pierced her finger in the process and her blood stained the cloth, but she had bled many times before on her husband's behalf. The incantation for the end of love was written on a slip of paper that she attached to a candle that burned brightly.

Let our bond be broken by the powers above. You will wish to run, and you won't look back. When I look for you, nothing will remain. You will not remember me and you will be nothing to me.

This was magic that needed words, for literary magic held the greatest power. Once home, Anne was to bury the poppet outside her front door, then burn the incantation and walk the perimeter of their property, laying down the ashes. When she went inside the house, she must dust his clothes with salt.

"This will drive him away," Maria said. "Once he leaves, his fate is his own and neither you nor I are responsible for what happens then."

Nathaniel Hatch was gone for a fortnight, then a month. Before long it was summer, and he still had not been seen. Anne ran the store herself, and after six months she went to the court and was declared a widow. A search party had found her husband's boots and his gun on the far side of Leech Lake. It was thought he had drowned while hunting the sea monster, as others had before him, for there was a pile of salt near his belongings, and salt was known to call to saltwater creatures. No one but Maria had seen the footprints of his bare feet continuing on past the pond, driven by an overwhelming urge to leave Massachusetts.

As a widow, without any male heirs, Anne Hatch was allowed to own property; the store was now hers. She never again charged Maria for her purchases, whether it be molasses or chicory or flour. When there were items that were difficult to come by, Spanish oranges, for instance, or myrrh oil from Morocco, luxuries that occasionally arrived when ships that had visited faraway lands docked at the harbor, Anne saved them for Maria Owens.

Soon after Nathaniel Hatch disappeared, women in need of cures began to come to Maria's door, always late, when most of the good people in town were in bed. Anne Hatch's mistreatment was not as much of a secret as she had wished it to be, and it quickly became known that she'd had assistance in righting her life. In these times, most people turned to homemade remedies that could often cause more harm than good. They believed babies who died in their cradles had the life sucked out of them by Satan's emissaries or by cats, which were thought to be untrustworthy, evil creatures. They thought that the skin of an eel could cure rheumatism, and believed that beating a child who had fits, with a thin switch cut from a young tree, would drive the devil from his body. Now, for the sake of themselves and their children, they turned to Maria Owens for other remedies.

Frustration Tea for granting good cheer, good for those who grieve.

Caution Tea for wild children, such as boys who carry shotguns or dream of running off to sea.

Fever Tea, to nip high temperatures in the bud, made of cinnamon, bayberry, ginger, thyme, and marjoram.

Courage Tea as an antidote for fear, grief, and facing the world's trials, one cup reminds you to always be who you are.

On these nights, Faith sat on her bed in the dark, with Keeper beside her, and her favorite old poppet close by as she listened to the voices in the kitchen. She quickly came to understand that her mother's visitors often came to deal with illness, and when it came to the matter of love, there were only certain kinds that Maria would approach. Love that made a woman willing to walk through the brambles late at night and beg for a remedy. As for herself, Maria never spoke John Hathorne's name; all the same Faith knew that her mother had been betrayed by a man who was a judge. When they went to town on market days and passed the courthouse, Faith would linger behind, close her eyes, and imagine her father at his desk. John always felt a chill when she did this, and he would go to look out the window. Each time he spied her standing in the cobbled streets, he closed the shutters and turned away.

"What's keeping you?" her mother would call.

"Not a thing," Faith would say. But each time she grew more convinced, and by her next birthday, when she turned six, Faith Owens had already made a vow that she would never fall in love.

III.

There was a woman who came through the fields at night, but unlike Maria's customers, she never once knocked on the door. Martha Chase didn't believe in magic, and yet she was drawn here, made to get out of her bed and walk through the fields in her nightdress. She had spied Faith Owens by the lake, running on the rocks without stockings or shoes as if she were a wild child. She had often returned to watch Faith play, hiding behind the inkberry bushes, crying hot, salty tears.

Martha wore her rope of pale hair pinned beneath a white bonnet, which she removed only once a month, to wash her hair in a basin in a locked room. She'd had a husband, but he died of the spotted fever, and she had to dig his grave herself and had been quarantined for three months after his death. It didn't really bother her to be rid of him. He had been a cruel and distant man and she would not miss him for a minute. If the truth be told, she'd had a fierce distaste for her husband and had never approved of his lust and the desires that coiled and uncoiled depending on how much rum he had to drink. What tore at her was that her future seemed to die on the day of his funeral, for his absence on earth meant she would not have a child of her own.

She did her best to have no pride, to follow the Scriptures, and to never veer from the righteous path. But she, too, had a desire, one that flamed so brightly there were times when a hole burned through her dress and singed the fabric at her chest, as if her heart could not contain what it wanted more than patience, more than obedience, more than honor, more than deliverance. She wanted a daughter. Her marriage had lasted years and she had tried every remedy. Now she stood in the woods, lurking in the dark as she watched the red-haired girl climb around the shore of the lake or collect vegetables in the overgrown garden, and she thought it so unfair that a witch should have what she herself wanted most in the world.

Martha Chase was at the shop buying fabric for a new gray dress, for her own dresses had been washed and pressed so many times they were threadbare, when she spied the child near the bins of flour and arrowroot and loaf sugar. For an instant she believed the Lord had heard her prayers and had delivered her heart's desire, this angel of a child she had been watching from afar as she slunk through the woods in her night-dress, for this time the girl seemed to be there all alone. She was about to go speak with her when quite suddenly the dark-haired woman, the one people said was a witch, came down the aisle to take the child's hand.

Martha felt a storm of spite rising inside. She was a plain woman, but not as simple as she proclaimed to be, she was haughty, for she believed she had been chosen to be in the Lord's light. Her jealousy was turning into a ruthless desire, and with such an emotion came a plan. The girl and her mother wore colorful dresses that Maria had sewn, with purple skirts, dyed with cedar and lilac leaves, and yellow bodices, tinted with bayberry leaves. They went up and down the aisles of the shop, like chattering birds. There were barrels of Indian meal and rye, stored with a cold stone in the flour to keep them cool and stop them from fermenting, which could cause all sorts of maladies, including nausea and hallucinations. The girl's mother was buying beans to soak, along with a tub of local honey, some dried plum-colored currants, and a bag of flour. Martha overheard the witch tell the little girl she would fix Indian pudding and that treat would be their supper. The witch then bought a bag of English tea, at a dear price. Martha didn't waste her funds on expensive coffee beans or tea when there were homegrown substitutes, like Liberty Tea, made from loosestrife or a mixture of strawberry, currant, and sage.

Some people in town were so nervous when they spied Maria Owens, they made the sign of the fox, holding up the pinkie and pointer fingers of their hands to protect them, but there were women who nodded to her as if they knew her, or perhaps they merely thought it prudent to be polite. As for Martha, she said nothing. She was waiting for an omen that would instruct her on what action to take. She felt something green and bitter inside her; the seeds of jealousy had quickly grown into tendrils that circled her lungs and liver and heart.

The witch left the child on her own when she went to speak with Anne Hatch, who, instead of tallying up Maria's charges, showed her a bolt of fabric that had recently come from England, an aniline-dyed calico, colorful and far superior to the homespun most women used for their clothes, perfect for a little girl's dress if you were not a Puritan who wore gray or brown, the shades of dead leaves.

"My gift to you," Anne Hatch said, clearly in a good humor, as she always was when Maria came to town.

While the two women were examining the fabric, Martha went up to Faith, who was busy with a tray of buttons, counting out each one.

"You're very good at numbers," Martha said. Children loved compliments, though such things could stir a child's vanity.

Faith turned to the stranger. She could see inside this woman's heart and was bewildered by what she saw. There was something dark there, as if a cloud had passed over the sun.

"Are you sad?" Faith asked.

Martha's eyes were brimming with tears. "Of course not." She quickly wiped her tears away. She was well aware that crying in public was as shameful as wishing to steal something that didn't belong to you.

"My mother could help you." To Faith, Martha seemed no different than the women who came to the door at night, leaving their shoes on the porch so they wouldn't track mud inside, women who wanted something, whose lives had not turned out as they'd imagined they would, who could not sleep or eat, who worried over the fate of a son or a daughter. Faith saw a smudge around the stranger, but she was too much of a child to understand the dark turn desire might take.

"Could she?" Martha felt a chill. She stared at the witch, who was gathering provisions in a basket. She wore her black hair loose and red boots; a black crinoline peeked out from beneath her dress. Who was she to wear black undergarments? Martha was a widow and had worn mourning clothes for the prescribed period, then had once again dressed in a proper gray dress. "And how could she do that?" she asked the child, thinking to herself that the answer was simple. Witchery.

It was then Maria turned and spied Martha. At once she believed that something was not right.

She saw the shrewd cunning in this stranger, and the craving that was so heated a hole had burned through the bodice of her dress. There was a puff of smoke in the air that Martha caught in her hand.

"Come here, Faith. Stay by my side," Maria called. The girl grinned at Martha, then ran dutifully toward her mother. "Did you want something?" Maria asked the stranger.

Martha's face flushed and her desire shone through her, aflame. She wanted something most desperately. Among the town fathers she was thought to be mild; she had been a good wife who didn't complain, and was now a widow on her own in the world. But Maria spied a woman who plotted, one who was jealous beyond words. To know another's mind was evidence of witchery, and Martha began to burn more hotly beneath Maria's gaze.

"If you want something, speak up," Maria said.

"I want nothing from you," Martha replied curtly. She turned on her heel and found her way to the back of the shop, fearing she would be struck dead if she dared to look behind her, for she had told a lie and she knew it.

When Maria and her daughter left, Martha went to the counter to pay for a box of glass jars she needed for her raspberry jelly. The property her husband had left her would soon be claimed by the magistrates, for she hadn't the means to cover their debt and the land would pay for all they owed. The only thing that would grow there was a thicket of raspberry bushes. All through the summer she made jam and jelly, which she sold door-to-door. But every jar added to her bitterness, and every family she saw inflamed her, until at last her skin burned with a scrim of envy.

"What do you think of that one?" she asked Anne Hatch, nodding to Maria as they watched her through the window. The witch was skipping alongside her daughter as if she were a girl herself, without a care in the world, her red boots showing. There was a big black dog following them, a slinky creature with strange pale eyes.

"I would consider Maria Owens to be a good and generous woman," Anne Hatch responded.

"Would you now?" Martha said thoughtfully. She had her doubts about Anne as well, for where was her husband? And how had she come to be so cheerful with the burden of running the shop set upon her shoulders? Martha kept her suspicions tucked beside her desire, close to her heart, where it continued to burn. She had seen what she wanted and she intended to have it: a daughter, one with red hair who could already count, who skipped down the street as if she hadn't a care in the world and had no fear of strangers, even if it would have been best if she had.

· · ·

The letter was dispatched to the courthouse on a spring day when the pear trees had begun to bloom. The sun was shining, as it was said to do every Wednesday for at least an hour a day. There was no signature on the parchment and the handwriting was shaky and difficult to read. It took all morning for the clerk to decipher the message, and when he did he brought the complaint before the magistrates, who were meeting to discuss the growth of the harbor, as well as a list of grievances they must attend to: a pig delivered but not paid for, a fence constructed over the landholder's property line, the switching and caning of children in public places. The content of the letter was baffling at first, but when they really considered the charges it contained, no one was surprised this day had come. The complaint concerned a woman who flaunted the rules, who sold the bars of black soap that so many husbands had found in their wives' possession. The anonymous note accused Maria Owens of a variety of evil deeds including speaking to spirits, dispensing poison, stealing souls, bringing on the loss of unwanted babes, and enchanting innocent men.

John Hathorne was quiet during the debate among the magistrates, but his heart was racing. By the end of the afternoon he would not have recognized the man he'd once been in Curaçao.

252

That fool had gone swimming in his clothes; he had broken his marriage vows and his vows to God. He was most certainly not the John Hathorne who threw in his lot with his fellow judges, agreeing that witchery would only lead to more witchery and to women who believed they could do as they pleased. At the end of the day John Hathorne stood up and declared there was reason enough to prosecute Maria Owens. That night in bed, his hands began to bleed. He rushed outside and poured water from the rain barrel over his palms, but he could not wash the blood away. In the morning, Ruth noticed that he wore gloves. Her mother had told her that this was what guilty men did after they committed a crime; they could not look at what they'd done, they hid it away from others and from themselves, but the mark was there all the same, for what was done could not be undone.

There was a rapping on Maria Owens' door the following night. It was late and dark and the frogs were singing, as they did each spring. It sounded for a moment as if Cadin had returned, but when Maria woke she saw that the flame in the fireplace burned black, and she knew there was evil outside. She stood by the door in her white nightdress, reciting a spell of protection, but whoever had come was still there. It was then that she felt the same chill she'd had when

Thomas Lockland and his brothers rode across Devotion Field with murder in mind. She took the wooden box of salt she kept in a bureau, then poured a thin line along the walls and the door. But the salt evaporated in a white cloud as soon as it was laid down. Nothing would stick; it was too late for protection. Keeper had begun to growl and scratch at the door.

"Tie up that dog of yours," a man shouted.

Tell a witch to bind a wild creature and she will do the opposite. Maria opened the window at the back of the house. "Go," she told Keeper. The wolf refused to move. He would listen to one voice alone. Faith had been woken by the ruckus and she sat up clutching her doll, terrified by the shouting outside.

"Tell Keeper to run," Maria told Faith. She knew he would fight to the death to protect the child, and she sensed the men outside would be grateful for any excuse to shoot him. "It's for his own good."

Faith asked the wolf to go, and he reluctantly leapt through the window, tail between his legs. They could hear him out in the woods, howling. It was at that moment that Maria wondered if she shouldn't have sent Faith with him, as Hannah had sent her away. But it was too late to reconsider. The door was flung open by a constable with an axe in his hand, for he'd been ready to break it down. As Maria was about to utter a curse, sending them on their way, to hell if need be, the constable grabbed her, though he wailed when he did, his jabbing fingers burning from the heat of her flesh. The second constable now had the opportunity to snap iron cuffs on her wrists. This is how a witch was caught, while she worried over her child, and fought off one man, forgetting there was another. The men saw a pile of books Maria had bought while in Boston, and collected them as evidence. Then Maria was taken barefoot, in her nightdress with no belongings, pushed out the door into the night as her child choked back tears.

Fate is what you make it, or you will be what it makes of you.

"You damn well burned me!" the first constable cried. Blisters were rising on his hands where he'd grabbed her. He didn't dare touch Maria again. "You've rightly been accused."

"Of what, I'd like to know," she said.

"Do you see how she is? Prideful," the constable muttered to his brother constable. He would have caned her then and there if he hadn't been so afraid of her powers. He did have the nerve to tear off the amulet she wore, with Cadin's feather inside; and when she protested, he insisted her distress was proof of witchcraft. They led her away in chains they'd attached to the cuffs. She was informed she was being taken to the jail. In the morning, she would be brought to the courthouse.

"I have a child!" Maria protested. "You cannot separate us."

Faith had followed them, clinging to the skirts of her mother's nightclothes. The child was very quiet and pale. She did her best to recall the remedies and enchantments she'd seen in the *Grimoire*, but nothing suited this moment, other than one dark spell that caused flames to arise on the ground when you tossed down six black stones. But she had no such stones, and she was too terrified to call up any of the magic from Agrippa's *Occult Philosophy* that had been carefully transposed into the *Grimoire*.

"I don't know which words to say," she told her mother.

Maria silenced her girl with a warning. "Say nothing." She could already tell that any words they spoke would be used against them, and even a child might be considered an emissary from the sinister world these men imagined to be everywhere. "They will get what they deserve."

"Do you hear this witchery?" the first constable said to his brother. They stuffed their ears with grass so they could not be further bewitched.

Maria had no choice but to take Faith with her, as women who were confined to prison often did. She had once passed the jail, a small wooden building on a leafy corner of Federal Street, and had heard childish voices from within, and the crying of babies. What sort of world is this? she had wondered. This second Essex County was in many ways worse than the first.

As they walked on, Maria took note of a woman standing on the path, a hood draped over her head to stave off the chill of the evening.

"What brings you here?" the first constable asked the woman who'd appeared in the field.

"I'm just a simple neighbor," the woman said. "I cherish my town and am here to see a good result from tonight's events."

The woman now came to walk side by side with Maria. She was Martha Chase, who was at the heart of the events now conspiring. "I'm here for your sake, sister." Martha was plain and pale and her mouth was set, but there were bright spots on her cheeks, perhaps caused by excitement or fever or perhaps a bit of both. She threw Faith a look and her gaze softened. "You don't want them to take the little girl as well."

Maria looked into the dark and saw silver eyes watching them. "Stay away," she told the wolf, who had hidden in the darkness. She could not stand to have Faith see her wolf's blood shed.

Martha took the message for Keeper to be meant for her. "I'm only a neighbor wishing to help. The child knows me."

Maria glanced at Faith and saw in the girl's eyes that it was true. "How so?"

"She was in Mrs. Hatch's store. It was there we met." Faith felt that she had done something wrong in keeping their acquaintance from her mother. "She likes buttons."

"Does she?" Maria took more notice and recognized the woman as the one who had been speaking to Faith. So she had wanted something after all, and Maria thought it was likely she had come to the cabin to ask for a cure.

Martha introduced herself. She whispered that she was only a neighbor who wished mother and daughter well. "It's said you have powers. Can you not speak words that would free you or enchant these men?" Martha urged. "Surely you can utter a curse and stop them in their boots. Be rid of them."

Maria gave her a dark look. "Whoever told you that is what I do is wrong."

"I mean no harm in saying so. But you don't want a little one to be taken to that filthy jail," Martha Chase said, now satisfied that Maria would not or could not defend herself by using the Nameless Art. "There are rats there, sister, who like nothing better than a sweet child. It's damp and cold and many who walk in do not walk out."

They had reached the field where the crows had been shot. There were sharp stones littered about that pierced Maria's feet, or perhaps they were the thin bones of birds. She lifted Faith to carry in her arms. The girl was heavy, for she was already falling asleep, her head tucked against her mother's shoulder.

"There have been children judged to have carried out witchery," Martha Chase said. "They are beaten with switches, taken from their homes, treated like common criminals." Martha had bathed in a wash of salt and vinegar that evening, to make certain she washed away her desire. She was now clean, a good and serious woman with a good deed in mind.

Maria had slowed down, for each step she took brought her closer to the jail. Hannah would never discuss the time when she was incarcerated, when she was believed to have a tail people said was cut off with a carving knife. Her jailors kept her naked, so that they could spy her tail the moment it began to grow back.

"Keep moving." The first constable scowled, expecting treachery from Maria at any given moment. He wouldn't be tricked again, and rather than touch Maria he shoved her in between her shoulder blades with the butt of his rifle. The grass was dewy and the hem of Maria's nightgown was soaking wet. Faith was talking in her sleep, as Samuel Dias had been known to do, and although it was only a murmur, Maria understood her. "I want my dog, I want my bed, I want to sleep until morning."

"Let me do this for you, sister." Martha placed

a gentle hand on Maria's arm as she reassured her. "We are both women, and we understand a child's needs come first. Give your burden to me."

A drizzle had begun and Maria ran her hand over her daughter's damp hair. She thought of how chilly a cell would be, for the floors were dirt and the walls bare brick. They were at the edge of the field where there would soon be sunflowers. Maria could hear them growing up through the earth right now.

"You must do so now while you still can," Martha said. "Before we reach town and it's too late. Do so and we can both praise God."

It was dark as ash when Maria gave her daughter over into Martha's arms. Faith grumbled and Martha hushed her. Maria looked over her shoulder and saw that the wolf was following.

"You'll take her dog as well," Maria urged. "She must have him."

"A dog is the least of your worries." As Martha leaned in close, Maria picked up the scent of something odd, as if a fire was burning inside of this neighbor of hers. "Make it so they pay attention to your actions and they will not pay attention to mine."

They were near the homestead of the farmer who'd shot at Maria when he believed she was a witch who could turn herself into a crow. It was here, in the field where Cadin had died, that

Maria threw herself onto the ground. She began to utter a curse in Latin; it would not have any effect while she had iron cuffs on, and in fact each word burned her tongue, as if the curse had been reversed, but it was successful all the same. It took attention away from Martha. The constables panicked and gathered round, careful to keep their distance, poking at her with their rifles.

"Rise up now," the one in charge said. Her nightgown was stained by mud. She glanced over her shoulder as she turned, to see Martha duck behind the farmer's barn; she spied the shine of her daughter's red hair. When she arose from the ground, she glared at the constables.

"You had best hope I am not practiced in black magic," Maria told the men.

Later they would swear she'd had a smile on her face, and that she made the rain fall in torrents, and the toads came in masses through the mud so that the earth itself moved beneath their feet. They could see through the fabric of Maria Owens' nightgown and soon enough they felt the devil close by, breathing on their necks, rattling their souls. When they saw her young, near-perfect body, it made them think of all they might do to her, and for that they blamed their prisoner. She was the cause of their evil thoughts, and if evil deeds followed, she was to blame as well.

By then there were tears in Maria's eyes. She looked over her shoulder toward the empty field, and she saw there were indeed the sharp white bones of murdered birds in every furrow. This is the way it began; she knew that from the day Hannah told her that she must run. A woman alone who could read and write was suspect. Words were magic. Books were not to be trusted. What men could not understand, they wished to burn.

They gave her nothing of comfort in her jail cell, not a blanket or a cup of water. In the morning a woman came with porridge and a jug of water. She was a local woman named Lydia Colson, whose eight-year-old granddaughter accompanied her. Elizabeth Colson was a shy child who always kept her head down to conceal the fact that her face and neck were often covered with a bumpy scarlet rash that grew worse when she was nervous. Lydia had come to Maria on another occasion, desperate for a cure when her darling granddaughter had been stricken with a coughing disease that had caused her to hack up black phlegm, and Maria had given her an elixir of cherry bark and elderberry boiled into a syrup. In time the child had improved, and there had been no charge for the cure. Lydia had not forgotten Maria's kindness. She'd been told not to speak to the accused, or to look her in the eye, but she had compassion for the prisoner and had brought her a loaf of bread hidden in her granddaughter's shawl.

"Will you return the favor I once did for you?" Maria begged. "All I ask is that you make certain my daughter is well."

When Lydia Colson agreed to do so, Maria took her hand. She asked her for one more favor, that she bring a book for her to write in, along with pen and ink. "You can hide it in little Elizabeth's shawl." Later in the week, Lydia returned. She hadn't yet managed to see Faith, but she was able to smuggle in a blue paper journal. In return for this favor, Maria had Lydia bring her granddaughter back into the cell. Once the child and her grandmother were there together, Maria told Lydia to draw a circle of protection around them. Maria was bound by iron, so she had Lydia recite an incantation Hannah had taught Maria which called for good fortune and good health. When Lydia and her granddaughter left the jail that day, the blotchy rash that had always plagued the little girl had disappeared and her skin was clear and fresh. They were silent in the light of this miracle, and when anyone asked, little Elizabeth's grandmother said the child had fallen asleep in the woods with her face resting on weeds that had a healing property.

Once she was alone in her jail cell, Maria began

to write in her journal. She did so with her cuffs in place, biting at her skin. She kept the book hidden behind a loose brick. She wrote for the future, for her daughter and the granddaughters she might have one day.

Beware of love. Know that for our family, love is a curse.
He should have been my enemy, instead I thought I fell in love with him and I made the mistake of declaring my love. I was wrong to think that was love. I was too young to know any different.

The constable's wife was brought in to cut off Maria's black hair with a rusty tool she used to shear sheep. Hair was known to make women powerful, and in fact Maria moaned as if in pain while the constable's wife cut her hair so short that her scalp shone through. Then she was paraded through town to the courthouse in the sharp sunlight. Maria was still in her muddy nightdress, wearing nothing underneath. Men and young boys came to stare, although when she stared back they quickly glanced away, mortified and shocked by their own dark thoughts. Maria remained in chains, and by now her wrists were bleeding, yet she'd managed to write all night, until there was no longer any ink.

The courthouse on Endicott Street was built of granite brought down from the cliffs of the White Mountains. Maria was chained to her seat to face three magistrates. John Hathorne was among them, and she hoped he would not act against her and that what they'd once had would fill his heart with compassion, but when he looked past her as if she didn't exist, she knew she was alone here. Maria was asked her name and her date of birth, both of which she gave freely, and then she was asked the name of her husband, to which she replied, "None." The letter the court had received was then read aloud, accusing her of all manner of evildoing, including turning herself into a crow who flew above the fields, and a succubus who stole the souls of men. In spite of herself, Maria laughed.

"Does this list of evil amuse you?" the oldest magistrate asked.

"I find it to be ridiculous." She turned to John, who looked away. "Some among you know these are lies," she dared to say.

"Do women not come to you for potions?"

"For herbs to cure illness, yes."

"For magic, for vengeance, for spells, for the devil's work."

"No." She was freezing, as if a block of ice had been set upon her. Even now John said nothing. "I'm a healer."

"Did you not think of enchanting the sheriffs

who came for you and consider killing them?" she was asked. But these were not questions, she understood that now, they were statements of facts in these men's eyes. This is the way it must have begun for Hannah. With lies, with fear, with a man who refused to look at her.

"I did not, sir," she managed to say.

"Speaking falsely is a sin, you understand," she was told. One constable had sworn he had a bite mark on his shoulder. The other had been in a fever since he'd touched her.

"Treating someone falsely is a sin as well." Maria glared at Hathorne. He must have felt her eyes upon him, for at last he returned her glance. It was as though they had never met.

"Thou shalt not suffer a witch to live," the old magistrate said, quoting from Exodus. It was the same quote used on the title page of *The Discovery of Witches*, written by Matthew Hopkins, who had overseen the deaths of so many in the first Essex County in England.

A woman in disguise was called into the room; she'd been covered in a veil that reached to the floor to hide her identity. As a witness against Maria, she had pleaded to remain anonymous, fearing for her life. To turn against a witch was dangerous business and her pleas had been answered. When she was seated before the council, she was to respond by nodding, so that Maria would not know her by her voice and curse her. Without the iron cuffs Maria would have known her in an instant through use of the sight, but now this enemy of hers might have been any woman in town. The veiled witness nodded yes to enchantments, yes to a promise of murder, yes to curses, yes to sexual perversities, yes to speaking with the devil. Had she seen her fly? Yes, indeed, she had. Had she seen feathers fall away and flesh appear to cover the witch's bones? Yes as well. Black plumes sprouting upon her skin? Yes, a thousand times yes.

"You are a liar," Maria said before she could stop herself. "And you will pay for these lies."

"Are you threatening witchery right here before us?" the chief magistrate asked.

"Where is her proof?" Maria wished to know.

"Her proof is the word of a God-fearing woman."

Maria sat back in her chair. Hannah had told her how God-fearing people had nailed her cat to her front door while it was still alive. How they had given her moldy bread and no water in jail. How she'd been stripped and searched to see if she had a tail. Already the metal cuffs had drawn blood on Maria's wrists, black blood that was burning through the wooden floor. *Let no one see it, let no one know,* Hannah had warned her, should her fate ever lead her to a prison cell. *Do not speak or argue. Do not proclaim your innocence. They want you to be guilty, they want to mock your sins, they want to keep you in irons, and they would most certainly like to see you burn.*

The trial lasted three days, during which time there were several accusers, some Maria knew and others she had never seen before. The farmer who had shot her; a woman who had lost her sight and insisted Maria had climbed through her bedchamber window, causing her to go blind so the witch could have relations with her husband; the husband himself, who agreed and wore a blindfold so he would not have to look at Maria and perhaps fall under her spell yet again; a local fruit vendor, who had tried to sell her rotted lemons, for which she had refused to pay.

John Hathorne was the one who said she should not be kept in her nightdress, and in truth, many of the wives in town had complained. There were scabs on her wrists from the rubbing of the metal against flesh. Lydia Colson managed to sneak her another small bottle of ink, and all night she attended to the blue journal.

Wherever you are, she wrote to her daughter, *I did not wish to leave you.*

She was guilty, proven so by spectral evidence, rumor, and gossip that could not be proved, only believed, based on nothing more than a random bite mark, or a black crow feather, or a man who swore she had come to him in his dreams. They intended to test her by water. If she was a witch she would float, if she was a woman she would drown. Either way, she was likely to die. They fitted her with a pair of heavy black boots filled with stones that would sink any normal woman, and she was made to wear a white garment with pockets in which she could carry more stones. She was so weighed down she could not walk and had to be carried to the chair she was then tied to. They were at the lake that had no bottom, with its weedy shore and dark water. Maria gazed at the green leaves on the trees, wondering if they would be the last beautiful things on earth that she would ever see. She recited her daughter's name, her mother's name, and Hannah's name. None of the names were said aloud, but her lips moved quickly, in a silent chant. Certain people in the crowd swore she was calling down an incantation and that all of Salem would pay a price for what they did on this day when there were damselflies drifting over the black water, when the sun was strong, when those who had doubts did not dare to come forward lest they be accused of giving aid and solace to a witch.

They carried her chair into the water, though the men who did so quaked with fear, for they all believed there was a monster in the lake. Still, they went deeper, convinced that the devil might appear before them if they called him by his name. They were up to their ankles, then up to their knees, then they pushed the chair out into the water, the bottomless depths, where stray lilies floated, creamy white blooms on pads whose tendrils reached toward shore, wrapping slimy strands around the men's legs so that it seemed they might be pulled down as well until they charged backwards.

In the middle of the lake, the chair began to sink. The stones carried Maria down, for no witch could float when she was so weighted with rocks. For Maria the whole world turned green, the green leaves of the trees above her and the green water rising over her. She wished for one thing and one thing alone, to see her daughter, and yet she was grateful that Faith was not there and would not have to see her own mother murdered. Once you witness such brutality, it can never be unseen; it changes who you are and takes your childhood from you. It had happened to Maria when she stood on a hillside and watched Hannah's house burn. For hours she had cried, but the smoke had turned her tears black, and she realized that her weeping would never bring back what she had lost.

From under the water, Maria could spy the men on the grassy bank of the lake in their black coats. She viewed them as though they were the ones dissolving before her eyes. Fish floated by, small bright silver shadows. She would have no choice but to give up; it was impossible to fight the strength of water. When the serpent came to her, she felt it before she saw it, winding its way past her legs. It was not scaly but smooth, reminiscent of the cover of her *Grimoire*. The creature had adapted to this lake, eating frogs and leeches, but it had also been fed crusts of bread from Faith's hands and so it had been tamed. A creature that knows kindness can repay such deeds. The serpent swam beneath the chair, lifting it up through the green bubbles. On the banks the men blinked and stepped back when they saw the chair rising and moving toward the shallow water. Riding there, like a queen tied to her throne, was Maria Owens, nearly naked in her wet garment. She looked like an angel, but this was clearly the devil's work, for it went against nature. A woman tied to a chair must drown, and this was not the case.

Maria spat out water. The ropes had slid from her, and she stood with her feet in the mud. There were women in the crowd who fainted straight-away at the sight of her, now safely on the shore, and men who sank to their knees. Maria walked past the water lilies in the shallows, then went through weeds that were as tall as a man. Beasts could be humane, and men could be devils, Hannah had told her. Beware of those in power, of kings and judges and men who think they own you. If Maria hadn't been wearing iron cuffs, she would have caused the grass the magistrates stood upon to burn beneath their boots, but her natural talents were blocked by iron; she could not resist when they grabbed her and covered her in sackcloth so she could not work her evil upon them. They turned the fact that she had not drowned against her, declaring that she had given them all the proof they needed. She was a creature who couldn't be drowned, who called monsters and beasts to her and brought forth all the most foul urges in men. What they had in their grasp was a witch. By living, she had proven that she was an emissary from the dark and invisible world.

Maria Owens sat in jail, knowing her fate. She saw the hanging to come in the palm of her left hand, the fortune she'd made by coming to Salem. When Lydia Colson brought her supper, Maria was unable to eat. Not because the bread was hard and the stew cold, but because all she could think about was her daughter.

"I found her for you," Lydia whispered. She had her granddaughter stand guard to ensure the constable wouldn't overhear.

Maria looked at her blankly.

"I went to Martha Chase. I've told her you've asked to see the child." Maria was overcome with gratitude, but Lydia shook her head, for the visit hadn't gone well. "She refused. A jail is no place for a child, she said, and I had no business doing your bidding. She looked at me in a way that frightened me, as if she suspected me of some foul deed, when all I did was bring a message to her. And what of you, she said to me, right in front of my Elizabeth, are you certain the devil himself hasn't sent you here?"

Faith was kept inside the house during this conversation, but afterward Lydia had spied the child looking out the window before a hand drew her away.

"Go back," Maria pleaded. "Ask again if she'll bring my girl here. I'll pay any price!"

"I dare not go. That woman said she would report me as your accomplice if I returned. She would write to the magistrates if she had to, as she did to call their attention to you."

That was how Maria learned that Martha had implicated her for her own satisfaction. She'd been a fool to trust her, that simple woman who cherished her neighbors and her town. Some people can lie while they look at you and manage to hide their falseness; it's a form of witchery to be so disloyal, a terrible talent that is both rare and despicable. "Surely they won't believe her lies. They'll see she's stolen my daughter."

"You're a stranger here," Lydia said. "I've lived here all my life and I know that people see what they wish to believe."

"We're all strangers if they should decide for us to be so," Maria responded. "They can turn on anyone if it benefits them." She then asked if Lydia would keep an eye on Faith, from a distance if necessary, to make certain she wasn't being mistreated. "I would do the same for you if you needed me. Someday I'll pay you what I owe you."

Though the child was only eight, Elizabeth Colson vowed she would try to watch over Faith, and because of this her grandmother relented and said she, too, would try to see to the girl's well-being as best she could.

That night, Maria dreamed of her daughter, for although iron cuffs did away with the sight, they couldn't prevent dreams. In Martha Chase's house, where the raspberry bushes hit against the windows, and rabbits gathered in the yard, Faith Owens dreamed the same dream. She heard her mother tell her that when you were loved by someone, you never lost them, no matter what might happen next. Despite the curse, despite the losses you might endure, she knew now that love was the only thing that lasted. It was inside you and with you for all eternity.

The day drew near. It was spring and the world was green, but in jail the earthen floor and walls were cold. Maria heard the beetle calling, the same one Hannah had searched for in her cottage, the warning sign of a death to come. Maria covered her ears with her hands, yet heard it still. She closed her eyes and tried to dream even in the daylight hours, for it was her only escape from this dank and terrible place. In her dream snow was falling, with huge flakes dashing against her cheeks and eyelashes. When she opened her eyes and gazed out the window, there appeared to be white flakes, though the morning was warm and fine.

Maria went to the window and reached her hands through the bars as far as her cuffs would allow, so she might collect the snow and let it melt and drink what was left. It was then she discovered it wasn't snow that fell, but large creamy petals. She wondered how this had come to be, and if indeed it was a miracle. And then she saw a face she recognized, and dark eyes staring at her. The man who couldn't stop talking had come to Essex County to bring her a flowering tree belonging to an ancient genus, twenty million years old, existing before there were bees, so that it was pollinated by beetles. This one had come all the way from the Martinique, where people referred to it as a tulip tree or a sweet bay. It was said that the original flowers on earth were much like those on this tree, with white leathery petals and tough waxy leaves, impervious to the work of beetles or ants.

On the island the Carib people called *Madinina*, "Island of Flowers," Samuel Dias had met a man who told him of a sort of tree people swore could make a woman fall in love if she stood beneath its boughs. Perhaps, if he brought Maria Owens this tree, it would open her heart, for he was already convinced that he belonged to her and that he had ever since she had saved his life.

He'd hired two men to take him into the hills, and when he saw the tulip tree he sat down and wept, which had shocked the native people who accompanied him. They lowered their eyes as they dug up the roots, and refused to take the coins he offered. Clearly he was a man who'd been cursed and loved in a way that was too strong for most men. By the time Dias arrived in Salem, he had been traveling with the tree that would someday be called a magnolia—after the French botanist who would classify it—for so long he had grown fond of it and had begun to talk to it, telling it stories of other trees. His mother had once told him about a man who loved a woman but couldn't tell her so, for when he tried to express himself, his words got stuck in his throat. He brought a tree to his beloved, and when it bloomed she understood what was in his heart. Perhaps his mother's advice had been given to him to use when he needed it most, and he needed it now.

After leaving the *Queen Esther* in Boston, he'd found a horse and a cart and traveled here to Essex County. He'd gone through the green fields and dark forests filled with birds that called with songs he'd never heard before. He preferred light and heat, and what he'd seen of the city of Salem already caused him to loathe the place. He'd had several offers for his miraculous tree, the likes of which had never been seen in Massachusetts, but he turned each proposal down and hurried on. He had no interest in these people dressed in gray with their pale faces and their pale eyes. His father had given him one week away from the ship to complete his mad plan of winning Maria with the gift of a tree. It was obvious to Abraham that his son was in love, but not so clear that his attentions would be reciprocated. The notion of dragging a tree around the Massachusetts Bay Colony seemed unnecessary, especially for a man who knew how to get what he wanted simply by talking.

"Just tell her how you feel," Abraham Dias had suggested, though he knew how hard it was to dissuade Samuel once he had an idea in mind.

"The tree will tell her," Samuel said.

As soon as they'd arrived in Boston, large buds had appeared on the branches, which had drawn a crowd. Dias had shrouded the tree in muslin to ensure that no one would attempt to steal it. Now, here in Salem, he had walked the cobbled streets, asking people if they knew Maria Owens, but no one could help him and most eyed him with suspicion.

When he came to the store, Anne Hatch quickly said she knew nothing of the woman he asked for.

This dark-skinned man was a stranger who wore gold studs in his earlobes and clearly belonged at sea. "You should be on your way," Anne said. "There's no one here by that name."

Samuel Dias knew a lie when he heard one. It sounded soft, but it was sharp when it landed on the counter between them, a wasp made of words. He waited until Anne left for the day, then followed her home and stood outside her door. Hours passed and he was still there with his cart and horse and his tree. At last, he decided there was only one way to win this woman over to his side. He drew the muslin from the branches, and there was the magnolia, glorious even though it had not yet flowered. As far as he could tell, it was hours away from blooming and he had no time to waste.

Standing at her window, Anne was enchanted to see the buds that would soon be opening into white stars. Perhaps the magnolia spoke to her, and if it did, it told her that no man with ill intentions would travel with a large, flowering tree. She came outside, bringing Dias a plate of fricasseed chicken with onions, for which he was grateful.

"What do you want with Maria?" Anne asked.

"I'm a friend," Samuel said. When the woman gave him a look, for the relationship undoubtedly was more than that, he added, "She saved my life."

"If you are a friend, and you wish her well, then you won't like what you discover," Anne warned.

She directed him to the jail, where he'd sat all night, waiting for Maria to come to the window. He could tell this city was a cold and heartless place, one of the worst he'd known. He had seen the women with their heads covered, their eyes downcast. He'd passed by the stocks on the hill and the frame of the gallows built between two linden trees beneath the mottled sky. Dias wore his black coat even though it was spring, for he still was affected by breakbone fever even when he was not in the grips of the disease. He despised cold weather, but here he was in Massachusetts, a place that mystified him, for the righteous in this new country were no different than the inflamed mobs in Spain and Portugal.

When Maria saw the snowy flowers, her heart opened to the world she did not wish to leave, and when she spied Samuel Dias, who had been waiting all night, she heard what the tree told her, everything that the man who could not stop talking could not bring himself to say. The tree convinced her that he was in love with her, but just then she heard her jailors grab their chains and their keys. It was too late for her to feel anything in return.

Maria had saved his life, and now Samuel was meant to save hers. Before the jailors came for her, before they told her the court's decision and allowed her to wash her hands and feet a last time, Samuel Dias told her the truth of the world as he knew it. *They always want to burn a woman who defies the rules. They want to turn lies into the truth.* This time they were not so barbaric as to set her on fire. They thought themselves too godly for such pagan practices, and left fire and water to those heedless fools in Europe. They would dole out her punishment in a civilized manner and hang her at the gallows on the hill at the edge of town where wild purple nightshade flourished. There was already a crowd, and boys and young men had climbed the linden trees for a try at the best view.

Dias thanked the tree for bringing him to Essex County. He felt undone by how badly they had already treated Maria; her hair had been cropped so hastily she had only patches left, her beautiful face was so pale and drawn. She was near starved, for she said she could not eat a bite. When she told him her little girl had been taken by a neighbor who refused to give her back or even allow the child to visit, Maria looked broken.

"How can you help me? What will you do?" she asked through the bars. "Will you talk to them until they change their minds just to stop you from talking?" She smiled despite her wretched situation.

Yes, he could most assuredly talk, but he

intended something quite different. "I can tell you this. You may be hanged, but you will not die."

"You know the magic that will accomplish this?" she asked, unbelieving. "Perhaps you speak directly to God?"

As they held hands through the bars, Dias spied a black beetle burrowing through the wood of the jail. It made a horrid clacking sound. It was said there was no way to stop this beetle's ticking off the hours of a person's life, but Samuel Dias had never heard of a deathwatch beetle. He went over and stomped on it with his boot, crushing it completely.

"What did you do?" Maria said, stunned that she could no longer hear the horrid clacking.

"It's a beetle." Samuel shrugged. "I killed it." Such a thing could happen when the fate of the person who was to die shifted. Samuel Dias could not save his mother or his sisters, but he had learned many lessons since that time. His presence had changed Maria's fate, and death no longer chased after her.

"Trust me," Samuel said, and because the beetle was no longer pursuing her, and because this man had carried a tree a thousand miles for her, she told him that she would.

By morning the magnolia had been planted in Maria's garden. Dias had worked for hours with a shovel he'd stolen from a farmer's field. There was a light green rain spattering down, and toward the end he'd been digging through soppy mud, arms and legs streaked black, but at last the job had been completed. He awoke before dawn to find the tree in full bloom, a bower of cream-colored stars on dark, leathery leaves. He heard it speak to him when he leaned his head against the gray trunk.

You were only a boy before; now you're a man who understands you must take action against the cruelty in the world.

Samuel was fortunate to have a sailor's knowledge and skills other men might not have. He had circumvented bad fortune dozens of times, so many that the lines on his left hand were a jumble, all possible fates he had managed to avoid. He wondered if he'd brought the tree to speak not to Maria but to himself, to give him courage and remind him of who he was, a man ruled by love. Morning was about to break. It was certainly not a day to die, but rather a time to rejoice in the beauty of the world. He rode through the grassy fields in the dark, to the hill near town that was deserted, except for the birds waking in the bushes. This is where the gallows had been built. He tied his horse to a tree at the edge of the woods. The grass was damp and he was still unaccustomed to being on earth rather than at sea; he walked with a rolling gait, as if the ocean was below him rather than the black earth of Essex County. Over one shoulder he carried a leather satchel that was stained with salt. He had a grin on his face despite the circumstances. Inside the bag was the one thing that could set Maria Owens free.

A woman who went to the gallows must be barefoot. She was to walk through town in iron chains, and then be taken up the hill in a cart drawn by oxen. There were horse pastures on either side, for all the trees had been chopped down, and groves of locusts would be planted here when at last men realized only fools cut down nearly every tree, except for the few where boys sat in the branches waiting for the gory event to occur. Maria wore a long white shift and nothing more. She was not allowed the comforts of this world, for she would next be judged in the hereafter, and here on earth she was beyond all help. She had been found guilty of witchery, of conversing with spirits, of evil deeds done for her benefit and the benefit of Satan. The old magistrate came to her and told her to list her sins, and repeat her conversations with the devil, and she would not do so. When he made his report to the court, John Hathorne asked for a chance to speak to the witch. He was a learned man, from a well-respected family, and so the court agreed. Hathorne stood outside her cell, and called for the jailor to leave them alone.

"Have you come to free me?" Maria asked.

She sat on the floor, for there was no bed, although Lydia Colson had brought her a woolen blanket.

"Tell them what they want to hear," John Hathorne said. "Confess you have worked with the devil. I'll help you leave here."

"With false gems?" How could it be that he seemed a complete stranger to her?

"With silver and a wagon to take you to Boston or New York. I can keep the girl."

Maria rose to her feet. She could feel something flicker inside her, despite her iron chains.

"I've discussed it with my wife," Hathorne went on. "We've agreed this is the right course. We'll take the child and treat her as if she were our own."

"She is your own. But you will never have her."

He backed off, seeing the fever in Maria's eyes. "Then take her with you when you leave this place if that's what you wish. Just sign a confession."

"I confess that I was a fool and a young girl who knew nothing. But what is your excuse?"

"You refuse my help?"

"Unlike you, I am not a liar. I have nothing to confess. Not even who the father of my child might be."

Hathorne bowed his head and wished the world were a different place. But it was not. There were no turtles in the sea, no courtyard filled with Jamaican apple trees. He stepped outside, where the jailor was dozing on a bench. The air was bright and the day was blue. A man had no choice but to live in the world he was granted.

"Go forward," Hathorne told the jailor before he walked home to Washington Street, where the black leaves were falling, and would continue to fall until not a single one was left.

When Maria was marched along the street, Hathorne closed himself into his study. He could not watch her pass by, but Ruth Gardner Hathorne went into the yard and stood at the fence, her hands wrapped around the wooden pickets. She did not know why her eyes were burning when she saw Maria, or why her face was wet with tears. She wished she could walk past the gate, out of the yard, and out of her life. Maria was instructed to stare at the ground, but she lifted her eyes to Ruth, who felt a burden of guilt even though she'd had no voice in all that had happened and all that was about to transpire. Perhaps it was because they had the same love line in the center of their left hands, one that altered halfway across their palms as their paths diverged.

John Hathorne was so chilled to the bone, he

285

went out to stand in the sunlight. It was then he saw his wife there with tears in her eyes.

"You must take the child," she said.

He had never heard her speak in that tone before. Perhaps the girl was their burden. He nodded and left the garden, but before he went to inform Martha Chase of his decision, he made his way to Gallows Hill. He went to offer Maria grace in her final moments, a prayer book in his hands.

For Maria it had been a long walk to the hillside, and it was meant to be so. Let it be difficult and painful, as the sentence for crimes of witchery must be. The accused's feet were to bleed; in her white shift, which was as sheer as her nightdress, she would remain unprotected from brambles and thorns. All the while, Maria thought of Faith. *My darling,* she thought. *I have written down the lessons you need to know in a blue notebook.* She'd told Dias where the notebook was hidden, in the wall of the jail cell, and also where he would find her *Grimoire,* in the bureau drawer of her cottage, should his plan not work as he intended. *There will be no need for me to do so,* he had assured her. *You'll be here to give her those books.*

But if, she had said.

Anything you wish, he had assured her.

Maria had little faith in this world, where every woman must behave. She had grown up without a

286

mother, and now Faith would likely do the same. She trusted that Martha would keep Faith inside today, and close the shutters, and that when she spoke of Maria she would say, at least, that she had loved her daughter, and that when Samuel Dias came to the door she would unlock it, for he had agreed to take Faith and raise her as his own if need be, and show her that there were other worlds, far across the sea.

There were swifts in the air as they crossed the pasture where Cadin had been murdered. Maria concentrated on the blades of grass and the warmth of the sun on her shoulders. When they came to the hill, there was a crowd assembled, not a raucous, wild gathering, but a solemn throng, as if they were attending a church service, and, in fact, there were those who held hymnals. The constables acted as the gallows men; the older one had overseen a hanging, but the young one, named Ellery, had not, and he had been sick all morning and had come to the gallows late and had rushed to prepare. The frame was a simple hanging construction, hastily built for the event. There were not even stairs leading up to the platform. Maria was lifted up by the jailor, who wore heavy gloves so he would not have to touch her and risk becoming bewitched, for to look at her was said to be dangerous.

Risk or not, people couldn't take their eyes off Maria Owens. Most of the women who had come to her for help stayed home, refusing to attend the hanging; some feared they would somehow be implicated, others could not abide such a terrible wrongdoing; still others, the most grateful among them, were in attendance. Anne Hatch was there, doing her best not to cry, losing her faith on this day, not in God, but in mankind and in those who sat in judgment and saw evil where there was none.

It was a fine day, of the sort when it was possible to forget the snows of winter, for the world was fresh and green. Maria was asked if she wished her eyes to be covered, but she waved the blindfold away. She remembered that when she had looked in her black mirror, she had not seen her fate conclude at the end of a rope. The magistrates had gathered to watch their will be done. The air was so still the cries of the swifts echoed, and a mass of swooping crows called to each other, gathering as they were known to do when one of their kind was threatened.

If it was Maria's fate to live, she wished to make sure everyone in attendance knew it. She waved the hangman away so that she might speak. "If I do not die, am I then innocent and allowed to go free?" she asked the magistrates. She looked so young with her hair cropped short, there in her billowing white shift.

"Sister, you would," the first magistrate said. "But that is unlikely."

As they placed the rope around her throat, Maria gazed at the tree line. She saw the white horse tied to a tree and she thought about the day her father came for her mother, and the look of joy on Rebecca's face. That was the moment Maria had decided she would never fall in love. That was her mistake.

After the noose was looped around her throat, the constables unlocked the iron cuffs. Maria once more felt the stirring of the heat of her bloodline, carried from mother to daughter for as long as time had existed. She saw John Hathorne among the crowd, and she couldn't stop herself. She cried out a curse that opened the skies, and a squall arose, a drenching rain that would flood every farm and every house. The man who had brought her to Essex County stood in the field and nearly drowned as he gulped down rain. She would protect herself and her daughters and all the daughters who might follow from any such betrayals in the future. "To any man who ever loves an Owens, let this curse befall you, let your fate lead to disaster, let you be broken in body and soul, and may it be that you never recover."

Had anyone bothered to look at the magistrate, they would have seen he was chalk white and shaking, even though he was still the same strong man he'd been when he'd come to Gallows Hill.

289

If he had looked at the palm of his hand, he could have read the truth. His fate had changed on this day. He thought to run, but could not move. He could not stop watching her.

Maria leapt from the platform, the rope around her throat. The rain stopped as suddenly as it had begun, and there was silence as the trees dropped their leaves. The crowd drew a breath, expecting to view the horrible contortions of a hanged person who dangled in the air, but instead the line of rope broke. It snapped in two, and Maria landed with her feet in the mud, the rope still around her neck, as alive as anyone, as alive as she'd ever been.

People began to run away. They dashed through the muck in the field, hauling the startled children they'd brought to witness the hanging. Men who'd previously thought they were brave were afraid to turn back, for they remembered that an individual who looks back on evil may be turned into a pillar of salt. There were those who saw the horse approach, and the stranger who took Maria's hand to pull her up to ride behind him. Later some people said it was the devil who'd been waiting for her, and that they had been tested and had failed, but there were others who said God always grants a pardon to those who are blameless and the fact that Maria couldn't be killed was proof of her innocence.

Those who ridiculed the Nameless Art began to

doubt that courts and laws could control magic. There was no need for them to know that Samuel Dias had replaced the constables' original rope early that morning with one he'd used at sea, an old length rotted through by salt and exposure to the weather. He'd used it to tie up the magnolia tree, and when the rope split, he grew convinced that the tree had saved Maria. When spring came to Essex County, years later, the magnolia would bloom on the same day every year, a miracle and a joy to all who saw the white flowers blossom, the glory of the world.

They rode to Martha Chase's house, where the chimney was falling down and the windows were shuttered. There was no sign of life. Maria felt a wave of darkness as they approached, which hit her like the heat from an oven. Her child was her heart and now she was hollow. When she pushed open the door, she saw that jars of raspberry jam had been left to cool on the table, and the place smelled sticky sweet. There was the small pallet where Faith had slept. Everything else was gone. They had left in a hurry.

Maria went into the garden. Samuel tried to comfort her, but she could find no comfort here. Then she heard a moaning from a storm cellar where Martha Chase stored her provisions and jars of jam. Samuel came to help unbolt the lock and then open the heavy wooden doors. When they peered into the dark, there was the wolf, Keeper, chained to the wall, his ribs showing, starved and abandoned. Made vicious by his ill treatment, he growled when he spied a human form.

Samuel put a hand on Maria's arm as she went forward. "That's a dangerous animal," he said, concerned.

"Every mistreated creature is dangerous," she replied.

She ran down the rotted wooden steps into the dark and let the wolf off his chain. He only glanced at her with his silver eyes, before he lurched past her and ran up the steps and into the house, in a mad search for Faith. When he found she wasn't there, he lay down beside the pallet where she had slept, exhausted and hoarse from weeks of howling. Martha had duped him, tricking him into the cellar by tossing Faith's clothes down the stairs. She'd then thrown a chain around his neck, attached to the mud-caked wall. Whenever Faith had heard howling, Martha had said it was the wind, and she'd vowed that the wind here always sounded like crying, and it was best to ignore it.

They went through the woods, the wolf following at a distance. At the lake Maria stripped off the white shift she had worn for weeks. Dias could not take his eyes off her, so he didn't try. He gave her his coat to wear once she had bathed, then spoke to her in Portuguese. "We'll look through every house in this damn county."

But the sight had returned to Maria and she could see and feel what an ordinary woman could not. She knew her daughter would not be found in Massachusetts. The green rain she had called down upon the people of Salem had also washed away any trail that might have been left, making it impossible for the wolf to track Faith. Keeper knew it as well. The girl was gone.

They spent the night at the cabin, with Dias setting up his hammock on the porch. When she couldn't get any rest, Maria came to lie beside him.

"What made you come here now?" she asked.

"The tree." They could see the magnolia, the blooms like white stars. He had come here to let the tree speak for him. His heart was hitting against his chest, and he hoped Maria couldn't feel its ragged rhythm, despite the curse she had called down from the gallows. He, a man who could talk to anyone in six languages, was now tongue-tied in her presence. If he could speak he would say the magnolia was his heart, given to her to do with it as she wished.

When Maria awoke in the dark of morning, she found that Samuel had gone to the harbor and returned with news. Martha had paid for two passages to New York. She'd had a red-haired girl with her. Maria threw her arms around him, as she had when he was so near death. She'd thought he didn't know how close he'd come to the end, but he'd always known, just as he knew that she would ask him to take her to New York Harbor, and that he would agree.

"You will not find New York to be like any other place," he warned her. "You can go there as one person and become someone else entirely."

Searching a city of nearly five thousand people would be all but impossible. It was easy to disappear in New York. It was here that men who wished to avoid their marriages vanished without a trace, women who yearned for a world where there were no rules settled in, sailors who jumped ship found that no sheriff could find them, and Dutchmen went off into the wild land beyond the wall that marked the limits of the city and were soon forgotten.

Before they left, Maria went inside her cabin one last time. She'd been barefoot, and now she pulled on the red boots her mother had bought in the first Essex County. She took the blue blanket and the poppet Samuel had made for Faith and packed them along with the *Grimoire* and the black mirror. She peered into the glass before she stored the mirror, but didn't recognize herself. Maria was more magic than mortal, but even a witch can be changed by sorrow. Nothing would ever be the same, but Hannah had taught her that there were times, rare as they were, when what was done could be undone.

PART THREE

Divination

I.

They took up residence in Manhattan on a street called Maiden Lane, not far from Minetta Creek, where the surrounding land was farmed by free men who had once been slaves. Originally called *Maagde Paatje* by the Dutch, the street began as a footpath near a stream where lovers often met and women gathered in the mornings to do laundry. At the most southern end stood the Fly Market, where fish and vegetables and fruit were sold, a crowded, filthy place where housewives could find anything they might need and witches could find rare ingredients, such as the bark and berries of the *Dracaena draco*, the red resin tree of Morocco and the Canary Islands, if they knew where to look.

The house on Maiden Lane was well furnished, with hand-knotted rugs from Persia dyed with indigo, and satin curtains. There was white tableware from France and expensive cutlery that had immediately blackened as soon as Maria unpacked it, though every knife and spoon had been marked by the stamp of a fine silversmith in London. There was a yard in which to grow herbs, including tall plumy sage and aromatic rosemary, along with feverfew and wormwood, and currant bushes whose young leaves made a fragrant mixture when lemon zest and rosemary were added for Maria's Travel Well Tea that helped to prevent scurvy. In the rear of the garden, there was a spiky fence to ensure that children from the neighborhood would not stumble upon certain plants and mistakenly ingest herbs that would make them ill, the darker ingredients such as bittersweet nightshade, foxglove, laurel, castor beans.

Samuel's father, Abraham, often sat in the garden on fine days, wishing he were at sea alongside his son. He still had on his leather hat that he'd always worn when sailing. The old fellow was a charming man with a thousand stories, more even than his son, but he had been ailing and Samuel had purchased the house so that his father could comfortably live out his final years in Manhattan. He'd bought the small manor from the first Jewish resident of New York, Jacob Barsimon, who had arrived in the city in 1654, traveling from Amsterdam with the Dutch West India Company. Although Samuel bought the house for his father, he'd chosen it with Maria in mind. Right away he had a team of workers come to stake out the garden plot and cut down the weeds and nettles that grew wild, and he made certain there was a chamber for Faith, ready when she was found.

When they first arrived, Maria had locked herself in her chamber with the *Grimoire*. She attempted every spell that might bring a missing person home. She lit candles, laid out stones and bird feathers on the wooden floor, slit the palms of her hands so that her blood could call out to Faith. She cut up one of Faith's dresses and dropped the fabric into a flame, then added pine needles and marigold flowers, a spell meant to call a person to arrive on your doorstep in less than twenty-four hours. None of it worked. Try as she might she could not use the sight to find her daughter. When she gazed into the black mirror, all she saw was a land that seemed to stretch on forever where hundreds of rabbits gathered, nothing more.

During her first weeks in New York, Maria didn't eat or drink or sleep, and she didn't answer when Samuel knocked at the door. Her loss was too enormous. She could not bear to speak to another person. Early in the mornings she sneaked out to search the city streets, hoping that luck would allow her to spy a girl with red hair. In time, she found several, but none were her daughter, and she came home exhausted. After a while she seemed to give up, and she took to her bed and slept for days, until Dias woke her and said if nothing else she must drink water or she would make herself ill.

"When she does come back, she will need you alive," he told her.

He made *adafina*, a chicken stew his mother had often served, consisting of chicken, fava beans, onions, chickpeas, garlic, and cumin, and a sponge cake called *pan de España* that had been baked by Jews in Spain since the year 1000, often using potatoes instead of flour. When Maria sat down at the table, she realized she was starving. She was still eating her supper long after Abraham had gone up to bed.

"Do you think this will win me over?" she asked Samuel Dias when she was done. The food had been delicious and he had spent hours making it. He also baked a chocolate cake, using his mother's recipe, a sweet so drenched in rum a single slice could make a person tipsy. For some reason Maria felt alive again, and guilty that her heart still managed to beat, though it was broken in two.

"I don't have to win you over." Dias shrugged. "I already won."

Maria couldn't help but laugh at his arrogance. "That was before. Now there's a curse."

"I don't care," Dias said. "I loved you before there was a curse."

They were both stunned by this admission, so they said nothing and ate more, tearing apart oranges from Spain that were fragrant and sweet. Then they discussed their situation and the terms of their living arrangement, including the fact that he must not love her, it was too dangerous to do so. She thought back to the gallows, how she had looked at John Hathorne and set a curse upon anyone who might fall in love with a member of the Owens family. She'd sought to protect herself and her daughter and any of their descendants from the grief she'd known.

"You can't be in love with me," Maria told Samuel.

"If you insist, I will say that I'm not."

The butter in a dish on the table had already begun to melt, a sign that someone in the house was in love.

"Why is that happening?" Maria asked when she saw how it melted.

"When it's hot, things melt."

"I see." Maria was burning as well.

"What's love?" Samuel shrugged. "You can't hold it in your hand. You can't see it. It's something you feel. Perhaps it's not even real." He thought his argument was excellent, until Maria laughed at him.

"How many women have you told this story to?" she wanted to know.

Then Samuel was serious. "Only you."

With that, he won the argument and they went up to bed. Maria insisted they make no vows to each other, no contracts of love, no promises, nothing that could call down the curse. Of course he agreed; he would have agreed to anything in order to have her. When Maria woke the next morning, she gazed at Samuel's broad back as he slept, and she felt something that she couldn't name in the pit of her stomach. Perhaps it was desire, or affection, or perhaps it was more, the thing you couldn't hold in your hand or see with your own eyes, but was there all the same.

Whatever it was, it was a mistake. At the age of ten Maria had vowed never to be in love; she had seen what it had done to Hannah and Rebecca and the women who arrived late at night, desperate for spells. She'd only been infatuated with John Hathorne, the flirtations of a girl, and there'd been disastrous results. She set stricter limits for herself with Samuel. She would sleep in his bed when he was at home and she would care for his father when he was at sea, but he must never ask her for more. The problem was, they couldn't keep to the rules and they couldn't keep their hands off each other. They lived like this for nearly a year, their life at night a secret, so that Maria often entirely ignored Samuel during the daylight hours. And then one morning Maria saw a beetle in the yard and she felt a chill. Upon examination she found it was not the wretched deathwatch beetle; all the same she feared for Samuel's safety. She was grieving over Faith and she didn't think she could survive losing someone else. From then on she locked her door and didn't answer when she heard Samuel at night. One morning she found that he had slept in the hall.

When she woke him, Samuel stood to face her. It was clear that he was stung by her rejection.

"If you want me to leave, say so," he told Maria. "I'll go now. Today."

"This is your house. Are you sure *you* want *me?*"

He did, too much, but he didn't respond.

That night she recited an incantation to send love away. The next morning he packed to leave.

"You shouldn't go away," Abraham told his son. "Life is short and getting shorter. I know you want Maria. Stay with her."

"She won't let me." Samuel continued packing his bag. "She says we're cursed."

"Everyone is cursed," the old man assured him. "That's life." He shook his head and thought that young people were fools. "You might as well do as you please."

Samuel did one thing he knew Maria wouldn't wish him to do. He left a leather pouch on the table. Inside was a sapphire on a silver chain.

This one is real, he'd written in the note he left behind.

Você não pode finger algo real não existe.
You can't pretend something real doesn't exist.

After Samuel left, Maria and Abraham Dias settled into the routine of two people in mourning. They comforted each other, for each knew sorrow. Men who were sailors rarely became accustomed to living on land, and Abraham Dias longed for the life he'd once had. He spent his days waiting for his son, even though Samuel might be gone for months at a time. The old man's memory had begun to fail more each day, still he knew that he was in New York, and that he lived in his son's house with a beautiful woman whose name he sometimes forgot, especially in the evenings when Maria returned from searching for Faith and poured him a glass of port. All the same, Abraham shared his stories with her as he sipped his nightly drink. He always remembered these stories, even though he'd often forgotten what he'd had for his supper that very day. He told her about the joy of riding on the back of a whale, the salt spray filling his mouth, and about a land where all the bears were white and it was so cold the earth was covered with ice even in the heart of August, and about the Barbary Coast, where the leopards and lions would eat beef from the palm of your hand if you had the nerve to reach out to them, and where diamonds glittered up through holes in the earth, as if there were stars not only above but below. The stories that she loved best were when Abraham recounted his son's early days at sea, when the young Samuel was so captivated by the starry heavens above he didn't sleep at night, but instead lay on his back on the deck memorizing the position of the stars so that he might chart the sky.

Abraham Dias tired easily and went to bed directly after he had his nightly meal, which was just as well. He would have been confused by the women who came to the door in search of remedies once darkness had fallen. He likely would have looked among them for his wife, who had been gone for so long. She had been young and beautiful when he first met her and he had loved her too much, so much that she still appeared in his dreams, although she had been burned to ash long ago. Her name was Regine, but she was called Reina, for to Abraham she was a queen.

Maria had a deep affection for the old man, who had taught her how to make Chocolate Tipsy Cake, and she hated to leave him on his own when she left the house, for he was prone to wander, often finding his way to the rough area of the docks. Once he'd been tied to a post by a gang of unruly boys and left there in the rain, unable to escape from the ropes that bound him until Keeper at last tracked him down and Maria cut him free. From then on, whenever she went to search for her daughter, which was her daily habit, she employed a hired girl named Evelyn to watch him, even though he was annoyed when left in another's care.

"She doesn't give a damn about stories," he would complain about his caretaker, a dull girl who often fell asleep when she was supposed to be watching him. "She's not like you."

"Pretend she's me and before you know it I'll be back," Maria said to soothe him.

Maria continued to search for Faith, and each time she came home, unsuccessful, she turned to the *Grimoire*, also to no effect. She had no idea what thwarted her, making it impossible to locate Faith. She'd begun to think she'd lost the sight. By now she was known in the neighborhood as the woman with the stolen child, for she'd gone door-to-door asking if anyone had seen her daughter. The other mothers pitied her when they saw her in the short black veil she wore when she was in public. She paid informants, but those who said they had seen a red-haired girl in the care of a tall, thin woman were either out of date or inventing sightings in order to collect some silver.

Keeper was always beside Maria as she searched farther northward, in the wild area beyond the wall built by the Dutch to keep out native people, and pirates, and the British. Wall Street, built in 1685, ran beside the ramparts and crossed the old Indian path now called Broadway. Maria trailed the river on the west side, taking the road called Love Lane, a nighttime trysting place, hiking into the highlands where there were still large Dutch farms, and making her way through the woods where some Lenape people remained, hidden in the old forest where the trees were so big it would take ten men to circle the trunk of a single one. People grew accustomed to seeing Maria and Keeper; some of those they passed called out a greeting to the purposeful black dog and the woman wearing a veil, but there were those, such as the old farmers who had been among those who settled New York more than sixty years earlier, who recognized the wolf for what he was. The Lenape people did as well, but they called him brother, for they knew that when the Dutch and the English claimed the land they'd treated Keeper's kind as they had the original people, with the intent to own and destroy.

Nothing helped Maria Owens, not even the back pages of the *Grimoire*, which contained those spells from Agrippa and *The Key of Solomon* only to be used in the most dire of times. At last, she performed an act of desperation. She lay on her back, naked on the floor, inside a pentagram she had drawn with charcoal. She was surrounded by burning candles, a brass bowl of blood and fingernail clippings and strands of hair on fire. She had made a small wax figure of Martha that twisted in the heat. This was left-handed magic, dangerous to one and all.

Use only when you must, Hannah Owens had written in her perfect handwriting. *And know you will pay a price for doing so.*

There was always a price when magic was

used selfishly, for the practitioner's own benefit, but Maria no longer cared. The wax figure was stabbed with a single sharp pin and the wax shuddered as it dissolved. This was sympathetic magic; do unto an object what you would wish on an individual. One becomes the other.

> *Ut omnia quae tibi. Take all that you want.*
> *Quid enim mihi est meum. Give me what is mine.*

Maria sat by the window in the early morning light before she went out to search. Perhaps one day Faith would walk up the gravel path. She might return on an ordinary day, whether it be a blue morning in May or a snowy afternoon in the midst of winter. One day Martha would be the one to disappear, Maria's spell would see to it, and once she did, Faith would find her way to the house on Maiden Lane, where Maria had planted lilacs by the back door, for where there are lilacs there will always be luck.

In the spring of the third year after their departure from Salem, Samuel Dias returned to Manhattan beset by his old illness. He came back every few months, to sleep in the barn, doing his best to ignore Maria. By now they barely spoke, and she missed the man who could not stop talking.

This time, he said nothing at all. Breakbone fever was the devil inside him, but the disease was his teacher as well, for it reminded him of his own mortality and instructed him in the ways in which men were powerless over their own fates.

He arrived in a rented carriage and was helped out by the driver, for he was too weak to navigate the street. Maria had insisted she wanted nothing from him; all the same, she wore the sapphire hidden beneath her collar. She often thought of the other gift he had given her, the magnolia tree in Essex County that had predicted her freedom. It was a tree of fortune, blooming not in season, but whenever it chose to do so. Even now, in the bitter and austere Massachusetts Bay Colony, where women were being jailed every time a neighbor accused them of hexing sheep and cows or setting a pox on their children with the devil's help, often from miles away, while the accused was asleep in her own bed, the magnolia tree had bloomed all winter long. Some people said that it, too, was the work of the devil, but others went to sit beside its flowering boughs, even when there was snow on the ground.

No other specimen could compare to this miracle tree, and yet Samuel brought back other trees for Maria every time he returned. Each time he did so, he gave her his heart. The trees did his talking for him now, if only she would listen to what he had to say. He'd given her date palms and bridal bloom, jujube trees called *zufzuuf*, tamarisk, thuja trees, monkey puzzle trees, floss trees—some of which were too delicate for the climate and needed to be kept in pots in the parlor through the winter. Maria never said she was pleased, but he could tell that she was from the look on her face. This time he'd found a specimen on St. Thomas called the Tree of Heaven. He'd gone hiking with some local men to find it, and they'd mocked him for being so love-struck he had been willing to hack through the weeds to get to the perfect sapling. In the spring, the hillsides on St. Thomas turned red as blood and birds came from northern lands a thousand miles away to build nests in its branches; even if it wasn't a miracle tree, it would be one of a kind on the island of Manhattan.

Dias appeared more hardened than he had in past years. Now that he commanded the *Queen Esther*, he was often put in a position where cruelty was the only choice, even for a fair man. There were strands of gray in his coarse black hair, but when he grinned he still looked like a young man in his twenties, as he was when Maria first met him. As time went on, he had discovered that it wasn't that he merely enjoyed talking, he wanted *someone* to talk to, not the strangers he encountered in foreign lands that he would never see again, not the sailors who drank enough so that they forgot his stories as he was telling them.

He wanted someone who truly knew him. He wanted her.

When Maria spied him through an open window on the day of his return, she knew something was wrong. She went to meet him without bothering to pull on her boots or close the door behind her. No matter how much she wanted him to stay away, he was the man who had saved her life with a rope trick and had been beside her as her heart broke apart in the second Essex County. She quickly paid the driver and helped Dias into the house. As always, he'd arrived without notice and had no idea how long he would stay.

"We weren't expecting you," Maria said to reproach him, worrying over the state he was in. Usually he cared about his appearance, but now his clothes were in disrepair and hung on his frame. He'd lost a good deal of weight, and some of his strength was gone. Still he was the handsome man whose stories Maria could listen to again and again. His dark hair was tied back with a leather band and his boots hadn't been cleaned for months. Maria, too, was not at her best. "I'm not at all prepared." She had dirt from the garden under her fingernails and her hair was in knots.

Samuel's fever was raging, and he was still a man who either said too much or said nothing at all. When they went inside, he immediately felt at home, a comfort he experienced only when he visited New York. But it was all too much on this day. Samuel found he needed to take a moment to sit and catch his breath before greeting anyone properly.

"What do we have here?" Abraham Dias said, his voice trembling. There was a handsome man with dark eyes who seemed exhausted and wore a familiar black coat. "You look like my son."

"He should," Maria assured the old man. "That's exactly who he is."

Samuel gathered his strength and went to embrace his father. The two men were not afraid to show their raw emotions when they were together. They had seen and done terrible things and had worked side by side for a lifetime, until Abraham could no longer stand upright for more than a few minutes at a time without the pain in his back and legs overwhelming him. Age had come upon him quickly, like a thief, and an injury he'd suffered when they first took their ship from a royal merchant and renamed it the *Queen Esther*, had worsened with the years so that he limped and could no longer walk very far. On this day, neither man could stand for long. Abraham could deal with his own failing body, but to see his son in such bad health caused him to weep.

"It's that damn fever," Abraham declared. "It won't leave you alone." He turned to Maria, frustrated. "I thought you had cured him!"

"I cure him every time. That is the only way to

treat this disease. Some things return no matter what, and we must deal with it when it does."

"I'm fine," Samuel insisted. "I can stay in the barn."

But Maria insisted he must take the chamber being saved for Faith's return. Samuel was mortified that she had to help him up the stairs, and yet he wondered if perhaps he had willed the illness to return, if he wanted nothing more than to have her arms around him, despite the price. Everything inside of him hurt, as if his bones were made of glass once more. A single touch was agony, and yet he yearned for Maria's embrace, for glass could burn as well as break. Once in bed, he moaned and turned his face to the wall. He hated to show his weakness; all the same he hadn't enough strength to take off his boots.

"You should have come home before this," Maria told him. "I can tell you've been ill for a while."

Abraham had a right to fault her, but breakbone was a tricky disease that lurked inside a person's body. You chased it away, only to have it return unexpectedly. Samuel found he was comforted by Faith's belongings that were stored in this room, the blanket with the blue stitching, the poppet doll he had made.

"There it is," he said, happy to spy the doll. "You've kept it safe."

"Of course I have," Maria answered. "Didn't you tell me I must?"

She went to collect the dried Tawa-tawa leaves that were stored in her herb cabinet so that she might fix a pot of the curative tea, and when she returned, Samuel was already asleep. He was talking as he dreamed, this time about the burning of his mother. The prisoners had been dressed in sackcloth, with dragons and flames painted upon their shirts and hats; they had ropes around their necks, and were forced to carry rosary beads and green and yellow candles. Dias was haunted by the shocking scene he had witnessed as a boy, and in his dreams he often revisited the square where it had occurred. The smoke that arose from the burning bodies was bloody and bitter. He could hear his mother's voice ringing through a crowd of a thousand. Maria removed his boots and slipped into bed beside him so that she might hold a cold, wet cloth to his head. She reached under his shirt to find that he was burning, his heart red-hot.

"Don't leave me," he said, convinced it was she who was the true remedy, not the bitter tea she insisted he drink or the broth she made for him out of fish bones to keep him strong.

At first, Maria thought he was speaking to his mother in his dreams, until he embraced her and called her by her name. This was what happened every time he was home. If she kissed him once, she would not stop. It was wrong, and she knew it. It was dangerous as well. She spoke both to him and to the curse. "Don't say any more, and do not speak of love, this is not love, this is something else, it's my life twined together with yours. You are only home because you are ill, not because you look at me the way you do. You must go away as soon as you can, far across the sea, where you will be safe. This is a dream, it isn't real, it won't affect you. I will never be yours."

Samuel Dias tore at his clothes, and Maria helped him. He was burning and so was she. The broth on the bedside table would wait. The world could wait as well. Outside, rain had begun to fall. Maiden Lane was silent and green, but nothing outside this chamber mattered. Soon the quilt began to burn and they tossed it away. The city had grown so small it only included one room. Samuel kept his eyes open so that he could see Maria at all times. The world was her and her alone. He remembered the way she had leapt from the gallows, her eyes meeting his as he waited in the trees with his heart in his mouth, praying the rope was frayed properly so that the jute would split apart. The world ended and began when it did.

Do you know how much I wanted you, still want you, will always want you?

In the small bed, in the room under the eaves, she told him he must not love her. "If you want to live," Maria said, "you must stay away from me. That's why I always tell you to leave."

"That's the only reason?"

"You're very annoying, it's true."

They both laughed.

"As are you," he said, his arms around her.

He was convinced what they did didn't matter. He was ruined already. What sort of curse could be worse than the way he'd been cursed on that burning day in Portugal? Let his life be over if it must be, let the last thing he see be the rain on the window glass, the white plaster walls, Maria's black hair falling over her shoulders, the line of daybreak over Manhattan, a sky that was the purest cobalt-blue, the blue of heaven, which, no matter what they might wish or what they might do, signified the end of a night of love.

The old man knew about them. He often didn't remember what year it was, or what country he was in, but certain things were unmistakable and unforgettable. The sounds of love, for instance, were obvious. He heard them at night, and was glad that his son could find pleasure in this cruel world. Now Maria was late to breakfast, and Abraham chuckled to think of the reason. He was sitting at the table, having managed to get himself down the stairs. The black dog and he were both waiting to be fed. They were patient even though the hour for breakfast had long passed and their stomachs grumbled. On most days, Maria was awake long before the old man rose from bed, while the morning was still dark. But today the sun had been up for hours, and the old man and the wolf were still waiting.

When Maria finally came downstairs she was wearing her black dress, neatly buttoned. She had taken the time to comb the tangles from her hair and she had washed her face with black soap. She looked refreshed even though she'd barely slept.

"I thought I heard something last night," Abraham said when Maria finally came downstairs. "Very late, when people should be asleep."

"You heard nothing," Maria insisted as she boiled water for Abraham's tea. Abraham Dias liked his tea strong, with a slice of lemon when Maria managed to find one of those precious citrus fruits at the market stands.

"I know what I heard. Maybe now he'll stay." The old man always had bread and butter in the morning, which Maria set before him. Keeper was fed a portion of meat and bones.

"He won't."

"New York would be good for him," the old man insisted. By now, Samuel Dias was a wealthy man and could easily turn his attentions to another line of work, one that was within the realm of the law. He could import rum from Curaçao, or bolts of silk from France; he could find himself a warehouse, and an office nearby if he lived on Maiden Lane. "If he were here, you'd know when he was coming down with the fever. He'd be in your care."

Maria threw Abraham a look. "That won't happen," she assured him, brewing herself a cup of Release Me Tea, a mixture that loosened love's hold on a person, especially when combined with bitters and fresh radish root.

"He could be convinced," Abraham said. "Especially if you helped me do so."

In Abraham Dias's opinion, if a man had to live on land, there was no better choice than Manhattan. Portuguese Jews from Brazil had come in 1654 when Portugal reclaimed Brazil from the Dutch, bringing the Inquisition with them. These original Portugals were greeted by governor Peter Stuyvesant, who had been unwilling to accept the group of twenty-three souls with no country and no home until he was pressured to do so by the original owner of the house on Maiden Lane, Jacob Barsimon, who had worked for the Dutch West India Company. The new immigrants were not allowed to build a synagogue, but the men met daily, and Abraham Dias had gone to these gatherings on Friday evenings in a small house near the harbor. In 1655 Jewish taxpayers had paid for nearly ten percent of the price to build the wall, later the site of Wall Street, to separate the city from the wilderness beyond. Although they were outsiders, Jews were watchmakers, tailors, butchers, importers of rum and chocolate and cocoa. Manhattan was a tolerant city, and if you didn't provoke your neighbors or call attention to yourself, you could do as you pleased and worship as you liked.

"Let your son be who he is," Maria told Abraham. "A man who lives at sea."

"A man can change," Abraham Dias assured her. After all, he was about to plant vegetables in the garden, his hands deep in the earth, which, at this late date, he found to be an unexpected pleasure.

Maria went to the North River on the west side of the city to buy haddock and cod so she might simmer a broth of fish bones for Samuel's supper, to strengthen his constitution. He had been healing all through the month of his recovery and was much improved. In the afternoons he sat in the garden with his father in the pale green sunlight, listening to stories he'd heard dozens of times before, and enjoying each one. He'd recently helped his father put in a row of lettuce, which distressed Maria. Why would Samuel bother with planting vegetables when he wouldn't be there to see them grow?

She predicted he would be gone by the end of the week, and once away from her, he would be safe. The *Queen Esther* was docked, and it was likely most of the crew had begun to run out of funds and would soon be ready to be back at sea. If Maria wasn't mistaken, she could see a flicker of longing for the sea in Samuel's eyes when the wind picked up and the sea chilled the air, a hunger for his old life in which he didn't have to sit at the dinner table at an appointed hour, here where the stars weren't half as bright as they were out at sea. He was drawn to the harbor, where he stared out beyond Hell Gate. New York was blue and gray, a city surrounded by water, which called to him even though he wished to stay. The broad North River, later to be renamed the Hudson, ran two ways: seawater rushed to the north; fresh water flowed into the ocean. It was a river that couldn't make up its mind, and Samuel appreciated that. He was born under the sign of water, and was himself often of two minds. He yearned to leave and he didn't want to go. He had recently constructed a boat out of parchment by folding it this way and that for Maria's amusement. Men on ships found all sorts of entertainments to while away the hours at sea. How to make a valentine out of shells, how to turn paper into cranes and birds and fish and boats, how to tell stories, how to be completely silent. When Maria set the paper boat in the river, it had turned one way and then the other. In the end, it did not set forth on either tide, north or south, but instead continued on in a circle until Samuel plucked it from the sea. It was a sign of his own indecision. On some mornings he packed his bag, on others he could not imagine ever leaving New York.

At the Fly Market on the far end of Maiden Lane, Maria noticed a person of interest farther down the row of stalls, buying lemons at the fruit stand. The shopper was an elegant woman who wore an embroidered mauve dress stitched in France; her pale hair was caught up with small combs, all of which were blackened silver. A small white dog followed at her feet, devoted beyond all reason. If Maria wasn't mistaken, the woman wore red boots.

"I wouldn't look at Miss Durant for too long," the fishmonger warned Maria as he weighed out haddock. "It wouldn't be wise."

"Why is that?"

Maria wore a black veil over her face whenever she was in public. On the day when she finally found her daughter, she would throw the veil away, or burn it over a pile of sticks, or tear it to shreds. For now, it had its desired effect: people steered clear and avoided her, for no one wished to step too close to tragedy. And yet there were still those who took pity on her, the fishmonger among them, for she was unmistakably a woman in mourning.

"Catherine Durant is an enchantress," the fishmonger confided in a low tone as he nodded

323

to the other shopper. "You might call her a witch."

"Is she?" Maria craned her neck to see, for the woman they spoke of was already leaving, her back turned to them. Her little dog gazed at Maria with bright eyes before hurrying after his mistress.

"I sold her fish she said wasn't fresh, and for the next two months I didn't sell another thing," the fishmonger went on. "Not a scrap or an ounce. People walked by as if I was invisible, and those who saw me held their noses, as if my wares stank. So I had a bushel of mussels delivered to her house, and after that it was business as usual. Now I send a gift of mussels or clams to her on the first of every month. It's worked out well for both of us."

Maria soon made her way to the fruit vendor, but before she could choose any of the produce, he handed her a satchel.

"Sir," Maria said, surprised by his forwardness. "I don't yet know what I want."

"It doesn't matter. She knows." He nodded in the direction in which the woman had disappeared. The vendor looked sheepish, but when a witch suggested you do something, it was best to comply. Inside the satchel were ten apples, already paid for, shiny red. "She said to bake a pie."

"Did she?" Despite herself, Maria smiled.

Someone had seen her for who she was, most likely a sister in the Nameless Art.

"She said you wouldn't regret it. And to bake one every week and set it on your windowsill."

If this was magic, it was made of simple, practical stuff. All the same, Maria went home and cut up the apples, then made a crust. She rolled out the dough, and when she added the apples to the mix, the white slices turned crimson. Perhaps the fruit was not as ordinary as she had first thought. She felt her hopes rise as the pie baked in the brick oven beside the fireplace as she sent a message to Faith, wherever she might be: *Do what you must until we are together again, but never believe a word she tells you. Believe only in yourself. You are my daughter and mine alone, whether we are together or apart.*

When the pie was done, Maria let it cool on the windowsill. It sat there, red as a heart, the crust brown, perfectly done. From then on she baked a pie each and every week, with apples that turned from white to red. People passing by sniffed the fragrant air and were reminded of home, and many longed to find their way back to their loved ones. That was all Maria wished for. That was all she wanted in the world. To look out her window and see her darling girl, to have her walk up the stone path and fling open the door.

II.

In a place called Kings County, originally called *Breuckelen* by the first Dutch settlers, newcomers arrived to find a land of marshes dotted by snow-white clouds where the horizon reached out in bands of blue until at last it met with the sea. This low land had reminded the Dutch of home, and many had sunk to their knees and wept upon their arrival in this wild place where the sky was filled with ducks and geese, and fish jumped in the streams. Rough workingmen, both farmers and fishermen, established the original villages on land where the native Lenape people had once lived, before they were slaughtered and driven out, first by the Dutch, then by the British who replaced the original invaders. In a world that had begun with murder, there was always cruelty, despite the beauty of the shore and the sea.

There were five towns originated by the Dutch in the county, and the sixth, Gravesend, was populated by those who wished to disappear from their previous lives. It was built in 1645 on a parcel of land originally belonging to Lady Deborah Moody and her son, Sir Henry, both of whom had fled from the Puritans of the Massachusetts Bay Colony in search of religious freedom. Lady Moody had been fortunate enough to have the Crown grant her a small wedge of Kings County. She'd begun her life in England, close to royal life, and had happily ended her time on earth in Brooklyn, where she'd been free to do as she pleased and had been buried in the one cemetery, at the end of an Indian path. Her son had disappeared. Some people said he'd been buried beside his mother, others vowed he'd left for the unknown territories in the West, and that he preferred native people to Englishmen.

The original settlement had been destroyed by the war-ravaged native population, who had lost more than a thousand to the Dutch aggression and hundreds more to the British, though they did their best to fight back. In the end, they were defeated, and their population had all but vanished. When Faith was brought to Gravesend, it was the farthest outpost of what was called the Flat Country by detractors and admirers alike, populated by hardy souls who did not fear isolation. Martha Chase paid a pittance to the village elders for the use of an abandoned house overgrown by weeds and vines. She wished to be in a place that was on very few maps, and the farther she was from the crowds of Manhattan the better, for all the previous year there had been an epidemic of yellow fever which had killed ten percent of the population. Gravesend was cold in the dead of winter with ice coating the cattails and reeds, and it was equally hot in the blazing summer when the sun beat down. Their house was far enough from the village so that hundreds of gulls and terns wheeled across the sky all through the day and not another sound was heard. It was a worthwhile spot, for they could fish in the streams and have a garden, though the sandy soil was a trial. It was easy enough to hide away in this desolate location where there would be few questions asked concerning the girl with her hair dyed pitch-black from a tint of crushed inkberries and the boiled bark of a black walnut tree, a quiet, thoughtful child who didn't resemble the pale nervous woman who insisted Faith call her Mother. When Faith repeatedly told her she already had a mother, Martha Chase calmly said that Maria hadn't wanted her, and had given her to Martha, otherwise she would have been in a workhouse. Faith wept at night; when she looked at the inky sky she wished for a sign that her mother still loved her, in her dreams or in her waking life, which would let her know her mother was still thinking of her.

By the time they had arrived, Brooklyn was populated by two thousand souls, and although it was set just across the river from Manhattan, it was a world away. When they'd first left Massachusetts, Faith had been told there were evil people who were chasing after her and that they must escape or the devil would have them.

Faith's mother would approve of their move to New York, the girl was told; after all, she had given her only child to Martha for her protection and wasn't that proof of her wishes?

Faith might be in disguise, but she was who she was, and her natural inclinations arose time and time again. When she closed her eyes and sang a song in a language Martha had never before heard, a soft green rain would begin. When she whistled, sparrows came to sit in the palm of her hand. She could foretell storms and sunny weather, light a candle with her breath, find drinking water merely by following its scent, and Martha once heard her speaking to her mother, asking Maria to please come and find her.

Martha had heard that there were ways of curbing magic, and that witches had an aversion to iron, for it took away the sight and was the element that decreased their powers. After Faith picked a flower that bloomed in the palm of her hand out of season as she stood in the snow, Martha had a blacksmith come to solder iron bracelets around Faith's wrists. It was costly, but worth it as far as Martha was concerned. In a proper, pious household, any form of blasphemy could not be allowed.

"This is so I can always find you," Martha had said, to comfort Faith when the torch stung, but the truth was she wanted to make certain that Faith would not escape.

After the bracelets had been locked onto her wrists, Faith felt a pale dullness inside of her. She could no longer call birds to her or see what was to come. She could not make the clouds move or ask the sky to rain. When she dipped her hands in the streams, the fish swam away from her. She was a prisoner, without talent, without hope. But at night, she was free to dream, and in her dreams she saw her mother crying as she stood beside a flowering tree. That was how Faith knew that her mother was still alive.

She hadn't been forgotten.

They had traveled constantly at first, living in lower Manhattan, then on a farm in the settlement of Bergen in New Jersey, a place plagued by mosquitoes and lawlessness. Wherever they went, the door was always kept bolted to ensure that none of the bad people from Massachusetts would snatch the child. Who these bad people were, Faith had no idea, for all she could remember was a loving mother, a man who told stories when she was little more than a babe, and a black dog that followed her faithfully. And yet she was told they must always remain in disguise to protect themselves. Martha called herself Olive Porter and Faith had a new name each time they moved, even though changing a person's name was known to bring bad luck. She had been called Temperance, Charity, Patience, Thankful, and Verity. When she was alone, she wrote down these names in black ink, then crossed them out with thick blotchy lines, as if doing so could block out her false identities.

At last they had come to Kings County, where the blue air tasted like salt and seabirds dropped clams onto the dirt roads to crack them open to feast upon. It was the last outpost, and the place where they would stay. As always, Faith was made to call the lady who took care of her "Mother"; the word continued to stick in her throat. She was certain that if she waited long enough her true mother would find her, and that one bright morning when she opened her eyes, Maria Owens would be there.

Faith had turned nine when they first came to settle in Gravesend, the land of seabirds and outcasts. There were few outsiders who passed through this place, and most residents who abided here had reasons to be in a town that seemed to be perched at the end of the earth. There were husbands who had quit their wives, and women who'd been cast out, and robbers who were tired of running from the law.

"We'll be safe here," Martha told Faith, although safe from what, Faith wasn't quite sure. She was now called Comfort, a name she despised, not that there were many to call her by name. Quiet was a certainty here, and it was possible to be alone for weeks on end, whether one was walking along on the dirt roads or through the sandy fields. Other than the changes in the weather, each day was the same as the one before and the one to come. People in town waited for the peddler, who appeared on the last Friday of the month, and all were excited to see an outsider. They went to him for bolts of fabric or nails or pots and pans and would have to go without until he appeared, for no storekeeper had found the courage to open shop in this remote location.

Faith Owens could spy the sea from her room in the attic, where the previous tenant had died of the fevers, for in this low-lying land there were clouds of mosquitoes drifting by on summer nights. One out of every three children born out here would be dead before a first birthday was celebrated, and several of the women in town wore mourning black no matter the year or the season. As the years passed, Faith had more questions all the time, but because she dared not ask, they went unanswered. If Maria was alive, why hadn't she come after her? Where was her loyal wolf-dog who would never leave her side of his own volition? Why must Faith not show the true color of her hair? Ever since that day when the constables came to call in Essex County, her life had been torn in two. There was the *before,* when she'd lived with her mother, and the *after,* the time that had accrued ever since Martha had taken her aboard the ship bound for New York, leading to these years in Brooklyn.

Faith often walked to the end of the old Indian path, which led past the cemetery. She left seashells to decorate Lady Moody's grave, for she felt this Englishwoman who had made her way in this wilderness to be a kindred spirit. On the shortest night of the year, she left the house after dark when there were only patches of silvery light slipping through the clouds. She brought along a white candle to honor the town's founder. Never hide who you are inside, she'd always been told, but all that she was had been hidden, even from herself.

By now Faith understood that she was living a lie. Over the years, she had slowly gained her foster mother's trust. She was always well behaved and did as she was told without complaint. She didn't talk back, and when they went into town on the day the peddler came, she knew well enough not to talk to strangers. Martha Chase told Faith that she was the perfect child, and if being perfect meant she could see into Martha's bitter heart and know she was deceitful, then perfect was what she was. By the time she turned eleven, Martha agreed to let Faith be called Jane, a simple name Faith far preferred over Comfort, which made her feel as if she were a blanket or an old dog. In time, Faith was allowed to wander the beaches, and even to go into the village on the last Friday of the month when the wagon came to town. She stole pennies from Martha and bought a hand mirror from the peddler, an affable English fellow named Jack Finney, a modest individual who had few attachments in the world and wore a shabby blue jacket and boots that were too large for his feet. Faith asked if she might have a bit of black paint, which she used to coat the glass, and when the paint dried she peered into the dark mirror. There was her mother, in a black dress, crying in the night. There was her dog, standing at the gate. She dreamed that her mother spoke to her: *Do what you must until we are together again. But never believe a word she tells you. Believe only in yourself. You are my daughter and mine alone, whether we are together or apart.*

Whenever she could, Faith did as she pleased. She bought old water-stained volumes from the peddler, and she could often be spied with her parcels, walking the lanes while reading a book, which she made sure to hide before Martha Chase could catch her. As far as Martha was concerned, one learned to read only to have access to the Scriptures; all other reading was the devil's work, inflaming men's imaginations with stories that weren't true and ideas that could lead a reader to a path of rebellion. A streak of independence and a curious mind meant trouble. In Martha's

335

opinion, a woman who spent her time reading was no better than a witch.

Martha Chase believed in evil. She was absolutely certain that it walked alongside them every day, on the road and in the fields, tempting them to leave the grace of the Lord. Witchery was a brand of wickedness Martha had hoped they'd escaped when they left Massachusetts, for in that colony witches were born and bred. She would have been stunned to know that Faith climbed out her window at night to go to the graveyard. Faith had set up a kettle in order to make the black soap her mother had been known for. She bought or pilfered ingredients that she remembered as useful from the time when she'd watched Maria practice the Nameless Art. Ginger, lemon, salt, the bark of the elm, chokeberries, cherry pits, white candles and black candles, black fabric, red thread, blue beads, feathers, wild belladonna which was dangerous and agitated the spirit, bright yellow-green ferns, for lightning never strikes where ferns grow. She'd begun to trade her soap for books and herbs, and Finney, the peddler, said every woman who bought a bar of the fragrant black soap had returned to beg for more.

On Saturdays, Faith sat with Martha to read from the Geneva Bible, the Scriptures that formed all Puritan beliefs. She always washed her hands and face before they read, so as not to smudge the pages. In Martha's eyes, Brooklyn was a land of disbelievers, where all denominations other than Quakers were welcome to own land; there were Dutch Reform Protestants and some Catholics, and even, some people said, a few Jewish families from Amsterdam. It was a free and wild place compared to the Massachusetts Bay Colony, and one had to keep watch at all times to remain on the narrow path.

Faith looked unnatural with her black dyed hair and the oversized gray dress her foster mother insisted she wear at all times, along with a pair of heavy black boots that she kicked off whenever she walked to town, preferring to go barefoot. People considered her to be the oddest of creatures, a well-mannered girl, sure enough, with unnatural raven hair and pale eyebrows, who always had her nose in a book. When she wasn't reading, she was talking to herself, reciting recipes to make certain she wouldn't forget them. Be True to Me Tea, a boon for lovers; Travel Well Tea, a tonic for good health on a journey; Frustration Tea, which granted good humor and cheer even on the outskirts of Kings County; Clairvoyant Tea, concocted from mugwort and rosemary and anise, which helped the drinker see beyond the curtain of the here and now; and Faith's favorite, Courage Tea, which provided bravery and grit and was made of vanilla and currants and thyme. Every time Faith recited a remedy, she felt a thrill, as if she were unlocking a door to her true self. Whenever she did so, the iron bracelets burned and chafed, but she had learned to ignore them as a dog ignores its collar and a horse its reins.

Faith was walking through town one afternoon on her way home from seeing the peddler, a treasured new book of Shakespeare's sonnets in hand, when she heard sobbing. A woman stood outside a small cottage with a tilted roof, convinced that her child would die of the wracking coughs that plagued him. In that instant, Faith remembered a cure for this affliction. She'd only been six when she was taken from her mother, but she had always paid attention when the Nameless Art had been called upon. She ran back to the peddler and asked him for quince seeds and honey, which she heated on a stove in his wagon.

"What is that supposed to be?" the peddler asked.

Jack Finney had grown fond of this odd girl through his dealings with her, for she had an endearing sort of charm. In his travels, he always looked for editions of books she might favor. He was a Cornishman who'd come to this country with nothing, after his wife and child had died of the pox. He'd wanted to be as far away from England as possible, but now he felt lost in this vast, flat land of Brooklyn, and it was a pleasure to speak to someone with whom he felt at ease.

As far as he could tell, the girl was an outcast just as he was, a loner by nature or by design. Though she was now eleven, and had lived at the end of the world for nearly three years, she was less a child than anyone of her age the peddler had ever seen. She spoke with assurance and without the vanity and self-centeredness of childhood. Faith bit her lip when she was thinking and narrowed her eyes, and now she paid strict attention to the concoction on the stove.

"It's a remedy," she told Jack Finney. "If you let me have one of your glass jars, I'll tell you the secret."

She went on to teach him how to cure a cough. He wished he'd been aware of this cure when he'd had a child of his own who'd been ill with a similar disease, heartbreaking to watch when at the very last his daughter could not draw a single breath.

Finney gave Faith a jar with a cork top for her mixture. "How did you learn all this?" he asked.

Faith shrugged. She remembered bits and pieces, and sometimes whole spells, but the truth was, she'd been born with the knowledge. She returned to the house where she'd seen the crying woman, then knocked at the door and told the distraught mother that a spoonful of the tonic given twice a day would stave off the boy's coughs. The woman was suspicious, but after Faith went on her way, she tested the cure by tasting a spoonful herself. There were no ill effects, so she gave a dose to her son. His coughing stopped that very night, and before long he was out and about, healthy as anyone.

The women in Gravesend took note of the child's healing. Though Faith was only a girl, they began to seek her out. Perhaps she was too young to be a proper witch, but she seemed to have a natural talent for the Nameless Art. In time, people in need knew where to find her, within the cemetery gates on Friday evenings, the traditional time for working love spells, mirror magic, health tonics, and potions for reconciliation. Faith often suggested castor oil, milk, and sugar, a children's tonic her mother had fixed in Boston, along with summer savory for colic. She made most use of the recipe for Fever Tea, to nip high temperatures in the bud, made of cinnamon, bayberry, ginger, thyme, and marjoram.

Faith climbed out her window no matter the weather, as soon as Martha Chase was in bed, for she hated to disappoint one of her clients, some of whom waited hours for her to appear and came from the far-off towns of Bushwick and Flatlands. Faith had recently bought a black book from the peddler to use as a journal. Finney had added a small bottle of ink and a pen, and she'd written down all she could remember from the nights when women in need came to her mother's door. How to end toothache and insomnia and skin rashes, how to cast away bad dreams and regret, how to make amends, how to find happiness.

For her services, Faith was paid whatever a client might have. A bag of apples, forks and spoons, coins, pies, and once she was granted a pair of heavy black stockings. The payment didn't matter. What mattered most was that Faith was still herself, even though the iron bracelets kept her from using her full talents. She had to trust in what her clients told her, for she was unable to read the lines on their right or left hands, the first of which, she remembered, revealed the future you are given, the other which allowed you to view the future you made for yourself.

By now, Faith Owens had grown into a gawky, tall girl, and the iron cuffs dug into her flesh. She wondered if without them she might be able to fly far from here and find her mother. She knew the map of the sky and could chart the world, north and south. She'd once known a man called Goat who could divine the stars and had pointed them out to her. Faith considered running away, but she didn't know the name of the place they had come from so that she might return, only that there had been a bottomless lake nearby, and a water serpent who ate bread from her hands, and a wild black dog she'd found in the woods who never left her side.

Most of those who came in search of Faith were illiterate, and the fact that she could not only read and write, but could recite passages in Latin and Greek that she'd taught herself, amazed the women of Gravesend. As it turned out Faith had a prodigious memory and could recall the charms of Agrippa and Solomon that had been written down in Maria's *Grimoire*. It was clear that sorcery was second nature to her. In New York magic was not outlawed and magic books were sold on the streets, hidden inside black covers, available at a high price for those willing to pay. It was possible to find copies of *The Greater Keys of King Solomon*, the conjurations and curses and spells written out by hand, explaining the knowledge and wisdom of that ancient king. *The Mystical Alphabet*, *The Mystical Seal of Solomon*, *The Pentacles of Solomon*, along with *The Lesser Key*, a *Grimoire* written by Cornelius Agrippa, a most secret explanation of the mysteries of mankind and nature—all could be found, if one knew where to look. Finney had managed to get his hands on a few of these books, but the prices he quoted to Faith were too dear. She had to depend on her memory and the notes she jotted down in bits and pieces in her black notebook.

I am with the All and the All is within me.

The letters flickered on the page and then disappeared, but when she ran her hand over the parchment she could feel them. In this way, alone and abandoned, shackled by metal cuffs she could not remove and pretending to be someone she was not, she began her practice of the Nameless Art, for one does not have to have the talents of a witch to be called to the Art. She simply has to have the desire to see beyond what is right in front of her.

Martha Chase had planted thirty raspberry bushes when they came to Gravesend, but the soil was too sandy, and one by one the plants had withered until there was only one spindly specimen left. Faith had been given her own patch of land, and despite the soil, her garden grew so well it would not keep within the bounds of the fence that kept the rabbits away. Rabbits were everywhere in Brooklyn, and there was a place near the sea where there were so many of the creatures that the land there was called Rabbit Island. There were deer and turkeys and all manner of wading birds and ducks in the marshes, but the land itself was fairly barren. It was a miracle that Faith's garden was such a marvel. She grew feverfew for health, rose hips and skullcap for healing, lavender for luck. She'd plucked wild black nightshade to start from seed. Martha spied it snaking out of the ground, its black flowers already in bloom. She saw Faith standing among the blossoms, her dyed hair blue-black in the harsh light, her lips moving as she recited an incantation to Hecate, the ancient goddess of magic, who held power over heaven and earth and sea. Martha watched and grasped at her chest. Despite all her efforts she'd come to believe that Faith was permanently infected by her mother's blood, and even the iron cuffs were not enough to change who she was. The older the girl became, the more convinced Martha became that it was her duty to cure the child of her heritage. The daughter of a witch must be carefully watched. Once she planted nightshade, anything might happen.

III.

In the month of June, Abraham Dias went to bed and he didn't get up again. At first he tried; Samuel and Maria held him under his arms and lifted him up, but he soon sank back down, shaking his head. Abraham had no strength and no appetite for life. He knew this weakness, for he had seen it in others; it came at the end of life, it appeared that a person was giving up, but it was an acceptance of the end. He stopped eating, even refusing a bite of his favorite chocolate cake, and what was even more telling for a man of the Dias family, he stopped talking. That was when Maria heard the deathwatch beetle. She got down on her hands and knees to search beneath the furniture, then investigated the attic and every inch of the damp brick cellar, but she couldn't find the wretched insect. It continued with its clacking call, for once begun the sound could only be ended by a death in the house. Samuel hadn't stopped the deathwatch beetle by stepping on it outside the jail in Salem; rather, the beetle's death had foretold that Maria would not hang. This was not the case now, for the beetle didn't show itself, always a dark sign. She remembered Hannah searching the cottage at Devotion Field when she heard it, never managing to get it out

345

of the walls no matter how she might try, for it predicted the day of fire and destruction, when she was nailed to her own front door and her house was burned to the ground.

Maria turned to the book, reading the *Grimoire* for hours, trying every remedy that might help the old man regain his vitality. Vervain, feverfew, nightshade, horehound syrup. None of it worked. As Abraham's condition worsened, Maria was willing to delve into the darker magic that practitioners of the Nameless Art were taught to avoid, though she could find no death spells in the *Grimoire*.

That is not our business, Hannah had told her. *When you go inside darkness, the darkness goes inside you.*

She found the spell she was searching for at the very end of the book, on a page she had never noticed before. It was invisible without bodily fluid, but Maria could feel it there on the page, writhing, ready to be called up. She licked her thumb, then ran her damp finger across the page. The letters appeared in small, perfect script. *Do not use unless you must.*

When Samuel entered his father's chamber that evening, the scene he witnessed stunned him. They had never discussed where Maria had come from, or more importantly, what she was. Now it was clear; there was no mistaking witchery. Black candles were lit around the old man's bed, so many that the smoke scorched the ceiling and billowed into the corners of the room. A line of salt had been poured along the walls so that no evil could enter, and herbs were strewn over the bed. Maria sat before the old man, naked, slick with sweat, as she chanted an ancient spell so dangerous and powerful the words turned to ash as she spoke them and her mouth burned as she called to Hecate, the goddess of magic and sorcery and light.

Avra kadavra, I will create as I speak, I will force into being that which is impossible and illogical, all that is against the rules of men. A shield to prevent death, no matter how dark the results might be.

"Enough." Samuel Dias seized Maria from the bed and covered her with a blanket. He stomped on the candles as if they were bugs, extinguishing the flames, then opened the window and waved the smoke out. At last Samuel turned back to her. He wasn't often angry, but when he was, he burned. "Is my father an experiment for your Art?"

"It's a cure! When I cured you, your father was happy that I did. Why can't you be?"

"This is not the same! The only cure for old age is death. There are things you cannot change. That you should not change! We'll let him go, as he should."

Samuel was right, and she knew it. What was

forcibly brought back from death never came back as it was. One lived or died as fate saw fit. It was possible to shift one's destiny depending on choices that had been made, but some things were meant to be, they had been written and could not be unwritten. Abraham Dias's time had come. On both hands, his lifelines had reached the ends of his palms. Maria stopped fighting a war she couldn't win. She washed and dressed, then watched Samuel from the window as he sat alone in the garden, waiting to lose the last member of his family.

When it was clear that Abraham was about to die, Maria intended to call Samuel to his bedside, but the old man stopped her. He placed a hand on her arm and managed to speak. The man who could talk for hours at a time, and had taught his son to do the same, still had some breath left. When a person was about to die, nothing could prevent him from talking if he had something to say.

"I need you alone," he told her. "So you understand Samuel." Maria sat beside Abraham to listen to his last story, and she wasn't surprised to hear it was about his love for his son.

"My boy was eleven years old when it happened," he began. While he spoke, he appeared younger, as if he'd gone back to that time. "I will not begin to tell you how clever he was, every father will tell you that about his son. But I

348

will tell you that no one has as big a heart. The midwife told us so when he was born, she said it filled up his chest, and even before his birth, I could put my ear to my wife's stomach and hear it beat, it was so loud, I knew he would not be like anyone else.

"We were not home when the terrible thing happened. We had gone into the forest, to meet with the owner of a ship, a man who swore he would take us far from the perils of Portugal. Everyone wanted to go to Amsterdam, and we were willing to pay whatever was asked. It turned out the man we met was a liar and took our most precious belongings: a strand of gold that belonged to my wife, a silver prayer cup, and two strands of pearls my daughters were meant to wear on their wedding days.

"We rushed back home, expecting to fetch my wife and the girls so they could join us in the woods, but it was too late. My wife was taken; my daughters were gone. I told Samuel not to leave the house, but as you know he will never do as he's told. He went out into the square, searching for his sisters and mother. Our family had come to Portugal from the city of Toledo in Castile, Spain, then known by its Arabic name, *Tulaytulah*. We thought we would be safe in this new country, we had paid a high price to enter Portugal. Our family had been forcibly converted, but we practiced our religion in secret.

349

The madness continued, with *autos-de-fé*, mass murders of *conversos*. It was a world of black and gold and then a world of blood. Samuel saw everything that day. The hoods they made our people wear, the lashings they gave them, the fires that burned. Flesh became ash; body became soul. Afterward he did not speak, not a word.

"We stole the ship we were promised with the help of our neighbors who were to travel with us. I murdered the ship owner and his captain; I kept the crew who would be loyal to us and killed the rest. I made them jump into the sea and had no compassion when they drowned. That was what my life had done to me.

"Samuel sat in silence with the navigator, a Jew named Lazarus, and that was how he learned to follow the stars. I thought he might never speak again, but he did, almost two years later, soon after his thirteenth birthday. He had become a man while we were searching for a place where we might be safe. We went to Brazil, but the Inquisition had followed the Portuguese to the new land they had claimed. At last we made our way to Curaçao, where people such as ourselves were allowed to live. We were in shallow seas when Samuel jumped off the bow. He yelled out 'Look, Papa!' I didn't even recognize his voice because it had changed. He was a man with a man's voice, but he still had a boy's joy, for on this day he recognized the beauty of the world.

There he was, riding on a dolphin's back. I could hear him laughing. It was the day I had hoped for. I knew that as long as he kept talking he would be all right. That is why I'm telling you this, Maria. Don't let him be silent."

The old man had taken her hand in his. He still wore his wedding ring, for Jews had given such tokens to one another since the tenth century as a declaration of love and faith. His was decorated with Hebrew symbols for luck, fashioned out of gold filigree and blue enamel. It was his greatest treasure. He had worn it for so long he could barely move it past his swollen knuckle; now when he did there was a deep indentation around his finger, the mark of his married life. He asked Maria to give the ring to Samuel, then told her that after his death he wished to be wrapped in white cloth and placed into the ground without a coffin so that he might become one with the earth. He was accustomed to living on land. He had come to love New York, and the sea was only a memory. You never know what you want or need until you are old, for old age is a mystery that is impossible to unwind until you step into its maze. Thorn, blood, earth, love— that was the riddle that Abraham Dias held in his hand.

Maria wept as he was dying. Her tears burned her and left red marks on her face, and Abraham asked her not to cry. Instead he asked for some-

351

thing else, a last wish that could not be denied, one he had been thinking about every minute of every day during his last months. He wished for her to take care of his son.

"Of course," Maria assured him.

"I mean in every way," the old man urged. "The way a man needs to be cared for. With all your heart."

Maria laughed. "That is none of your business," she told Abraham in a firm, gentle voice.

"Love is my business," he insisted. "Long ago I was an artist. You didn't know that, and why should you? You don't know everything about me. That was what I did before I went to sea. I made the most beautiful marriage contracts that could be had. A bride-to-be would have her family pay any price for my work. I constructed them from a single piece of parchment that I cut into shapes and words with a small pair of shears. When the brides-to-be saw the documents, they wept. The grooms fell to their knees, grateful to be alive in the world. Believe what I say. I know about love."

Maria was forced to lean close, for she could hardly hear him. His voice was a whisper; it was leaving him now. The light inside him was rising up. She opened the windows so his spirit would be free once it left his body. *We are birds,* Hannah had once told her. *They sit inside of us waiting to fly away.*

"No one can fall in love with me," Maria told Abraham. "Don't wish that on your son."

"I know love when I see it," Abraham Dias insisted. "I see it in you."

He gave her his ring and told her the secret that he had learned about love during his time on earth. Then he closed his eyes. He had nothing more to say; he wasn't even in the room anymore, not in Manhattan, not in the year of 1691, not in a house on Maiden Lane. He was with his wife when he first met her. How beautiful she was, with her straight black hair that was so long she could sit on it, or wear it wound atop her head so that she looked like a queen who wore a dark crown. When you fall in love like that, time doesn't matter. This was the secret he told Maria, the last words he ever said.

What belonged to you once, will always belong to you.

Be grateful if you have walked through the world with another's heart in your hand.

Abraham Dias was buried in the First Shearith Israel Graveyard near Chatham Square, wound in white linen, as he'd wished to be, placed into his grave without a coffin so that he might become a part of the earth without delay. He had belonged to a congregation of Sephardic Jews who had wandered the globe, searching for a safe place in which to live and die. They had found what they were searching for in Manhattan. The burial took place on a blue June day, and the achingly beautiful weather made the loss cut more deeply. It would have been more fitting had there been rain or hail or black storms blowing in from the sea, a world from which a man wished to escape, not this perfect day. The women stood on the fringes of the gathering, their heads covered, and the men wore prayer shawls that their wives and daughters had stitched. The men joined in the mourner's Kaddish, the ancient Aramaic prayer Jews recited to honor the dead. Samuel Dias did not practice his religion, but with a borrowed prayer shawl over his shoulders, he, too, recited the Kaddish and sang laments in Portuguese, as his father had done on the night of their family's murder. Then he got down on his knees at the gravesite and wept. He had refused to shave and his hair fell to his shoulders; he looked rough, but he cried more than any man the congregation had seen before.

The unmarried women watched him, so moved by his raw emotion they felt their feet lift off the ground. How could a man feel so much? What else was inside of him? If only they could find out, if only they knew, a great mystery would be revealed to them. The married women gazed at their own husbands with disapproval, for the men looked away from Samuel's passionate display. It was too much for them, it was a story they had forgotten a long time ago, when they were thirteen and became men and locked their emotions away so they might navigate the cruelty of the world.

That night the house on Maiden Lane felt much too empty. Samuel had torn his clothes, as mourners are commanded to do. For seven days he sat outside, even when it rained. He wept until his dark, handsome face was swollen; he had stopped talking, as his father feared he might. Instead, he began to drink rum and he didn't stop, growing more silent and moody with every drink. When he finally came inside, Maria brought him his father's wedding ring, hoping it would start him talking. Samuel held it up to the firelight, squinting to see it more clearly.

"There's a reason my father left this with you," he said.

"Because he wanted you to have it."

Samuel Dias shook his head. He knew the way his father approached the world and he knew the meaning of the gift. This ring was a message, one he was grateful to receive. One he hoped Maria would accept. "No. He wanted you to have it."

Maria shook her head. "It's a family treasure. I couldn't possibly."

"If he wanted to give it to me, he would have placed it on my hand," Samuel said. "No. It should belong to you. We should do as he wished." Dias knelt before Maria and slipped the ring onto her finger. "This is what he wanted. For you to be mine."

She didn't wish to hurt him. "It cannot happen if I don't agree to it, and you know I can't."

"But you have agreed. See! It won't come off. We're married in my father's eyes," Samuel insisted. He was making a fool of himself, but he didn't care. "That's why he gave you the ring. That's our tradition."

Maria attempted to slide the ring off, but it was stuck; even when she took a bar of soap to the band, the ring would not move past her knuckle. It seemed impossible, her hand was so much smaller than Abraham's.

"The ring fits the person it should belong to," Samuel told her.

"Are you trying to annoy me?" Maria said.

Samuel shrugged. He didn't care if he was annoying. He'd certainly been called worse. "I'm trying to tell you the truth."

Rather than argue, they went upstairs. The bed was small, but it didn't matter. Rain began in the middle of the night, but they didn't care. Once more and then never again. That's what she told herself, but it was a lie and her mouth burned even though she didn't say the words aloud. He saw that she wore the sapphire and he laughed out loud. She was his, he was sure of it, certainly she was his in bed when she told him never to stop. But in the morning, as they sat across from one another at the table, Samuel took Maria's hand, and she drew away. She'd thought they had a tacit understanding. No love, no commitment, and certainly no marriage. He, of all people, should understand, for he'd been with her on her hanging day.

"You wanted me here last night," Samuel said. "Was that a favor because my father died?"

"It was a mistake," Maria said.

"Because of a curse?" He was as outraged as she'd seen him. "That's a fool's belief."

"Because words have power. And they can't be taken back."

Samuel Dias was a practical man, yet in his travels he had seen astonishing things he would never have believed could exist. Such miracles had changed him, convincing him that anything was possible in this world. He had seen golden lions sunning themselves on the rocks of the Barbary Coast, whales with long twisted horns floating under the sea, stars falling from the sky, parrots that could speak as well as a man, clouds of pink birds on the coast of Africa all taking flight at once, a woman with dark hair whom he wanted no matter what the cost.

"A curse can be broken," he told her, convinced that miracles were not so difficult to find.

She shook her head and refused to agree. Causing him harm was not a risk Maria was willing to take. "Sell the house or keep it. I can find somewhere else to live."

Dias talked for an hour, then two. He was good at it, and had learned from the best. He told her what it was like to stand in the woods and watch her on Gallows Hill; his heart had been ready to explode, it was a bird, he said, struggling to be free of the cage of his ribs to be beside her. But she told him that what was done could not be undone. A witch who cast a spell upon herself could not escape its chains with her own magic. No ritual she called forth could undo the damage. It had happened to her mother and now it had happened to her. There was only one woman she had known who would have been capable of undoing such damage, and Hannah Owens wasn't there to break the curse.

"If your answer is no, then you stay here," Samuel told her. "I'll go."

He wished that he had told her he loved her before her hanging day. He wished he had admitted that as soon as he knew, when he thought his life was ending in Curaçao and he realized that she was the miracle who had come to him. As they sat across from one another at the table, he gazed at her, doing his best to memorize everything about her. Her black hair, her gray eyes, the mourning dress she had worn since her daughter's disappearance with its mother-of-pearl buttons, her throat, her moon-shaped fingernails, her beating heart, her beautiful mouth. There was much he hadn't told her, hundreds of stories, perhaps a thousand, and it pained him to think that it was quite possible that he never would. He should have told the story of stumbling upon the magnolia, how he'd sunk to his knees and cried, overwhelmed by its beauty. He should have told her that while they were on the *Queen Esther* he'd wished they would never reach Boston, and how he had worried over her fate in Essex County, and how he would worry about her still.

He stood so quickly the chair skittered backwards and fell to the floor. "If you tell me to go, and you mean it, this time I won't come back."

Maria Owens looked away, and he had his answer.

She felt something pierce through her as she watched him go out the door and walk across the garden. Hollyhock, lilac, sunflower, lavender, thyme. There were all the trees he'd brought to her, each rarer than the next. If Abraham had still been among them, perhaps there might have been a chance for them; the old man was as persuasive as he was intelligent. As Samuel walked into the garden, he thought he glimpsed his father reclining in his favorite chair near the rows of lettuce and beans, but it was only a shadow. What was gone was gone. The ground was muddy, and the herbs in neat rows turned the air spicy and green. It was a good time of year to plant the tree he had brought from St. Thomas, ignored for as long as he'd been here, its roots wrapped in burlap, its leaves still coated with salt. It was not a magnolia, the one genus that might have convinced even the most contrary woman to fall in love, cursed or not. All the same, the roots of the Tree of Heaven would take hold long after the red flowers fell off and scattered. Samuel hoped it would tolerate the chilly climate of New York and did his best to help it do so, choosing a sheltered place beside the barn where it would be protected in winter. The mourning period had ended. For seven days Samuel had wept. He had torn his shirt and cut off his hair as offerings of his grief, which was twofold now. When it was time for him to leave, he did so. He left most of his belongings in the barn, for he didn't need much in the world. He didn't stop to say good-bye and he didn't plan on returning. There was nothing for him here without Maria. Still, all the while he was gone he would think of her and wonder why if she didn't want him she had stood at the door on that seventh day. If she had been another woman, he would have sworn there were tears in her eyes.

A witch's tears burn, they turn her inside out, they are not meant to be, and yet once they began they were difficult to stop. A witch could drown in her own tears if she wasn't careful; she could scorch the ground beneath her. As Maria watched

Samuel go, she was thinking of Abraham, buried a mile away, an expert on love, who had told her in the moments before his death that he saw love inside her. It looked like a dove, he said, but appearances could fool you. Some people mistakenly believed it was peaceful and calm, but that wasn't what love was. It was a wolf. If you open the door and call it inside, you must sink to your knees and say its name, you must do so whether you are cursed or not.

That was the mystery Abraham had come to understand. Always and everywhere, love was the answer.

PART FOUR

The Charm

I.

One morning Faith awoke to the scent of apple pie, the fragrance so strong she could have sworn that her mother was in the kitchen, baking her favorite treat. She looked out her window to see that her foster mother had pulled up all the plants in her herb garden by their roots, and was busily tossing them into a bonfire. Faith had carefully planted the ingredients for Courage Tea, currants and thyme, and now they were little more than twigs, along with all the rest. Martha hadn't worn gloves and her hands bled, pierced by thorns and brambles; all the same she ignored her wounds as the pious must, and stood close to the heat to make certain it flared.

When Faith came into the yard, she was distressed to see her ruined garden. She let out a sob that chased the sparrows from the trees, and a wind rose from the sea, filled with stinging salt. Martha grabbed Faith's hand and surprised her by stabbing her with the small paring knife she'd used to cut down the stalks that now lay in shambles. Two drops of black blood fell onto the ground, burning through the grass.

"It's still inside you," Martha cried when

confronted with this sight. After all she'd done to save the child, the girl was still tainted. She'd given up everything for Faith: her home, her house, her past. A bloodline witch could not be cured or changed or charmed or made to obey, even if she pretended to be perfect. Martha went upstairs to search the girl's room and soon found the black mirror and the notebook. She ripped the notebook into shreds, and when Martha broke the mirror, the glass shattered into a thousand black pieces, one of which stabbed her directly below her eye, leaving a small deep mark, as if she'd been pecked at by the beak of a bird. From then on the windows in Faith's chamber were nailed shut. Her door would be locked from the outside at night.

"I'm saving you from evil," Martha said to Faith calmly, when the girl raced up the stairs to see her room had become even more of a prison than it had been before. "Will you do as I say?" Martha asked.

"Of course, Mother." The words burned her mouth, for Faith was not a liar by nature and she didn't intend to follow this woman's twisted rules.

It was a Friday. Faith knew there might be women waiting for her that evening in the cemetery, perhaps they would stay until morning's first light if she didn't appear and they were desperate enough. She sat on the floor of her room, a prisoner, and yet even with the window nailed shut she imagined the scent of apple pie, made with cinnamon and brown sugar, a treat her mother would make especially for her on every birthday. Her true mother, the mother she had lost, the one who told her to always be true to herself, even if she had to hide that truth from others. Her life in Essex County came rushing back to her due to the scent of apples. She imagined the woods where the ferns grew so tall, and the bottomless lake, and the serpent that would eat bread from her hand. She recalled her mother's voice singing her to sleep, and the doll the man named Goat had made for her, and the wolf who had slept beside her bed, and her own natural red hair before it was dyed with bark and ink. She remembered the women who came to the door at night, and the tonics and spells her mother created for them, often asking nothing in return. Apples were used in many of these charms, the seeds worn in an amulet, or a red apple itself pricked with a needle while the name of one's beloved was repeated. A woman was then to sleep with the apple under her pallet, make a pie out of it, and feed it to the one she loved. Faith remembered the book in which everything she needed to know had already been written.

It was that night, while locked in her room, that she realized if she continued to obey Martha she would betray herself, perhaps even lose herself. She must do what she believed to be right. She would not spend another year pretending to be someone she was not.

It was the last Friday of the month, and she knew the peddler would be in Gravesend; perhaps he would help her. As soon as Martha went to bed, Faith took up a garden spade she kept hidden beneath her bed. She hit the cloudy window glass until at last it cracked beneath her touch. When she pushed it out, tiny glittering shards rained down into the garden. She threw down a satchel of belongings, then climbed down the vines, holding onto the prickly, twisted creepers. As soon as she touched the ground, she took off running. She knew where the peddler kept his wagon, and she rushed to the Indian path that led through the flatlands of Brooklyn where he and his horse were settled in for the night. Faith gave him everything of worth that the women of Gravesend had given her. Frankly, it wasn't much, and when she handed over the silverware she'd been given, she worried that he might reject it, for it had all turned black in her hands. All the same Jack Finney knew real silver when he saw it. He'd heard stories of women back home in Cornwall who turned silver black, and he knew what they were thought to be, but he was a practical man, and he stayed away from anything considered to be magic. He believed in buying and selling, and in taking good care of his horse, and in staying off the back roads at night, when robbers might be searching for a man such as himself who might have a tin box filled with silver and coins. He thought Faith was quite calm for a child who was running away, but he could tell she was serious. She slept in the wagon, beneath an old quilt he'd picked up when a recently deceased woman's belongings were sold at a good, cheap price. When Finney woke in the morning, Faith had already been up for hours.

"We have to leave right now," she told him. "We must be as quick as we can."

Martha had fallen into a deep sleep and dreamed she was tied to a chair and drowned in a lake. She was turning blue, struggling for one more breath. When she awoke she was drenched. Pools of water had formed on the floor around her bed. Some dreams connect to the past, some to the future, some to the very moment you are in. Martha went to Faith's chamber to find that the window was shattered. She peered outside to spy footprints in the sandy earth. They disappeared halfway down the road. Perhaps a wind had come up, or perhaps it was what occurred when a witch's foot wasn't nailed to the ground: she managed to escape. It was then Martha heard a clacking sound. It was somewhere in the wall, and when she put her ear to the plaster the clatter was so loud she felt deafened. She went downstairs and the clacking followed her, mocking her it seemed, tracking her like a dog though it was nothing more than a black beetle that had come out from the walls.

Martha grabbed her cape and left the house, the door swinging open behind her as she took off running. She wore the white bonnet she'd sewn years ago, in Essex County, and she spoke to the Lord as she raced up the lane, for she considered herself to be doing His work on earth. She refused to lose what she had gained and was ready to fight evil with everything she had. When she got to the Indian path, she saw the treads of the wagon and followed. Her breath rattled inside her. She had not come to the end of the earth here in Brooklyn to lose what she wanted most in the world, whether or not it rightly belonged to her.

By now it was early morning and the air was pale but growing brighter, throwing down bands of shadows and light. The peddler had stopped in the village to deliver an order of several bolts of cloth on his way out of town, for he would likely not be back to Gravesend for a long time, and the transaction—how much the fabric was worth was at issue—had slowed down their departure. Faith was anxious, her stomach a nest of nerves. As she waited, she bit off her fingernails, but knowing a

370

person's nails and hair could be used in a spell, she swallowed the bits of her nails, then felt them scratching inside her.

"That took long enough," she said to the peddler when at last he returned to the wagon. She already knew some things were not worth bargaining over, not when you were in a hurry, not when your future depended upon it. The air still smelled like apples, though there was not a single such tree in all of town, and Faith was aching to leave. She knew she was being called home. She thought of her mother's clear gray eyes and the song she had sung.

The water is wide, I cannot get oe'r it
And neither have I wings to fly
Give me a boat that will carry two
And I shall row, my Love and I.
Love is handsome and love is fine
And love's a jewel while it is new,
But when it's old, it groweth cold
And fades away like morning dew.

"Don't worry so much," Finney told Faith. He supposed he had no choice but to escort her. "We're on our way."

They headed through the flatlands as the seabirds were circling above the dirt road, dropping their breakfasts of mussels and clams so the shells would split open. Martha had been running through town when she spied the cart in the distance, as it was about to go over a small wooden bridge. She still heard the echo of that beetle in the wall, even out here where there was nothing but marshland. The sky was a brilliant blue, and foxes in the marsh were walking through the muddy shellfish beds, the vixens calling to their kits. Martha called out for the wagon to stop. When she shrieked, the foxes grew silent.

"What on earth?" Jack Finney turned to see what he at first thought was a ghost in a white bonnet, her gray cape flying out behind her. "Good God," he said, for she looked a terrible sight.

"Don't stop," Faith Owens told the peddler. She was changing the future right now, minute by minute. If she hadn't been wearing the iron cuffs, she would have seen the fate she had made in the palm of her hand, a path that led across a deep river. Though her sight was gone, her courage was not. She thought of the tea her mother often made her. *Never hide who you are. Do what you think you cannot.*

"If that's who you're running away from, I can't say I blame you," Finney said as he charged his horse to go forward. The horse was an old steed, one that had been treated cruelly before Jack Finney stole him, and Finney didn't regret his thievery for a moment. He'd needed a horse and he'd seen this one being beaten by a farmer on the shores of Gowanus Bay. The beast had one eye and a resigned expression. Finney, himself, never used a whip; all he need do was say a word or two, and the horse was ready to comply.

"Let's go," the peddler told Arnold, for that was the name of the horse, dubbed so because his shaggy white mane reminded Finney of an old uncle in Cornwall, a plodding kindhearted gentleman who could always be relied upon.

Martha was behind them doing her best to keep up with the carriage.

"You're stealing that child!" she called. "I'll have you arrested!"

Finney looked over at Faith, who was staring straight ahead, as if she couldn't hear the woman's voice. "I'd hate to be arrested," he said.

"You won't be," Faith assured him. She was more herself than ever, despite the iron cuffs. It was freedom that gave her a bit of the sight, it was the wind and the clatter of the horses' hooves, and the opportunity to say whatever she pleased without being punished for her thoughts. It was simple enough to see this Cornishman's fate. He talked about his homeland in his sleep. "I've seen your future and you live to be an old man in a place called Penny Come Quick," she told Finney.

He was a good man and deserved good fortune. In fact, he'd been born in what the Cornish

373

called *Pny-cwm-cuic*, a village on the Fal River, referred to as Penny Come Quick by outsiders. It was here that his wife and daughter had been buried, and his one wish was to return before he passed on, so that he might be buried beside them. He felt a chill along his backbone. No one on this side of the ocean knew where he'd come from. He thought perhaps he had a special little passenger. As a Cornishman, he understood there were those who had the sight, and this girl was obviously such a person. Whatever she was, he wasn't likely to let her fall into the hands of the shrew at their heels. He told old Arnold to race; all he need do was to ask him nicely to please gallop and the horse picked up speed. That was when Martha Chase tried to catch up, on the small wooden bridge where there was barely space for a carriage, let alone a woman charging ahead. Arnold was lumbering and huge, and there was not enough room for this woman to run past the carriage on the narrow bridge so that she might reach Faith. They heard her cry out, a sharp cry that chased the gulls from the marshes. The birds rose up in a flapping cloud of white and gray, circling in a swirl above them. There was a thud and then the shouting stopped.

Jack Finney called for the horse to halt, and Arnold complied, heaving from his exertions. Finney and Faith turned to look over their shoulders. Behind them the bridge was empty. There were hundreds of gulls still wheeling through the sky, as they often do when they spy something that might make a meal.

"Stay here," Finney told the girl.

The peddler climbed down and walked back to the bridge. He had long legs and he wore a brown jacket he'd had for nearly twenty years that had served him well. Finney was a rough man with a tender heart and he had a lump in his throat. He didn't need the sight to know that something was wrong. He put a hand over his eyes, for the sunlight was bright, and his vision wasn't what it once was. The peddler was forty, but he'd let himself go, for he'd had no reason not to do so, and the fact of it was, he drank too much. All he saw below the bridge was the brackish water and the weeds and the black stones and the sand, and then he saw that the water was red.

Finney went in, even though saltwater was bad for his boots. He turned the lady over, but it seemed she was no longer alive. There was blood coming from her skull, a small trickle that mixed with the water in a red swirl. A shadow fell across Finney and he gazed up to see Faith standing behind him, her face set. There was a white bonnet, floating downstream; there was the woman herself in the water, exactly as she had dreamed it, lying in the shallows beside the cattails that were as tall as a man.

Finney shook his head. "I told you to stay where you were."

"I thought you might need help." Faith gazed down at Martha. The bright light didn't bother her one bit. She could feel the cold water reaching up to her ankles. She didn't mind if her boots got wet.

"I think she's gone." Finney waited but Faith was stone-faced, and when there was no response he added wryly, "I can see you're broken up by the situation."

Faith was taking the opportunity to study Martha, something she had never dared to do before. She reminded her of the thin, tall, poisonous weeds that grew in the marshes and burned your skin if you tried to cut them down.

"Shall we bury her?" Finney asked.

"If you want to live long enough to go back to Cornwall, I suggest we leave her where she is." For an eleven-year-old Faith sounded very sure of herself. "If a sheriff is called, we should have the flatlands behind us when the body is found."

"It's not as if we had a hand in killing her. She's done that all on her own. I suppose we should feel sorry for her."

"She took me from my mother and locked me in a room. For five years I've been waiting for this day," Faith told her companion.

Finney felt it was their duty to honor the dead.

He dragged the body to the shallows and set her on the watery bank, beneath the bridge. It was the least he could do even though she was heavier than he'd imagined and he was sweating through his clothes. He felt as old as Arnold, who huffed and puffed at the end of the day.

"Perhaps we should say a word or two?" Finney asked Faith once he'd scrambled back up to the dusty road. The girl was still below the bridge, on the stony bank, the water running over her boots as she contemplated the scene before her. One of Martha's legs had been crushed by the wagon and was twisted underneath her body, her stocking torn off, her flesh white among the black stones.

"What you do comes back to you threefold," Faith recited. "That's what happened to this woman." Faith had a pretty, serious face, but that dyed black hair didn't look human and wasn't. She couldn't pretend to feel sorrow. Now that this day had come, it was no surprise that Faith had no feelings at all. It wasn't just the lines on her left hand that had changed.

"If what you say is true," Finney said, "this woman was evidently responsible for some terrible actions, for this is a terrible death."

"She made horrible jam," Faith said. "And she tried to have my mother drowned."

"That's enough for me." Finney felt lucky to have such a smart horse, and an even smarter girl beside him. It was only now that he was in constant conversation that he realized how much he had despised being alone. "We can leave her where she is and let her discuss her actions with the Lord."

"I'll take a minute, if you don't mind."

Finney nodded and walked back toward the wagon. Faith stayed there beside the creek while he hoisted himself back on the carriage bench and took up the reins. It was then that Martha spit out some water, which trickled into the rising tide. Faith didn't move or shout out. She had been told lies for so many years: why they had to leave on the ship to New York, how evil would find her if her hair was red, how her mother had never cared for her. Standing in the shallows, she closed her eyes and let the person she'd been forced to be go, that obedient girl Jane she'd pretended to be, who did as she was told. She breathed in the chill morning air, the salt stinging her lungs, and she might have forgiven Martha her wrongdoings, but she could not forget that she had been robbed of five years of her life. She would not allow another minute to be stolen. Inside Faith's mind Martha Chase disappeared, a shadow growing smaller until it was the size of a wasp, then a stinging ant, and then no size at all, a spirit vanished. A death wish can be a powerful spell, by witch or mortal alike, and Faith shook with the bitterness she felt and her willingness to ignore the rules of magic. If Martha wasn't quite dead yet, she would be by the time she was found, her eyes open, looking at the flat blue sky. And if she was aware of her surroundings at the very last moments of her life, if the black beetle crawled out from the folds of her clothing, if she called out Faith's name, no one would have heard, for the seabirds were screaming like mad and circling above and the tide was rising quickly, the way it does in the marshes, so that one moment it was possible to see a figure of a woman, and the next it seemed that a long gray dress was floating in the deepening water.

Faith climbed up the embankment, then hopped into Finney's carriage. The soles of her boots were covered with muck and her stockings were soaked. The lines on her left hand were changing before her eyes and she noticed a red splotch in the palm of her hand, as if Martha's death had marked her. She paid it no mind. The past was behind her now and the future lay ahead. And yet she blinked back tears, not for Martha, but for all the years that woman had cost her. Finney wasn't the kind of man to speak about such matters. Anyway, the likely cause was the bright Brooklyn sunlight.

"Where are we going?" he asked, practical as ever.

Faith's mouth was set. She might be eleven, but

she was extremely sure of herself. "To look for my mother."

Finney might well have argued against that notion. Brooklyn was a big place, but since this girl had shown herself to know more than most, he decided to do as she said. He found that he was suddenly more curious about the future, nearly hopeful, which was something he hadn't felt for many years.

"And what happens when we find her?" he asked.

"Then I'll be where I'm meant to be," Faith said. "And you'll be rich."

When they stopped for the night, Faith looked through the cart until she found a handsaw, which she quickly handed over to Finney. She nodded to the iron bracelets.

"Work away," she told him.

Finney took a step back when he realized that she wished him to saw through the iron bracelets she wore, fitted tightly to her wrists. He didn't have great confidence in the steadiness of his own hands. He often drank to forget, and had tremors, along with a lack of faith in himself. And he was a gentle man, who hated to cause anyone pain. He shook his head and put down the saw. "I might hurt you."

"I couldn't be any more hurt than I already am," Faith replied. "I lost everything. You're just helping me find it again. When we get to where we're going, you'll be rewarded. You'll have more than you've ever dreamed of."

"So you say." Finney laughed. "I assume you have hidden riches?"

"I assure you," Faith said, sounding insulted. "My mother will see that you're repaid."

When she stared at him so pitifully, he had no choice in the matter. Faith sat perfectly still, and if the handsaw nicked her now and again, she didn't wail or complain, not even when there was a line of blood, which was black and sticky and burned through the floor of the wagon. She had grown up drinking Courage Tea, and the effects of that brew had lasted. When the bracelets came off, blue marks circled her wrists, and where the skin had been pinched for so long there were deep indentations in her flesh. She would have these marks all her life, and they would serve to remind her of what some people were willing to do for what they told themselves was love.

Faith could feel her power increasing immediately. A breath, a sigh, and she was herself again. She glanced at the sky and knew it would rain if she wished it to. She gazed at Jack Finney and with the sight was able to see through him to the young man he'd been when he lost his wife and child; she saw the grief he carried with him in a tight web that sat beside his heart. When they stopped to rest, she spied the souls of the murdered Lenape, the original people who had lived in the marshes, for their spirits had gathered in the blue dusk and their weeping sounded like the cry of the seabirds. Faith was overcome with emotion, and if she'd been another girl she might have wept, but instead she walked out to where Finney couldn't spy her and she danced as the moon rose. She was herself again, it was true, but she had also been changed. Inside there was a line of bitterness that reached directly to her heart, so strong it brought her to the brink of tears. This is who she was: the girl who had climbed through the window to save her own life.

They stayed at a farmhouse on Rabbit Island, called Konijon Island by the Dutch and Coney Island by the English, referring to the ancient name for these creatures that was used in the King James Bible. It was here, near the seaside, where a Cornishwoman named Maude Cardy lived on her own. Although she and Jack Finney had forgotten how they were related, they had cousins who were cousins, and she always had a room for him should the need arise. Maude loved Brooklyn and how wild and lonely it was, for she was wild and lonely as well. She'd come across the ocean because of a man, but that affair had been short-lived, and many other men had been in her life; forty years had passed since she'd thought of that fellow, except once in a while when the tide was high or the moon was full she remembered to be grateful to him.

"Who's this?" Maude asked when she saw the strange dark-haired girl. Maude was suspicious no matter the circumstances, and wise to be so, for she lived all alone in this odd blue land where it was possible to see for miles and where robbers and ruined men had settled among the good people of Brooklyn.

"I'm his niece," Faith was quick to say. Her gray eyes gave nothing away, but for every lie she told a white spot appeared on her fingernails.

Maude pursed her mouth and studied the girl. She wasn't sure what she was looking at.

"That's who she is," Finney agreed, wondering how he'd ever gotten so involved when he'd spent all his years on this side of the Atlantic having nothing to do with other people.

"Is she now?" Maude had lost a few husbands and children herself and had a dozen nieces in Cornwall. She knew a bit about the world. There was something else at work here. "She doesn't look a thing like you."

"She's lucky, then," Finney replied. "The good Lord didn't make a mistake there."

That night Faith slept outside, so that she could see the stars. She thought of men and women who spent years in prison, unable to see the heavens. That did something to you; it drained you inside. In the morning, there were white and red roses growing in the place where Faith had slept; they had bloomed from the withered plants Maude had brought with her from England that had never grown well in the sandy soil. Maude had wondered about Faith from the start; now she was certain this was no ordinary girl. To be sure she was protected from any witchery, Maude carried a piece of rose quartz she had collected from the beach in Cornwall, a stone that is known to cure most ills. One look at the stone Maude Cardy had tucked in her sleeve, and Faith knew she'd been found out. It was best to make friends out of enemies.

"I'd like to repay you for letting me stay," Faith said to the old woman.

"Would you?" Maude said. "Can you make me young again?"

Faith gave her the last bar of the black soap she had made in the cemetery. It wasn't quite her mother's recipe, but it could take a few years off anyone's age.

"Well, I won't be twenty again using that," Maude said.

Faith couldn't debate that fact. "Then ask me for another favor."

And so the two went out in the dark of morning so that Faith could help the old woman chase the rabbits out of her garden. It was a thankless task; for every ten Maude had chased away, twenty more appeared. Because of these creatures, most of the farms here had failed.

"I can get rid of them, if that's what you wish," Faith said. "But once they're gone, they won't come back."

"Do so." Maude had her hands on her hips. "I won't miss them."

Maude noticed that where the girl's inky hair was parted there was a pale red line of color showing through. Red-haired people were said to have talents others did not. Perhaps this girl had a knack for making things disappear. The rabbits were multiplying as they stood there, and Maude was interested to see what this girl was capable of.

Faith put down salt around the garden as she spoke words Hannah had taught Maria, to keep unwelcome pests out of a garden. It was a Latin spell, and it sounded otherworldly spoken here in the flatlands. Coming from Cornwall, Maude knew something about the Nameless Art. She most certainly could spot a witch. As soon as the spell was cast, the rabbits moved on to Maude's neighbor's place, a good ten miles away. There were so many that the sandy ground shook as they ran east. Impressed, Maude invited Faith into her parlor, her best room, one Jack Finney had never set foot in, for there was a precious Turkish carpet there that was far too good for the peddler to stomp upon with his muddy boots. To

Faith's surprise, a black mirror was set upon a small wooden table.

"One favor deserves another," Maude Cardy said. "Perhaps you'd like to look into the future."

Maude came from a long line of what people called the cunning folk, not among those born to be a witch, but practiced in healing, descended from a tradition of women who could see what others could not. She'd sat at her grandmother's knee and heard about how to bring a baby along when it refused to be born and how to save a man in the throes of a fever.

Faith sat in a hard-backed wooden chair and gazed into the mirror that had belonged to Maude's grandmother in the time when not many could afford mirrors. It was an old piece, in use for more than fifty years, and though the glass was silvered and the black paint thick and peeling, its power was strong. Many women had seen what was to come when looking into it, for it was pure and asked for nothing in return.

Faith placed her elbows on the table, and looked down. Immediately she felt as if she were being pulled underwater. There was the lake with no bottom, and the serpent she'd fed crusts of bread, and the blue-green sea they had crossed while aboard the *Queen Esther*. There was the marsh where Martha Chase lay dying, her eyes fluttering open to see how bright the world was before she left it behind. In that black mirror,

Faith saw the time she'd been away pass quickly, like pages turned in a book, five years that had vanished in the blink of an eye. For all this time, Keeper had searched New York for her. He was full-grown now, not a leggy, skinny, half-starved creature, but her familiar, her heart and soul, in pain over his loss. When he howled at night, those who heard him shivered in their beds, well aware that there was never a dog that made such mournful cries. Faith could hear him now, across the water, her other, her familiar, who had chosen her.

She dove in deeper as she stared into the glass, so deep that all that she saw was underwater, both the present and the past. Floating there, between worlds, she could spy her mother in the silk mourning dress she had worn ever since she'd lost Faith, a black veil shielding her face. She saw Maria walking through the muddy streets, crying even though it is said witches cannot cry. They can, but doing so changes them, and leaves them unprotected, for that's what real love can do.

Faith was drowning in the black mirror, going deeper and deeper. She held her breath; she peered through the murk of the muddy currents. She had come to the river of hell, a dark, bottomless canal that was filled with bodies of those who could not swim. Faith might have never surfaced, she might have been trapped there inside her mind, drowning in that cold brackish place, if Maude Cardy hadn't grasped her arm and firmly pulled her away from the table.

"That's enough, girl," Maude said. "Let's get you back here."

Faith gasped, and when she did she spat out river water.

Maude went off to retrieve her smelling salts so she might revive the child. She returned to find that Faith was dripping wet, a pool of black water around her feet. Whatever she was, whoever she was, Maude knew she was powerful. The girl's face shone and her hair was damp. Faith's heart was pounding because of the flash of vision she'd seen. "Where did you go off to?" Maude asked the child.

"It's on the other side of the river that crosses hell," Faith replied. She had no idea where that was, only that her mother was there waiting. She'd been waiting all along. Faith didn't need any more answers. Her mouth was set and she felt fearless, as if she had consumed a pot of Courage Tea. She felt like a bird that was about to fly away from this cloudy blue countryside. "That's where I must go," she told Maude.

"I know the place," Maude informed her, pleased she could figure out the puzzle of the girl's vision. The East River was divided by Hell Gate, a natural rock sill where there were swift currents and jutting ledges that had caused many ships to sink and many men to drown. Still, it was the way to cross over to the docks that were teeming with sailors. "You'll be wanting to go to Manhattan," Maude Cardy told Faith. "And if anything's a vision, it's that city. Remember, once you're there, keep your purse closed and your eyes open and every wonder will be there to see."

II.

Keeper escaped from the yard one fine August day. One minute he was there, and the next he was gone. Maria went to search for him, at last spying the tracks of his huge paw prints in the muddy lane. He was heading east, to the riverside, a dangerous place populated by the sort of men it was best to avoid, sailors and criminals alike. Both Britain and France hired pirates to bolster their military, lawless men who dressed however they pleased, happy to offend those who believed men shouldn't dress in Persian silk and calico, and happier still to fight for whoever paid the highest price and to thoroughly enjoy their time in New York. The city's most famous pirate, William Kidd, was so devoted to Manhattan he'd had his men hoist the stones to build Trinity Church and would, in only a few years, pay for much of the first Anglican parish. But that didn't mean many of the others did as they pleased, and that the lawmen in New York had little hope of controlling such men once they went riot.

Maria followed along to Dock Street, the location of the first printing shop, then to Wall Street, the only paved road in the city, where a wharf had been built near Broad Street. The first coffeehouse in the city had opened nearby and there was a crowd milling around outside. Despite the strong aroma of coffee, it was still possible to smell apples, even here by the riverside, as if the scent of the pie Maria had baked that morning had reached this far and made people's mouths water.

Maria finally spied the wolf on a pier, not far from the ferry building. He was staring across the East River, alert, his hair standing on end. In his gaze was a ferryboat, so packed with passengers it appeared to tilt as it made its way past the currents of Hell Gate. The sky was bright blue and it pained one's eyes to stare into the shimmering distance; Maria shielded her eyes with one hand. She could spy the fading moon, still a white slip in the sky. A ferryman was perched at the edge of the dock, ready for the incoming boat, there to tie up the ropes when it docked; he kicked the beast at the edge of the pier, and shouted for the creature to get away, but Keeper stayed where he was, his lips pulled back so he could show his teeth to his abuser, making it clear that he could not and would not be moved.

Seagulls wheeled in the clear sky, their quick yellow beaks ready to snatch any fish they might spy in the flat water below. Maria dashed toward the ferry as it docked, elbowing past an unruly throng of people waiting for the boat to be unloaded so they could then have their turn to board and be taken across the water. She pushed back her veil, so she might see what was before her more clearly. And then she felt it; the heartbeat she had once carried. Her daughter, born in a circle cast for protection on the luckiest day of the month of March. The time had come. It was happening right now. Maria felt weightless, as though she were rising, as the first of the arriving passengers pushed and shoved to make their way onto the dock, alongside carriages pulled forward by teams of horses, some calm, others in a panicked state, desperate to get to solid land. There were wagons piled high with vegetables grown in the sandy flatlands, barrels of potatoes and cabbages, and men carrying bags of live chickens and ducks, and women who had never before left Queens or Kings county and now blinked in the mad whirl of Manhattan. The crowd disembarked, all headed in the same direction in a crush of flesh and blood, some ready for the chaos that awaited them, others cringing at the sight of the mass of humanity before them. None of it mattered to Maria. They might as well have all vanished. She saw not a single one.

The wolf bolted on board before the boat was completely unloaded, leaping onto the seat of a wagon before anyone dared try to stop him.

"Keep it moving or I'll charge you double," the ferryman called to the petrified wagon driver who now found a wolf beside him.

It was Jack Finney who sat motionless, a block of sheer terror in his chest, even though his young passenger laughed when the beast leapt up. She threw her arms around the wolf, insisting the huge, devilish creature in the wagon was a dog and nothing to worry over.

"He's mine," she assured Jack Finney. "And I am his."

Though it seemed madness to Finney, this girl could convince him of nearly anything, so the peddler clucked his tongue to urge his horse on, even though poor, gentle Arnold was shaking from the nearness of a predator.

From where Maria stood on the dock all she could see was the nervous Cornishman driving a wagon drawn by an old horse with one eye, and Keeper beside a girl who scrambled in order to stand on the seat of the wagon. Maria narrowed her eyes. This tall, angular girl had raven-black hair falling to her shoulders. She was pale and lanky and wearing a dress that fit like a sackcloth and fell nearly to her ankles. She was all arms and elbows and freckles, unfamiliar in every way, and yet she was calling out *"Mother,"* waving her arms as joy spread across her face. There was her darling girl, her vanished daughter, who now, five years after she had disappeared, stood on the carriage seat, a fearless eleven-year old who had gleefully journeyed through Hell Gate on an ordinary day when miracles happened.

• • •

In the time they'd been apart, Faith's gray eyes had paled to silver; her red hair had been dyed with ink, although a few blood-red hairs shone through. Her narrow, expressive face was marked by a sharp intelligence that included both wit and suspicion. It was possible to see the woman she would become, and yet something of the child she'd been when she'd been taken still showed in certain aspects of her features: her wide grin, for instance, and the brand of mischief in her eyes, the black mark of her bloodline on her left hand, which Martha Chase had tried her best to scrub away with the use of a stiff wire brush and lye soap, rubbing until Faith yowled with pain. Try as she might, none of Martha's efforts had made the slightest difference. When you are so marked, you are marked for life.

Faith climbed down from the wagon and raced to her mother, and Maria hugged her close. Her child smelled of salt, for she was still a girl of the flatlands, sunburned and wild. Yet in her mother's arms she was a child again. Maria might have never let go of her if she hadn't caught sight of Jack Finney climbing down from the wagon. She didn't take the time to look inside him, for the instant she spied him she imagined he'd had a part in abducting Faith. Maria ran toward him in a fury. Before he could step away, she held up a paring knife she always carried, so close to his throat he felt the blade.

"What you've done, you'll pay for," she told him.

"You have it wrong," Finney assured the outraged woman. He'd broken into a sweat, which made him appear to be a guilty man all the more. "I'm the hero," he said in a voice that wavered as he spoke.

"Don't bother to lie." The blade had already nicked Finney's throat so that a bead of blood oozed through his flesh. If he was a liar, he was a good one, for there were no white spots on his fingernails and no blisters on his tongue and she saw no evil within him. Still, he had her girl, didn't he?

Faith ran to her mother. "He *is* the hero." She spoke with the authority of someone twice her age. When a child is forced to save herself, she is a child no longer, and Faith had no issue speaking her mind, even to her mother. "He should be rewarded. Without him I'd still be in Brooklyn."

Maria apologized to the peddler, and was soon convinced to invite him to stay with them on Maiden Lane, for he had nowhere else to go and Faith was insistent that they treat him like family. Truthfully, she knew him better than she knew her own mother.

"Thank you. Much appreciated." Finney could use the rest, for sleep had eluded him ever since they'd left Gravesend. Each time he closed his eyes, he saw an image of the tall, awkward madwoman who thought she could outrace a horse over a narrow bridge. He couldn't help but wonder if she'd cried out at the moment she fell to the marsh below, and worse, if she'd still been alive when they left her there. That was the thing that haunted him. When he'd gone to peer down into the shallows, the woman was facedown, her gray dress and bonnet soaked with saltwater, unmoving. She didn't give any sign of life when he dragged her to a higher watermark. And yet, looking back on it, he could swear he'd seen the flutter of her back as she inhaled more water than air before he climbed back into the carriage to wait for Faith. *Go on,* Faith had told him. And he had. He had done as an eleven-year-old girl ordered him to do because she was fearless and he was not. Finney had actually been shaking as he stood there gazing into the creek. He knew the difference between life and death—a flutter, a heartbeat—and yet he had climbed up in his wagon and he hadn't looked back.

"What's done is done," Faith had told him when at last she'd scrambled back onto the carriage seat beside him, her boots and dress soaked, her hair streaked white with salt. He'd looked at her and nodded and knew it was likely they had killed someone. But the sky was blue and there were miles to go before they made their way across Brooklyn, and it was true, what was done *was* done and could not be undone.

Faith and Keeper walked side by side, completely at ease with each other. Maria had grown dizzy with emotion, but fortunately Jack Finney brought out smelling salts to revive her. "You'll be fine," he told her, but she wasn't as certain. It was a shock to see someone come back from the great unknown. What was gone could return, but not necessarily as it was.

"I assume she was with the lady who took her from me?" Maria asked once she'd recovered her senses. Finney had helped her into the wagon, and they followed after Faith, who seemed to welcome the mayhem of Manhattan.

"She wasn't a lady," Finney said. "I'd say she was more of a monster."

Maria looked at him more closely and she liked what she saw, a kindhearted, wounded man. Perhaps he was a hero after all.

"Anyway, the girl's the one who found me," Finney went on. "She's got the sight, you know."

"Does she?" Maria's back was straight. She had been taught never to discuss the Nameless Art with outsiders.

"I've known such people before, in the town where I grew up, but none as young as your girl. She's a special one. Seems it's in her blood."

• • •

When they reached Maiden Lane, the first thing Maria asked Finney was to build a fire in the yard, and as soon as it was lit, she tossed her mourning veil onto the flames. Without the veil, the light of day was so bright there were tears in her eyes. Finney led Arnold inside the barn and unhitched him from the wagon. Maria felt a tug inside her, thinking of the nights Samuel had slept there, and how long he'd been gone.

Maria and Faith sat in the garden as the fire burned and the sky darkened, together for the first time in five years, ill at ease, as if they were strangers. Now that she was in her mother's presence, Faith had questions, ones that had haunted her.

"Martha told me you gave me to her. You didn't want me."

"They had me in jail and she promised she would take care of you. She would do so until I could come for you."

"And you believed her?" Faith's eyes were narrowed, a suspicious daughter glaring at her mother. Somewhere inside herself Faith had always wondered if any of Martha's claims had been true. A monster makes you hers in small ways, each time she insists you must behave, you must not disagree, you must never show your feelings, and if you're not careful, you may start to believe what she tells you. *No one else wants*

you, no one else cares, you are nothing without
her, you are nothing at all.

Maria pulled at the collar of her dress so that Faith could see the mark of the rope. "They tried to hang me. I had no one to turn to and I didn't want you to be in jail."

"But I *was* in jail," Faith said softly, eyes shining with resentment. She was picking at the black mark on her hand, a nervous habit. "I couldn't escape." She held up her hands so that her mother could see the indentations from the metal bracelets around both wrists. "She had me in irons."

Maria blamed herself for all that had happened and mostly for trusting Martha, though it could be so difficult to see inside someone who was bound and determined to trick you, who hid her intentions beneath a scrim of false kindness. Even a witch can be betrayed.

Faith nodded to the barn, where Finney was seeing to his horse. "He was the one who sawed off the cuffs. That's why we must reward him. He deserves whatever his heart desires. You should see that he gets it. I wouldn't like to be thought of as a liar."

"Of course. I'll see to it." Maria had a strange lurching feeling in the pit of her stomach. Faith had power, that much was certain. This girl of hers was a complicated being.

Faith was thoughtful, biting her lip. "Does a

400

person have to pay for any life they've taken?"

Finney had begun to wash off the carriage, carrying buckets of water from the well. Maria assumed he was the reason Faith had asked about penance. "Did he kill Martha?" Maria asked.

"No," Faith said grimly. "It was me."

There was a film of black behind the girl's pale gray eyes, the mark of guilt. Still, she was a child.

"No," Maria said. "You didn't."

"I might as well have," Faith admitted. "I watched her die. I could have pulled her out of the tide, but I left her there to perish as it rose around her."

If anyone was to blame, Maria felt it was herself. She thought of the wax figure and the pins, and the fire that had melted it into a black pool as Martha's name was recited. You get what you give. You walk into the dark and the darkness abides within you. "I wished her ill and tried to cause it to be so," she told her daughter. "I used the sort of magic we must never turn to."

"What sort is that?" Faith asked, her eyes bright.

Maria shook her head. "We should not discuss it."

Faith showed her mother the red blotch in the palm of her hand that had appeared as she climbed up from the stream in the Flatlands, away from the rising tide.

"A bar of black soap should wash that away,"

Maria said. "You are not responsible. And likely, neither am I. Whatever we might have wished for, the truth is, Martha Chase made her own fate."

Faith shrugged, defiant. She knew precisely what she'd done. "What you put into the world comes back to you threefold. I watched her die and was happy to do so."

Faith had walked through the door into vengeance, and in doing so she had lost her childhood, but she was still young, and there was time enough for her to reclaim her life. "For every evil under the sun there is a remedy," Maria said as she embraced her daughter. Let love be one, let it heal what had been broken, let it open the door to hope for the future. Time had passed too quickly and not at all. What was done could not be undone, but they were in Manhattan now, under the Tree of Heaven, and after all this time, they were together.

Faith was delighted to discover the small room under the eaves that had been waiting for her since the day the house was purchased. It was a child's room, but still she adored it, even though she hadn't the thoughts or emotions of a child. There was comfort to be found here, and for a few moments she could imagine she was the person she'd once been. She grinned as she held up the poppet she had loved when she was little more than a baby. "I remember this. Gogo made it for me. Poor Goat. I wonder what happened to him."

"Poor! That's far from what he is. This is his house."

"Is it?" Now Faith was curious. She had noticed the ring on her mother's finger and wondered if there was a man. She was accustomed to looking at details, no matter how small, for her life had depended on such things: the door unlocked, the window open, the mint or sassafras growing by the side of the road, the blink of her foster mother's eyes when she was beginning to anger. "And are you his wife?" she asked her mother.

"The ring is a token, nothing more. I'll never be anyone's wife. I lived because Samuel Dias changed the rope on my hanging day, but before I leapt I vowed that anyone who fell in love with an Owens would be ruined. I did so to protect us all."

"I don't care," Faith assured her. "I never want to be in love. But poor Goat. He was always in love with you."

"You were only a baby! You couldn't know how he felt."

"I saw the way he looked at you, and how hurt he was when you teased him."

Maria did her best to make light of the topic. "What do you know about love?"

"Only that I never want to have anything to do

with it." Faith had learned that during her time with Martha, who had so often professed her love for her. *You are mine, now and forever my daughter. No one else's. Remember that.* Faith had never once shown Martha the pools of black hatred behind her eyes. She'd been a perfect child so as not to receive any punishments. No nights locked in a dark cellar, no beatings with a switch. But then, and now, love in all its forms dismayed her. She wasn't sure she could love anyone, not even her own mother, who could not do enough for her, baking apple pies, ordering new clothing from the dressmakers, reaching for her hand every time Faith was near. Faith kept her thoughts to herself, as she had for all those years in Brooklyn. Now that the iron bracelets had been removed, she could see into people's hearts, but most of what she saw was a disappointment.

"I'm afraid that one day you may be angry at me for what I've done," Maria said thoughtfully. "You'll despise me for setting down the curse. You'll want to be in love."

It was then Faith knew it was her mother herself who regretted the curse. "I doubt that, but I intend to learn all I can about love. How to make it behave and how to stop it. Teach me and you'll see. I'm a good student."

Fortunately Martha had allowed Faith to learn to read the Scriptures, and she had become a compulsive reader, hiding books in the hollows of old trees, and in the cemetery, and beneath the floorboards. Now that she was living in the room under the eaves in Samuel Dias's house, she set up a lantern so that she might read magical texts late into the night. These were the books she'd brought along and kept hidden from her mother, for there were those who might say she was too young for these volumes, and others who might believe no one should have access to this knowledge. She'd taught herself Latin and Greek so she could immerse herself in Agrippa's *Occult Philosophy*, the *Ars Notoria*, a section of *The Key of Solomon*, which included ways to increase one's mental abilities and focus. Jack Finney had found a translation of the ancient Arabic text *Picatrix*, which contained all manner of enchantments, and a copy of the *Arbatel*, a spell book the peddler had uncovered in an abandoned farmhouse which he kept swathed in cotton batting, for it had burned his hands when he'd first taken hold of the book, as many powerful texts did. Faith was fairly certain this was the magic her mother didn't wish to speak of, black magic, blood magic, left-handed magic, powerful and ancient and dangerous.

Often Faith sat on the stairs, listening in when women came to see her mother to ask for charms and cures. Maria avoided love as best she could, but when women came crying, when they felt they had been destroyed, she gave in. The hue of henna that had been mixed with lime and roses, the tea boiled and simmered overnight, would reflect the strength of a woman's love; the deeper the color, the more genuine the love. For love to last one must wear an amulet with apple seeds. Rosemary and lavender oil would give a person willpower, and to break a simple hex one must use salt, coconut oil, lavender, lemon juice, and lemon verbena. Faith memorized many of Hannah's remedies when she read her mother's *Grimoire*, but was even more intrigued with Rebecca's runic spells that bordered on dark magic. In a few weeks' time, she was delighted when her mother presented her with a book of her own. She saw the rules of magic that must never be forgotten written on the very first page.

Do as you will, but harm no one.
What you give will be returned to you threefold.

The lines on Faith's left hand had changed so radically they were unrecognizable; the red splotch that had appeared was still there, and sometimes it burned. She dyed her hair with madder root, which turned it a blood-red color. In truth, she didn't care for rules of any sort; rules made little sense to a person who had grown up in a world without compassion or pity, where there was no moral code by which to abide. The rules that applied to the Nameless Art seemed childish. What she desired most of all was to find a *Grimoire* of the dark arts. She wanted protection and revenge, all that she might have used to defend herself when she was made to wear iron bracelets and pretend she was a perfect child; magic without rules, dark and deep and endless. Some people grow weak when they are victimized, others grow stronger, and still others combine those two attributes to become dangerous, even if the person in question is a girl who has recently turned twelve.

Faith soon grew accustomed to Manhattan and came to know the markets quite well. She regularly visited bookstalls to search through old piles of water-stained manuscripts. She would know the text she needed when she found it. It would feel like a nest of bees when she touched it, swarming and alive, ready to do damage once it belonged to her. Keeper followed at her heels, clearly disapproving of her mission. He growled at the booksellers and at those searching through the stacks. Occasionally, Faith was asked to leave a stall and take her hellhound with her. She began to leave him at home when she went searching, though the poor beast clawed at the door and howled, startling the birds in the branches of the Tree of Heaven.

And then one morning, in a bookstall on the

outskirts of the Fly Market, among piles of ruined and rotted manuscripts, Faith found a handwritten treatise of the Dark Arts, a *Grimoire* that should have been burned on the day of its author's death, but had managed to escape the fire. It was called the *The Book of the Raven*, dated *1600, London*. The prose was written on thin pages of vellum in alternating red and black inks, then bound in black calfskin that had been tied together with knotted black thread. When Faith set her ear to the spine, she could hear it humming as the book came alive.

The *Grimoire*'s mysterious author was a woman with a huge range of knowledge, writing in both Italian and English. She'd been born in Venice and had become a member of the court of England; she knew more than most educated men about politics and falconry and music and myth. The author maintained that she was a poet, which was thought to be impossible for a woman, yet her claim was true enough. She had been the first woman to publish a volume of poems, a text that had gone largely unrecognized, not due to the quality of the work, but to the particularity of the sex of the writer. On the first page of her *Grimoire* was a quote from a man who many claimed had written love songs of admiration and desire for her, celebrating her strengths.

In the old age, black was not counted fair, Or if it were, it bore not beauty's name.

The author of *The Book of the Raven* was dark in every way, not a traditional English beauty, but a beauty all the same. There was no cure for the sort of passion her admirers felt for her. It was an illness, a devastation, and, often, a crime. Those who desired her wondered if their love was natural, or if it had been induced by the use of magical incantations.

Love's fire heats water, water cools not love.

The author of this *Grimoire* knew more about love than most, for at thirteen she'd been given over to a lord of the court who was three times her age. She looked at love with a cold, clear eye and a heart that was as practical as it was passionate. *The Book of the Raven* was the author's book of spells and enchantments, lost at the time of her death, nearly fifty years earlier.

Know what you want, and be sure of it, for regret gives birth to more regret and nothing more.

The author could call up strange maladies, force a liar to tell the truth, conjure demons that would haunt men's dreams. She had studied astrology with a great master in Italy, and the written conjurations and charms formed by the power of her words were so intense and beautiful they turned silver in the dark and could be read by the light of their meaning alone. She had been trained to be charming, but she gathered knowledge solely to make certain she would never again have to do anyone's bidding. The men who had used her, she used in return. Always it was words that saved her and renewed her and gave her freedom, even when she appeared to be chained to her life by love.

THE BOOK OF THE RAVEN

What I have sacrificed, what I have given, what I have hidden from the world, what is needed to do the same.

A wand of hazel will be needed.

Rose water should be beside you at all times.

The pentacle of Solomon should be drawn on the floor to summon the spirit of Oberon, the king of magic.

Stand in a circle that unites the four sections of the world and the four elements, then burn myrtle wood and sandalwood. Burn white nettle, the herb of the archangel.

After this process one would be able to see into the future, control the elements, enchant mortals, subdue enemies, and invoke a malediction for enemies.

I conjure you by fire, by blood, and by memory so that you may perceive your eternal sentence.

Let it be so.
This thing of darkness I acknowledge to
    be mine.

What had been done to Faith, she would give
back to the world three times over, then three
times again. Darkness begets darkness, and
nothing could be darker than her own imaginings
while locked away in Brooklyn. Had she been
capable of ridding herself of her iron cuffs, she
would have burned the house down. To carry
such vengeful thoughts was a heavy burden, and
it was a relief to have found a volume whose
author seemed to know her very soul. As Faith
paged through *The Book of the Raven*, her fingers
were burning, her mind was inflamed, and her
hair turned a deeper, darker red. It was on this day
that she became a woman, for there was blood
between her legs, and the woman she had become
was one who wanted magic more than love. She
would have stolen *The Book of the Raven* if need
be, but the bookseller considered it worthless and
gave it to her for a single silver coin. A woman
with a small white dog was watching, and she
looked displeased. "These are not rants meant for
children," the woman warned, for it was such a
strange and unsettling volume. Faith was young,
with freckles dusting her cheeks and a somber
expression in her pale eyes.

The magic books at this stall were concealed

by a white shroud, to keep them from catching on fire and from influencing both the bookseller and his buyers, for such texts were known to change a person's temperament so they became nearly unrecognizable, even to themselves. Though Catherine Durant did not introduce herself, she was concerned, for she recognized the girl to be Maria's daughter; she saw inside her, and she worried for her future.

"I think it's best if you don't sell it," Catherine Durant told the bookseller.

"Be assured, the book is not for me." By now, Faith was a brilliant liar. She couldn't be shaken from a false statement even when interrogated, a skill she'd learned at Martha's hands. *Have you tried to work magic? Have you spoken to anyone in town? Have you collected herbs? Have you been yourself?* "I can't read," Faith told the woman, a white spot appearing on her fingernail as she spoke. "It's for my grandfather."

"Sold," the bookseller said. So few females could read or write, it was easy for the vendor to believe her. And there was yet another reason he didn't argue with the girl. He knew enough of the Nameless Art to know that he didn't wish to quarrel with someone who could turn silver coins black, and he now realized that the coin Faith had paid him with had turned so; nor did he wish to return it to her, magic or not. Coin was coin, no matter the color. And the woman, Catherine

412

Durant, was not a customer of his. The *Grimoire* was wrapped in black paper so that it might remain hidden as Faith carried it home; even in New York, witchery was a private endeavor, one best kept to oneself. As for the bookseller, he sold not another book or manuscript all that week; it was only then he realized he would have been wise to take advice from the woman with the small white dog.

On her way to Maiden Lane, the binding of the text burned through the paper wrapping. The package throbbed, as if it had a beating heart, as the most potent books sometimes do. The dark *Grimoire* itself was a protective talisman, one so strong that when a thief suddenly approached Faith in an alleyway, he stumbled back as if pushed when he tried to grab the package. Faith could hear the snap of a bone breaking in his hand. The thief cried out, then glared at her as if it were she and not the book that had been responsible for his pain.

"Wait," Faith called out as the thief ran away, about to do her best to apologize. But then she thought better of it and stopped herself. The truth was, she wasn't at all remorseful. The time for apologies was over and her mouth was set in a thin line. She'd had enough of being a victim and never intended to be one again. She made a vow then and there to do harm to anyone who might wish ill upon her and those she loved.

That very night she began to study *The Book of the Raven*. She told her mother she had a stomachache, forsaking a supper of spring chicken with cream sauce, locking herself in her small chamber. She didn't stop reading until the first light of day. By then Faith was in a fever, her imagination on fire. She would no longer practice the tradition she'd been born into, she'd forsake the Nameless Art in favor of left-handed magic, black magic, the most ancient form of all such arts, begun before Babylonia had been built, before the flood washed away most of the world, a practice that originated with a secret text titled *The Key to Hell*. She'd thought of hell quite often while she was in Brooklyn, and how she might send Martha there. If only she had possessed *The Book of the Raven* then, she would have known what to do, even when restricted by iron.

Wax, pins, fire, hair, fingernails, blood, bone, Bella donna, skullcap, henbane. This thing of darkness I acknowledge to be mine.

Faith was still a novice, but she practiced the black art faithfully, learning maledictions by heart, until she was skilled at her craft. Soon enough she was nearly thirteen, the odd age between childhood and womanhood when a

414

person becomes more of what she is. A locked door was not enough privacy for her studies. She kept a blanket thrown over her to shroud the magic and contain it within a circle, then drew the pentacle of Solomon on her floor with invisible ink. It was easy enough to hide her practice. Maria Owens had the sight, but all mothers see their children as they wish to, and the truth of Faith's studies escaped Maria's sight. Faith had helped that to happen, casting a See What You Please spell so that Maria viewed Faith as a perfect child who set the table for supper, swept the floors, tended to the garden, and kissed her good night. Yes, her hair was a darker shade of red, her skin had a new pallor with the freckles disappearing, her eyes were indeed fevered. She had learned to be deceptive from her years with Martha, and now she did so again quite naturally.

She was in the midst of the left-handed magic of revenge, using malice and spite to get what she wanted. In no time, the magic had changed her. When she found a baby swallow and lifted it off the ground, it turned to ash in her hands. She dusted off her hands and felt a shiver of fear over what she now carried inside her. But what was done was done. She had chosen her path. In her practice she used the wild purple orchids that have two tubers, one for white magic, one for black, a plant that could heal or hurt and was called "Dead Man's Fingers" in a play written by

415

the man who adored the author of *The Book of the Raven*. Near the Minetta Stream there were old trees with hollows in their trunks, doors to other worlds where words were said backwards, widdershins, spinning left, the witch's path that was counterclockwise. It was here that Faith gathered blackberries, long used against serpent's bites and for setting curses. *The Book of the Raven* had taught her transference magic, shifting the sorrow or disease or the ill fate that a person carried into another object or being. She had small glass bottles filled with hate and fever and rage and grief, which were stored in a cabinet in her chamber, and at night they glowed with green light, as if stars had fallen from the sky.

In time she could turn a blooming flower black, stop a bird's heartbeat, confuse men so they forgot their own names or lost the power of speech. Love was a common thing to her now, the foolish territory of those without her discipline. She knew that to undo an attraction one needed black paint, blood, a bird's broken wing, pins, and a thin strand of lead, handled carefully, and with gloves. One night she cut her arm and let her blood sink into the ground, and in that place a stem arose with a single red rose. That rose was the magic inside of her, and every day the rose grew darker, until one morning the petals and the stem were black and the thorns were so sharp not even the bees would come near.

Faith wrote down the skills she had studied onto slips of paper to see what practice would best suit her. *Invisibility. Sight. Healer. Love Magic. Revenge.* She left the papers to float in a bowl of water overnight to see what her future might be. In the morning one scroll had bloomed opened. Faith's heart beat quickly as she reached for her fate.

Her place on earth had been decided. She'd known what it would be before she read the floating word, for it was already in her heart, and the black rose in the garden had grown to be as tall as she.

Revenge was what she wanted.

III.

Magic continued to flourish in Manhattan, for most New Yorkers looked the other way when faced with the unusual, be it magic or not. There was a freedom of spirit in the city that couldn't be found in the other colonies, perhaps because of the settlement's Dutch heritage. Respected Amsterdam minister Balthasar Bekker had published *The Enchanted World*, arguing that Calvinism was mistaken in stating that Satan walked through the human world. The devil was nothing more than a symbol of all the evil that resided inside mankind, and belief in witchcraft was the work of ignorant, superstitious men. The governor, Peter Stuyvesant, agreed that the search for witches was far-fetched nonsense. He'd been schooled on this issue when his own sister-in-law Judith Varlet was accused in Hartford in the witch craze of the 1660s and rescued from Connecticut in the dead of night to avoid prison. That near-tragic incident was close enough to the governor to give him pause when it came to supernatural claims. He was a logical man who demanded proof; proving Satan's existence was a fool's errand, and he had declared so in his remarks concerning such arrests, stating that sentences for witchcraft should not end in execution, no matter how dark the accusations might be.

In Massachusetts scores of people had been arrested and held for preposterous reasons, with claims that they were in league with the devil and could torment people from miles away. Though not present in bodily form, those charged were said to be able to ruin crops, induce babies to fall ill, make loyal husbands go mad with lust. Serious men, including Cotton Mather, son of the illustrious Increase Mather, president of Harvard, believed that evil could be found in the personages of old women and fishwives and children, that it emerged from their mouths, that the dark world had encroached on everyday life so that the line dividing the two had vanished into thin air.

Cotton Mather was at work on *The Wonders of the Invisible World*, a treatise that claimed Satan wished to overturn the Massachusetts Bay Colony and used witches to do so. He was convinced that black magic grew in the woods and in the pastures, a bloody black weed. Magistrates continued to rule on spectral evidence, which was supernatural and invisible and therefore impossible to refute. A madness had taken hold in the colony, and each day more women were arrested: those with property, those who were poor, those who had married the wrong man, or who were spinsters, or had angered a neighbor. The original accusers were young girls, beginning with the daughter and niece of Reverend Samuel Paris and their slave Tituba, who had little choice but to agree when questioned, and the mania spread like a fever to more girls and young women who swore witness against satanic acts they had witnessed. Bite marks, bruises, cows whose milk ran red with blood, stars that exploded in the sky, a black horse seen from a window, a mark on a woman's face in the shape of a moon or a star or a sickle, all could be counted as proof. In a wicked turn of events, several of the accusers soon found themselves suspected of witchcraft. Many of the settlers of the town of Salem had come from Essex County in England, home of Matthew Hopkins, the witch-finder general who had sent one hundred women to their deaths, persecuted simply for being women without power in the world.

No one in New York had been arrested for any such reason. The two trials that occurred decades earlier, one in Queens County, the other in the town of Setauket on Long Island, both involved people from Massachusetts and no one was found guilty. Still magic continued, the sort of practical magic that cured and healed and helped both with love desired and love gone wrong. Everyday people had their horoscopes written out and visited fortune-tellers on Miller Street, also known as Mud Avenue after downpours in the spring. There were magical items for sale in many of the markets, often hidden behind the counter or found in a back room or kept under cloths. Most residents did not trust doctors, who were often unschooled and lost more patients than they saved, using worthless remedies: saltpeter, tinctures of distilled powdered human bone used as a cure-all, a false remedy that was called skull moss, a plant grown from the remains of violent criminals who had been hanged which was inserted into a patient's nostrils and was said to staunch bleeding and stop fainting and fatigue. Folk medicine was far less dangerous than the work of medical doctors. Practitioners of the Nameless Art were held in high regard when it came to their talents and their knowledge of curative tonics, seeds to induce sleep or cure insomnia, packets of dried lavender and rose hips for teas that would calm the nerves.

CURES FOR COMMON ILLNESSES

Linden root and yarrow for racing hearts.
Oatmeal and almond meal for cleaning one's face.
Rosemary oil for the hair, or a tonic of lemon and rosemary.
Lavender for sleeplessness.
Ginger root for diarrhea.
Cabbage leaf poultices for wheezing.

Darker ingredients were in demand as well: squid ink, thought to make tangible whatever was written in script, the hollow bones of birds for divination, mushrooms for erotic adventures or for revenge, seeds and oils to end a pregnancy, a knotted rope to burn and the ashes then eaten to bring forth a child. And there was love, always love, which was in the highest demand. Some unscrupulous vendors sold merchandise that was nothing more than wilted weeds, or a smudge of ashes said to be made of a dove's heart but were nothing more than pipe leavings swept into tins, or perhaps rosemary oil flecked red with paint pigment or madder root, all of it dubbed with false Latin names. These unprincipled merchants played at magic, cheating clients in exchange for false cures that either wouldn't work or, in some cases, might cause real harm if ingested. The names of those who were true to the Nameless Art and could be trusted were passed from friend to friend and sister to sister, as valued as silver.

Women came to the door of the house on Maiden Lane, as they had in both Essex Counties. They came at dusk, making certain they would not be recognized by neighbors or friends. Some had recently traveled across the sea in search of missing husbands, of which there were many, men who had left their wives behind in Ireland or England so they might disappear into new lives in Manhattan, often claiming not only new

423

names after they'd vanished, but new wives as well. Try as Maria might to avoid love, it arrived at her doorstep, time and time again, and, despite her resolve to stay as far away as possible from the madness of raw emotion, she gave her clients what they wanted most in the world.

HOW TO BRING A LOVER HOME

Cook honey with nightshade, add a curl of his hair and let it rest on the windowsill. If your beloved is nearby he will appear, but if he has disappeared into the wilderness a bird will take his place. Tie a scrap of paper with your name written upon it to the bird's leg and let it fly out your window. If your beloved is alive, the bird will find him and he will return, though it may take months or years.

Nail a wishbone over your front door.

Stick two silver pins into a red candle. When the flames burn down to the pins, your lover will arrive.

Are you sure you want him? Maria would always say about the man in question before she began an enchantment, for it was possible for a woman who had been unburdened by a husband to begin a new life in New York, one that she alone commanded. *Oh I'm sure,* most would say, not minding Maria's disapproval. These women had put effort into their desires, arriving in the dead of night, leaving the rented rooms of their boardinghouses or the cots set up in the parlor of a relative's flat, all to regain what they'd lost. But every now and then there were those who reconsidered, leaving without any help from Maria. And then there were those who found the men they'd searched for only to return for a different sort of remedy. *He's changed,* these women said, *he's not the one, it's all a mistake, save me, help me, give me back my own life.*

Love was complicated; Faith had understood that even before she took to sitting on the stairs to watch these women come and go. She shook her head in wonder at what fools humans could be. Let them throw their lives away and weep over lovers who would only cause them pain and agony. Let Maria Owens trade in the thing that had caused her grief. Faith had studied love, but it wasn't her business, and it never would be. She had something else in mind.

She had been in Manhattan for close to two years, and had grown up faster than most. By now she was tall, with a newfound grace, and a cool, distant gaze. She hadn't left the practice of acting like an obedient girl, but she was anything but mild mannered. Faith climbed out the window on Maiden Lane, just as she had done in

Brooklyn. Habits died hard, and she had the habit of doing as she pleased, even if that meant there were those who must be deceived.

She set up her practice near the grove of linden trees beside the Minetta Stream, where indigent men lived in canvas tents and the poor were buried without stones to mark that they had ever walked on this earth. This was where her craft had led her, to a hollow where the ferns were as tall as she and the earth was muddy and damp and vengeance came easily. Faith felt it inside her, spreading out from the red splotch in the center of her left hand that she had never been able to wash away. She was called to dark places, such as this. The birds did not sing here and the frogs did not call, although there were hundreds of peepers on the banks of the stream. If a woman wanted something other than what she could find in Maria Owen's kitchen, she came here. If she had been mistreated and damaged and betrayed, if she wanted revenge, she came up the path, no matter how perilous it might be to walk alone in the dark woods.

Come to me and I will never judge you. I am just a girl and you can tell me anything, who hurt you, who you wish to defy, who should pay for their acts against you.

The hysteria in Salem began in the winter of 1692, stretching into the spring. Bridget Bishop was the first woman to be arrested, and the first to be hanged, on June 10. By September, twenty people had been executed. When the news about what was occurring reached New York, there was shock, especially among the Dutch community, who did not agree that the devil walked among men, or that it was proper to make use of spectral evidence based exclusively on dreams and visions, with no practical proof. The original Dutch settlers were serious-minded people who believed what they saw with their own eyes, but such was not the case in the Massachusetts Bay Colony.

In May of that year one of those set to be arrested was a sixteen-year-old girl who had first seen a jail cell when she was a child who accompanied her grandmother, Lydia Colson, visiting Maria Owens after her arrest. When young Elizabeth Colson heard there was a warrant drawn out for her signed by the magistrates, she disappeared into the woods. Her grandmother packed a basket of food and told her to go to New York, where she could find a woman Lydia Colson had once helped who might assist them in return. One could hope that their kindness would be remembered, and perhaps repaid.

By the time Elizabeth arrived in Manhattan, she was exhausted and terrified. She'd stopped in Cambridge overnight, then made her way to Connecticut, where the witchcraft mania had spread to New Haven. Her cousins there had helped her leave in the middle of the night, but the hired carriage driver had beaten her and stolen what little she had. She made the rest of the way alone, all the while in fear of the large wildcats in the hills of Connecticut. At last she reached Manhattan, taking a ferry that disembarked near the Fly Market. She asked vendors if they might know a woman named Maria Owens. The fruit seller knew such a woman and the fishmonger did as well, although neither knew her address. The fishmonger's daughter, however, called Elizabeth aside, for she had gone once for a love charm, and she knew exactly where Maria Owens could be found.

When Elizabeth rapped on the door, a suspicious red-haired girl appeared, her black dog at her side. Faith was an unwelcoming figure, glaring at the unexpected guest with narrowed gray eyes, for the sight allowed her to know where the girl had come from. "You're from Salem," Faith blurted.

"I've come to see Maria Owens." Elizabeth lowered her voice. "I fled before the constables could arrest me."

"For what crime?" Elizabeth certainly didn't appear to be a criminal, but then neither had Martha. People could surprise you, each and every time. When Elizabeth hesitated, Faith assured her that she could be trusted. "I'm Maria's daughter. We have no secrets."

It was hardly true, but Elizabeth wished to believe Faith; they were not so far apart in age, and perhaps she imagined she had found a friend in whom she could confide. She glanced over her shoulder to the crowded street. There was a good deal of foot traffic and several carts and wagons, but no one paid the girls the least bit of attention. "Witchcraft."

Faith held back a laugh. "You're not a witch."

"True enough. But the truth won't save me from hanging."

Faith took the other girl's hand and looked into her palm. "I see that you'll live."

"Are you a fortune-teller?" Several of those arrested in Salem had practiced palmistry and other forms of parlor magic in which they promised to divine who future husbands and wives might be.

"Not at all," Faith said, drawing the visitor inside. "I just know that if you're here with us, you'll be safe."

They had a dinner of chicken pie closed into a coffin of crust that had been flavored with rosemary, and to celebrate their guest's determination to make her way to New York, Maria fixed a delicacy called Hedgehog Pudding, consisting of bread and raisins, sweet cream and eggs and butter, which was then decorated with slivers of blanched almonds pointing upward like spikey spines. She was delighted to see Elizabeth so grown up and remembered what a dear child she'd been, but the evening took a turn when Maria heard the details of what was transpiring in Salem. She felt a deep sense of foreboding, and when she asked who was at the heart of the witch mania, she was not surprised when John Hathorne's name was spoken. He was one of the magistrates hearing the cases of the accused, well known to be the most unforgiving among the judges, badgering the women who were called before him, forcing admissions from prisoners who hadn't eaten or slept but had been beaten with sticks and leather straps, accepting spectral evidence of the worst sort, pure madness and gossip masquerading as truth.

Faith noticed that her mother shivered when she heard about this judge and his deeds.

"Do you know this man?" she asked.

"I don't believe I ever truly did."

But she certainly knew what he was guilty of: seduction, betrayal, lies, abandonment, pride.

Despite the Owens' hospitality, Elizabeth had decided she would not be able to stay. Her Connecticut cousins had confided that when the constables came to arrest her and found her missing, they had taken her grandmother in her place. She realized she had erred in coming to New York.

"You can't go back," Maria told Elizabeth Colson. "It's far too dangerous."

Still, it was clear the girl wouldn't desert her grandmother in the old woman's time of need. Elizabeth had an honest heart and was young enough to believe that she was dealing with reasonable men who would release her grandmother when she gave herself up. She stayed a single night and left in the morning. Before they'd gone to bed, Faith had whispered she would leave something for Elizabeth that might be useful, in the rear of the garden. She'd kept her word. There between the neat rows of rosemary and cabbages was an amulet for Elizabeth to wear close to her heart. Inside the velvet pouch was powdered vervain, used in dark acts of magic, and a slip of black rope tied into knots to protect her three times. A note had been written upon black paper with red ink that disappeared as soon as it was read.

Travel well. Trust no one.

Jack Finney was happily ensconced on Maiden Lane. He'd planned to accept a few days of hospitality, but he'd stayed on for a year, and then another, putting to use his talents of seeing to odd jobs, fixing the roof of the barn and fashioning a room for himself inside the stable, replacing the wooden windowsills so they would close tight against bad weather, setting out a new garden gate. He had traveled for so many years that he still never knew where he was when he opened his eyes in the morning.

Maria had rewarded him financially for his help, and though he was far from rich, he was no longer poor. He'd spat on the pile of blackened coins he'd been given, shining them up with a handkerchief, grateful to possess what he considered to be a treasure and perhaps even more grateful for a home in Manhattan. He'd had enough of Brooklyn. When he thought of Kings County, he imagined the woman in the gray dress chasing after them across the flatlands, an image that caused him to shiver. In the past he'd always moved on when he wished to escape bad memories, hoping against hope that a different landscape would renew his spirits and help him to forget. But now he felt at home on Maiden Lane and had taken a stand at the Fly Market to sell his wares. He'd seen Faith slinking about near the vendors that dealt in foul merchandise, poisons, dangerous herbs, books hidden in black covers.

One afternoon, Faith came to sit in the grass while Finney polished his coins, a habit he'd come to enjoy, for counting his money was a new pastime. He grinned and tossed a coin to Faith. As soon as she caught the disc, the silver turned black.

432

"Never do that in public," Finney advised.

"I'll do as I please." She made a face at him and the peddler shook his head.

"So said the criminal on his hanging day," Finney said. He worried about Faith for he believed that a man was responsible for whomever he rescued, although sometimes he was confused as to which of them had saved the other.

"If you insist," Faith said. "I'll pretend not to be what I am."

"Join the human race. That's what we all do."

Faith had a spot in her cold, dark heart for Finney. She believed she would still be in the attic bedroom in Gravesend with iron bracelets around her wrists if not for his help. He was a man who carried his sorrows close to his heart and never discussed them, who would surely never mention what had happened on the bridge. If he suspected that Martha was still breathing when Faith left her there in the water, he never said so and he never would.

"You should have something better than silver as your reward," Faith decided.

"I'm happy with all I have. Your mother has been very generous." Jack found Faith to be amusing and intelligent, but at times she was a bit frightening. She looked like a girl, but her thoughts were often those of a grown woman, one who was more canny than most.

"You should have a wife," Faith decided.

Though he never said so, she knew how lonely Finney was. He talked in his sleep, and when they'd shared nights in the wagon he'd often called out for someone named Lowena, and had wept until morning.

"I had a wife." Finney's mood darkened with this topic of discussion. He didn't wish to think about all he had lost. Mourning the life he'd once led wouldn't bring it back and who was he to complain? Every man lost all that he loved in this world by the time his life was through. It happened to some sooner and some later. For now he had his horse, his wagon, his freedom, and a huge pile of silver. He could do as he pleased, as no married man could, even if Finney wasn't quite sure what good the freedom he'd claimed did him.

"I don't see anyone breaking down the door looking for someone like myself," he informed Faith. "Maybe the old washerwoman down the street would like to have tea with me."

"I can find the right woman." Faith was utterly sure of herself. "Let me try."

"Try?" Now Finney had good reason to tease the girl. "Are you saying I'd be the first to benefit from this service?" He was well aware that Faith had talents, he had seen so himself in the flatlands of Brooklyn when she chased away the rabbits and dreamed of crossing hell to find her mother. That didn't mean he wished to be part of an experiment. If she was a witch, she was a novice, and beginner's luck was rare. "I don't think I want you mucking about with my fate. For all I know, I could wind up living in a cave with a bear, or married to a turtle under the sea, or sleeping with the washerwoman, and I'm not sure she would be the best of those bargains."

"I'll find someone who will bring you happiness." Faith was serious about this matter. "You deserve that. You can't stay in the barn forever."

"You think too highly of me," Finney responded. "To be honest, I didn't even want to save you, but it was easier to let you tag along with me rather than leaving you with that old bag."

Another man, even a good man, would have left her to fend for herself in Gravesend. Finney was more than decent, and therefore he deserved more than silver. Faith knew he still had dreams of Martha chasing after them, her white bonnet flying into the air. He'd given up salt, for it reminded him of the air that day, which had been so salty and blue.

"You know I drowned her." Faith almost sounded like a child, though there was nothing childlike about her admission or the cool expression on her face.

"Not rescuing her isn't killing her. Listen to me, girl. You didn't kill her."

Faith had a habit of biting her lips when deep in thought. Her dark red hair was braided and she wore a dress that was the same color as her silvery eyes. She might be beautiful someday, but not yet. "I've already decided," she told her friend. "I intend to pay you back for all you've done." Finney eyed her, uneasy, as she brought out a small bottle. "It's the Tenth Potion, the strongest there is. We're told not to make it, but I broke the rules. It can make anyone fall in love with you, and you with them. It's unbreakable."

Finney gazed at her, concerned. "Does your mother know?"

"This is between you and me."

The elixir was set before him. It looked like wine, but the scent was of something that had been burnt. Finney had put up a good fight, but now he relented; he took a sip and considered. He'd had worse.

"Trust me," Faith said. Her hands were folded in front of her. She was a very serious girl. Love was not her business, but repaying Finney for all he'd done was.

"I trust you to bury me if I die," Finney quipped. Then he grew silent as he thought of his deep loneliness and all he'd lost. He gulped down the elixir. "God help me," he said.

Faith ignored him and recited the incantation.

"Let the one who drinks this wine be granted true love divine."

Nothing happened. "Your experiment has failed," Finney was quick to say.

"I have to decide on who the right woman will be and she must drink as well. Once she does there is no going back."

"That's not exactly comforting." Finney patted Faith's head as if she were a child, then got up to see to Arnold. "I only hope it doesn't work on horses."

Faith laughed and went into the house. She and Keeper set off for the butcher, where she would get a bundle of bones and meat scraps. She had a few women in mind for Finney. The fruit vendor's daughter at the market, a neighbor who had recently lost her husband, a woman who sold books. She'd planned to take the Tenth with her, but in her hurry she left it on the garden table. Faith was happy to be with her beloved Keeper, forgetting that once magic has begun it cannot so easily be put away.

The Tree of Heaven was blooming with the last of its red flowers when Maria set to work in the herb garden that day. She had been attempting to grow *mampuritu*, an herb from Curaçao that was accustomed to warmer climates. It was a very stubborn herb. She had tried lighting a fire near it, to warm its roots, to no avail. Perhaps she should rid the garden of the herb, for it made her think of Samuel Dias, even when she didn't wish to, and she was glad to be interrupted when Catherine Durant arrived at the gate, her little white dog following close behind. Catherine had been using Maria's black soap, which so refreshed her that she looked ten years younger than her age. "Is this what happens to all of your customers?" she called to Maria, who was down on her knees, weeding between rows of parsley and sage. "Once we use your soap, we can't live without it?"

Maria laughed and clapped the soil from her hands. She would always be grateful for the simple pie magic that had brought her daughter home. "For you," she told Catherine, "the soap is always a gift."

Catherine was thirsty from her walk from the Bowery, and when she saw the glass of wine on the table she sat on a metal chair and took a sip. Her dog jumped on her lap, barking, but Catherine ignored him, and, intrigued by the taste, she continued to drink. Her mouth began to tingle once she'd drained the elixir, as if she'd eaten nettles. She immediately knew there was an enchantment at work. Ordinarily she would have been indignant, but not on this day. What was meant to be would be, whether or not you approved. The truth was, she was curious to see what would happen next.

Finney walked out of the barn, smelling of horseflesh and sweat. He intended to tell Faith to stop the spell. There was no point going any further, not in his case. Love was an impossible, ridiculous goal for a person such as himself. What he'd had, he'd lost, and he thought it better to accept his life as it was. Finney would leave Manhattan and the false notion that he had found a home. He would go back on the road, perhaps to Connecticut, unknown territory devoid of memories. He was meant to be alone, and he'd become quite good at a solitary life; his horse was more than enough company. But there in the garden the peddler stopped as if struck. A force went through him, heart and brain, body and soul. The whole world seemed a wonder, the table and the chairs set out in the grass, the red flowers falling to the ground, the beautiful woman before him.

Catherine could read the man in the yard—a peddler, a widower, a man who was lost—but she viewed him through the power of the Tenth and therefore saw that he was a hero who put others first, who cared more for an old horse than most people cared for their neighbors and friends. She could see the young man he'd been, before his heartaches, when he liked to balance on stone walls and raced through fields on his father's horses, when the women in his village claimed he was the handsomest man alive. Her little dog ran at Finney, barking protectively, but when the peddler reached down, the dog flopped over on his back, ready to be petted, as if Finney were a long-lost friend.

Faith came home with her purchase from the butcher shop to find Maria waiting for her, furious. "You've created mayhem, and it's unbreakable. There's nothing I can do to amend it. I told you, you aren't ready to work magic."

Faith returned her mother's gaze and held it. As it turned out they were now the same height. "I am ready."

Maria felt a chill go through her. "When I say so."

"It's my fault," Finney was quick to claim. "She did so on my behalf."

"I believe it was on my behalf," Catherine said.

Already, Catherine Durant could not be kept from him or he from her. They had an unspoken pact that they would never be parted, two spell-bound people who left together for Catherine's farm on the Bowery without looking back.

Maria narrowed her eyes. It had been too long since she had really looked at her daughter. Now she saw the edge of darkness inside. "You haven't enough practice for such things."

Faith shrugged. "It's only love."

"You think love is so simple?" Maria thought of the day she saw John Hathorne in the blue dining room in Curaçao and the morning Samuel had brought the magnolia tree to Salem so she

440

thought that snow was falling. "Take my advice," she told Faith. "Stay away from it."

"If that's how you feel about love, why are you still wearing Gogo's ring?"

Maria had tried everything to remove the gold band from her finger, but the wedding ring wouldn't come off. It was likely the reason she thought of Samuel Dias so often. She wondered if Abraham had known that would happen and why such rings were worn, to make you think of the one who had given it to you.

"You're the one that played with love," Faith said to her mother. "You called down a curse on us. You didn't care what I thought or what I wanted."

Try to do what's best for your children, and still it could all go wrong. What you knew today, you didn't know yesterday. What you wished for then, you might come to regret.

"You never told me what happens if someone falls in love with us."

"We ruin their lives," Maria told her daughter.

"It seems you've already ruined the Goat's life," Faith told her mother that day. "You might as well love him."

PART FIVE

The Remedy

I.

There were so many women in love and in trouble in the city of Manhattan that Maria hadn't time for all who came in search of a charm or a cure. Often a dozen or more waited in the garden, some disguised by shawls or cloaks, others so desperate they didn't care who might spy them visiting the witch's house. What was a witch if not a woman with wisdom and talent? Here in New York, such things were not a crime. Maria's clients perched on benches or sat in the dewy grass counting out pieces of silver, removing wedding bands, reciting small prayers that Maria Owens might help them find health or solace or love. When she looked out the window to see how many women were in need, she was overwhelmed. A woman who had renounced love should not be so close to so much emotion. It would surely affect her. Love was contagious, it passed from soul to soul, it woke a person up and shook her even when she wanted to be left alone. There were times when Maria looked in the black mirror to search for a client's fate and all she could see was Samuel Dias. She had no heart, she was sure of it, and yet something inside of her ached.

"I could be your assistant," Faith said as they looked out the window at the women waiting there. "In Brooklyn, people came to me to be healed." She had recently learned how to construct figures out of the bark of the black hawthorn; when melted over a fire the love for the wrong person would melt as well and a client would be freed of foolhardy desires.

"Well, that was in Brooklyn," Maria responded. "They should not have gone to a girl."

"I know more than you think I do," Faith insisted. She knew the expression on a woman's face when she realized she had only a few more breaths to take in this life, she knew that when she was in a cemetery at night she could hear the heartbeats of the dead, she knew that a girl whose father doesn't want her will be both stronger and weaker than she might have been had he ever loved her. "I'll take the ones seeking revenge," she chirped.

"We don't do that here," Maria said.

"You do all sorts of things," Faith said archly.

"For the benefit of those in need."

"Maybe you don't think I have the power."

"That's not true. I believe in you. You're just not ready."

"I have been ready since I was six years old and you left me."

Maria stepped back as if slapped. "I told you I never wanted to leave you. I had no choice."

"I thought we all had choices," Faith said, her gaze turning to ice. "If you hadn't gone to Massachusetts, none of it would have happened."

The lies Martha had told Faith had done damage, and she carried the scars of abandonment. She went inside and sat on the floor beside Keeper. He had a distant, somewhat removed character and resembled Faith in that way, but now he put his head in her lap and she stroked his fur. Here she was, in her own home, and she was still invisible, her true self lurking in the shadows. Every witch wishes for a pair of red boots, and Faith had hoped her mother would grant her a pair as a gift on her thirteenth birthday, but when the day came she was given a sky-blue shawl. She didn't need protection. She didn't need luck. She wanted her one and only life and the freedom to live as she pleased. She had been paid well by her clients, which was a good thing. She would order her own boots at the cobbler's.

Anyone who had the sight and the ability to see inside Faith to her core would see the damage there, the iron wound, the nights in a locked room, the open window, the cemetery in Gravesend, the salty land and the seabirds in the sky, the loneliness, the bitter taste in her mouth, the father who never showed himself, the mother who wished to believe that all was well with her daughter when there was a crack in everything and the world was coming apart. Faith would be ready for magic when she said she was ready, not when her mother allowed it. She had said yes to magic years ago in the flatlands, with the salt stinging her eyes so that she almost cried, not that she had the ability to do such a thing, not then and not now. Maria Owens could cry, but that was unusual for a witch, and was likely a sign of weakness in Faith's opinion. Faith, herself, was nothing like that. Even if Maria had wanted to see inside her daughter, Faith had blocked her from doing so. It was a murky and solemn spell she had worked at the Minetta Stream, a fitting place for dark acts; she had used her own blood and hair and the bones of a small sparrow, and had thereby grown invisible to the person who loved her best in the world.

A part of her longed to be saved from the path she had taken, so that she could become the person she might have been if she hadn't been a stolen child, if she hadn't learned early on that there was evil in the world. What plunged her further into the dark was an ordinary day when she was cleaning out the barn after Finney moved out. She stumbled upon an old satchel, one that belonged to Samuel Dias. Inside was a rope, a book of maps, and a letter from Maria Owens, left for him when the *Queen Esther* docked in Boston after their trip together from Curaçao. He had kept it all this time, though he could only tolerate reading it once, for once was more than enough.

I don't know what might have happened between us. I am in search of a man named John Hathorne, he is my fate and the father of my child.

Faith sat back on her heels, her heart pounding. She had never known her father's name. To her eyes the letters were sharp as glass. She could hear her mother calling to her from the garden, where she was planting rosemary and mint. Instead of answering, Faith lay in the straw. She paged through the book of maps until she reached Essex County. Navigators can never touch a map without plotting the journey ahead, and Samuel had marked the path with spots of ink. Faith thought of the unfurled paper that told her future, and how vengeance had settled inside her like a bird in a nest, fitted close to her heart. From the start, she had been ready to seek revenge.

That evening she had supper with her mother, a cod baked with spring onions and cream, then Faith went up to her room under the eaves. She had been trained to keep her feelings to herself. She set the lock and burned a black candle. Her father was the magistrate who had judged the women who stood before him with their wrists in iron chains and their legs bound by ropes. If she reached back inside of herself she could

449

recall his appearance, a tall man who had stared as if willing her to disappear. When your father doesn't love you, a stone forms inside of you, hard and sharp enough to pierce through bone. The dark was rising in her soul and she was glad of it. She was at the age when innocence seems like a flaw. Do what you must or do what you will. Adhere to the rules or break them in two. Faith would not be thirteen forever, but that's what she was now. She had picked up her red boots at the cobbler and they fitted her perfectly. Before she left she wrote a note to her mother, folded it, and placed it upon her bedside table.

Faith had been stolen once before, and she wanted Maria to know that this time she was leaving of her own accord. She would stand before the magistrate and *she* would judge *him,* although she already knew she would find him guilty. She would see that he paid the price for all that he'd done.

On the day that Faith left New York, the air swirled with a cold mist that soon changed to a smattering of hail, for out at sea there was an unexpected storm that raced toward harbors and coastlines. Everything was white, air and sea and sky, but the weather and the high seas didn't deter her. She had looked in the black mirror and had seen that it was her fate to go to Salem. She paid for her passage with coins earned from women in need of her talents, those who wished for revenge and escape and reprisal, and she silently thanked them as she stood on the dock, equally ready for revenge.

The ship's purser thought the coins were false, for Faith was only a girl and how had a girl come into possession of such a sum? Then he rubbed one with his kerchief and found that it shone in his hands. "Go on, then," he told Faith, though his gaze was on Keeper. "But that beast stays."

Faith certainly didn't intend to leave Keeper behind, for the loyal creature would have leapt into the freezing river to follow her if he must. When the purser went off to see to his other duties, Faith withdrew a figure made of hemlock bark. She held a match to it and recited an invocation from *The Book of the Raven*, watching as the wood melted into a black pool. Each time she recited a spell from the text she felt a change inside her, as if her blood burned more hotly and her bones became sharper. Her hair was so darkly red it looked black in the shadows, as if the person she once was and the child Martha had stolen had magicked into one being. She was made of blood and heart and soul, and it was blood magic that she practiced. She was no one's little girl now. From a distance she appeared to be a full-grown woman and men were attracted to her; she seemed different than other girls. It was the manner in which she looked at the men who stared at her, so directly, as if to see who they truly were.

When the purser returned, he no longer noticed Keeper and failed to say another word about the wolf's presence. In fact, the purser's vision was cloudy and would remain so. It was the first time Faith had used left-handed magic for her own selfish reasons, and later, in the evening, when she bit into a slice of bread she'd brought along for her supper, she tasted blood and found that a tooth had broken. Blood magic had a price. Faith felt a chill, and she wondered if she was about to go too far. What you send out comes back to you threefold. What you give to the world returns in kind. Blood begets blood.

She huddled close to Keeper to stay warm. Several of the sailors looked her over, for a girl of thirteen traveling alone was considered fair prey. Keeper growled low down in his throat to warn them, but that was not the only thing that kept the sailors away. It was Faith's silver eyes, cold as coins; it was how she appeared to be one thing, a red-haired girl, and then suddenly she seemed to be a woman with black hair it was best not to cross.

They arrived in the morning light with Salem glittering before them in the cold spring sun. The harbor had nearly frozen solid even though the new leaves on the trees gleamed green. Men in rowboats had to cut through the forming shell of blue ice so that the ship might dock. It was foul weather and people on board whispered it was a sign of foul things to come. As for Faith, she pricked her finger on a piece of wood and her blood boiled on the deck and red steam rose into the chilly air.

She remembered little of arriving in Salem when she was a babe, only the bumpy carriage ride and the deep forest and the trees with black leaves that were strewn along the path to an imposing house with diamond-patterned glass windows. The docks were quiet now because of the storm, and Faith's red boots made a clicking sound on the ice. She went to a tavern where there were sailors who were more raucous than usual, trapped on land as they waited for the ice to thaw and their ships to set sail. When Faith took a table, no one disturbed her as they might had she been another girl who had wandered in unaccompanied. They were wise enough to let her be, for she had a protector who lay at her feet, his eyes glinting. Not one of the men in the tavern had ever seen a dog that looked like this one. The girl and her beast appeared as a single creature that had been joined in some wicked way, she in her black cape, he with his long black fur. A young serving maid was told to wait on her, for the older server could already tell this red-haired girl was trouble.

Faith asked for two bowls of stew, one for herself, one for Keeper, and a pot of boiling water for her own brew. Tea was dear and often unavailable; and so Faith carried her own Courage Tea. She placed a tarnished silver coin on the table. She could see the serving girl's hunger, as well as a silence she had been trained for. The girl was being mistreated on a regular basis. Across the room, the owner of the tavern was watching them with a lazy eye. He had the nerve to nod at Faith.

"Is he the one?" she asked the girl.

The maid was quick to look over her shoulder and even quicker to turn her gaze away. "I don't know what you mean. He's nothing."

"If you say he is, I should believe you." Faith knew from her own experience there were times when it was impossible to do anything other than lie. "I want to find a man named John Hathorne," she went on to say. When there wasn't a flicker on the serving maid's face, Faith set another coin on the table.

The server swept the silver into her hand before anyone could see. "You'd do better to stay away from the magistrate," she murmured. She confided that a cousin of hers had been brought up on charges and was awaiting trial. Her only crime was to have taken a walk with another woman's betrothed. She'd been accused of witchery shortly thereafter. "Most of us don't dare to say his name aloud."

"Do I look as though I'm afraid of any man?" Faith's voice was soft, but steady. "And you shouldn't be either." She reached into her satchel and handed the girl a figure stitched from red cloth and black thread. "Burn this and the man causing you trouble will disappear."

"Will he die?" The mild serving girl was shocked by the idea, despite her wish to be rid of her abuser. In her experience, punishment came with every attempt at freedom.

"He'll only disappear." When the girl continued to appear nervous, Faith added, "To Rhode Island or Connecticut, not to hell, just far enough away not to bother you."

Faith and Keeper were given two heaping bowls of stew, and by the time they left, the serving girl had managed to unearth the address of the magistrate's house, south of the courthouse on Washington Street. Faith's breath came hard as she walked through town. The streets were slippery and the roofs of the houses looked slate-blue in the dusk.

She saw the elm trees before long, the leaves unfurling, the black bark slick and wet with melting ice. The temperature had risen, and the ice storm was all but forgotten. Now that she had returned, Faith remembered the banks of white phlox in bloom and the boy she had waved to and the shock on her mother's face when she saw him. She felt her heart beat faster as she approached the door. Her heart had been beating just as fast on the day they ran away from the little boy in the garden and the woman who was calling out to him.

Keeper went off toward the woods where he could go unnoticed, for he certainly would not be welcome here. Faith, however, was just what Ruth Gardner Hathorne had been looking for. There was a hired woman who came to help with the laundry and another to cook on the Sabbath, but the household work was never done. When Ruth opened the door to find a lovely girl in need of work, one who declared herself an orphan, but solemnly promised that she could cook and bake and clean as well as anyone, and had no aversion to using strong lye and washing sheets in the large kettle set over a fire pit in the yard, Ruth Hathorne thanked the Lord for this day and for His wisdom. Caring for six children had worn her down. This girl with nowhere to go was a godsend.

"You must be freezing," Ruth said, as she drew the girl inside. "Snow in April means a hot summer to come."

Ruth was a kindhearted woman; you didn't need magic to discern that, all you had to do was gaze into her calm blue eyes. She had been a year older than Faith when she was married with no say in the matter, having lost her parents to exile in Rhode Island because they were Quakers and considered to be enemies of the Puritan colony. Her experience had caused her to be generous to girls who had nothing other than their own abilities, for she wished someone had come to her rescue and let her be a girl awhile longer; perhaps then she might have had a choice in whom she was to wed. She no longer thought about the years when she stood at the garden gate, her hands gripping the posts, wondering what would happen if she walked down Washington Street and just kept walking, through the colony, through Connecticut, going as far as she could. But she had the children, after all, and the fact that her husband paid her little attention suited her fine. He assumed she was still a foolish girl who had cried when he took her to bed, and wept when she was confronted with running a household at such a tender age. He thought she knew nothing at all. But she'd learned quite a bit during their years together. She had seen the mud on his shoes back in the time when he would disappear at night; she remembered the woman with black hair who came to knock at their door. If anything, these things made her even more compassionate to those who had nothing, for no matter how fine her house was, or how much china and silver were in her pantry, she some-times wished she could change places with them.

"I hope you'll be happy here with us," she told the reserved girl who had appeared at the door, calling herself Jane. Faith had given the last name she'd been made to use in Brooklyn, when she was her other self, the well-behaved girl. To Ruth's eyes, she looked in need of a good meal and a place to lay her head.

"I'm sure I will be," Faith assured her. She was now fully the obedient girl who never talked back. She had a certain smile when she acted this part, a shy, innocent expression.

"Then you were meant to be here."

Ruth was happy to lead the girl through the house, reciting a litany of what her duties would be. The snow had all but ended, and was just a flutter of soft flakes. The April sun was strong and beneath the ice the world was already green. It would be a perfect day. Ruth Gardner Hathorne showed Faith the cot in the scullery where she could sleep, and the peg where she could leave her damp coat, and if the inappropriate red boots the girl wore gave Ruth pause it was too late, the offer to work had been extended, and the girl had hugged her as if Ruth were her own mother, then carefully hung her coat upon the hook.

II.

A woman who loses a child twice will be acquainted with sorrow, and yet the second loss will hurt just as much as the first. It is a snake that circles around to bind you hand to foot, heart to soul. If it comes to pass that the child runs away again, there is no magic strong enough to bring her back to you. In the natural order of things, children do leave, but not with bitterness and in secrecy. Maria knew Faith was gone before she opened the door to her daughter's room. She had dreamed of a dark wood where the birds were silent. She saw *The Book of the Raven* in a hollow tree. *I know more than you think I do,* Faith had said in the dream. Maria could hear her voice, but the girl was nowhere to be seen. She awoke in a panic and sure enough the window in Faith's chamber was open and there were footprints in the damp grass. On the bedside table was a note written with red ink on black paper.

Do not follow me. You should have told me who my father was. If you try to stop me, then you will be the one I never forgive. This is my life to live.

Making her way to the farm in the Bowery, Maria went immediately to Finney, who seemed to know Faith better than anyone. Finney was working in the garden, the white dog digging up mud to bury a bone, but he put down his shovel when he spied Maria.

"Why would she run off?" Maria wanted to know. "And to Massachusetts of all places."

Finney told Maria of Faith's vision in Brooklyn in which she had to cross through hell to reach home. They'd assumed the vision had been of Hell Gate in the river, but perhaps there was another meaning entirely, and it was her fate to return to Salem.

"She's as smart a girl as there ever was," Finney assured Maria. "Surely she's got her reasons to go."

But Maria disagreed. "It's a dangerous place, and no matter how smart she might be, she's only a girl."

"If you decide you want to go after her, I'll leave with you today."

Finney insisted they go first to Catherine for advice, and although Maria felt humiliated to ask for another woman's help in such a personal matter, she agreed. She had a new admiration for those who came to her for cures, for they opened themselves to reveal their most private thoughts and deeds, an act that now mortified her.

"Have you not worried about your daughter?" Catherine asked Maria.

"No more than any mother would," Maria said.

It was a wonder how those you loved best were often the ones you could not fully see. "She's gone over to the dark," Catherine told her. When Maria's expression was still puzzled, Catherine explained, "You didn't want to know, so it was easy for her to fool you. She works left-handed."

"No. That's impossible." Maria looked up at Finney, who couldn't meet her eye. "Isn't it?"

"She's a good-hearted girl," Finney assured Maria. "No one is saying she's not, but she was locked away for five years. It could turn anyone."

"You had lost her before she left for Massachusetts." Catherine had the little dog on her lap, ignoring how muddy he was. "Now let's see if you can get her back."

Catherine filled a glass bowl with cool, clear water. She placed two sticks of bramble into the bowl, which helped to invoke the spirit of the person in question, along with a stalk of thistle, for protection. The water turned black, the better to see into. On one side of the bowl was the future as it was now, on the other side the future as it might be. There was fire on one side, waves on the other that leapt from the bowl, splashing onto the table.

Catherine turned to Finney. "When the girl dreamed of hell, how did she cross over?"

"Through water," Finney said.

The women exchanged a look. They both knew that meant a drowning to prove witchery was at work. Maria rose to her feet, thanking her hosts, ready to leave, telling Finney he need not accompany her; she would find her daughter.

Catherine held her back. "Listen to me," she said. "I have seen this before. I know black magic. I have seen more than you could imagine. Following the girl isn't the answer."

"I know what people are capable of in Essex County. I know what they did to me."

"But this is her fate, not yours. She has to cross through hell to come out on the other side. Otherwise she will be trapped in her own darkness."

Maria shook her head. She held back tears that burned her.

"There's only one way for you to help," Catherine told her. "The first and second rules combined."

Maria saw then that Catherine was older than she appeared to be, older than any mortal should be. Women in the Durant family lived too long, and in the end lost everyone they had ever loved. That was why Catherine had come to New York, to begin anew. She was grateful to Faith for invoking the Tenth and giving her a new life with Finney, a good and decent man. She would now return the favor and help Maria win her daughter back from the dark side.

"If you want your daughter, save someone. That's the way to win back her life. Wait and the chance will come to you. When it does, don't let it pass you by."

For weeks Maria looked out the window, barely able to eat or sleep. Days passed and then one bright morning a minister's wife came to Maiden Lane. Catherine had vowed that a sign would appear and now it had arrived at her door. Maria could feel her caller's sorrow; another grieving mother, one she must help at all costs. The woman was the English wife of a well-known Dutch minister who introduced herself as Hannah Dekker. As soon as Maria heard that the stranger had the name of her beloved adopted mother, she was certain this stranger was the woman who would lead her to her daughter's rescue.

You receive what you give threefold. Save someone else's daughter and you'll rescue your own.

Hannah Dekker had searched out Maria Owens in desperation. Her daughter was in the throes of a fever that had grown worse with every passing day; there seemed nothing to do but watch the poor child sink more deeply into sickness and pain. The family's dear friend, Dr. Joost van der Berg, an esteemed elder with the Dutch Reformed Church and a physician, had found no success in fighting her affliction. He had given the girl an elixir made of crushed bones collected from crypts, thought to heal bone pain, but to no effect. If anything, the girl grew weaker.

Hannah Dekker had overheard furtive conversations about Maria Owens that took place among women when they thought no one could overhear. She didn't believe in witchcraft and had no experience with the Nameless Art, but when there was nothing left to try it could not hurt to believe in something, however preposterous it might seem. Hannah made it clear that she was willing to pay any price for a cure.

"When your daughter is well again you can decide what it's worth," Maria said as she gathered her cape and her black bag of herbs. She would have her payment, but it wouldn't be silver or gold. *Save a life, win a life.* She knew of Jonas Dekker by reputation; he was prominent and well respected within both the Dutch and British communities, and had lived in Boston, but was more comfortable in New York, among more freethinking individuals.

Seeing as the girl was too ill to leave her bed, Maria would call at the Dekkers' home, something she rarely did. When she arrived, the family's lavish mansion appeared to be a house in mourning with the damask curtains drawn and the candles and lanterns snuffed out. Maria was led upstairs by a servant, then asked to wait in the dim hall. Dutch paintings lined the wood-paneled walls and hand-knotted French carpets could be found on every floor. All the same, wealth was no protection from sorrow, and when Maria entered the bedchamber she felt great compassion for the

464

patient, a pale ten-year-old girl named Anneke, who writhed in pain. Anneke was in a fever, her bedclothes drenched, her delicate face set in an expression of agony. The girl's mother could not look at her without bursting into tears. They had tried leaching and cupping, none of it effective, and Dr. van der Berg had been stymied in his diagnosis, for he was most familiar with diseases of the Netherlands and New York and the Massachusetts Bay Colony, and this girl was in the grips of a tropical disease. Maria immediately recognized the illness as breakbone fever, so common in the West Indies. The family had been to Aruba to visit relatives, and when questioned closely, Hannah recounted that the children had often been at the shore, where mosquitoes clouded the sky on hot summer evenings.

Maria had brought along a selection of dried and fresh herbs, including two it was clear the girl needed: dried blue violets as a tincture for mouth sores and linden root and yarrow for a racing heart, for the child's heart was pounding so hard she kept her hands on her chest, frightened her heart would fly out from her body. Fortunately, Maria kept Tawa-tawa at hand, and grew it in pots on her windowsill, ready if Samuel Dias should return with a recurrence of the disease, though it seemed unlikely he would ever come back, for she hadn't received a single letter from him since his departure.

The Dekker girl's illness was far worse than Samuel's. She had begun to bleed internally, and when she cried her tears were red. There were purple bruises blooming along her arms and legs; she could barely stand to be touched without crying out. She could not open her eyes when asked to do so, for she was too weak. Maria decided she would stay beside her patient until there was some improvement. On her way via a small corridor to the kitchen that was attached to the house, she passed a room that was filled with books. She went inside and stood at the desk. The minister had been working on a letter, open on his desk.

Too much is attributed to the devil and the witch or sorcery.

The minister was well acquainted with the Mathers, a family that had been instrumental in the witch trials, whose beliefs Dekker had come to believe were ridiculous opinions for godly, rational men. Maria thought over the minister's writings as she soaked clean rags in cold water and vinegar to bring down the girl's fever and then asked the cook to begin a fish bone broth. She boiled water to make Tawa-tawa tea for her patient and Courage Tea for herself. There was a reason fate had led her here, and she wished to be strong enough not to back down from what would come next. She was fighting darkness, which arose when it was least expected, in this case in the heart of a young girl, her own daughter.

Though the minister's wife did not believe in magic, she said nothing when Maria poured a line of salt along the window ledge and hung the brass bell above the door, or when she dressed the child in a clean blue nightdress. Maria rubbed rosemary-infused oil over Anneke's aching bones before spooning Tawa-tawa tea between her parched lips. The poor child had been speaking to herself in a fever; she wished to be put out of her misery and no longer had the will to live. Hannah sat on a chair beside the bed, quietly weeping until Maria whispered they must show the girl they had faith in her recovery. She then went to tend to the child.

"We will rid you of misery and you will live until you're a very old woman with white hair," Maria assured Anneke. *But you will never be a child again,* she thought, *not after such pain. You will be a person of compassion, who will be unable to walk past another's suffering without doing your best to aid them.* She crooned Hannah Owens' song, the one that had comforted her when she was a babe, and that she had then sung to Faith on board the *Queen Esther* and in the woods of Essex County. Anneke begged for her to sing it again and again, and Maria was happy to comply, for the song always reminded her of home.

The water is wide, I cannot get o'er it
And neither have I wings to fly
Give me a boat that shall carry two
And I shall row, my Love and I.
When Cockle Shells turn Silver bells
And mussels grow on every tree,
When frost and snow shall warm us all,
Then shall my love prove true to me.

The minister heard the tune and came to stand in the doorway of the bedchamber, dismayed by the old folk song as he stood watching the stranger care for his daughter. It was a song sung by the cunning folk, people he held in low esteem. He watched as Maria washed the child's matted hair in a bowl with warm water and black soap that had a distinctive sweet scent. Rose and rosemary, sage and lavender. Maria had a beautiful, clear voice, and Anneke, who had tossed and turned in the throes of pain, at last lay quietly, taken up by the song. Her improvement was so quick it appeared that magic was at work, had there been such a thing, for the minister didn't believe in enchantments, only in the ignorance of those who had faith in sorcery. Maria did not leave Anneke's side, remaining by her bed, where she hemmed the girl's nightdresses with blue thread.

The minister drew his wife into the hallway. "We don't know a thing about this woman you've brought here. Who's to say she won't poison our daughter with her potions?"

Hannah Dekker went to her knees and begged her husband to allow Maria Owens to continue to treat Anneke. When he saw how distraught his wife was, the minister had no choice but to agree. Still, when he returned to the room later that night he found that Maria was burning a white candle onto which she had carved the name of the disease, the name of the child, and the date. He was ill at ease, and insisted on tasting the tea Maria was feeding the child; once he had, the bitterness of the drink worried him. "Will this not make her more ill?" he asked.

"I know breakbone fever and you either will trust me to do my best, or I can assure you, your girl will not live."

The minister sat beside Maria and watched the candle flicker. He had one child, and Maria knew what that was like. You carried your heart in your hand.

"You can have me thrown in jail if I fail you," she told him. "You can have me hanged."

The minister exhaled a soft, brittle laugh. "I prefer not to do so. I prefer that my daughter lives."

"Then we're in agreement. That is what I prefer as well."

Maria was in the corridor carrying a basin of cool water and vinegar when the minister's close friend Dr. Joost van der Berg arrived. The doctor was a tall man of huge influence who regularly visited the governors of both New York and Massachusetts and was highly regarded by all. She overheard the doctor speaking with Dekker about the trials in Salem. They were both skeptical that a human being could make contact with the devil, causing death and destruction at that person's will. The doctor believed there were issues with the accusers rather than the accused. It was clear that both he and Dekker saw the entire process of witch hunts as insanity. Neither believed that any of the accused could hit and bite victims when they had been seen miles or more away at the same exact time as the attacks. It was lunacy to think such acts were possible, with Jonas Dekker stating that the accusers were ill and deprived of their sanity. The two men were not alone in their opinions. There were many who were in power in Massachusetts who had begun to see that the trials were a sort of hysteria, although some would not understand the horror of what had been done until later. Increase Mather, the president of Harvard, had published *Cases of Conscience*, making an argument against use of spectral evidence in witch trials, in direct opposition to his son Cotton Mather's *The Wonders of the Invisible World*, which insisted spectral evidence was valuable in a court of law, with the elder man writing, *It is better that ten suspected witches should escape than one innocent person be condemned.* One man among those in power who had not changed his mind at all, however, was the chief examiner of the witchcraft trials, appointed in 1692, John Hathorne.

He had once been a man who had dived into the water fully clothed, who had stood in the moonlight to pick apples from a tree in the courtyard. When she'd asked him why he had abandoned her, he'd merely said, *People change.* Perhaps he wanted to believe this was true, but you were who you were. A person might be changed by ill fortune or circumstance, as Faith had been, but every individual carried a soul within him, unchanging and eternal, a light, a heart, a breath.

Dr. van der Berg brushed by Maria, barely glancing at her. At this moment his only concern was the patient he'd come to visit. He examined the girl, then went into the study, calling Maria to join him, closing the door so they might speak privately. Van der Berg's brow was creased and he looked disturbed, not over the state of his patient, who was much improved, but rather in regard to his own apparent lack of judgment and expertise.

"I suppose you think I'm a fool." He was certainly looking at Maria now.

"Not at all. I've had experience with this illness

in Curaçao and merely recognized it for what it was. You cannot know what you haven't seen."

The doctor was grateful for her kindness, though he believed that in this case he had indeed been an ignorant fool. He was known to be a somewhat arrogant man, assured of his vast knowledge, but he now humbled himself and asked for her method of treatment, and she shared the curatives she'd used, all of a practical nature. Wet washcloths with apple cider vinegar, basil tea with ginger, fish bone broth, all simple enough, but most important was the use of Tawatawa tea, which she would be happy to supply if he came upon more patients with the disease.

"If she first became ill in Aruba, among her cousins, she was likely infected by them. It travels in the breath," he concluded.

"No, by the bite of an insect. It is not like the pox. You cannot be infected by a person who is ill."

"What was your name?" the doctor asked, quite taken with her.

"Maria Owens."

"And mine—"

She stopped him there. "I know who you are, sir." Everyone in New York knew of him, he was so esteemed, a friend to those in power and those in need.

The doctor poured two glasses of port from the minister's glass carafe. "I celebrate you," he said.

People were usually so dull in his opinion, but not this woman. "I must say, I can't help wonder what it is you'll do next."

Maria glanced at his hand. His fortune was changing as he spoke. She had never seen a man's fate change as quickly. When she peered into her own palm, the same thing was happening, a twin to the pattern on the doctor's hand. Their meeting had changed everything that was to come.

Fate is what you make of it, Hannah had told her. *You can make the best of it, or you can let it make the best of you.*

Maria and the doctor were now tied together, by choice, by intent, by happenstance. Fate had made it so, but Maria would make certain it continued to her benefit. When they said their good-byes later that evening, it would not be the last time they met.

While Maria was watching over the vastly improved Dekker girl, she came to understand what she wished to receive as her payment for this cure. She knew why the line on her hand ran identically to the doctor's. She found paper and pen and ink in the minister's study and stayed awake till dawn writing, producing a letter that was three pages long. By noon, Anneke was sitting up in bed, starving and calling for fish bone soup. She wolfed down buttered toast and was strong enough to bathe and have a change of clothes. The girl's mother had been directed in what she must do should the disease reappear, and was aware that it might be a constant fight, though one she could win.

"Must you leave?" Hannah Dekker asked when Maria began to pack up.

"I have a daughter of my own," Maria said. "And you know how to care for Anneke." She asked if she might meet with the minister before she left for home.

"I've told him to give you whatever you ask for," Hannah told Maria. "I am always indebted to you, no matter what you might need."

"I might want something he doesn't expect me to ask for."

"No matter what it might be, it's yours," Hannah assured her.

The women embraced, for they had been through the darkness together and come into the light of day. It was true, when you saved someone, they belonged to you in some small way, but it was also true that you belonged to them. They would stay with you and enter into your dreams and your thoughts, as you would enter into theirs.

Maria found her way downstairs. She had not slept, or washed, or eaten; still she felt elated. She knocked on the door of the library, then ran a hand through her hair before entering when the minister bade her to do so. She thought of the girl she'd been, breathing in smoke, watching everything she had ever known and loved burn, knowing that Hannah Owens had saved her not once, but twice. That was when she'd made a vow that she would never watch another woman burn.

"I'm told I must give you anything you ask for," Dekker said, gesturing for her to sit across from him. He was grateful to her beyond measure, but also glad that the ordeal was over and that Maria Owens would be leaving. "Name your price."

Maria placed the letter on his desk. She had lovely handwriting and a fine turn of phrase. "I want this delivered."

Dekker picked up the letter, but after only a moment, he turned to her, confused. "This is addressed to Governor Phips. Why are you handing it to me?"

"We share the same beliefs. Neither of us wishes for innocent women to hang."

He gave her a look, then turned back to the letter. Once he'd begun reading in earnest, he could not stop. Maria sat in a velvet chair that had been fashioned in Amsterdam, its feet and arms made of polished wooden claws streaked with a patina of gold leaf. She watched the minister's increasing concern as he read on. Two hundred people had been arrested, and already nineteen people had been hanged on Gallows Hill and one man had been crushed to death by stones. Maria had heard that Elizabeth Colson and her grandmother were both in jail awaiting their sentences. Essex County had become a truly dangerous place for women and girls.

"I could not have done any better," Dekker said when he'd finished reading Maria's letter. "I'm impressed by your logic and your prose. It's convincing beyond all measure. But what shall I do with this missive?"

"Ask Dr. van der Berg to sign it and present it as his own to the governor of Massachusetts." When Dekker stared at her, mystified by this request, Maria went on to explain. "He's your dearest friend, and he believes as we do. I can tell he's a good man who wishes to do right." Dekker shook his head, displeased, convinced that to have a man sign a letter he hadn't composed was trickery, especially if that letter was written by a woman. But Maria was not about to give up. "He would have no trouble signing a letter his scribe had written at his bequest. Anyway, it doesn't matter if you think it's a wrongdoing. We are beyond that. Your wife said you must grant my wish, whatever it might be. If you won't help me with the doctor, then I'll have your daughter."

"Pardon me?"

Maria stood, as if to leave the room, and the minister followed her into the hall. If he'd been another, less genteel man he might have grabbed her arm.

"You can't be serious," Dekker said.

"Anything I want," Maria reminded him. "Your wife will not deny me. I gave the girl her life and that life now belongs to me. Send her to my house."

"She's our daughter," the minister said, shocked by the turn in the conversation. "I could have you arrested." He looked into Maria Owens' gray eyes and saw that she was not alarmed by his response. "My words are not just a threat," he said.

"You could do many things. But I hope you will choose to speak to Dr. van der Berg. And I wish to go with him when he travels to Boston. I don't think he'll mind my presence."

Maria went home and packed up everything that mattered to her. Jack Finney would take care of the house, for she might be away for a long time; she might never return. She tossed her clothes into a small satchel so that she could use her trunk for herbs and plant cuttings and bulbs, all wrapped in brown paper. What was most precious was her *Grimoire*, which she would carry in her purse. She went into Faith's room, to collect some of her daughter's clothing, then, overcome by emotion, she sat on the bed. In her hands was the poppet Samuel Dias had made on board the *Queen Esther* when he thought he would die, even though Maria had vowed that he wouldn't. *Do you believe me?* she had asked him once. *Should I?* he had responded.

She took the poppet downstairs, and as she tucked it into the satchel, the fabric tore. It was sailcloth, strong, but hastily sewn, a crude toy that Samuel Dias had told her she must never lose. She'd kept it for thirteen years. She had been a girl of sixteen then, and was now a woman of nearly thirty. When the poppet split open in her hands, she began to cry, an act she should not be capable of, but again and again, Samuel Dias caused her to weep. Perhaps she had inherited this trait from her father, who could cry on command when he was a player in a tragedy. Maria's tears were hot; they burned through the sailcloth as the poppet split in two. Inside there was a small blue pouch, embroidered with the letters *SD*. When she emptied the contents she held seven small diamonds in her hand.

This is what she had seen in the black mirror when she was only a girl, the man she was fated to love, one who never stopped talking, who wasn't afraid to love a witch, who searched for a tree with white flowers that was so ancient it had grown on earth before there were bees, the man whose ring she wore, whose bed she had slept in, who, she had foolishly not understood, had always been the one.

The house on Maiden Lane was shuttered, the doors locked, the garden put to bed. Maria wore a pale blue dress and her red boots, her dark hair wound up, clasped with the two silver clips that had belonged to her mother, which had blackened even more with age. It was not acceptable for a woman to be a scribe, so they would say she was the doctor's serving woman when they arrived at the governor's home. Dr. van der Berg was impressed by the document Maria Owens had written and he had signed his name with a flourish. He thought Maria to be quite extraordinary, in both her literacy and her strategy. Everything about her appealed to him.

"I've asked if you can stay at the governor's house when we reach Massachusetts," he informed her.

"There's no need. I'll be going on to Salem." When he gave her a look, she added, "I lived there once."

"You were fortunate to leave it." He studied her. "But you'll still go?"

"There are things I need to accomplish there." She'd come to enjoy his company, and said a bit more. "Save a life, win a life."

"Whose?" he wanted to know.

"For you? Every woman who will not be hanged. Each of their souls will be saved by you, and all that is righteous will come back to you."

"And you? What's in it for you?"

"I have a daughter in Salem."

"I see." Joost van der Berg looked out at

479

the hilly green landscape. They would spend one night at an inn in Connecticut, but he was beginning to see there was no hope for him. Maria wore a gold ring, and when he'd asked if she was a married woman, she told him only that it was indeed a wedding ring, a very old one, fashioned in Spain. "You're such a logical woman, I'm surprised," he said to her. When Maria gave him a look, he laughed and said, "You clearly believe in love." Van der Berg was a reasonable man who felt sentiments and passions could be tamed and cured, as diseases were, and that raw emotions were nothing more than a nuisance. He had always believed that madness could easily be born from an excess of feeling. That was what happened in Salem. People's emotions had gotten the best of them, and jealousy, hatred, and fear had turned into self-righteous vengeance.

"Love is many things to many people," Maria said.

"It either is or it isn't," the doctor responded. Maria smiled. She enjoyed arguing with this man, a great believer in the rational mind. A fly was buzzing around and now the doctor reached to catch it in his hand. "This creature exists. We can hear it. Touch it. See it with our own eyes. Can we do the same with love?" He was, in his own way, arguing that she should spend the night with him, that such an engagement was the logical conclusion of minds that were so in tune.

He was not afraid of a woman who was his equal, both in his bed and in his life. "Would you say it was fate that brought us together, or simply that it was the practical outcome of our interests? It's sensible that such a connection leads to desire."

When he offered to take her for his own, his hand held out to her, Maria politely declined. That afternoon, she served the doctor a cup of Fall Out of Love Tea, made of ginger, honey, and vinegar. It was one recipe that worked every time. Once they'd reached Boston, it was over and done between them. They were partners in dismantling the witch mania, nothing more. They shook hands and Maria thanked the doctor for all he had done, both for her and for the accused women of Essex County. He had changed the world, and her world had changed as well.

Never deny who you are, Hannah Owens had told her, *no matter the price.*

She had a heart, and there was nothing she could do about it. That was why she had left a letter on the table at Maiden Lane in case Samuel returned. She certainly couldn't give her heart to this good, serious man, a logical doctor who didn't even believe in love. What was meant to be had already begun. The future had already been written in a tree, a kiss, a vow, a rope that would fray, a man who did not believe that love could ever be a curse.

III.

John Hathorne didn't often eat with the family; on most days he left early, and came home when everyone was already asleep. But one morning he came into the room like a windstorm, very much in a hurry, for there was to be a meeting of the magistrates called at the last moment by a clerk who ran from one judge's house to the other. Fortunately the courthouse was steps away and he would have time for some tea and toast at least. He was tall and dark and self-important and handsome, though he was more than fifty. His coat was perfectly pressed and his shoes well polished despite the muck in the streets. Faith took a step back, her breathing labored; it happened to her whenever she saw her father. This man and no other was to blame for crimes against her and her mother and the women of Salem. They had the same high cheekbones and long legs. He pursed his mouth when deep in thought, as she did. And, just like Faith, he was particular about his diet.

She had made cornmeal pudding and fresh speckled eggs cooked with parsley. She'd risen from sleep while it was dark so she could bake an apple pandowdy, a crusty pastry, perfect for afternoon tea. Apples were used in love charms, but also in spells of remembrance. For that purpose she had also added rosemary, an entire sprig, finely chopped. Let him recall his actions against them. Let him be haunted by them. Let him repent. That was why she had come all this way, to face him and damn him so that he would be the one pleading for mercy for once in his life.

Faith wished to be thought of as a servant, and to not have him look too closely at who she might be. So far he hadn't even noticed her. To assist in the effort of being invisible, she had pulled her hair tightly away from her pale face and drawn it into a knot atop her head. Over that she wore a white cap so not a strand of her hair showed forth, for he surely would have recalled her red hair, if he remembered her at all. She used ink to darken her eyebrows, and a bit of pencil shaving to turn her eyelashes black.

Faith could see that the magistrate carried ambition and worry in his heart. She intended to bring bad fortune into his house with its dull mohair-covered chairs and pine tables. Already her presence was affecting the household. She'd noticed that the oldest son, a handsome boy a year or so older than she, couldn't keep his eyes off her. Had he never seen a girl before? Perhaps due to their Puritan beliefs he had never been as close to one as he was to Faith, for his bedchamber was directly above the storage room where she slept, and she had a habit of appearing in his dreams.

The younger children paid her no attention at all, which was just as well. They were innocents and had likely suffered from having the same father as she. She had told the mistress of the house that her name was Jane Smith and said she had grown up on a farm in Andover, and was an orphan who was grateful for any honest work she could find.

"My husband will take tea," Ruth Hathorne reminded Faith when she stood there staring. "And perhaps a slice of the pandowdy, for he won't be back this afternoon."

"No cake," John said, his nose in his notes for the day's meeting. His children knew well enough not to interrupt when he was at work, and he was always at work.

Faith poured him a cup of Tell the Truth Tea. She spilled a few drops on the tabletop. He noticed her then.

"Who is this?" he asked his wife.

"A godsend," Ruth responded. "Jane. She's been here for weeks. She can help me with everything. She's a wonderful baker and very knowledgeable about cooking. She even makes her own tea." The tea supplied from England was so expensive many people drank raspberry tea, called liberty tea, which was not half as good as

485

Faith's mixtures. "We're so fortunate," Ruth was happy to say.

"Do you have a voice?" the magistrate asked Faith.

"I do indeed," she answered.

They gazed at each other, and for one confusing moment each seemed stunned by how similar the other's tone was. Arrogance and intellect. Fine for a magistrate, not so fine for an orphaned girl. Before another breath was drawn, Faith lowered her eyes, though she was reluctant to do so.

"I expect I will not be hearing much of your voice while you live here," he said to her. "My house is a quiet one. The voice we listen to is the Lord's."

"I thought it was yours," Faith said bluntly. "Sir."

The younger children gazed up at her then, and the son, also called John, who had once been a little boy peering at Faith through the white phlox, and who had swallowed his emotions for a lifetime due to fear and fidelity, had a rush of color in his face. The magistrate looked at her again, puzzled.

"Go on," he said. "Do what's expected of you."

Faith went to fetch the biscuits, knowing young John watched her as she left the dining room, turning to give him a quick smile. It did not hurt to have an ally here. He was her brother, but by half, and that half did not include the blood that made her who she was. Faith simply could not puzzle out what on earth had made her mother fall in love with John Hathorne. She assumed he must have presented himself wrapped up in a lie, as many men were known to do. When she returned to the dining room, his tea was gone.

"The oddest thing just happened," Ruth told the girl called Jane, for she was dazed by her last interchange with John Hathorne. "My husband announced that he was afraid to go to his morning meeting. He thought the magistrates might be disciplined. He's never said that he was afraid of anything before. Perhaps your presence is a good influence," she murmured.

"I doubt that, ma'am," Faith was quick to say.

Tell the Truth Tea could affect even the most challenging of liars, those who were false not only to those they loved, but to themselves as well. It seemed her recipe had worked wonders. He'd told the truth to his own wife, an uncommon occurrence.

"I'm sorry he missed the biscuits," Faith said. "I think he would have enjoyed them."

Ruth patted her arm. "You're a good girl." The maid appeared to be an innocent and a poor judge of character who wished to see the best in everyone, even in Ruth's own husband, who was, after nearly twenty years of their marriage, still a complete stranger to her.

• • •

Faith stowed away bones and leavings from her supper, wrapped them in a handkerchief, then sneaked them into a basket and went off, saying she would return from the market with some vegetables and herbs. She wore her cloak and her boots even though the weather was fine. The fiddlehead ferns were unfolding; bloodroot and trout lilies grew in profusion in the marshland. There was a shadow following her, as there always was. Her dear wild heart, her other, who pretended to be what he was not just as she did. People looked out their windows and swore they spied a black wolf that wore a dog's collar, skulking down the cobbled streets, though most in the area had been killed for bounties or for their fur.

Faith found her way across the meadows and headed into the woods, allowing memory to lead her. The town had grown, but there was still plenty of wild land and acres filled with pine and oak, old chestnuts and elms, witch hazel and fragrant wild cherry, with its delicious fruit and poisonous seed. At last, Faith came to a muddy clearing where Maria had made a path. When she scraped at the ground with her boot heel, the blue stones Maria had carried from the ledge of the lake were still there. The roughly made slatted fence ringing the garden had tumbled down and was covered by wild ivy. There was the tiny tilted house, a neglected hunting shack her mother had worked so hard to make into a home. The windows had been covered with thick translucent paper, but that was torn apart now, for raccoons and weasels had taken up residence inside, and one year a bear had made its home in the cabin through summer and the last smoldering blaze of autumn. The seeds of the grapes he had eaten had sprouted and there were now wild grapevines growing over the roof, with wide green leaves unfolding. And there was something Faith didn't recognize, the tree Samuel Dias had brought here from a thousand miles away, planted in the hours before Maria Owens left Massachusetts. People in town said that if you stood beneath the magnolia, your beloved would come to you, no matter the season or the time, and when its flowers bloomed those who passed by became confused, imagining there had been snow in May, or that stars had fallen from the sky.

Even a bitter, hard-hearted girl could feel wistful upon returning to the first real home she'd known. Faith climbed over the broken-down fence and cleared away the ivy. There she discovered what she was looking for, the apothecary garden. It had gone wild, and there were jumbled weeds abounding, but there were still stalks of belladonna, along with the root that took the shape of a man and was said to scream when plucked from the ground. Faith filled the basket with the ingredients she needed, then noticed that a small sparrow had tumbled from its nest. One more ingredient, fallen into her lap. She took it in her hands for it was what she needed for her dark spell, the bones and heart and liver. She closed her eyes as she wrung its neck, and as she did so she could feel the wrongness of her deed pulsing as if a hive of stinging bees were under her skin. Whoever was charmed by this spell would feel the pain he had caused others; his deeds would be pulled out of him and bite him, as if all his wrongdoings were sharp teeth, and he would feel the stab of remorse.

As Faith took the life of the sparrow, Keeper threw back his head and howled, overcome by loss, as if Faith had been stolen from him once again. The sound sent shivers along her spine but she didn't stop. Her blood was on fire. When she opened her eyes the bird was lifeless in the palm of her hand, and Keeper was gone. He was done with her. She was not the person that he had been attached to, the one he'd come to of his own accord, for a familiar can never be called, he must make his own choice, and Keeper had made the choice to leave her.

Faith wrapped the bird in a bit of flannel cloth and placed it in the basket of herbs, then went to search for Keeper. There were muddy footprints that led past the lake where she had fed handfuls of bread to a huge eel, but when she searched the cliffs and caves, Keeper was nowhere to be found. Faith cried out for him, she whistled and clapped her hands; still there was no sign of the wolf. Her most loyal friend had deserted her, and for good reason. She was not the girl he knew. It is easy to become what your actions have made of you.

"Go ahead," she called in a broken voice. "If you leave me, then you were nothing to me anyway!"

Her face was burning as she ran through the fields. She went back to the house with the elm trees and began to simmer her cursed stew over the fire in the kitchen. When she cut up the bird, the lifeline on her left hand stopped. If she had glanced down that afternoon as she swept the Hathornes' house and boiled their laundry with ashes and lye, she would have seen that she had made her own fate out of bitterness and spite. According to the rules of magic, she would have to pay a price for the actions she had taken that had been born of vengeance.

Samuel Dias had returned to New York to stand at Abraham's gravesite, where he said the Kaddish to honor his father's passing from the world. He had been gone to Jamaica and Brazil, and to islands that had no name and seas where there was no wind. He'd spied dozens of trees he might have brought back, beautiful, unusual specimens that had never been seen in New York, pink trumpet trees, blue jacarandas, rosewood trees with green and white flowers, but this time his only cargo had been barrels of dark rum. Samuel left the trees where they were, though each one had made him think of Maria Owens. All the same, a gift given to someone who wants nothing from you is worthless. He knew that now, though he still dreamed of the expression on Maria's face when she looked out the window of the jail and declared the magnolia to be a miracle.

Samuel was growing tired of the sea and its loneliness, something he had always been grateful for as a younger man. At night he stood on the deck and watched the creatures beneath the water and thought of the first ship he'd ever sailed upon, when the navigator his father had enlisted took him under his wing and taught him to read the stars. Back then, he could still remember everything about his mother and sisters. Now it was difficult for him to bring up their faces, although there were certain things that he would never forget, his sisters singing as they walked up a hill, his mother telling him his first stories, the bonfire on her burning day, the white hood covered with stars that she was made to wear, how empty the world was without her.

He had felt the same sort of aloneness once again when Maria told him to leave; the sharpness of her dismissal was still as fresh as it had been the day he left Manhattan. He was deeply hurt, and it was this emotion that had made him stay away, but it also caused him to walk past the house on Maiden Lane, even though he had no intention of stopping. Samuel had too much pride to go where he wasn't wanted, and yet he was drawn there like a dog. He waited to see if there was a glimmer of life, perhaps a lantern when dusk fell, or smoke from the brick oven's chimney. When he saw none of these things, he went closer, pulled forward despite his will. Spring in New York meant horseshit in the streets, and sewers running into the footpaths, and crowds of newcomers. The city was so alive Samuel Dias felt his aloneness all the more here than he did at sea. He went through the gate in the falling dusk, for he was a fool, he admitted that to himself, and his hurt drove him on. The garden was filled with weeds and the Tree of Heaven was in need of water. He went to the well and filled a pail, then watered the tree, but he could already tell it would do no good. This genus belonged in the tropics, and was never meant to be here.

He went to try the door and found it locked. He had a sinking feeling in the pit of his stomach. All the while he'd been gone he had imagined Maria in this house, but now it appeared he'd been wrong, for the place was clearly abandoned, though he owned it still.

"You're to be off the property."

It was a man's voice he heard, English by the sound of it. Dias turned to see a fellow with a horsewhip in his hand, then glanced around and spied a spade he could use if he needed a weapon. "Am I?"

"Sorry, brother, but this is private property."

"I know. It's mine."

The other fellow laughed out loud. A Cornishman, that's what he was. Samuel had known many who'd taken to sea, though they all seemed to long for their homeland, and when they'd had enough to drink they cried, desperate to return to a place they couldn't wait to leave behind when they were young.

"Since I'm well acquainted with the owner," the fellow told Samuel, "I can tell you that you're wrong."

Samuel fished around in his bag and brought out his key to the door.

"If it fits the lock, I may have to believe you," the Cornishman, who said he was called Finney, now allowed.

When the key fitted perfectly, there was no fight to be had, and, although they were still cautious, the men shook hands. They sat down in the garden chairs where Abraham Dias used to spend hours when he realized he loved being on land and became an avid gardener. Finney was made to understand that this man, who was wearing a black coat in the fine weather, as he did every day of his life, for he'd never shaken the chill brought on by his disease, was indeed the owner of the house.

"I could tell you many things about why and how Maria came to be here, I could talk all day, but I'd rather you do the talking," he suggested to Finney.

He was told that Faith had disappeared and Maria had recently set off after her, traveling first to Boston, then to Salem. It was clear this fellow Finney knew the girl well and that Maria had placed her trust in him. She had gone to see him in the Bowery the day she left. Because he'd saved her life, Faith would forever owe him her loyalty, a situation Samuel understood, for his life had been saved as well, and his loyalty was unwavering.

"The way I see it, the girl owes me nothing," Finney said. Yet she had appeared with a gift before leaving for Salem, for they might never see each other again, and she offered him an elixir she called Live Well Tea. She advised that he drink it every morning. He had done so, for he trusted Faith Owens, and his life had indeed improved. His new wife, Catherine, could not have children, but a little girl had been abandoned in the Fly Market with a note pinned to her dress. *She is yours.* Finney and Catherine had adopted her and now called the child their own. It was his heart's desire to be a father again, one he'd never spoken of, and yet Faith had seen through him. She had given him what he wanted most in the world.

"I worry for her," Finney admitted. "The art she's working is dark, and it takes a toll. Maria's gone to save the girl from herself." Finney's eyes brightened. "Maybe you should go after her."

"No." Dias laughed. "I couldn't. I've been told to stay away."

"You don't seem a man who will do as he's told." When Samuel shook his head, Finney went on. "I'm asking you to go after them, and that cancels out what she told you. I'm asking on Faith's behalf. She thinks I'm the one who saved her, but she's got it all wrong. I was a dead man when I found her in the flatlands. My life was over and done with. She's the one who saved me."

Samuel thought this over after Finney had left. He was a man who enjoyed a good argument, but he was humble as well, and could admit when he'd made a mistake. He thought perhaps the Cornishman had been right. Samuel had saved Maria's life on her hanging day, so perhaps he was not the only one with a debt to pay. Perhaps they owed their loyalty to one another.

He sat in the garden until dark, when a chill sifted into the soft spring air, then he went inside, still trying to make his decision. It had been a

496

long time since he'd been home, and though the house was empty and dim, it was still so familiar it was as if he'd been here only days before. There was a lantern on the table and he took out the small brass tinderbox that he carried to strike a light. He sat hunched in his black coat. He could have started a fire in the fireplace or gone upstairs to sleep, but he spied a letter on the table, his name on the envelope that had been sealed with red wax. Samuel knew the script, those perfect black letters. Perhaps the sight had allowed her to see that he would come back. He took his knife and slit open the envelope.

We do things when we're young that we regret. I believed that love was my enemy, but I was wrong.

He folded the letter into his coat and made certain to lock the door when he left. It took less than two hours to get together a crew willing to sail to Salem, for there was no cargo and the lighter the ship the faster the journey. He was in a hurry, that much was true.

He recalled the woman who had given him directions to the jail and went to her house straightaway. Anne Hatch spied him through the window and opened the door, beckoning him to come up the stairs. "I remember you. The man with the tree."

As she had years ago, when he first arrived in

497

Salem, she fetched him a plate of chicken stew. He thanked her and ate, ravenous, and when he was finished he told her he had come for Maria once again.

"If she ever did come back here I figure she'd go out to that house she had," Anne said.

He took the path in the woods, headed to the spot where he had planted the tree. It was dark when he arrived and the air was damp and cool. Exhausted, he lay down in the grass, using his satchel as a pillow and his coat as a blanket, falling asleep so quickly he didn't hear the clacking sound in the ground beside him, a wretched noise he would have recognized as the one he'd heard outside the jail on Maria's hanging day, the sound of a beetle no one in this world wishes to hear.

Hathorne was enraged when he returned home, for the final meeting of the magistrates had been filled with petty jealousies and hostilities, with judges blaming each other now that Governor Phips had dispatched a decree that the witchcraft trials must stop and those in custody be allowed their freedom. A clerk whose aunt was currently in jail left the courthouse and was quick to spread the news throughout the town. Soon there were families all over Essex County who were celebrating. They praised the governor's wisdom; they lit bonfires in the fields, and brought wreaths of wildflowers to the hidden graves of those who had already been hanged, their bodies stolen by their families so that they might be secretly buried, for those deemed witches were not allowed even that last bit of dignity.

Faith was washing up after dinner. The family had dined, but Faith had made the cursed stew meant for John Hathorne alone, and had baked a crust for Revenge Pie, fixed from the bramble, what some people call blackberry, used in transference magic. Into the pie she baked the bird she had killed. After a few bites, his luck would turn; his roof would blow off in every storm, his son would set off to sea, he would not have a night of sleep. He sat at the table when he called for her; she brought out a tray with the stew and a plate of pie and a pot of Tell the Truth Tea.

Everyone else in the house was asleep. The peepers were trilling with their shivery song, for it was the time of year when everything comes alive, birds and bees and frogs. Faith had *The Book of the Raven* tucked inside her dress, burning her chest. She had a talisman in hand made after finding a blackthorn bush in the woods, a wild bitter plum whose shimmering black bark was covered by large black spines. She'd collected a handful of spines, even though her fingers bled, and she pressed them into a ball of wax and hatred, a charm to carry with her, which would increase her power and cause this man who was her father pain throughout his body, something unnamable and incurable. If she attached it to him, the revenge would be threefold, strong enough to burn a hole right through him. What she wished for was that forever after, throughout history, Hathorne would be remembered as a man who had no conscience as he had called for the murder of twenty innocent people. The colony itself seemed cursed. Crops failed, smallpox spread, and many wondered if God saw fit to punish them for acts against blameless people; a Day of Humiliation would be declared, a day of prayer and fasting, in the hopes that God would forgive them. But Hathorne would never ask for forgiveness; he would never ask for any sort of pardon from men or from God.

"At last," he said when Faith set down his supper tray, so annoyed he might have been waiting for hours rather than minutes. Faith watched as he ate the stew. Afterward he downed a large tumbler of water. He was parched from the start of the enchantment. Faith felt quite thirsty herself. Perhaps being in his presence affected her more than she would have imagined.

"I have no need of an audience," Hathorne said when he realized her eyes were on him. "I'm ready for my tea." He, like so many men in Salem, most often took his meals alone, away from the distractions of his family. Faith cut him a piece of pie. Hathorne didn't usually like sweets, but after one bite he couldn't stop eating the blackthorn Revenge Pie.

"Ruth was correct about one thing," Hathorne allowed. "You know how to bake."

"I know more than that. I know you. But you, do you not know me?" Faith asked when he was through.

"I know when a girl is rude and improper if that's what you're trying for." He felt defeated, for the governor's edict and letter had made those who had judged the witch trials seem like fools, and worse, like criminals themselves. It was said that a Dutch doctor had influenced the governor to end the trials. John thought perhaps he would fight it. He had time before all of those now incarcerated could be processed and released, if they ever were. Lydia Colson, Elizabeth Colson's grandmother, had already died in jail due to the harsh conditions and her frail health.

Hathorne would have chased the housemaid away after his supper, but he had a sudden urge to tell someone the truth about his life. Now that the governor had stopped the trials, he feared how the world would judge him. They would laugh at all he had tried to do in an attempt to rid the world of evil. Tonight he himself wavered in his beliefs. Perhaps all along the beast had been inside of him.

"I thought you might tell me something about love," Faith said.

He laughed at her sheer nerve. Ruth really had no business taking in strangers. Hathorne stood up, for he knew the intimidating effect of his height on most people, although right away he could see this girl wasn't the least bit cowed. "I'll have you let go in the morning. You should pack tonight."

"So you know nothing about love?"

He gave her a dark look. Girls her age were foolish, dreamy things. "You marry as you're expected to." He was blathering on for no reason, telling her the truth of his feelings. Well, what did it matter? She'd soon enough be gone. "So yes, I know nothing about love. Perhaps I'm incapable of it."

"Wasn't there a woman some time ago? You must have loved her."

"In Curaçao," he said before he could stop himself. "I left without saying a word. I didn't know what to do with her. She wanted too much and all I wished for was to be left in peace. It all went wrong before I thought it through."

He had no idea why he'd said all that. It made him sound as if he were a coward and then, quite suddenly, he realized that he was. His eyes and throat burned. As a child he was caned if he wept, but now he feared that if he weren't careful he'd soon be crying in front of this housemaid. Love

502

was nothing he thought about. It hadn't affected him in the least, except for a day or two when he was enchanted, when he seemed to be another man entirely. Hathorne thought of his wife on their wedding night, weeping for her parents. He didn't say a word to comfort her, he just did as he pleased. He imagined the women on trial begging for their lives, the ones in prison, the ones who'd been hanged. Hathorne had seen evil everywhere, but now it resided within him. That was the truth if he was to tell it. That was what he was saying now.

"I would change things if I could. I would be another man." He shook his head and pushed the tea away. "I was that for a while."

"Men don't change who they are deep inside. You must have hid yourself from her."

Hathorne narrowed his eyes. It had been a hellish day and that hell continued now. "Who do you think you are?"

"Who do *you* think I am?" the girl replied.

And then he knew. He looked closely and saw what was directly before him. She was indeed his daughter, too smart for her own good. He was impressed despite himself. The cool gray gaze, the fearlessness, the way she could hold her own against him. He wished his son could do as well.

It was then that the black charm fell from the folds of Faith's garment and rolled upon the floor. Hathorne knew it for what it was, some sort of wicked curse. He should have expected as much; she was not only his daughter, but also the daughter of a witch. Evil is drawn to evil. Truth is drawn to truth.

Before he could reach for it, Faith picked up the charm though it pierced her hands.

"I've decided not to use it," Faith said. It was true, she'd done enough damage and had already changed his fate. She had seen her likeness in his eyes. A wounded person who wounded others. "I had it with me in case you acted against me with ill will, for my own protection."

"I think we shan't wait till morning," he said. "You can leave tonight."

"I will do so." Faith untied her apron, then pulled off her cap. Her red hair shone in the dim light of the room.

"You've been making me say all I've said tonight. You'll leave here now and not come back. If you were anyone else I would have you arrested." But the witch trials were over, and if anything he might face charges for having a child outside of his marriage. Best to be rid of her, as he'd rid himself of Maria. He took out a purse of coins, which she quickly refused. He shook his head. She was nothing but trouble. "You're very like your mother," he said.

"Thank you." Faith's eyes were burning. "I was afraid I might take after you."

She threw out the rest of the pie, so no one else in the household would mistakenly eat it; inside were the bird bones, fragile little things that made a sob rise in Faith's throat. This is where left-handed magic had brought her, to the black edges of revenge. As it was the cursed stew would change John Hathorne's future and his standing in history.

Faith left a note for Ruth, thanking her for her kindness. She wondered if Ruth had known who she was, and had taken her in to make up for how John Hathorne had wronged her. It didn't matter anymore. Faith no longer wanted anything, not even revenge. It had changed her into something she didn't wish to be, and the price was too high. She made sure to lock the door when she left. She had met her father and he had met her, and she didn't know which of them was the worse for having done so.

Two farmers spied her in the field, in her black cape and red boots, running as fast as she could. They knew immediately what she was. She was followed by a dark shifting shape, a wolf with silver eyes. When she left the Hathornes, she'd found that Keeper was waiting in the garden. No matter what she had done, he still belonged to her, and she to him. She went on her knees to embrace him before they ran off together, stumbling into this wretched place where men found evil in everything they saw, in shoes, in cloaks, in wolves, in women.

The farmers would later tell the constable that she had set their barn on fire, but in fact they themselves overturned a lantern in their hurry to chase after her, guns in hand. When there is murder intended, murder will be the result. They shot into the dark as if the dark itself were their enemy. They had both been there on the day the crows died, and it was an event that still thrilled them, for they had embroidered the story with an attack of murderous crows sent by the devil himself. When they heard a howl, they thought it was a she-wolf, but it was Faith, crying out as Keeper fell into the grass. She sank to her knees and held her hands over the bloody wounds, reciting an incantation of protection, but it was impossible to staunch the flow of blood. She was reaching for *The Book of the Raven*, so distraught she didn't notice when men came up behind her, guns ready. The barn was in flames now, and the men blamed her, though she had only passed by. A witch's presence can cause mayhem, and now that they had her, they feared her. They wrapped chains around Faith and studied her as she cursed them, a girl drenched in wolf's blood, powerless at last, the sort of girl they'd like to drown.

Dr. Joost van der Berg was kind enough to hire a carriage to take Maria to Salem. Governor Phips had changed the way an alleged witch could be tried; by October the trials would be completely outlawed. Because of this success, the doctor had offered Maria an appointment to be his personal secretary, but she kindly turned him down. She did, however, accept his offer to find her a solicitor, and on her way out of Boston the carriage stopped so that a fellow named Benjamin Hardy could draw up a trust and a will. She had come up with a plan to build a grand house in Salem, one that could never be sold, and always remain in the family. This trust would ensure that the Owens women would always have a home.

Maria had not been back to Essex County since the night she left for New York with Samuel. She had been so young the first time she'd seen these green fields and the marshy land abutting the North River, only seventeen. It was impossible to know then what she knew now. The carriage stopped on Washington Street. Maria had looked in the black mirror to see Faith standing on the path to the door, empty now, and covered by fallen leaves. She thanked the driver and went up the path. Ruth heard a knock at the door and she knew who had come. She felt a shiver inside of her, the same feeling she'd had when she was a girl and the sheriff had told her that her parents were gone.

When Ruth opened the door they recognized each other as if it had been only days since Maria had been driven along the road in an oxcart wearing a white sackcloth, her hair shorn. The truth of it was that Ruth had imagined running after her, but she had stayed here, behind the gate.

"All I want is my daughter," Maria told her.

Ruth understood a mother's love and concern. "I knew she was his daughter. She resembles him. But she's not here now. He sent her away."

Hathorne had punished Ruth for taking on the girl without his permission. Look where it had led. He was still coughing up small bits of bird bone. Ruth had been made to get on her knees and recite passages of Scripture for hours without a drink of water or a bit of rest.

Maria could hear the thudding of Ruth's heart. She did not envy her life. "Tell me where she's gone."

"If I knew I would. I promise you that."

"Did he know her for who she was?"

During Ruth's punishment the tea Hathorne had been given was still at work and he'd told her the truth. The girl was his flesh and blood.

"He did. I could tell he thought she was clever," Ruth said. He had not said as much, but she knew from the way he looked at the girl each time she hadn't backed down. "Now I see, she's very much like you."

"Did she hurt him?" Maria asked.

"Oh no," Ruth said. "If anything I suppose she was hurt by him."

dark water and when she woke she was drenched, even though there had been no rain. Samuel was sleeping still, holding onto a bough of the tree.

Long ago, before they'd ever met, before either of them had come to the second Essex County, they had each made the same promise. They would never watch another woman burn. But there were other ways to be rid of a woman who didn't behave, who did as she pleased, who had courage, who talked back. You held her head under water until she could no longer speak.

The farmers locked Faith in a neighbor's barn, for their own barn was smoldering ash. They would have brought her to the magistrate, but the governor had outlawed the witch trials, so they tried her themselves and found her guilty. They had been the judges, and they would be the executioners. It was the Lord's day when they dragged her to the lake in chains. It was early morning, with a mist rising and the sky breaking into bands of color. The men had frightened themselves with their own cruelty and their own imaginings. They had convinced themselves they had caught a servant of the devil and not a thirteen-year-old girl who pleaded for her life until she realized it wasn't any use to beg. Now she was speaking backwards, an incantation from *The Book of the Raven*, hidden in her cloak, that beautiful book a woman had written to help other women save themselves. Women who were bought and sold, women who had no voice, women forced to have secret lives, women who knew that words were the most powerful magic. Faith had vowed to leave the left side and forsake black magic, but she turned to it now. She was wrapped in irons, therefore the spell couldn't do much damage; still the men's throats began to close up, and when they tried to speak to each other they could only grunt, as if they were animals. Their hands appeared to be changing, as if they had claws rather than nails. It was the spell of the beast, when an individual shows what resides within him, and it is only dark magic if there is darkness within.

The farmers were brothers, Harold and Isaac Hopwood, cruel men who were even more brutal after drink, and they had been drinking all night. Their barn had burned down and they needed someone to blame. Blame a woman, drown a woman, let the Lord be the judge. They carried her to the lake, which was as deep as the end of the world, the waters where her own mother had been tested as a witch, a lake that no man, woman, or child would enter for it was said to be cursed, and certainly there were leeches in the shallow reedy water, and the lilies were attached to black weeds that reached all the way to hell.

The brothers carried a chair that Faith had been bound to with rope. There were still irons around her arms, chains the farmers used to keep their cows in place. Ready to be rid of her, they could tell she was bad luck, and even though she was a girl, they feared her. They sent her out as if on a boat, so that she drifted out from the shore. Courts and magistrates meant nothing to the brothers; they would make their own law on their own land. The Hopwoods were sweating through their clothes, but they were chilled as well, and they still felt the tightness in their throats. What was done was done, and surely they were in the Lord's favor, and yet there was fear seeping into their bones, as if they were as brittle as twigs, as if they might break and turn into a heap of dust.

Faith's black cloak rose up, a dark flower that was disappearing as it sank below the surface. Her face was white, a lily. She remembered when she had a vision in Maude Cardy's parlor in Brooklyn, when she was underwater and about to enter hell, and she knew this is what she had foreseen, the dark water rushing in, and her own tears, a witch's tears, tears that burned as if they were made of fire.

When Maria climbed down and stood in the grass, she saw a dozen crows winging across the sky. The day was bright and she could spy the blue center of the lake in the distance. She took off running without a word. Samuel Dias called to her, but she wouldn't stop, and so he followed through the woods, not knowing where he was going, disoriented as he made his way through the brambles. Maria was in front of him, and when he looked through the trees she seemed to be flying, untouched, whereas he had to dodge tree stumps and branches, cursing as he ran.

Maria spied the men at the shore. She knew right away they were the ones who had her daughter. Metal, ropes, fire, water. She saw a long red hair on one of the Hopwood brothers' coats. She spied the aura of disaster, a dark, ashy shade. Maria was almost upon them when she stumbled upon a book that had been dropped on the rough path. Once held in her hands, *The Book of the Raven* fell open to a spell of protection meant to stop an attack and hold the assailants at bay. She began the incantation right then, and as she spoke the branches swayed and leaves fell down and turned the water green. She could not stop speaking it; she must continue until they were driven off. There was the scent of fire, and the brothers felt as if their skin was burning; still they waded into the water, pushing the chair out farther.

It was then Maria heard the deathwatch beetle. Her breath was sharp and cold. The clacking sound was louder; it echoed now. She continued the incantation. She would not lose Faith a third time. She recited the spell faster until her lips were burning, until the brothers' skin was aflame.

They turned to see her, and later they would swear she was levitating, standing in the air rather than on the ground. They were cursed and they knew it. There were leeches in their boots and they had forgotten their own names. They let go of the chair, unable to do any more harm to Faith, watching the witch on the shore as she hexed them. The chair was sinking into the center of the lake that was so green it seemed made of grass. Faith's red hair was still above the water, the color of blood and of hearts torn asunder.

By now Samuel had reached the lake; he had already stripped off his black coat as he ran into to the shallows, nearly stumbling as he pulled off his boots. The Hopwood brothers tried to stop him as he raced past, perhaps they thought he was the devil himself and it was their duty to attack him, but Maria still had the book of magic in her hands and she made it impossible for them to cause any more damage. They were stuck where they were, unable to move, hip-deep in the water, yet convinced they had been set on fire. The water had turned from green to black, so murky it was impossible to see anything at all. For a moment Maria stopped speaking. Faith and Samuel had both disappeared. In that moment of silence, when she stopped reading from the book, the brothers all but trampled one another as they ran to shore and through the woods, afraid for their lives, desperate to be as far away from Maria as possible, as if distance made any difference to a curse.

Samuel resurfaced, then dove again. He was an expert swimmer, but the lake was muddy and he had to feel his way. A dark creature swam beneath him, a huge eel he could barely see, but the eel pushed Faith upward so that Samuel could grab the girl by her cloak, hauling her out of the chains that bound her to the wooden chair, which now sank and went on sinking to the endless bottom of the lake. When Samuel tried to swim to the surface, he realized the waterweeds had hold of him, wrapped around his ankles and legs. He was caught, but he pushed Faith upward and watched her rise to the surface through the bits of sunlight that pierced the cloudy water.

Samuel knew that he was drowning. His leg was trapped no matter how he tugged. He moved his arms, still trying to swim, not yet giving up, but it was happening whether he fought against it or not. He had seen other men drown, they had fallen from the riggings of ships, or leapt into the currents while drunk, and he had wondered how it felt to be taken by the water, if it was a struggle or if it was more like a dream. He hadn't had a breath for so long his heart was stopping. He thought of Maria on the dock in Curaçao and how he had fallen in love with her then, even though he was bent over with pain.

Samuel now felt an even sharper pain across

his chest from the pressure of the water; it began in his heart and seared through his arm, then his throat, and finally his head. He had a single thought and it was she, and then he gave that up as well though it burned inside him. The way he was dying felt like a dark bonfire in a lake that had no end.

Faith was spitting water, alive, and so Maria didn't wait another instant. She quickly filled her boots with stones, then shoved them back on. She repeated the incantation for protection, calling to Hecate, offering her devotion if only she could be granted this one thing. One time underwater, that was all she wanted. Maria ran into the lake, past her shoulders, past her neck. She dove and went under, the stones in her boots weighing her down. She saw through the darkness and there was Samuel Dias, floating in the mucky water, already a dead man. She dragged him out of the tangle of waterweeds that had held him down. The threaded roots were green and slimy and black, even though they opened into flowers on the surface. To float once more, Maria kicked off her boots, and as the stones fell into the bottomless darkness, she arose.

She pulled Samuel toward the marshy shore, a sob escaping from her mouth as she shivered; water streamed down her back and into her eyes. Maria had always been able to hear Samuel's heartbeat when he was near and now she heard nothing at all. She tore open his shirt and pounded on his chest, her own breathing ragged.

Faith crawled over, drenched and in despair. "Goat," she wailed. "Wake up." There was no answer and Faith began to cry. She was on her knees beside her grieving mother, both coated with mud, weeds in the folds of their clothes, lake water dripping from their hair. Dias's skin was pale and he was so very quiet. It was clear that he was gone. "You have to stop," Faith told her mother. She knew death when she saw it. She'd seen it before. "Mother, he's no longer with us."

His spirit had left him and he was motionless. The beetle had stopped its clicking, for its work was done. Maria would not let this be their fate. She pounded on Samuel's chest, again and again, in a fury. They had wasted time because of a curse; death was always possible, with or without magic. Her own mother had confided that there was an ancient bargain a person could make with the darkest powers, one that would bring back the dead to walk among the living. *He will never be the same if you do. He will be a shadow self, a dark creature, but you will have him.* Mothers had done this with children, only to have the rescued child run away into the woods, a feral creature with no memory of the past; wives had brought back husbands who had afterward left them for other women, or stolen from them, or murdered them in their sleep. Maria didn't care. She was ready to make the bargain. She hit Samuel's chest one last time, ready to take up a knife so that she might cut her arm to mix her blood with his, the beginning of this dreaded spell, but before she could, Samuel opened his eyes.

He had been dead until Maria forced his heart into beating. He'd returned from the dark water, from the darkness of the endless depth where he had seen his father sitting in a garden chair, waving him away. *Don't be a fool,* Abraham Dias called to his son. *She's waiting for you, you stupid man.*

Maria lay beside him in the grass, her arms around him. You cannot curse a man who has already died and come back. He has rid himself of one life and begun another, a life in which love is everything. He had been dead but now his eyes were open and the woman he loved was singing to him.

A ship there is and she sails the sea,
She's loaded deep as deep can be,
But not so deep as the love I'm in
I know not if I sink or swim.
The water is wide, I cannot get o'er it
And neither have I wings to fly
Give me a boat that will carry two
And both shall row, my Love and I.

Samuel had to strain to hear Maria's voice, but soon he understood she was saying she wanted to be with him no matter the cost.

"Are we ruined?" Samuel asked. The world was so bright and beautiful. Like his father before him, he had a new appreciation of the earth.

"No," Maria said. She was as sure of this as she'd ever been of anything. "We're just alive."

While Samuel slept in the grass, Faith and Maria sat together in the falling dark. They had made a bonfire and sparks rose into the black sky. Faith gazed at her left palm. The line that had stopped when she found *The Book of the Raven* had begun again. She would live to be an old woman, she saw that now, but one who couldn't work magic. That was the price she paid when she ignored the rules. She'd lost the sight and with it her bloodline gifts. She was ordinary now.

"If you don't want me to be your daughter, I would understand," Faith told her mother.

"You'll always be my daughter." Now and forever, in this life and the life to come, no matter what separated them or what brought them together.

At the first light, Faith would return to the field and bring Keeper back to the bonfire so that her loyal companion would be turned to ashes here in the woods, where he belonged. They watched the bonfire burn and remembered when they first saw fireflies and thought stars had dropped from the sky, when Keeper was a pup and drank goat's milk, when Cadin brought gifts of buttons and keys, when they plucked apples from the trees, when the world of Essex County was brand-new.

Samuel Dias was asleep in the grass, his black coat still soaking wet. He was still dreaming when Maria Owens leaned in to tell him a story, one he already knew and had known ever since he saw her on the dock in Curaçao when she was fated to save his life, and he was fated to save hers in return.

PART SIX

Fate

Twelve carpenters had worked for a year without stopping to build Maria Owens' house. Fifteen varieties of wood were used: golden oak, silver ash, cherrywood, elm, pine, hemlock, pear, maple, mahogany, hickory, beech, cypress, cedar, walnut, and birch. The house was tall, with a twisted vine of wisteria that ran along the porch, in bloom at the first surge of spring. In the kitchen there sat a huge black cast-iron stove; in the pantry were dozens of shelves on which to store herbs. Two staircases had been constructed, one led to the attic, turning and twisting as if it were a puzzle bending in on itself, the other was made of the finest oak, with a broad landing that offered a window seat framed by damask drapes imported from England, ones very like those that had hung in the Locklands' manor house in the first Essex County. Beside the front door was the brass bell that had hung outside Hannah Owens' door.

When a traveling portrait painter came through town, he was hired to capture Maria's likeness in oils, rendering her image perfectly, down to the bump she had on her hand from the day she pounded on John Hathorne's door. When sitting for the painter, she wore her favorite blue dress, with her dark hair caught up in a blue ribbon and the sapphire that she never took off fastened at her throat. She wore her new red boots, ones Samuel Dias had had fashioned in Boston, which she wore every day. It was said that her eyes followed you when you passed by her portrait, and that she could see what was inside you and that you would know in that moment whether or not you had been true to yourself.

There were dozens of green glass windows, imported from England, and two brick chimneys that towered above the roof. The house was so well made that when a hurricane struck, every other house on the street sustained severe damage, but not a single shutter blew away from the Owens house. Even the laundry out on the line stayed exactly where it was on that day, which led neighbors to gossip even more than before. Maria kept chickens and goats in a small barn, and there was a renegade swan that arrived one day and refused to leave, soon enough spoiled by the crusts of bread he preferred to wild food. Maria called him Jack, and he waited outside for her on the porch each morning, and followed her about all day long, accompanying her on city streets and into shops, so that the children in town whispered that he'd once been a man who'd been turned into a swan, though no one dared to come near him, for Jack had a nasty temper and was devoted to one person alone.

In the garden there grew lily, rue, and arnica, along with fiery onions that could cure dog bites and toothaches. Maria planted Spanish garlic in great abundance, peonies to ward off evil, rows of lettuce, parsley, and mint, and lavender, planted for luck, by the back door. The original shed had been attached to a glass greenhouse so that herbs could be grown all year long, even in the dead of winter. Behind the foggy windows there were pots filled with lemon balm, lemon verbena, and lemon thyme. The more dangerous plants were kept inside the locked shed, which now boasted a murky glass ceiling so that light could enter. Belladonna, yarrow, black nightshade, wolfsbane, foxglove, lords and ladies with its pretty toxic berries, pennyroyal, which could end a pregnancy. It was there that Maria kept her *Grimoire* in its black toadskin cover, a book that would belong to Faith upon her mother's death so that she might learn magic all over again, from the start, but not until she was a very old woman who had come to understand the importance of the rules. On the first page Hannah had written the rules of magic, and now Maria added a third, doing so without hesitation. Some lessons you have to learn for yourself, others are best to know from the start.

Do as you will, but harm no one.
What you give will be returned to you
threefold.
Fall in love whenever you can.

Perhaps the *Grimoire* was the reason toads collected in the garden, or perhaps they merely enjoyed the varieties of greens Maria grew— sorrel, dandelion, spinach, and chard. At the rear of the large yard there was a small orchard of fruit trees—plum, peach, pear, and several varieties of apple—all having been set into the earth in the dark of the moon. Maria left the acreage between the house and the lake as free and open land, there for all to enjoy, a gift that would bring a blessing to her family. The fence that circled the house was of an unusual construction, black metal with spikes, laid out in the form of a snake with its tail in its mouth, ensuring that the only way someone could reach the door was to walk through the front gate where the ivy grew wild. Maria nailed the skull of a horse she had found in the Hopwoods' pasture to a post to send a message to unwanted visitors. That pasture was deserted now that the brothers had disappeared in the middle of the night, headed west, still unable to speak, dreaming every night that they were drowning in a dark, bottomless lake and waking each morning with mouths full of water.

Twenty blue stones from the old path to the

shed had been used to fashion a pathway to the house. Every night women came for what they needed most, red pepper tea for an upset stomach, or butterfly weed for nerves, or a bar of black soap that could take years off their age, or a charm for love. Love was what Maria was best at, and she didn't fight it anymore. Let the rumors be spoken, logical people knew that a woman in trouble would never be turned away from Maria Owens' door. If she went anywhere in the middle of the night, wrapped in a dark cloak and carrying her bag of curatives and teas, it was to visit an ill child. All the same, there was always bound to be talk about a household of women, not that it stopped people from coming to the door late at night in search of assistance, particularly in matters of love. Other houses were dark, but the light on the Owens' porch was always kept on. On some occasions baskets of cakes and pies were left at the door, or freshly made cheese, or hand-knitted sweaters, left there by those whose loved ones had been accused of witchcraft, then freed by the governor's decree, for there were those who were convinced that Maria Owens had something to do with his decision, and for this they would always be grateful.

The Owens Library opened in May, the most beautiful month of the year, when it was possible for people in Massachusetts to forget winter, at least until it came again. Maria bought the empty jail after Samuel Dias made a donation that would cover all costs for its renovation. While the carpenters were at work, they discovered a blue journal hidden behind the bricks. Work stopped for the day. Even the most serious-minded of the men were afraid of that slim blue volume and not one would touch it. When, at the end of the day, Maria came to see what had been accomplished on the project, the carpenters were sitting in a semicircle waiting for her, their faces ashen. She thought perhaps they had found the remains of a body, for surely there were those who had never left their cells alive, and when she saw that it was her journal that had stopped the men from working and was the reason they stared at her, unsure of what to do next, she was reminded of the first lesson Hannah had taught her. Words had power.

Maria kept the journal in the library to remind those who passed through the doors of what had happened in this building. Before it was filled with dozens of volumes, there was a book that had been written here when women were not allowed to speak on their own behalf. In the evenings there were lessons for those who wished to learn how to read. At first only women attended, many of whom sneaked out and said they were going to a quilting party, but after a while their husbands came to peer through the door, farmers and fishermen who entered the room with their hats in their hands, shyly picking up a book, then fitting their tall, strong bodies into chairs meant for children.

The Maria Owens School for Girls held its first classes soon after, with ten girls in attendance, aged six to thirteen. Faith Owens taught both Latin and Greek, along with poetry and classics. There were still many in town who thought it was a danger and a disservice to society to educate female students; all the same, several local residents allowed their daughters to register for classes, despite the rumors about the Owens women. Faith was not yet seventeen, but quite well respected by the girls and their families, who ignored the rumors that vowed both Owens women became crows who flew above the fields after dark, and that they would put a curse on you if you wronged them, and that they swam naked in Leech Lake. It was true that Maria went to the lake on summer mornings. She could only float, but that was enough, for she'd been able to dive the one time she needed to do so. If she wanted to swim there, among the waterweeds and the lilies, with no clothes on and her hair tied up with blue ribbon, who was to say such a thing wasn't a pleasure and a delight?

No one knew whether or not Maria was married, but there was a man who spent winters with her and went to sea cach summer. Some people swore he'd come back from the dead, and that love had returned him to life. His sailors said little about him when they frequented the taverns, other than to note that he paid them well and was a brilliant navigator. They laughed about his personal habits. He liked to tell stories, he always drank a special tea to give him courage, and wherever they might be, he searched out a certain variety of tree, bringing home so many that the road that led to the Owens house was now called Magnolia Street. It was rumored that if you stood there in May, on the day when the trees bloomed, you were bound to fall in love, but no one believed tall tales such as that, except for those it had happened to, and those couples often married there, rather than in church, and were said to be exceptionally happy.

Faith Owens was regularly seen in town with a book in hand, reading as she walked. She wore a wide-brimmed black hat and men's trousers, and she carried a satchel of books to ensure that if she should finish one volume she would be handily prepared with the next. There was rarely a time when she didn't have her nose in a book, and people would come upon her in the woods, sitting on a rock and reading, or on a ledge by the lake, tossing bread crumbs into the murky water as she turned the pages. She'd collected dozens of volumes for the new library, meeting with wealthy families throughout Essex County, as well as in Boston and Cambridge, convincing well-to-do patrons that the entire population, men, women, and children alike, must be literate in order for the colony to grow. Several men fell in love with her, but she turned them all down. If they called her beautiful, that was a mark against them, for what a person was could not be seen with the naked eye. She had learned from her mother's mistakes. If she ever fell in love, she wanted someone she could talk to.

Although women were not allowed to be students at Harvard College, the esteemed citizen Thomas Brattle, who had written a letter that was critical of the witch trials and was both the treasurer of the college and a member of the Royal Society, had made arrangements for Faith to study in Cambridge. She was closer to Brattle than most people might have supposed, despite their age difference; they appreciated each other's minds, and she was grateful to him for believing in her abilities as a teacher.

Faith sat in the back row of the classics seminar at Harvard, allowed only to listen and never to speak. She dressed in boy's clothing in her everyday life, which she found so much more practical than skirts and capes. At Harvard, she could be seen in a black jacket along with trousers and a white shirt and a black tie, the same uniform as the men, so that she might not call attention to herself and her gender, although she hardly went unnoticed due to the red boots she wore every day.

"Gentlemen," the professor had told his students on the first day of class when Faith Owens was present. "Keep your eyes on me, if you please."

Faith had been wrong about many things. She still had the red mark that had arisen in the center of her left palm when Martha Chase drowned; the color had faded, but the blotch was enough to remind her of the bad choices she had made in the past. Every midsummer's eve a sparrow came into the parlor of the house on Magnolia Street. If it completed a circle around the room three times, bad luck was sure to come. Because of this, Faith never forgot the bird whose life she had taken for her own benefit when she made the Revenge Pie for John Hathorne. Hathorne was a successful trader, but people in town avoided him. There was nothing she wanted from him now, because he had nothing to give her. She always chased the sparrow to the window, then gently urged it out with a broom.

Faith still had a penance to pay and much to set right. For this reason, she went from one farm to another on Saturdays to teach any girl whose parents wouldn't allow her to take time from the workday and attend school. She walked so many miles, and came home so late at night, that Maria worried she would exhaust herself. One dusky evening, as Faith was crossing a pasture on her way home in the gray light of early winter, a white horse approached her and followed her home. It was the field that had belonged to the Hopwood brothers, and the ground there was still ashy. Faith understood that she was fortunate indeed to be chosen again after Keeper's death. She called the mare Holly, and people became accustomed to seeing her riding through the fields at night, wearing trousers and carrying a satchel of books, her red hair tucked up under a black hat.

John Hathorne made certain to avoid the Owens women, but Maria and Ruth occasionally saw each other on the street, and when they did they embraced as if they were sisters. Ruth had begun to teach reading classes, and every time she went through her garden gate and kept walking until she reached the library, it occurred to her that she hadn't told her husband where she was going or asked for his permission, and she was grateful for the life she led.

There were times when Maria and Faith would glance at one another as they set the table for dinner, or worked together choosing ingredients for a cure, or baked the traditional Chocolate Tipsy Cake for birthday celebrations. They had not forgotten the dark time of left-handed magic.

But that time was over, and they had forgiven one another. There are none who can fight as fiercely as a mother and a daughter, and none who can forgive more completely. One evening, when Maria was turning on the porch light so that her clients would know they could come calling, Faith followed her outside and handed her *The Book of the Raven*. She was ashamed of her behavior and of the red mark she carried in the palm of her hand. "I used it badly. It shouldn't be mine."

Maria considered burning the book, for it was bound to cause trouble. There was no one to claim it, and by rights it should have been burned at the time of its owner's death. She might have made a bonfire in the rear of the garden and rid the world of it, but the book was so beautiful, and the writer so knowledgeable, she couldn't bring herself to destroy it. There were reasons dark books were written by women, those who were not allowed to publish, those who couldn't own property, those who had been sold for sex, those who had grown old and were no longer desirable, women in chains, women who dreamed, women who had turned left when it seemed the only choice. If used carefully, by the right person, the magic in this text could be a great gift. Hidden on the last page there was a spell to bring about the end of any curse, but the price for doing so was high, and the woman who did so must be fearless.

Instead of burning the book, Maria went through the fields into town late at night, in the dark, as she had long ago, when she was mistaken for a crow. She carried the keys that unlocked the library door. She hid *The Book of the Raven* behind the loose bricks where long ago she had hidden her own journal. She left that book of magic in the place where she'd looked out the window to spy the magnolia, thinking that a miracle had taken place. She worked a few drops of her own blood into the mortar. In time, an Owens woman would discover the book, and use it as it should be used, with love and courage and faith.

Maria always wore the sapphire Samuel Dias had given her. Sapphire was the stone of wisdom and of prophecy that allowed the wearer to be true to herself. When he was gone, she let herself miss him. He was too tall for the bed, but it was empty without him. Maria often sat beneath the magnolia tree when he was at sea. Even in foul weather she found comfort there. When he returned he would bring back stories of seashells that were as big as cabbages, and mysterious birds with blue feet, of white bears that lived on the ice, and islands where every flower was red. He was arrogant and difficult, a man who liked to argue, but he was a man who could do more than talk. He knew how to listen.

She had been wrong about love. She had thought it was meant for fools alone, only to discover it was a fool who walked away from love, no matter the cost or the penalty. They waited for the curse, to see if it could find him, but after a while Maria was satisfied that the curse was convinced Samuel Dias had remained in the lake that had no end. He wasn't the same person he'd been before he died, and a man could not be cursed twice. On dark nights, when she feared for the women in her family who were yet to be born, she found consolation in the knowledge that an Owens woman was made not only to seek remedies, but to fight curses.

Fate can bring what you least expect, and it brought them a daughter they called Hannah Reina Dias Owens, named after Hannah Owens and Samuel's mother. In this way two women were returned from the ashes and remembered each day when their names were spoken. The baby was born in January, a winter baby, with black hair and dark gray eyes. She could call birds to her with a single cry and unfurl the bud of a flower so that it bloomed in the palm of her hand, but she couldn't fall asleep unless her father told her a story. It was time anyway, Samuel announced one morning, he would stop going to sea. Like his father before him he had come to love being on land and spent most days in the garden, where he grew vegetables and kept

bees that were known for honey that was so sweet strong men cried when they tasted it. Samuel was out there every day, even in winter, spreading hay over the garden, starting hardy seedlings in the sun, wearing his black coat, the baby in a basket beside him. He was always talking, even as he worked, for he had a thousand stories to tell, and the baby listened so intently she forgot to cry.

On the last snowy day in March, when spring was greening beneath the ice, Maria left Samuel asleep in their bed. She tucked Hannah into her coat and walked over the grass that was brittle with frost. Crows clustered above them and ice shone on the birch trees. As she walked in the cold morning, her breath cutting through the bright air, Maria thought she heard Cadin's call. She could remember that day in Devotion Field, in the Essex County of her birth. The fields of snow, the bright blue sky, the forest that was so deep, the woman who taught her the Nameless Art, the quick black eye of the crow. It was then that she saw what was before them, what she had always seen in the mirror, a black heart in the snow.

A nest had been tossed from a branch when the wind swept through. Maria knelt to point out the small fledgling to the baby. The black bird ignored Maria, but he looked at the baby with his glittering eye, unafraid. You cannot choose a familiar, it must choose you. When Hannah held out her hand, the crow came to her and settled beside her, tucked into Maria's coat. Maria felt the beat of his heart inside him slowing to match the baby's heartbeat.

They would take him home and wrap him in a blanket and Hannah would feed him sugar water from the tip of her finger. In no time he would be hopping around the house, perching on the staircase and on the brass rods above the damask curtains. By the time spring had fully bloomed, he would be flying. He would never be far from the girl who had been born on a snowy day, whose father had come home from the sea so that he could tell her every story he knew, whose sister took her in her arms to read to her, whose mother would teach her all she needed to know. This is how you begin in this world. These are the lessons to be learned. Drink chamomile tea to calm the spirit. Feed a cold and starve a fever. Read as many books as you can. Always choose courage. Never watch another woman burn. Know that love is the only answer.

ACKNOWLEDGMENTS

To Carolyn Reidy, for all that she did for literature and publishing, and for her extraordinary kindness to me.

Gratitude to everyone at Simon & Schuster for their ongoing support, most especially Marysue Rucci. Thank you, Jonathan Karp. Many thanks to Richard Rhorer, Wendy Sheanin, Zachary Knoll, Anne Pearce Tate, Elizabeth Breeden, Angela Ching, Hana Park, Samantha Hoback, Carly Loman, and Jackie Seow. Thanks also to Richard Willett.

Gratitude to Suzanne Baboneau at S&S UK for so many books over so many years.

Gratitude always to Amanda Urban and Ron Bernstein.

Thank you to Denise Di Novi for believing in magic for twenty-five years.

Thank you, Joyce Tenneson, for your amazing photography.

Thanks to Sue Standing for your early reading of the novel.

Thank you to Miriam Feuerle and everyone at the Lyceum Agency.

Gratitude and love to the bookstores who have always championed my novels.

My deep gratitude to Madison Wolters for continuing assistance and literary insights. Thank you to Deborah Revzin for help in matters both practical and magical. Thank you, Rikki Angelides, for joining in with grace and enthusiasm.

A most special thank-you to my readers, who asked to know how the story began.

ABOUT THE AUTHOR

ALICE HOFFMAN is the author of more than thirty works of fiction, including *The World That We Knew*, *The Rules of Magic*, *Practical Magic*, the Oprah's Book Club selection *Here on Earth*, *The Red Garden*, *The Dovekeepers*, *The Museum of Extraordinary Things*, *The Marriage of Opposites*, and *Faithful*. She lives near Boston.

Center Point Large Print
600 Brooks Road / PO Box 1
Thorndike, ME 04986-0001 USA

(207) 568-3717

US & Canada:
1 800 929-9108
www.centerpointlargeprint.com